SUMMER'S REGENT

SUMMER'S REGENT

THE EISTEDDFOD CHRONICLES
BOOK FOUR

SARAH JOY ADAMS
EMILY LAVIN LEVERETT

Charlotte, NC

FALSTAFF
BOOKS
WWW.FALSTAFFBOOKS.COM

For all those who believe in our writing and our world, and with special thanks to Gerald Leverett, Janice Banducci, Oliver Morris, and Noel Adams, without whose presence our world would be much less fantastic.

1

In the private area outside the King's Box in Parliament, Deor waited. In the main chamber, the already full gallery buzzed. Only a few days had passed since Madeline, Duchess of Wellhall tried to steal the throne and Finn, the King, fled to Northfalls. In the aftermath, Deor had taken control and driven out Madeline Farringdon. However, when Finn had tried to return, the palace refused to open at his command.

Now Deor was Regent. Not Queen, as she reminded everyone who tried to call her that. She was the steward until Finn returned or died. Her regency wasn't official unless Parliament accepted it. If they didn't, she was nothing more than a traitor to be locked away in the Tower. She doubted she'd get out alive.

Nearby her new Cabinet stood with her. Victor, her new Sword, and Stephen, her once bodyguard, now Shield, were close. Lord Delaney Overton Sr., the mayor of London, had been in the Tower with her, and now eschewed his own Parliament seat to stand with her. Deor hoped that his support would matter.

A few feet away stood Bill, with no title but friend. He was all that remained of her human life.

Deor twitched at a fold in her skirt, picking at invisible lint, until Genevieve took her hand. Rafe's ex-fiancée and the most fashionable woman in the Winter Court, with a beauty that was said to rival the

Summer Court Queen herself, she was now one of Deor's staunchest allies.

"You look perfect," Genevive said in Deor's ear. "Your dress is perfect, the jewelry, your hair, even your high heels—"

"Perfect?" Deor asked with a smile.

"Yes." Genevive returned the smile. "You look the picture of a regent."

"Thank you." Her dress, strapless black velvet with a simple bodice and a flowing skirt buoyed up by layers of crinoline, had been intended for the great ball after Finn's tournament. The Aethelwing eight-pointed star, the sign of her house, sparkled over and over in tiny diamonds across the bodice and skirt. Now she wore it in the hopes of looking like a regent. Her short hair, chopped before Finn had her flogged, was tucked behind her ears and held with diamond bar pins.

Beyond the door, the Speaker of Parliament banged her gavel. A handful of sparkles spiraled uncontrollably away from Deor, an event that was happening more and more often.

"Ready?" Deor said. Her retinue nodded.

A Parliamentary guard opened the door to the Royal Box, and Deor stepped inside.

She'd been there before, but the sight still made her catch her breath. Every seat was filled and the viewing gallery was packed to standing room only.

As she reached her seat, Deor nodded to the Speaker and to the other nobles in the boxes. She also cast a wave and a smile at the galleries where the gentry and peasants crowded the few nobles without seats on the floor. She recognized a few faces: Holman Redfern, a pro-House-of-Commons guild leader, and Aiden, the red-faced university friend of Robbie. They, along with most of the gallery, whooped and applauded as she entered. Down in the main chamber, Roger, Duke of Northfalls sat in his seat. The look he gave her was a far cry from the gallery's cheers.

Deor settled into her chair as the Speaker read the agenda. First came the acknowledgment of recent events including a replay on a giant mirror of the moment Deor sat on the Winter Court throne and claimed the regency. Then to Deor's surprise, the Speaker turned to Deor.

"Her Majesty the Regent has the floor."

Deor stood. Victor slipped a tablet with her notes into her hand.

"Thank you," Deor said. An air faerie in Parliament livery gestured and her voice amplified, reaching everyone in the room. "I appreciate you having me here to speak today. I was going to recount what happened, but," she gestured at the large display mirror, "that is clearly not necessary. His Majesty King Fionnleigh is alive. He escaped the palace and is safe at Northfalls." A palpable sigh of relief went through the crowd. "However, the King is not fit to return and rule at this time." Murmurs and cries went up, and she waited for them to die down. "Until that time, I stand in his stead as Regent."

Behind her, Victor took her free hand and held it, squeezing gently. They'd been over this several times. She wanted to babble on about the kingdom choosing her, about the Palace itself locking Finn out. She wanted to plead with the people to understand that Finn had failed all of them, murdered her grandmother, and abandoned his kingdom. Instead, she squeezed Victor's hand and held her tongue.

The Speaker tapped her gavel and asked, "Ruler or Regent, the kingdom must have a Shield, a Sword, and a Consort. Where is the Princess Consort Astarte? Is she with the King or is she serving as your Consort now?"

"Finn left her for dead," Deor said. A gasp ran through Parliament. "The Lady Astarte is under her healers' care in the Palace, too ill to resume her duties as Consort. For now, I have chosen Victor Farringdon as my acting Sword, and Stephen Bolton as my acting Shield."

"Why did you replace Lord Farringdon?"

Deor scanned the crowd. A pale blue person stood in the Farringdon box. He was dressed well, but plainly, with no clear marking of his house. Next to him a woman stood, skin the color of the ocean on a clear day, with blonde hair arranged in a neat, simple bun. Like the man, she was dressed plainly.

"I'm sorry," Deor said. "I don't know who you are."

The man bowed his head. "I am Henri of Cote, a county that runs along the coast in the Wellhall duchy."

Deor drew a deep breath. She should have spoken about it when she mentioned the others. "I have no word of Rafe. He is currently missing." She managed to keep her voice steady, though pain shot through her as she said it. At her words, the man nodded sadly and moved to sit.

"What of Luc Monjoie?" the woman beside him said, stepping forward. "He, like Lord Rafael Farringdon, is a soldier of the palace." The man hushed her and laid a hand on her arm, but she shook him off. "They may be merely palace guards to you, Lady Regent," she said with palpable disdain, "but they have families. Luc has people who care for him."

"I do not doubt it," Deor said as gently as she could muster. "You are right that I should not neglect to mention the others involved in the protection of the King. A number of soldiers lost their lives."

The woman paled and sat. "Luc...?"

Deor continued. "All those that we found, we have identified. Their families have been notified." Deor blinked a few times, willing tears not to form. "We did not find Luc Monjoie," Deor said softly, "as we did not find Rafe." She chose not to mention that Luc and Rafe had been fighting on opposite sides. Now was not the time to tell Monjoie's friends and family that he was a traitor. "When I know anything, Lady...?"

"I am Juliette du Chanson."

"Lady Juliette," Deor corrected herself. "When I know anything, I will inform you immediately." She scanned the room. "That is true for all the soldiers' families. We are working now to account for all of the palace guards. Many fled." Deor glanced in the direction of those from Wellhall. "If you cannot account for a person, please contact my Shield."

Lady Juliette gazed at her for a long moment. "Thank you."

"Thank you, Princess Deor," the Speaker said. "We will now entertain the subject of the King's return and the Princess' regency." Deor stepped back and took her seat.

Delaney Sr. stepped forward, raising his hand. "Madame Speaker, I ask for the floor."

"Very well."

"My dear citizens of the Winter Court. I ask leave to speak not only as the Mayor of London, but as a citizen myself. I was imprisoned in the Tower with the Lady Deor. She was sick and in pain, yet she was kind to all of us. She spoke to both Bard John Dell and myself daily, seeking to learn as much as she could about her nation. Both she and Victor Farringdon experienced torture that left them incapacitated for days at a time. She stands before you not willing to sully the name of her father, a name that for many of us has long been sullied. Only a person devoted to the Winter Court would endure all she has and still consent to rule as Regent while the King recovers.

"It is not a disloyal thing to question the monarchy," Delaney went on. "Absolute loyalty serves no one well. This brave young woman could not have done what she did without a devoted love for our Winter Court, and I urge you to give her a chance, to not allow the long shadow of her father's sins to fall on her." He turned to Deor and took her hand, bowing over it. "I will follow Deor Smithfield Aethelwing."

Applause and cheers went up from the floor and the gallery and lasted until the Speaker gaveled them to silence. "Does anyone else wish to speak?"

Roger, Duke of Northfalls, stood. "My peers," he began, not even glancing at Deor. "No one here questions the lady's loyalty or bravery." His tone suggested otherwise. "But I do question her coloring of the current situation. His Majesty is healthy and of sound mind. Yet he remains my guest at Northfalls. The Princess claims His Majesty is unable to return. His Majesty asserts that he is unable to return to the Palace because his daughter remains Regent. And so I request the reinstatement of the King as soon as possible. The Regent has only to step aside."

Deor jolted. Of course, Finn would have complained to Roger, and anyone else who would listen, that she was denying him entry. Her fingernails went silver and she covered her hands in the folds of her dress. She wasn't afraid, and she wasn't even that angry, and yet, her magic was reacting as though danger loomed above her.

"Is this true?" A nobleman Deor vaguely recognized stood. "Do you prevent the King from returning?"

"Perhaps she is a traitor!" Another person, not from Wellhall or the surrounding areas, spoke. A growing swell of voices joined in.

"Oh, shut it, all of you." Tess McIntyre, the Countess of Mirrovere, stood. Fierce as always, her flaming red hair in a bun held in place by an arrow. Mirrovere had been destroyed years ago, magically broken, by Finn to punish a disloyal Count. Deor had reinstated Tess as the Countess of her lands only days ago. "You," Tess pointed at Roger, "profit from the King's stupidity. You and others like you are loyal supporters regardless of his actions. He'd slice you from neck to groin and you'd beg to lick your own blood off his boots!" She crossed her arms. "I'm for the Lady Regent. She's done more in a week to heal this country than the King has in his whole life. She stopped Madeline Farringdon and lifted the ban on werecreatures. The Tower was packed full of people wrongly arrested by the King's guard." She nodded to the Speaker of Parliament. "I was in a cell with your wife till the Regent set us free. Which d'you want back, her or the King? Cause I'll wager you can't have both."

The Speaker nodded, her mouth twitching despite her efforts at careful neutrality.

Tess glared at the peerage, her gaze darkening as it darted from family to family, crest to crest. "There's not a soul in here who doesn't know the King's a menace. Crops failed, babies never came, magic weakened. It's the monarch that does that."

Around the room, mumbles rose, some of agreement, some of confusion, and some stark rejection. Deor didn't move.

Finally, Tess spoke again. "We've got time," she said. "Let's give her a hundred days and see how she does. If the King," she managed not to spit at the title, "isn't back by then, and she's still here, we'll make it permanent. By then we'll have something other than our old biases informing us." She paused and grinned. "Me included."

That seemed to pacify most people as a quiet murmur of agreement rolled through the crowd. In the upper gallery, where the non-peers sat, the enthusiasm was stronger.

The Speaker tapped her gavel gently, drawing everyone's attention. "We have a proposal before us. Shall we vote, then?"

As the ayes began around the chamber, Roger stood again, his air faerie magic carrying his voice over the sound of others. "Wait! I have an amendment to the proposal." People groaned and Deor rolled her eyes.

"If the Princess wishes to be Regent, there ought to be conditions!" Roger insisted. "She must fulfill the proper role of a monarch. It takes more to rule than sitting on a throne." He smiled and bowed a little at the chuckle that drew. "We must have a Petition Day. It has been too long since the monarch heard directly and openly from the people. If the Princess wishes to rule, she must hear from those under her rule."

Under cover of the thunderous applause, Deor hissed at Victor. "What the hell is Petition Day?"

"It's a trap!" he whispered back. "You open the throne room to all comers and let anyone present their requests to the monarch directly. You have to say no! You'll be swamped with ridiculous and contradictory demands for favors, offices, boons. You can't possibly please everyone. By the end of the day half the kingdom will be angry with you."

She stood. "I accept," she said. "If you allow me to remain Regent for the next hundred days, I will do my best to prove myself to you. Beginning with a Petition Day. But I have a few conditions of my own. I can see my Shield is already having a heart attack at the thought of anyone and everyone crowding through the Palace doors. So, we will have a list. Anyone wishing to meet with me must contact the Palace Guard via stamp, not mirror, to be placed on the list. Petition hours will begin at seven o'clock in the morning, will pause at noon for one hour, and will end at six o'clock in the evening. Each meeting will not exceed ten minutes." She reached behind her to squeeze Victor's hand, feeling the flow of magic between them. He wasn't wrong in his concerns, but she hoped the gains would be worth the risk. He squeezed back. Agree with her or not, he had her back.

Roger nodded. "That is satisfactory."

"I'm not finished," Deor said. She locked eyes with Roger. "There will be only one slot for members of the nobility. Since they already have direct access to the monarchy, they do not need access through Petition Day. All other petitioners must be gentry and commoners."

Roger's jaw dropped as Tess McIntyre burst out laughing. Even Roger's protests were drowned out by the ocean's roar of applause from the gallery. Nobles quailed in their seats.

2

_____

Before Rafe opened his eyes, the smell of pungent green herbs tickled his nose. Light, bright enough to warm his eyelids, shone on his face. Someone hummed as they massaged his left hand. Blearily, Rafe blinked himself awake. He remembered the shoreline where he had washed up, swept through one of the thin places out of Fae and into the human world. He had walked toward a building, a fortress or castle of some sort. He remembered a door, but nothing after that.

He was in a narrow bed in a stonewalled room. At first he thought it might be a prison cell, but the walls were painted in an ochre zigzag, and there were no bars on the window.

A dark-skinned human woman with a thick braid of tightly curled hair and small golden rings in each ear sat next to his bed, humming as she rubbed the herbal-smelling stuff into his hand. Her cheekbones and eyes reminded him of Chloe, though her skin was darker, and she wore a plain brown robe with the sleeves pushed up to her elbows. She pressed her fingers into his wrist, humming a discordant note, and a sharp pain like acid-tipped pins and needles shot up his arm all the way to the elbow. He gasped and yanked his hand out of the woman's grip.

"I'm sorry you felt that," she said. "Though I'm glad to see you awake. Welcome to Mont Saint-Michel. I'm Aaliyah."

"What are you doing to me?" he rasped.

"Healing you." She reached for his hand, but he pulled away.

Rafe tried to prop himself up on his hands, but his left hand gave way, and he fell on his side. Aaliyah caught him and raised him to a sitting position in the narrow bed.

"Easy," she said. "You're not ready to put any weight on it yet. I only just reconnected that nerve. It's good you're wanting to get up though. Lying still too long isn't healthy for you."

"How long have I...?"

"Three days," Aaliyah said.

"I wasn't that badly hurt."

"Oh yes, you were, *habibi*." Aaliyah tapped her head. "You were in shock when you got here, so I'm not surprised you didn't feel any pain at the time. Something hit you very hard, and more than once. You're lucky your brain wasn't turned into pudding. The bones in your wrist...they were not so lucky."

The fight under the Palace came back to him in fits and starts. Monjoie had hit him with a block of ice the size of a couch. That much he was sure of. And then he'd called up a wave.

Steeling himself, Rafe looked down at his hand. The skin glistened with the green ointment, but no bruises, and no bones poked through the skin. The nerve in his arm still throbbed as if sending desperate messages to his brain, but the rest of his hand didn't hurt. Certainly nothing the palace healers couldn't fix as soon as he got back to the Winter Court.

As if she could read his thoughts, Aaliyah said, "The reason you aren't feeling much pain is that the nerves are damaged. Something very heavy crushed your hand. Nearly all the bones in your palm and wrist were shattered. I've been knitting them while you slept, but it will be some time before you can move your hand independently."

A slow rolling terror settled in Rafe's stomach. His *sword* hand. He tried to rotate his wrist in a habitual swordsman's gesture meant to keep the fingers limber, but nothing happened save a fitful twitch in the thumb and ring finger. Rafe gasped and tried again, willing his hand to close. Sweat stood out on his brow, and he panted with the effort. Three of his four fingers curled inward a fraction of an inch.

"Very good," Aaliyah said. "That's more progress than I expected at this stage. Keep it up, and you might get nearly the full range of motion back."

"Nearly?" Rafe shouted at her. He surged out of the bed, tossing the sheet and blankets aside, not caring that his ribs ached and his head pounded or that he was wearing some sort of nightgown that only went to his knees. "This is my sword hand!"

9

"Shhhh, shhhh. Calm yourself, *habibi*. This panic isn't good for you. You'll hurt yourself all over again." She took his wounded hand in both of hers, stepping close and turning her face up to his. "You will heal. But it takes time and patience and effort."

"Please, I need to get back to the Winter Court," Rafe said. "I need a healer."

"You are free to go any time you wish," Aaliyah said. "But there is no healer in any fae court who could do as well as I've done. If you don't let me finish treating you, you'll be lucky if your hand can pick up a cup."

A pain like a sob constricted Rafe's chest. His mind raced in a dozen directions at once, picking up and losing thoughts before he could finish them. Aaliyah smiled at him and the gentleness of her smile calmed his heart just a bit. She rubbed her fingers over the back of his hand and the prickling pain eased. "No one comes here by accident," she said. "You were sent to us for your healing and ours. Be patient with the process." She patted his hand. "I think that's enough healing for today. Why don't I help you dress and get some food? Broth is nourishing, but it doesn't satisfy like a solid meal."

Rafe's stomach growled loudly. "Yes, please," he said. "I'm starving."

Aaliyah took down a long brown robe, woven of soft wool and eased it over Rafe's head, guiding his hurt arm through the sleeve without a pang. "There you go," she said. "Come out and meet the cloister." She took him by his right arm, and Rafe followed her out of his narrow room toward the smells of a cooking fire and bread baking.

A stone corridor outside his room led to a kitchen and two more people in brown robes. The elderly woman with gray hair piled on her head tended a roast in front of a giant open hearth. The other, an older man with a shiny bald head circled by white hair, sat at the end of a long wooden table, peeling potatoes. As Rafe and Aaliyah entered the kitchen, the man looked up with a smile.

"You're up!" he said, waving the paring knife at him cheerfully. "Good sign. Come, have a seat. Do you remember me?"

As Rafe sat, he shook his head. His brain had gaps and foggy spaces.

"This is Caedmon," Aaliyah said. "He is our current Abbot. Mother Aelfburga is the lady by the fire. Don't be alarmed if she doesn't speak to you yet. Why don't I let you rest here for now? Caedmon can tell you anything you want to know about Mont Saint-Michel."

Caedmon smiled at her. "Going back to your garden before the sun sets?"

Aaliyah laughed and nodded. "I have to check on my other patient first. But you know I'll tuck in my plant babies before the evening chill sets in. I can feel a heavy wind gathering."

"Thank you," Rafe said.

As Aaliyah spoke, the old woman brought Rafe a mug of tea. She set it down beside him and rested her hand briefly on his shoulder. Rafe looked up to meet her gaze, but her eyes were unfocused and distant as if she were involved in a conversation he couldn't hear. She smiled a kind and gentle smile, but said nothing and went back to her cooking. Aaliyah kissed Aelfburga on the cheek, waved goodbye to Rafe and Caedmon, and went out by a different door.

Rafe raised an eyebrow at Caedmon.

"She's communing," Caedmon said, as if the word meant something. "She'll talk when she's ready. But she's glad you're here. We all are. You didn't say much when you arrived, not even your name."

"I'm Rafe, Lo-" he stopped. Telling them who he was might not be the smartest choice, no matter how nice they seemed. "Just Rafe."

"We welcome you, Rafe," Caedmon said with a smile.

By force of habit, Rafe tried to pick up the mug with his left hand. His fingers banged into the ceramic, refusing to close around it. Frustrated, he switched to his right hand, letting his left lie uselessly in his lap. "We?"

"The chapter. All of us here." Caedmon gestured with the knife again. "Not that there are many of us these days. Besides myself and the two you've met, there are only three others. You'll meet them at supper. Joan is especially pleased to have a swordsman among us."

The uniform robes and the words *abbot* and *chapter* stirred memories in Rafe's head of being tutored decades ago by the bard John Dell, who had been a part of a group of religious men. If he recalled, Dell's order had strict rules about obedience, silence, and a rigorous cycle of prayer. Rafe's eyes sought an exit. There was the door he had come through and a larger, open doorway on the opposite end of the room. A slight ocean breeze, damp with sea spray blew through. He could make a dash in that direction. His muscles ached at the thought.

"So this is a monastery?" Rafe said. "I'm not a monk." He framed his next question carefully, "Am I a guest in this place, or...?"

Caedmon chuckled. "Oh, you're not a prisoner. No one who comes here is. Well, I say no one. We had the Enemy prisoner here once, but he escaped. Now we guard against his return. But you're free to leave any time you like."

Rafe chewed on a piece of cheese and waited for the catch, but Caedmon simply flipped a peeled potato into the tub of salted water at his feet and selected another to peel.

"Where are we, really?" Rafe said. "I remember you told me the name Mont Saint-Michel before I fell asleep, but... What is this place? It feels different. Neither here nor there."

"That's as good a description for it as I've heard," Caedmon said. "You arrived from the human world, but I can see you're a Faerie. We aren't exactly in Faerie, nor out of it. We're not in the human world, nor out of it either. Mont Saint-Michel exists in both the faerie and the human worlds. Or rather it touches both and is in neither. The space where we are, the true place, if you will, is closed to either side unless we open it. Or someone like you comes to us."

Rafe narrowed his eyes at Caedmon, waiting for the explanation to make sense. Caedmon seemed distinctly bardic in his style of speech. He'd spent enough time with Dell and Ama Nefasta to know you couldn't rush a bard.

Peeling a potato, Caedmon went on, "If you were on the fae side of things, you'd have difficulty finding our island, the geography is tricky. On the human side, people come up the causeway all the time to stare at the old buildings and take pictures, but they're not exactly here with us either. It's a parallel space. I'd say less than one in a hundred is even aware that they've strayed near. Only people like yourself who are skirting the margins of death can truly get where we are without an invitation."

Rafe drank the tea and waited for further explanation. Outside, gulls called.

Caedmon dug out a potato eye, admired his work, and flipped the cleaned potato into the salted water. "Potatoes," he said. "One of my favorite imports from the new world."

"I need to find a portal to the Winter Court," Rafe said. "I have a duty." As he spoke each sentence settled like a weight on his shoulders. He had a duty. One which he had failed in every possible way.

He slumped, elbows on his knees, staring into the tub in which peeled potatoes bobbed. "There are people," Rafe said. "They need me."

Caedmon nodded. "Was it a war?"

"A coup," Rafe said. "It might be a war by now. I don't know. I don't even know who is alive."

"That's hard," Caedmon said. "Leaving behind people you love is often the hardest part of joining the cloister here."

"I don't wish to be rude," Rafe said. "You've been more than generous to me, but what makes you think I'm going to join your monastery? I'm not religious. I'm not even human."

"Oh, that's not a requirement," Caedmon said. "Some of us are. Some of us aren't. In fact, the cloister functions better if we don't all think the same way. No, the only rule here is that you must contribute to the Great Task. We guard the Source of life from the Enemy. That's our purpose, and yours, if you choose to stay. But there's no rush. Take your time. Heal. Very few of us came here on purpose, you know."

Rafe ached, inside and out. The thought of pulling on his uniform jacket over sore muscles and walking back through a portal into the Winter Court felt like an iron blanket around his shoulders. Where would he go? Back to Finn's service, wherever Finn was at the moment? Not unless he wanted to become a regicide. Deor, whatever she was doing now, was surrounded by people who had already served her better than him.

The kitchen was warm with the smell of meat slowly roasting. Aelfburga came and collected the peeled potatoes. She set down a large bunch of carrots by Caedmon and firmly pressed a slice of buttered bread into Rafe's hand. He took a bite, and she patted him on the shoulder before gliding off again.

"You said I was welcome here?"

Caedmon nodded. "For as long as you choose to stay."

"I think I would like that." Rafe ate his bread with his right hand and watched the old man methodically peel carrots, wondering if he'd ever hold a blade again.

3

Once back at the Palace, Deor hurried to change into slacks and a blouse. Donovan and Chloe were leaving for Romania, but they had agreed to a private farewell lunch with Deor before they left.

Deor had moved out from the Heir's official rooms on the fourth floor and settled into a smaller set of rooms on the fifth floor. It let her be closer to Astarte, but also got her away from Rafe's rooms. She couldn't bear to be in the suite. As she changed, she wondered when, or if, they would find Rafe's body. She couldn't say, even to herself, where their fling-turned-friendship would have ended if it had run its course, but now she would never know. Between the two of them, Finn and Madeline had robbed her of even the chance to say goodbye.

Deor's retinue for lunch with the vampires included only Victor and Bill, along with Brand and Rafe's dogs, Jake and Sam, who refused to leave her side. Stephen had his hands full sorting out the Houseboys.

Right before they entered the room, Deor glanced at Bill. "It can be a bit disturbing, watching them drink blood," she warned. "If you think it will be too much, you can meet them another day."

"I'll be fine." Every day he spent in the Winter Court, Bill looked stronger and more cheerful. Now he was bright-eyed and bushy-tailed, eager to meet more creatures he'd only read about.

Deor nodded at the guard at the door to let them in. Donovan and Chloe were already there, casually dressed.

Donovan wore what Deor thought of as his romance-novel-vampire costume: black leather pants, flowy cream-colored shirt, and boots, with his brown hair free down his back, nearly to his waist. Chloe wore dark jeans that could accurately be described as painted on, a tight, ruby red sweater, and black stiletto, knee-high boots, with her chin-length brown hair in tight curls around her face.

"Thanks for joining us for lunch before you head back to Romania. And thank you, too, for staying to talk politics with me." Deor smiled. "Please, sit." She took her seat.

"We're glad to," Donovan said with a fanged smile. He took his seat next to Bill, with Chloe between Donovan and Victor.

"This is my friend, Bill. We grew up together in Bakersfield." As she introduced him, Deor frowned at Bill. He now looked as pale as a corpse. Sweat dotted his brow and trickled down the side of his face. His breathing was shallow like he was heading for hysteria. Riveted, his gaze was focused on Donovan.

"Hello," Donovan said, reaching out a hand. "I'm Donovan, and this is my wife Chloe."

Bill said nothing but nodded slightly. He did not shake Donovan's hand.

Donovan withdrew his hand, scowling at Deor.

"Bill?" Deor asked. Maybe his illness made him stop shaking hands. Still, he should have said something. "Are you alright?"

He managed to drag his eyes away from the vampire and focus on her. "No." The word came out like a strangled gasp. "He's … they're … "

"Our allies and friends, Bill," Victor said sternly from his seat between Deor and Chloe. "Surely the human world taught you better manners?"

"Manners?" Bill glared at Victor. "Manners?" He repeated, his voice growing in volume. "That…man…is covered in blood. Can't you see it?" He stood, pointing a finger at Donovan. "It drips bright red down his cheeks, and cracks in brown clotted patches on his hands. His hair is matted with it!" Bill stepped back and stumbled over the chair, barely catching himself.

"And what about me?" Chloe asked with a purr, like Bill made some quaint observation. "Am I bloody too?"

Bill looked at her and swallowed hard like he was forcing himself to not throw up. "Bloody too. Less. And different. Splattered all over your face, your clothes, flecked through your hair. It drips from your chin, and your lips are stained with it."

"Hmm," she said conversationally. "I always thought my complexion made blood less visible."

"I can see every drop." Bill shuddered. "How many people have you killed?" He glanced back and forth between them.

Donovan seemed to consider the question, eyes glancing up, and a small furrow forming on his brow. After a few moments he shrugged, "I've lost count, but it's got to be in the thousands."

Bill slammed a hand over his mouth,

"I've killed fewer than my husband, but I'm catching up." Chloe's smile never faltered.

Deor stood and lunged for Bill, grabbing him by the arm. "What are you doing?" she said, quietly, though everyone could hear. He shook his head and tried to pull away from her.

Deor released him and turned to Chloe and Donovan. "I am so sorry. I don't know what's gotten into him." From the skeptical look on their faces, they didn't buy it. "He's been ill for years. He looked like he was better here in the Winter Court the last few days, but now..." She shook her head and looked back to Bill.

Donovan shoved back from the table and surged from his seat. "Right. Bards are all wise and gracious, and when they aren't, it's illness, not malice or poor manners. We'll be leaving."

"No, wait!" Deor had planned on reaffirming their alliance. Now it would be a miracle if they didn't leave enemies. Her nails sharpened and gleamed, and she curled her fingers to hide them. "You have to believe me. I didn't set this up—" Deor stopped. "What did you just say?"

"We. Are. Leaving." Donovan held his hand out to Chloe who took it and rose to her feet.

"No," Deor shook her head. "The bit before that."

"About bards? They don't think we're people." He switched his gaze to Bill who recoiled. "They made us, and then, like Frankenstein, rejected their own creations as monsters."

Chloe looked cooly at Deor. "Though I will say they've never been rude because I'm black. It's refreshing here in Faerie to have a different kind of racism."

"I'm so sorry," Deor repeated, clasping her hands behind her, the words' insufficiency making them sound false to her own ears. "But are you saying Bill is a bard?"

"Of course, that's what I'm saying!" Donovan snapped. "Did you think we were so dumb that we wouldn't see the insult? Maybe you are just like your father."

For an instant she flashed back to the classroom, to the moment when she'd stared him down, refusing to give in, even as her knees nearly buckled and her heart raced. Silver bled up from her nails, across her hands, a kind of self-defense armor. There was no hiding it.

"I am not my father!" Her own voice surged with power, and Donovan and Chloe bared their teeth. Chloe shifted her stance, ready to spring. The three dogs rose and growled, even Brand. Deor swallowed and composed herself. "Sit!" she snapped at the dogs. They did, though Jake continued a low rumble for a few moments.

Victor stood. "Please," he said to the vampires, "we would never intentionally insult you, you must know that." He gave Deor a look that suggested she should apologize again.

Deor focused her attention on Bill and thought about how he behaved in the human world. He cringed away from people who gave off even the hint of violence. He refused to walk past graveyards and he hated hospitals. At times he would stare at some object for a long while and then shake his head like he was trying to clear away thoughts that he never spoke.

"I am sorry, Donovan and Chloe." She shook out her hands, willing the silver magic away. "There has been a major misunderstanding. It's a comedy of errors, really, or would be if it were funny." She straightened her shoulders and looked Donovan in the eye. She drew power from the palace, willing her voice to carry the weight of her office, but this time under her control. "Until this moment, none of us, not even Bill, knew he was a bard. I swear to you on my throne and on my life."

Donovan gaped.

"You can't expect us to believe that nonsense!" Chloe said, though she sounded unsure.

"I swear," Deor repeated. "Bill and I grew up together. He was always sickly, always nervy. He's seen countless doctors, been given dozens of diagnoses—"

"And the barrage of pills to go with them," Bill managed.

"It never, ever occurred to me that his sickness might be fae-related. So, again, I am sorry for the insult, and thank you for making the connection we never, ever could have found on our own."

17

Bill steadied himself, keeping his eyes fixed on the table. "I thought bards had lutes, communed with nature, that sort of thing."

"There are all kinds," Victor said. "Some work with language, some numbers, some metals and swords, or animals, or plants."

"And very few are death bards," Donovan said. His tone toward Bill softened. "All these years, you thought you were hallucinating, didn't you? When you looked at a person and knew they would die soon. Or you saw someone like me and knew they carried death with them."

"Yes," Bill whispered. "That's why I hated hospitals. The ghosts weren't the problem. The doctors, especially ER doctors and EMTs. They carried so many deaths with them." His voice caught.

Deor touched Bill's shoulder. "Do you want to step out?"

"Yes." He nodded. He stared at a spot between Donovan and Chloe, not looking either of them in the face. "I am sorry. I wanted to meet Deor's friends."

"I've decided to take it as a compliment that you can see my accomplishments," Donovan gave a fangy grin. "It certainly isn't guilt."

"Ha ha." Bill croaked. "Thank you for understanding." He clamped his hand over his mouth again and hurried from the room.

Deor looked at the other three people. "Shall we eat? There's still a lovely meal set out for us."

The four made small chit-chat for a while, about the tournament before the attempted coup. About how much they all disliked Geoff. Anything but the current moment. Finally, Donovan spoke again. "About your friend Bill. Death bards are not particularly well treated in places like Eisteddfod. Some death bards engage in necromancy. For a while death bards were *neutralized* by other bards. That's what happened to the one that created vampires."

"What do you mean, created?"

"My ancestor lost a blood feud. His enemies slaughtered his entire family. He went to a death bard and offered the only thing he had left, his own life, for the opportunity to kill them all. The bard warned him that bloodlust would be his whole life. My ancestor replied that would gladly drink his enemies' blood."

"No one knows if the bard meant it to happen or if it was an unintended consequence, but after he took his revenge, my ancestor learned that he could turn other humans into vampires. By the time the Bardic Council knew what was happening, he created a new family for himself.

"The bards hunted down the death bard and destroyed him on the spot. They meant to do the same to my ancestor and his children, but a people conceived in blood and revenge are not so easy to kill." He paused, a bitter smile on his face. "They called us undead. And worse. But by the time we fought each other to a standstill, the vampires produced a bard of our own. And we learned we could bear children." He glanced at Chloe, taking her hand and squeezing it.

Chloe picked up the thread of the story. "The first vampire bard negotiated a temporary truce with the Bardic Council. And then he brought out his infant daughter. The legend says he asked them which was a greater monster, a person who lived by blood, or a person who would murder a child for the crime of being born. In the end, the bardic council decided we were people after all and could live. The vote was 51-49."

"Jesus," Deor said softly. "That's terrible."

"Yes." Donovan smiled. "It's one reason we flaunt what we are."

"A giant fuck you? That seems fair." Deor shook her head. "They were the monstrous ones. And I'll tell Bill to be careful." Deor leaned back in her chair. "And again, thank you for coming. I was hoping that we could reaffirm our families' agreement today. Nothing formal, just verbally."

Donovan nodded. "I have permission from the Vlad to do that. The vampires agree to not harm the royal family and to not wage open war."

"That sounds suitably vague," Deor said. "Would you support us in a war with the Summer Court?"

Donovan grimaced. "Not overtly. We can offer sanctuary. But my father is not willing to risk the wrath of the Summer Court. Most fae thoroughly believe we are monsters and would be happy to have a reason to demand our extermination. Declaring war, or even joining one, is risking our own genocide."

"I understand," Deor said. And she did. The vampires were not a powerful people, despite their individual strength, and their population was small. Still, some friendship was better than none.

Donovan rose, followed by the others. "It is getting late, and we are not traveling by portal. Thank you again for your hospitality."

Deor came around the table and hugged Donovan. "Thank you for your friendship and your understanding."

The four of them made their way out to the courtyard where a carriage waited. Victor and Deor waved as the two vampires climbed into the carriage and rode away. The dogs, as usual, guarded her.

"That could have gone better," Deor said. "I was hoping they'd give us more than just 'we like you a lot and hope you don't die.'"

"Me too." Victor offered her his arm. "Let's hope the goblins and the werewolves stay on our side."

4

Sitting idly with a broken hand didn't suit Rafe, but he didn't see many options. As Rafe ate his bread and cheese, a young man entered the kitchen. Red-faced and with short, sandy blond hair, he wore a patch over one eye. Scars extended above and below the patch. Unconsciously, Rafe touched his own scar. He hadn't thought to glamour it. Seeing the other man's scars made Rafe wonder if Deor was right in her attitude that scars held no shame. But it also made him wonder about Aaliyah's healing ability. After all, there were healers aplenty in the Winter Court who could restore sight to a damaged eye.

The young man piled an apple and some cheese on a wooden plate and came over to the table, sitting opposite Rafe, and introduced himself. "Evelyn, Shropshire Fusiliers," he said. "Pleasure to meet you." He stuck out his right hand. Rafe took it, wondering if this was courtesy since his left hand was disabled, or simply a human custom. Deor was left-handed like most fairies, but she had mentioned something once about humans being mostly right-handed.

"Likewise," Rafe said. "Call me Rafe."

"Wotcha," Evelyn said. He dug into his food with an efficient speed that Rafe recognized from young recruits in boot camp. The fellow couldn't be more than thirty. No, he was human, so probably ten years younger than that. Evelyn shoved the last of his cheese into his mouth, pitched the apple core across the room to land in a slop bucket, and picked up a tray that Aelfburga set with food and utensils. "Time to feed our other newcomer. Care to come along, Rafe? I'm sure he'll be glad to see you."

"Happy to," Rafe said, though he wondered who the other person was and why Evelyn was certain they would like each other.

Evelyn went down the corridor past Rafe's room to where a door stood partially open. "Are you awake, my friend?" he called out as he pushed the door open with an elbow.

"Just barely," a familiar voice said. "Whatever it is you're bringing me smells delicious though."

Looking past Evelyn, Rafe saw Monjoie propped up on pillows in a narrow bed. Without a second's thought, Rafe shoved Evelyn aside and drew back his hand, struggling to make a fist. The tray went flying. Broth splattered across the room.

"You!" Monjoie shouted. He seized the crutch next to the bed and swung it at Rafe's head. Rafe parried the blow with his good arm, gathering magic and hurling shards of ice at Monjoie's face.

"Hey! Knock it off, both of you!" Evelyn, a full head shorter than Rafe, somehow managed to seize him by the collar and shake him while at the same time wrenching the crutch out of Monjoie's hand. "What the blazes is wrong with you two?"

Rafe struggled in Evelyn's grip. There was no way this stripling of a human could be stronger than he was, but Evelyn held firm.

"Explain yourselves," Evelyn barked.

"I'm just defending myself," Monjoie said.

"You tried to murder me! I wouldn't even be here if it weren't for you, you traitor! If I could still hold a sword I would cut off your head and hang it over Tower Bridge!" Rafe bellowed.

"Ah. Silly me for thinking you'd be on the same side since you both arrived wearing the same uniform." Evelyn gave an exasperated sigh. "All right. Each of you keep your hands to yourself. Any man that makes a move in the wrong direction, I'll knock him down. Understood?"

Rafe glared at Evelyn while Monjoie sulked about already being down and that only cowards attack a man laid up in bed.

"You're not that laid up," Evelyn said. "You were up and hobbling around just this morning. You," he pointed to Rafe, "sit down. You, Luc, stay still and keep your hands to yourself." Rafe sat on a short three-legged stool in the corner.

"What on earth is going on here?" Aaliyah and Caedmon appeared in the doorway, faces full of concern.

"Apparently, our two newest brothers aren't as full of brotherly love as they should be," Evelyn said.

"That whoreson traitor's no brother of mine," Rafe growled. Monjoie picked up a mug and whipped it at Rafe's head. Rafe barely managed to duck and the pottery shattered against the wall.

"Keep my mother's name out of your mouth," Monjoie snapped. "You broke your own mother's heart. You don't get to talk about mine."

Before Rafe could lunge at him again, Aaliyah put a hand on his chest and Caedmon stepped in between them, shoulder to shoulder with Evelyn. The little cell was now so crowded that Rafe could barely see Monjoie.

Aaliyah's hand lay lightly on his chest, but she pressed down with an irresistible weight. Rafe looked up in surprise. Aaliyah was a sturdily built woman, but like Evelyn, her power exceeded her appearance. The weight of her hand was a command to calm himself, gentle, but also inarguable. *Calm yourself, or I will calm you.*

"Perhaps you should both breathe deeply and say nothing." She held eye contact with Rafe until he did as she suggested. It felt a bit like being five years old again and his nanny "suggesting" that he sit in a corner and think about his tone of voice. Inexplicably, he felt a tinge of shame at his behavior. He reminded himself that he was not the one who needed to be ashamed. Monjoie was the traitor.

"That's much better," Caedmon said. "Now, my brothers, perhaps you could explain yourselves. You both arrived together, wearing the same uniform, so we naturally assumed you were on the same side. More than one of our number has arrived after a battle." He glanced at Evelyn, who nodded.

"I am a soldier of the Winter Court," Rafe said, not sure how much these humans knew. Caedmon waved a hand impatiently, but Rafe went on, "This…personage… infiltrated the Palace Guard and gained the King's trust so that he could help the Duchess of Wellhall usurp the throne. I was swept out to sea fighting him off to cover the King and his Consort's escape. It's his fault I'm wounded the way I am." Rafe held up his bandaged hand in proof.

Monjoie snorted. "Thanks to you, I have a broken pelvis, so I think we're more than even on that score. And we wouldn't have been on separate sides if you had been loyal to the family that birthed you."

The three monks looked at each other for a long minute. Finally, Caedmon sighed and pinched the bridge of his nose. "Gentlemen," he said. "Whatever political concerns you may have in your former lives, they are of no consequence now. The work we do here matters far too much to be undermined by petty squabbles between brothers." He held up a hand as both Rafe and Monjoie protested. Silence fell over both of them against their will. "You are free to walk away at any time if you think being here is too onerous." As he said it, he raised an eyebrow at Aaliyah.

"They won't die just from leaving," she said. "Though I can't guarantee how well they will heal."

"Walk away into the human world," Rafe said, shocked at the idea. "The way I came? With no mirror, no money, and no way to find my way back to Fae?"

Caedmon nodded. "That is correct, yes."

"Exactly how far do you think I'm going to hobble on these?" Monjoie snapped, indicating his crutches.

"If you leave us, that ceases to be my concern," Caedmon said.

Monjoie rolled his eyes and threw his head back dramatically against the pillow, but misjudged the force and thunked his head against the stone wall. Rafe snickered as Monjoie winced and rubbed his head.

"Mutual support!" Caedmon bellowed. "That is the watchword of our order. Rafe, since you knocked over Luc's tray, you can clean up the mess and fetch him another. I expect no more violence out of the two of you." He swept out, followed by Aaliyah. Evelyn paused to give them a cheerful smile. "Chin up, lads. Joan called me 'that English dog' for months when I first got here. You'll come around in no time."

Rafe seethed at the enormity of being called "lad" by someone younger than Robbie while Monjoie muttered under his breath about preferring to suck a rotten fish out of the gutter than call Rafe a friend.

"You heard the man," Monjoie said. "Clean this mess up and fetch me my supper. Your lordship."

Rafe tried to flip him off, but his broken hand failed him. He cursed, and, using his right hand, sopped up the stew with the napkin, hurled everything onto the tray, and carried it back out to the kitchen. There he found another tray prepared for him. Rafe stomped back to Monjoie's room and set it down on the bedside table within arms' reach but without a word to Monjoie.

Even as Rafe stamped back down the corridor in search of some fresh air and open space, he vowed that the second, the absolute literal second he was able to use his hand again, he was leaving this den of lunatic humans and finding a way back into Faerie. In the meantime, he needed some pants.

5

After a long day dealing with Parliament, Roger, and Donovan and Chloe, Deor met with Genevieve to talk about Petition Days. As they sat on a couch in Deor's parlor, Genevieve took out her tablet to make notes and Deor idly stroked Brand's head. Jake and Sam watched her from in front of the fireplace.

A rapid knock came at the door, and Gordie rushed in. "I'm sorry to interrupt Your Majesty. But the Lady Robbie sent me to get you," he said. "It's Her Majesty, Consort Astarte."

"Oh, god." Panic rose in Deor's chest. She couldn't handle another loss, not right now.

"She's awake!" Gordie said. "She is asking for you."

Deor managed to pull herself together by the time she got to Astarte's bedroom door. She wiped relieved tears from her cheeks and straightened her shoulders. She knocked before cracking the door open and peeking in.

"Astarte?" she asked. "It's me, Deor. Can I come in?"

"Come in!" Astarte's voice, bright and cheerful, beckoned.

Deor opened the door and stepped into a room filled with light. All the curtains were thrown back from the windows.

Astarte had clearly showered and changed clothes, as she was in a lovely pale green nightgown embroidered with flowers. She sat back against a set of pillows. Next to her, in a tee shirt and jeans, Robbie snuggled against her mother. Astarte draped her arm around her daughter and held her tight.

"It is so good to see you." Deor hurried to the bed and stopped short. "Can I hug you?"

"Please!" She patted the bed next to her. "Come and sit. Tell me about all the things that have happened since I've been away." She glanced at her daughter. "Robbie has been a bit vague."

Deor sat down on the bed and leaned in to hug Astarte. The joy she felt at Astarte's health was drowned in the sorrow of the news she'd have to give. "What all has Robbie said?" She glanced at the girl, who shook her head slightly.

"A bit. Finn is gone?" Astarte sounded worried.

"He is. He escaped to Northfalls. He's there now." Deor shifted, uncomfortable for a moment. "I'm the Regent in his stead."

"You should be Queen," Robbie said firmly.

"Is he wounded?" Astarte asked. She dropped her gaze to the quilt covering her, picking at some unseen loose thread.

"Not a scratch." Deor drew in a deep breath. "When he left, the palace was hurt at his going. Now it won't let him open a portal and come back. When he can open a portal, he can come back. The palace can decide when he's fit to rule."

"And if it never decides he is?" Astarte looked up at Deor.

"I haven't thought that far ahead. I'm trying to take it one day at a time." She waved away her comments. "But we shouldn't be talking about dour things. You're awake! And feeling better."

Astarte smiled, but it was weaker than before, tinged with sorrow. "I am." She looked back and forth between Robbie and Deor and finally spoke again. "You haven't mentioned Rafe. Either of you."

Deor swallowed. "He was in the cave with you?"

"Yes. He and Monjoie fought on the dock. I couldn't leave Rafe. So Finn left without me. Then a massive wave came and dragged Rafe and Monjoie under. It's a miracle that I wasn't swept into the river too."

"We found you with Jake and Sam," Deor said. "They were guarding you. The palace told me where to find you."

Astarte frowned slightly. "I'm grateful for it and surprised. I'm not sure why it would care if a Summer Court Faerie died."

"I think it likes you."

Astarte picked at the blanket again. "So, no sign of Rafe?"

"None," Deor said. "No word. No body. Nothing."

"So there's hope!" Robbie insisted. "He might not be dead. Maybe he's hurt, or stuck somewhere, or, I don't know, but not dead!"

Astarte tightened her grip around Robbie, pulling her in closer. "Maybe." She didn't sound hopeful.

Deor bit her tongue. If Rafe were alive, he'd have contacted them if he could. There was no way he'd leave and not come back, if only to let them know he was safe. Especially now, when the Winter Court was anything but safe. She needed to stop pretending he was alive. And yet a small part of her, of her magic, insisted that he was still in the world, not close, but not gone either.

Astarte cleared her throat. "Let's leave off talking about him. There's nothing we can do."

Deor nodded. "When we found you, you were surrounded by vines. It looked like the ground itself was taking energy from you."

"I didn't see them, but now that you mention them, I remember. I remember falling limp on the ground after the wave, just trying to breathe. And then I felt the palace taking back its magic from me, draining me."

"That's horrible!" Deor said. "Why would it do that?"

"Because I'm no longer Consort." She sighed, relief softening her features. "I'm free of it."

"What do you mean? You're still married to Finn."

"Married to him? Yes. We have a marriage that we can't break." She scowled. "But a spouse isn't a consort. Finn made me Consort as a 'fuck you' to parliament when they refused to acknowledge our wedding."

"Okay, so what does that mean?" The book in the library defined a consort as a "keeper."

"There's so much power in the faerie palace. Too much for one person to contain." She pointed at a spot behind Deor.

Deor glanced back. A comet's trail of sparks floated behind her.

"So a consort holds some of that power. It's not my power. I have my own, though over the years the line has become blurred. I'm guessing that is why the palace taking back the magic nearly killed me. It will sound strange," she regarded Deor for a moment, "or maybe it won't, to you. The palace, as it took the magic, felt like it was taking a burden from me."

"Wow," Deor said. She'd never thought that *keeper* might be literal.

"You need a consort." Astarte pursed her lips. "You have to choose someone you trust. Someone who can say no to you, can stand up to you.

If you don't do that, it won't work. There will be power struggles, even if unintentional."

Deor sighed. "I've been putting that off because I have no one to choose. I am not ready to have any kind of intimate relationship with someone right now, let alone marry. But that was stupid of me. The Consort wouldn't have a book of its own, along with the Monarch, Heir, Sword, and Shield if it wasn't equally important."

"It shouldn't be a lover or spouse," Astarte said. "After I was already married, and already Consort, I read the book. We were the first. Most consorts are relatives, some are close friends. But being lovers adds so much other strife. Trust me on that."

An idea struck her. Deor knew it was a long shot, but figured she'd ask anyway. "Would you consider continuing your role as Consort?"

Astarte laughed. "Absolutely not. Never again will I tie myself to someone else's magic. I'm not sure that the palace would accept me again anyway. It tried to refuse the first time, but Finn has an iron will, and the palace bent to it, like everyone else."

"I understand." So who should it be? She trusted Victor as much as she trusted anyone. Could he be Sword and Consort?

Whatever she decided, it wasn't going to happen now. "Finn has asked that you join him," Deor said cautiously. "He tried to insist on it, but you were ill, and I was not about to move you, or have you portalled, to Northfalls."

Astarte nodded. "Whenever you want me to go, I will."

"No, Mom!" Robbie flung her arms around her mother and buried her face in her shoulder.

"Now hush," Astarte said, stroking Robbie's hair. She looked back up at Deor. "When would you like me to go?"

"When hell freezes over seems like a good time to me." Deor said. "If you want to join Finn, I won't stop you, but if you never want to be in the same room with that bastard again, I fully support that."

Robbie pushed away from her mom and stared at Deor. "Really?"

"Yes really." Deor grabbed Astarte's hand. "This is your home for as long as you want to be here. You and Robbie can come and go as you please."

"Thank you." Astarte squeezed Deor's hand and a couple of tears spilled from her eyes. "I want to stay here. But I can't stay here and be useless." She shooed Deor and Robbie off the bed and flung the covers back. She stood. "What can I do?"

Deor gaped at her. "You woke up from a coma today. How about rest?"

"I've rested enough. How can I help?"

Deor bit her lip. She had a very specific idea of how Astarte could help, but it would be work, and she felt weird giving the former Consort orders. "I need someone to run the household. I know nothing about servants. It's only holding together because of Jameson."

"You need a Seneschal," Astarte said.

Robbie scowled. "That's what she was to the King. That and a wife, a Consort, a—"

Her mother's sharp gaze cut her off. She shrugged. "I'm just saying…"

"I'll pay you," Deor said.

"What?" Astarte frowned.

"Robbie is right. Finn took that work from you, and that's not right. I've no idea how much I should pay you, or what that should look like, but you won't work for free, not for me."

"That sounds delightful!" Astarte beamed. "Now, I'll get dressed, and we'll discuss it. From what Robbie said there's a Petition Day coming up? That's going to be a nightmare to put together, but I'm sure we can handle it." The bright determined look in her eye would accept no argument, so Deor didn't even try.

6

Rafe spent the remainder of the day stomping around the rambling pile of buildings that covered the island, avoiding any members of the chapter. As it turned out, that part was all too easy. The island was nearly deserted. In some places crumbling masonry left corridors open to the sky. Moss grew over outside paths and up walls. At times Rafe felt as if he were about to walk into a crowded space only to turn a corner and find himself alone in a dusty room untouched for ages. The sense that he was in two places at once grew stronger in some areas than others. On the landward side, he swore he heard human voices talking, but he had no company except the gulls.

Eventually, he came to one large set of double doors where the ring-shaped handles had been wrapped in strips of leather. The doors were old, ancient even, but the leather looked relatively new, though shiny with use. Someone on the other side was whistling.

Rafe pulled the leather strap that dangled from the iron ring in one door and peered into what turned out to be a library. Unlike the library at the Palace, this one was crowded with shelves. A table in the center of the room was spread with scrolls and stacked books, some holding other books open. A man in a brown robe stood with his back to Rafe, his fingers tracing a line on a scroll.

"Come in!" the man shouted over his shoulder. He looked up, smiled at

Rafe, and said, "Just the brother I needed at the moment. How good is your ancient Faerie?"

Rafe winced at being called brother by a stranger yet again. His discomfort grew as he realized he was talking to a Summer Court Faerie. But the faerie held out his left hand and shook Rafe's, seeming not to notice that Rafe couldn't close his hand in response.

"I am Lachar," the faerie said.

"Rafe, Lord... Just Rafe here I suppose."

Lachar laughed and said, "You'll get the hang of it soon enough. It took me ages to stop introducing myself as Lachar, son of Sanbalat, Marquess of the Reaches and Third Junior Archivist to His Serene Majesty Currinan, King of the Summer Court."

Rafe blinked a bit. "So you came here when the present Queen's grandfather was on the throne?" Lachar didn't seem that much older than him. Certainly no older than Finn.

"Yes, I suppose I did," Lachar said. "So we have a queen now? Goodness. It has been a while since I heard news from home."

"You have a queen," Rafe corrected him. "I am of the Winter Court."

Lachar smiled at him. "Of course you are. I won't hold it against you."

Rafe's back stiffened, and Lachar laughed, slapping him on the back. "There are no courts here, my friend. Only the Source and our fight against the Enemy."

Rafe forced himself to give Lachar a cool smile, the kind that at court would have meant *you and I are not friends*, but Lachar seemed oblivious. Instead, he pointed to the scroll he was reading and said, "Is this a verb, do you think? It should be a verb. It needs to be a verb, but by all that's sacred I can't make heads or tails of it."

Rafe glanced down at the place where Lachar pointed. He read the sentence to himself, read it again aloud, and frowned. "I can't say..." He racked his brains for grammar lessons and came up with only the barest court formalities. "It must be a verb? It's placed immediately after the primary noun, yes?"

"That's what's troubling me!" Lachar exclaimed. "See here," he pointed, "and then here..." he launched into a complicated excursus on conjugation systems, strong verbs and their adverbial adjuncts, and something called the Great Vowel Shift. "So it can't be a verb," he concluded. "Except the sentence makes no sense whatsoever if it's not a verb."

Rafe blinked at him a few times. "You will have to pardon me," he said. "I am a knight, not a scholar."

"Ooh, and a courtier, too, I see," Lachar said. "Unless court manners have shifted quite a lot since my day, you've just told me to stop boring you with matters beneath your concern. But without giving cause for offense."

Blood rushed to Rafe's cheeks as Lachar said it. "Forgive me," he said. "I did not mean to be offensive. It's simply that I can't help you. I haven't set foot in a classroom in a very long time." Not that long ago, his brain reminded him. Only two seasons ago he had lurked in Deor's classroom, watching her parse human texts for her Fae students. Rafe looked at the sentence in question again and repeated it aloud. "Yes," he said. "It feels like a verb doesn't it? If I didn't know better, I'd have said the word was a Goblin curse."

Lachar leaned toward him, a gleam in his eye. "A curse? Tell me more."

"It can't be," Rafe said. "This scroll is…" He waved his hands at the gilded, carefully hand-lettered scroll. "This is a work of art. The word I'm thinking of is the lowest sort of oath, the kind you might hear a foot soldier use. It would make a sergeant blush. I've only heard it when around Goblin soldiers, and they didn't know I was listening."

Now the look in Lachar's eyes reminded Rafe of a cat about to pounce on a mouse. "Is it sexual or scatological?"

"Both, I'm afraid."

"Aha!" Lachar leaped around the table and began pulling books off a shelf. He flipped through one, tossed it onto the table, and moved on to another until he found an entry. "Of course!" he crowed. "No wonder I couldn't find the word in any dictionary. No one writes down obscenities. Stuffy old scholars." He grabbed a stylus and made a few marks on a tablet beside the scroll. "Yes. Yes! That unlocks so much. It's a borrowing from the Old Goblin, the Southern dialect. It has to be. Well, well, well." Lachar turned to Rafe, beaming. "An Ancient Faerie scroll with a Goblin scribe. He couldn't think of the right word for what he meant so he just took a Goblin word and slapped a Faerie verb ending on it. The blighter!"

"I see." Rafe did not see, but with archivists, as with bards, Rafe found it was better to let them rave and not ask too many questions. Questions led to more explanations. "I should be going," Rafe said. "I'm happy to have helped."

"Oh, you have helped!" Lachar said, beaming widely. "I've been working on this blasted scroll for sixty years now and that one passage has always baffled me. And here you are with the answer. I think the writer of this scroll knew more about the Enemy and his relationship to the Source than any of us alive now."

Far away, a bell rang two long slow clangs.

"An alarm?" Rafe asked. All the members of the cloister he had met so far were constantly speaking of this enemy of theirs. It sounded as if they expected an imminent attack.

"Supper!" Lachar said. "I don't know about you, but I'm starving. Come! Let's get to our meat." He carefully rolled the scroll back up and slid it into a protective ivory tube before snuffing out the lights and ushering Rafe out the door with a courtly gesture.

Lunatics. He was surrounded by robe-wearing lunatics, Rafe thought as he followed Lachar back toward the central kitchen. They and their invisible, probably non-existent, enemy could go to blazes.

His mood softened a bit when they arrived at the kitchen. Warm firelight played over the room, and the long wooden table was set with the roast that had been turning over the fire all day. Evelyn was just helping Monjoie ease himself into a high-backed seat as Aaliyah and a smaller, dark-haired woman brought mugs of beer to the table. Following Lachar in, Rafe found a seat at the far end where he didn't have to look at Monjoie's face. This put him near Aelfburga, who sat quietly, her face even more distant than before, as the others chatted and passed around plates. Caedmon stood at the head of the table, waiting until everyone had taken a seat.

When everyone was seated, Caedmon said, "Let us each give thanks according to our way." Around the table some bowed their heads, others lifted their hands or made signs. Some simply closed their eyes for a few seconds. Rafe closed his eyes.

"Thank you," he said quietly. And he felt better for having said it.

The thanks concluded, everyone dug into their meals without further ceremony. Rafe found eating with his right hand slow and clumsy, but the savory meat and potatoes almost made up for the struggle. Everyone else seemed to eat happily as well, except for Aelfburga who sat like stone, her hands folded in her lap and her eyes turned to things unseen. Occasionally Aaliyah, who sat opposite Rafe, would spoon a sip of broth or milk into Aelfburga's mouth as carefully as one might with a baby. No one else showed any sign of being worried about the old woman's lack of response and ate and drank and even addressed her in their conversation as heartily as anyone else at the table.

Just as Rafe was digging into a second helping of potatoes, Aelfburga rose from her seat and placed her hand on his shoulder. Instantly, the chatter around the table hushed. Her eyes fixed on some distant thing, Aelfburga spoke. "The end of our duty is soon. And an old beginning is to come." She drew a deep breath and looked around at the astonished faces around the table. For the first time since Rafe had arrived, the monks seemed shocked by her behavior. No one moved. They barely breathed. But Aelfburga said nothing more. She only returned their stares with a look of placid calm, her hand still resting on Rafe's shoulder.

Frozen, not sure what to do, Rafe let her hand remain, his eyes darting around the table for some clue as to how he ought to respond.

"The end, *memere?*" the dark-haired woman said. "The end of what exactly?"

Aelfburga smiled at her. "If I knew more I would tell you." She looked down at Rafe. "But I am so glad you have come to us. You are the bearer of good things, and we are blessed to have you. You will be with us at the end. Of that, I am sure."

She let go of his shoulder and resumed her seat, looking around the table with a calm smile as if she had not just announced the end of all things. "My, I'm hungry. Could someone pass me a plate?"

Half the people at the table lunged to serve her while the other half watched, mouths open.

At the head of the table, Caedmon pushed back his plate and said, "You've set us a fine riddle, Aelfburga. I suppose we'll just have to wait and see what the answer is." He reached for a stringed instrument like a harp and began tuning. "Shall we have a love song or a song of good life?" he asked the table and a merry argument broke out among the cloister.

Rafe, his appetite for seconds gone, leaned forward, his eyes meeting Monjoie's, who was staring openly down the table in Rafe and Aelfburga's direction. For a split second Rafe and his enemy shared a common look of confusion before Rafe retreated back into studying his own plate. Lunatics. He was surrounded by absolute lunatics.

7

Three days, it turned out, was not enough time to plan much of anything, and certainly not a full schedule of ten-minute meetings in the throne room. As Deor scanned the list of names, each neatly written next to a time slot, she realized that between seven a.m. and noon, she had scheduled no bathroom breaks. Maybe she'd get lucky and someone wouldn't show up.

It was summer, so dawn had long since arrived and filled the throne room with light. She stood at the base of the throne, staring at it like it might jump up and eat her.

"You have to sit on it," Victor said softly.

"I know."

"Today," Stephen added. "You have to sit on it today." He glanced over his shoulder at the door. "People have been here for hours making sure they get through security."

This was a bad idea. She shouldn't have let Roger goad her into it. She should have negotiated; she should have done something besides what she had. Too late now. Deor took a deep breath and sat on the throne. At once it shifted under her, making her comfortable. Perhaps it knew today wasn't the best day to try her patience.

She looked at the first name. She'd read over the list several times already, but the names ran together, mostly because exactly zero of them were familiar. There was one noble, the last appointment, listed as *an anonymous noble.* The doors to the throne room opened, and Genevieve came in. She was dressed in simple elegance—pink, as she often wore. Demure, with flowers tucked into her updo. She was the liaison, gathering people up at the throne room door and leading them to the dais to speak to the Regent. She would kindly, cheerfully, and firmly go over the rules. No more than ten minutes. No magic. No touching the Regent.

"I'm so sorry it isn't more organized. We had so little time," Genevieve said.

"Don't you dare apologize. I know you've been working nearly twenty-four hours a day to get this done. You and Astarte both, fielding calls until your voices gave out."

"It wasn't hard sorting through the first requests for a meeting. But after we announced that the list was full, that's when the bad calls started coming. You know, the 'my family has known the monarch for years' and 'do you know who I am?' and 'what do you mean there aren't any spots left, surely for my family...'" Genevieve shuddered. "We had to find dozens of ways to tell people that, no matter how special they were, they were not getting a spot. I confess, there were some who it gave me great pleasure to turn away."

Deor laughed. "I'm glad you got some entertainment out of this."

"I shall be off to gather the first person. A farmer, I believe, from about thirty miles outside of London. Berries."

Deor settled in. Victor and Stephen stood on either side of her. Both clearly armed. "Be nice. Or at least try not to look hostile."

Moments later Genevieve appeared in the doorway again, leading a middle-aged man. She stepped aside and waved him in.

The man gazed around the room, frozen in the spot, mouth slightly open. Behind him, Genevieve rolled her eyes and gave him a small shove. He jolted and moved forward, each step tentative like the ground might open up and swallow him. Deor felt that way the first time she'd stepped up to the throne, too.

The man was large, tall and broad. He wore brown leather pants and a beige shirt with a sloppy cravat certainly not made of silk. His shoes were scuffed, though recently polished. He had a wide-brimmed hat, yet another color brown, which he snatched from his head and pressed over his heart, letting brown curls streaked with gray tumble around his orange face. His bright green eyes were riveted on her, and he looked terrified. His free hand he held behind him, dragging something.

"Good morning," Deor said, trying for a cheerful tone that didn't sound manic. She glanced down at the list in front of her. "Jaccob Baker." She waved him forward. "Please come closer so I can talk to you."

The man bobbed his head but didn't change his pace.

"C'mon dad!" A small voice rang out behind him, and a child darted forward, apparently the thing Jaccob had clutched behind his back. The boy, an orange-skinned and brown-haired copy of his father, wriggled his hand free of his father's grasp and ran at Deor, barreling up the steps, stopping only on the second to the top, right in front of her. Deor held her hands out to catch him, but he caught himself and smiled. "Hello, Yer Majesty!" He bowed low, almost into her lap, and beamed at her.

"Hello." She laughed, and tension eased from her shoulders. She shooed back Victor and Stephen from looming over the child. "What's your name?"

"Jaccob, too." He glanced back at his dad. "I'm named after him. I'm the fifth Jaccob!"

"Really?" She glanced at his side. He carried a picnic basket.

Jaccob the fourth rushed up and hovered at the base of the dais. "I'm sorry, Your Majesty," he said, reaching for the boy, set to grab him by the back of his shirt. "He was born and raised on the farm, and doesn't know court manners."

The young Jaccob evaded his father's grasp by scampering up another step and darting to the side of the throne to stand in front of Stephen.

Stephen stared down at him with sharp eyes but then smiled. "Careful now, lad," he said gently. "You might get a right knocking once you get home."

The kid turned to face his dad, eyes wide. Then he shook his head. "Naw," he said, grinning at Deor. "My da's never raised a hand at me."

"That's good," Deor said. "So you and your dad are farmers? What can I do for you?"

"Do for us?" Jaccob the older jerked back like he had been slapped.

"This is a petition day," Deor said. "I thought you had a petition?"

"No!" He shook his head like the idea was absurd. "What could a que— Regent do for me?" He jerked his hat up, covering his mouth. "I apologize, I didn't mean … you're not useless." He went pale.

"That is good to know, Jaccob," Deor said, laughing. "I often feel useless. But if you don't have a petition, why did you come?"

"I can answer that!" the young boy said.

"Go on." Deor smiled.

Before his father could shush him, or perhaps in spite of his father's attempts, the boy told her. "See, when my dad and his friends heard about the petition day, they thought it was a right riot, yeah? Like there was no way that the new Queen—"

"REGENT!" his father corrected.

"Right. Regent. No way the new Regent meant it when she said she'd have space for commoners. So, on a lark, my dad said he'd ask for a spot. And then he got one! We had to go, yeah? Or else we'd be called cowards, yeah?"

"I see." Deor looked past the boy. "Is this so, sir?"

"Yes, Your Majesty," he said, blush brightening his already glowing cheeks. "But we didn't come just to stare." He waved his hat at the boy. "Go on now."

"Right!" The boy lifted the basket and offered it to her. "Here!"

Deor took it and sat it in her lap. "For me?"

Both Jaccobs nodded.

Deor opened one side and the sweet, sharp scent of strawberries filled the air. The basket was full to the brim of freshly picked berries. She reached in and took one nearly the size of an apricot. She took a bite.

"No!" Stephen and Victor said in unison, lunging for her.

But it was too late. The sweetness burst in her mouth, and she sighed. "Easy, you two," she said as the men glared at her. "There's plenty." She proffered the basket. "Try one."

"They could be poisoned!" Victor growled.

"Poisoned!" Jaccob the elder straightened. "Now just you wait here, mister fancy nobleman, sir. Sword or not, you've never worked a day on a farm! My berries never made nobody sick!"

Deor giggled. "That's right, Victor." She proffered the basket again.

"I'm game. They smell wonderful." Stephen picked up a strawberry and took a bite. "These are good. Better than we get down in Cornwall. It's too wet down there for the best berries."

The man and boy puffed out their chests.

From the doorway of the throne room, Genevieve waved.

"Thank you so much for these," Deor said. "And it was lovely to meet you. I'm afraid I do have to see other people. Are you sure there is nothing you want to petition for?"

"Can I kiss your hand?" Young Jaccob blurted out. "I mean, may I kiss your hand, Your Majesty?" He blushed as brightly as his father and broke eye contact, staring at his feet.

"Of course you can." Deor held out her hand to him. The boy gaped, but then took her hand delicately, like it was made of glass, and raised it to his lips. The touch was so brief that to call it a mere peck would be an exaggeration. He dropped her hand and bolted to the bottom of the steps where he flung himself into his dad's arms, hugging him.

"Silly boy," the man said, ruffling his son's hair. He put his hat back on and doffed it. "Thank you, Your Majesty. Me and the other farmers were talking, and, well, we've all been renters for generations. Some of us lived on the land even before the Count did. And, we know he means well, but a way for us to have a say…"

"Go on," Deor urged. "If there is any day you can say anything you like to the monarchy, today's it. You're not going to get into trouble, I promise."

Next to her Victor sucked air through his teeth. There would be words about promise-making later, she knew.

"A House of Commons, Your Majesty, we'd really appreciate it if you were on our side."

Deor smiled. "I'll see what I can do."

Jaccob nodded again and guided his boy toward the door where Genevieve was waving them out.

Deor glanced at the men next to her. "That wasn't awful."

"No," Victor said, reaching into the basket, grabbing a strawberry, and taking a bite. "But be careful with promises."

"I know." Deor said and finished off the strawberry. She waved a servant over and handed off the basket. "Keep this safe, will you?" She smiled.

The servant nodded and hurried back into the shadows.

Deor settled herself back into the throne and sighed. Maybe this wouldn't be a nightmare after all.

Most of the petitioners were courteous, and many were kind. A lot of them resembled Jaccob the older and younger, coming to see her just to see her. Often they brought gifts. She'd gotten a basket of beautiful citrus, and some lovely pork and venison. Another small group brought her a fine, perfectly woven handkerchief. They apologized for it being so little, but they'd only had three days. Her initials—DSA—were embroidered in the most delicate thread she'd ever seen.

One woman dragged her fiancé, and the woman he was apparently cheating with, in front of her. When it turned out the "other woman" didn't know she was the other woman, Deor thought she might be a witness to a murder. She'd have called it justifiable homicide. Cooler heads prevailed, though, and after the dust settled, the man escaped with his life, but no fiancée or mistress. The women, on the other hand, each seemed to leave with a newfound friend.

In the end, she got small snapshots of life all over the Winter Court. Farmers, merchants, teachers, parents, tradespeople, soldiers. Each showed her a slightly different facet of life. The day had been exhausting, but she had never loved a place more.

"Two left," Victor said. He and Stephen both had given in after lunch and had chairs brought for them to sit between visits. They were running a bit late, but not much. They'd finish by seven-thirty, a small miracle.

Deor glanced at her tablet. It was a name she didn't recognize. Liam. "Someone from Ireland?"

Victor looked at his sheet. "That's one of Rufus's cousins. He lives in London, but I didn't think he was involved in politics."

Genevieve, somehow looking as fresh and bright as she had at five-thirty that morning, led Liam in. He was tall, like Rufus, and looked like him too. Red hair, broad shoulders, a wide, cheerful trotting gait. A human-shaped puppy dog. In a good way.

"Greetings, Liam," Deor said. "What can the Regent do for you?"

Liam bowed, a stiff, low, overly formal gesture. "Thank you, Your Majesty." He straightened. "I have come to speak on behalf of the pack in Ireland."

Deor's hopeful cheer vanished. Whatever was coming, it wasn't good.

"Rufus himself would have you know that he does not hold you responsible for the actions of your father. Indeed, he appreciates the gesture you made the night your regency began. Your lifting of the ban on werecreatures was welcomed."

So far, not so bad. "I'm glad."

"Unfortunately," Liam continued, "after a lengthy discussion with the alpha himself, they decided that the werewolves will no longer maintain their association with the Winter Court."

"What?" Victor snapped. "You can't be serious!"

Deor touched Victor's arm. "Let him finish," she said, but her stomach had already dropped.

"While the werewolves have long been a protectorate, and we appreciate the protection offered, we no longer trust that the Winter Court is a safe place for us. Political instability in the nation makes our association too much of a risk." He bowed again and sighed sadly. "I will miss London." He turned, without salute or acknowledgment, and left the room.

Deor sagged back. "First the vampires and now the werewolves. That's two allies gone."

"I don't entirely blame them," Stephen said quietly.

"Are you mad?" Victor snapped.

"No." Stephen shook his head. "I'm gentry. The wolves have long been treated poorly. They're a protectorate with no seat in parliament. After the King's behavior, why should they risk staying for someone they don't know at all?" He held up a hand before Deor could speak. "I know you know Rufus and Penelope. You know them as people, not as the heir to the pack. This is politics. It isn't about personal feelings."

"Ugh." Deor sat back. In the doorway, Genevieve waved. "Let's hear this last bit of nonsense from 'anonymous noble'."

She forced the frown off her face and smiled politely as Roger, again, strolled into the room.

"Good evening, Your Majesty!" He said with bright cheer. "I was wondering if I might bring in some friends?"

Deor arched an eyebrow. Of course, it was Roger. Behind him, Genevieve looked alternately furious and worried. "Who do you have in mind?"

"I want to make sure this is public," Roger said. "The petition I am about to present. I want it seen in public, so there's no hearsay attached."

"You want to bring in the press," Victor said, rolling his eyes.

"Fine." Deor said and waved at those guarding the door.

A group of reporters, including several with mirrors, poured in. She recognized many from the press corps that had been at her speech, and at her beating, too. There were some she didn't recognize, either from smaller papers, or journalists chosen by Roger. "Ahem," Roger said. "I bring to you a petition from Parliament, for the good of the people."

"Good lord, Roger," Deor said, wincing. "You don't need to shout. I know you're an air faerie. Can you take it down a notch?"

"Forgive me." He bowed his head slightly. "I want to be heard."

"They have mirrors," Stephen said. "You don't need for everyone to be able to hear you from here."

Roger chuckled like he was indulging a spoiled but stupid child. "I bring a petition," he said at a loud, but much more reasonable volume. "That you are the child of Fionnleigh Aethelwing the King is a fact."

"Oh, thanks." Deor said. The reporters scribbled furiously. She should just keep her mouth shut. Keep a polite smile on her face. Let Roger get his political theater over with, and then have a bath and some food.

"If I may," he said, as though she'd silenced him.

When he didn't speak again she waved at him. "Go on."

"You are the child of the King; we know this. However, we do not know your capacity to rule. You have proven able to defend yourself with the traditional Aethelwing magic, but you have not demonstrated your power in a non-threatening situation. So we ask for a Proving."

"Absolutely not!" Victor snapped. He lunged forward like he might go after Roger himself, and Deor caught his arm.

"What is a Proving?" Deor asked. "I've never heard of it."

"No." Roger shook his head. "We know you're of the blood. We don't know you are of the power. In a neutral location, Mont Saint-Michel, you will call upon your magic for the verification of neutral witnesses. If you prove you have the magic, Parliament tentatively agrees to accept you as Regent, effective immediately, regardless of the hundred days. If you fail to do so, you will immediately step aside to reinstate the rightful King."

Deor saw silver. Roger stepped back slightly, the smug look on his face gone for the moment. "Let me get this straight, Roger. You speak for Parliament?"

"Yes." He said, recovering and standing tall.

"And they demand this Proving?"

"Yes."

"And if I refuse?"

"Parliament will declare a vote of no confidence. They will seek out the King, wherever he is, and either bring him back to London or let him rule from where he is." Roger rolled up the scroll and held it out to her. "For your perusal."

"I'll take that," Genevieve said, snatching it from Roger and moving up to stand by the throne. She scowled at Roger, a stare that had probably made several Harvest Queen contestants cry. Roger remained unmoved.

"When?" Deor asked.

"A week." He nodded at the scroll in Genevieve's hands. "The details are all there. The monks will be contacting you and your—" he took a moment to frown at Stephen and Victor in turn—"retinue." He crossed his arms and smirked. She wanted to slap his pale lavender face until his perfectly coiffed gray curls went flat. "The other courts have been invited, too. The Goblins, the Wolves of Ireland, the Vampires," he shuddered slightly, "the Dwarves, the Trolls, and the Pixies. All are allowed to send a small group of witnesses. As is the Summer Court."

Deor delicately took the scroll. No good shredding the document. She stood, and Roger stepped back. "It is settled, then. A Proving." She scanned the crowd of reporters, making sure to glance directly into every mirror she could. She wanted the whole of the Winter Court and whoever else to see and hear her. "I shall not disappoint."

8

Rafe tried to make himself useful around the monastery in gratitude for their hospitality and healing, but the habit of using his dominant hand kept spoiling his efforts. He didn't have the grip strength to carry any weight or the finesse to use an implement like a pen or a kitchen knife. When he tried to read the books in Lachar's library he found that most were written in languages he couldn't understand. His eyes ached, and the words swam after a few minutes of reading. Aaliyah told him that was because of the blow to his head and it too would heal with time, but he felt stupid nonetheless. Even simple tasks like helping Evelyn gather edible seaweed from the rocks were slow and tedious. He cursed under his breath as his grip slipped or he bobbled delicate items. More than one plate crashed to the floor as he tried to clear the table after a meal. When he cut himself on a hidden knife lurking under the suds in the wash basin, Aelfburga shooed him out of the kitchen.

Rafe walked out to the rocks overlooking the open sea and flopped down on the largest one. Here he was, a general of armies and the heir to a duchy, and yet he was unable to perform tasks the most menial servant could do. He picked up a shell and threw it, cursing in disgust as the throw hooked right and fell short of the water.

"I'm not fit to chase birds off a cornfield."

"Not with that aim," Caedmon said behind him.

Rafe yelped and jumped. "I'm sorry, Brother Caedmon." All the monks addressed each other as Brother or Sister. Copying their form of address seemed to be the polite thing to do. "I was... contemplating."

"Sulking is more like it," Caedmon said, though he sounded amused. "But I didn't come out here to comfort you, I'm afraid. I came out to give you a task."

"Anything," Rafe said. "I'm bored."

"Hmm," Caedmon said. "I'm glad to hear it. Aaliyah says that your hand needs more work than she has time to give and your brother Luc needs to spend more time on his feet. I have no one to spare for either task, so I am assigning you to each other. He can help you work your hand and you can help him walk."

"What? No. Anything but that."

"Hasty promises," Caedmon said. "You did say you would do anything."

Rafe groaned. "You don't understand."

"No, I'm afraid I don't. Not in a truly empathetic way," Caedmon admitted. "It's been a very long time since I cared much about what was going on in the outer world, and even when I did, there was no one I disliked enough to want them dead. It seems to me that you two hate each other entirely because your parents taught you to. A childish way to proceed, if you ask me."

Hot anger prickled up and down Rafe's back, and the slick algae on the rocks crystallized into ice under his fingers as Caedmon spoke, but the old Abbot seemed unaware of the chill pouring off Rafe. He folded his hands over his round stomach and stared contentedly at the sea while Rafe sputtered, at a loss for words.

"Cormorants," Caedmon said, pointing at the blackbirds diving in and out of the water. "They were thought to be birds of ill omen in my day. I've always thought they were rather elegant. Come along back to the cloister when you are done with your contemplation, my son. There's work to be done." He patted Rafe on the shoulder and turned, picking his way back over the rocks.

Rafe stared at the cormorants and considered diving into the surf to swim with them. But Caedmon's word "childish" rankled in his brain. After everything he had been through, the battles he had fought, the work he had done from his earliest training to become the youngest Sword of Peace and Justice in the history of the Winter Court, everything he had suffered to be Finn's heir, only to now be called childish by a bald old man who peeled potatoes.

He hurled another rock at the water. It plunked into the waves far short of the diving birds.

"I'll show you childish," he muttered. He tried to put out his wings to fly back, found them tangled in the shirt and robe meant for human use, and angrily stamped back up the slippery rocks on foot rather than wrestle off two layers of clothes. "Childish, forsooth."

Rafe arrived in the corridor outside Monjoie's cell where Aaliyah was helping him walk with crutches. Monjoie was breathing hard and gritting his teeth. After ten steps, Monjoie leaned on the wall, panting. "I can't do any more," he said. "Let me go back to my bed."

Aaliyah tutted at him. "No, no. No more lounging in bed. It's doing you no good at all."

"I'm in pain, woman!" Monjoie snapped at her.

"Yes. I know that. You need ice, salve, and gentle exercise. Fortunately, we have just the person to help you with that." She indicated Rafe with a wave of her hand. "Your brother is an ice faerie, I believe, and he can help you walk. You, in turn, can help him exercise his hand. Together, both of you will heal much faster, and you will discover that you can work together."

Rafe shook his head, arms crossed, while Monjoie sputtered. "Help me heal? He'd as soon help me off a cliff!"

"There's one thing we agree on," Rafe muttered under his breath. Not quietly enough judging from the look Aaliyah gave him.

"Is that any way for brothers to speak to one another?" Aaliyah said.

"We are not brothers!" both shouted in unison, but the healer only looked disappointed and shook her head. Heaving a sigh, she said, "Abbot Caedmon has given his orders, and I do not disagree. So you two will either make each other miserable until one of you leaves, or you will find your healing and your vocation here together."

"We could both leave," Rafe pointed out.

At that, Aaliyah looked truly grieved. She shook her head so that her braids rattled. "No. Even without Aelfburga's words, I do not believe that the two of you would arrive on each other's heels, just when our numbers are at their lowest ebb, for no purpose. Even if one of you departs, the other will be the help we need. You cannot have come here for nothing. I simply do not believe it." Her voice almost cracked on her last sentence, and she sniffed

47

hard against the hint of angry tears in her voice. "Now, the sun is shining, and there is plenty to be done. I expect the two of you to have gone a circuit all the way around the outside of the cloister before the sun sets." She strode off, the gold rings in her hair flashing as they caught motes of light in the corridor.

Rafe and Monjoie looked at each other. Monjoie glared from where he leaned on his crutches, and Rafe returned the look with crossed arms. Monjoie rolled his eyes and yanked himself around, making to go around Rafe toward his bedroom. "I don't care what she says. I'm going to lay down." He crutched away, a small *oof* of pain escaping through his gritted teeth with every labored step.

Outside the sun was shining. The seabirds were calling over the waves and small green plants were springing up between the stones. Rafe groaned and rolled his eyes at himself and the situation. "Let me help you."

Monjoie stopped but did not turn around. After a pause, he said, "Thanks, but I don't need you putting your icy hands on my ass."

"I wasn't going to, you stubborn git." Rafe crossed the distance between them and looped one of Monjoie's arms over his shoulders, stooping a bit to accommodate the height difference. "Lean on me, and I'll help you outside. Maybe some fresh air will blow the stink off you."

Monjoie grunted, but he neither argued nor struggled as Rafe supported his weight. They were both panting by the time they reached the outside air. With Rafe's help, Monjoie lowered himself onto a square stone that had perhaps once been a mounting block. Rafe placed his good hand on the stone, chilling the surface to ease the pain in Monjoie's hip.

Monjoie grunted something that might have been "thank you."

"Don't mention it." Rafe positioned himself nearby where he could look out at the waves.

The two of them sat in silence for a long time.

"How did you get here?" Monjoie asked.

"A pair of selkies rescued me. Then I walked," Rafe said. "You?"

"I washed up down there." Monjoie pointed to the base of the island. "I had just enough strength to call for help while the waves were bashing me against the rocks."

"Ow."

"Yeah."

They sat in further silence for a while.

"I don't know what Aaliyah expects me to do for you," Monjoie said. "I'm no healer. If your hand hurts you can make your own ice."

"It doesn't hurt much. Mostly, I don't feel anything." Rafe held his hand out to demonstrate. "I can barely move it." After another pause between them, Rafe said, "We should probably do what we're told."

"Always the obedient boy, aren't you?"

"There's no shame in doing what your host asks you to do," Rafe snapped. "And if you hadn't noticed, we're both at their mercy, no matter how good they seem to be. Do you want to test these people's patience?"

Monjoie groaned and tried to pull himself to his feet. Rafe quickly went to his side. "Lean on me," he said. "It's easier than those crutches." Monjoie said nothing, but he set aside his crutches.

Together, with many pauses to rest and more than a few bitter words, they inched their way around the circuit of the monastery. The sun waned, and their stomachs began to growl. At last, they made it back to the kitchen.

Aelfburga, her eyes more focused than they had been before, smiled at them both and Caedmon waved. On the table, silverware and plates were set ready for supper.

"Well done," he said. "I knew the two of you would rise to the challenge."

Both Monjoie and Rafe grunted in response. Rafe dumped Monjoie into a chair at the table, meaning to head elsewhere, but Caedmon stopped him.

"I think both of you deserve some small reward. Who would you like to see most in the world at the moment?"

Rafe's heart leapt. Of course, the monastery had a mirror somewhere around here. They had other forms of magic. "Deor," he said. "I need to speak to her."

Caedmon shook his head as he set a wide, shallow bowl on the table and poured clear water into it. "I'm afraid talking isn't an option, though if you concentrate you will be able to hear. Come closer." Caedmon stirred the water in the bowl and flicked the rim with his fingernail so that it rang with a single note. The water rippled as the note went on.

Rafe and Monjoie leaned forward on either side of Caedmon, peering into the water. As the ripples crossed and recrossed in the water images took shape. The throne room. Deor seated upon the throne with Lt. Stephen Bolton and...Victor? On either side of her. Roger stood before the throne, holding out a scroll with the seal of Parliament on it. Rafe swallowed hard and focused all his attention on the scene.

"We ask for a Proving," Roger said.

"What?" Rafe shouted as Victor snapped something at Roger. Deor's eyes glowed silver, and her nails gleamed. Rafe clapped a hand over his mouth and concentrated to get the sound back.

Roger spoke again. "Parliament will declare a vote of no confidence in you as Regent. They will seek out the King, wherever he is, and either bring him back to London, or let him rule from where he is." Roger rolled up the scroll and held it out to her. "For your perusal."

Genevieve snatched it from Roger and moved up to stand by the throne. What the devil was Genevieve doing there? Rafe watched in stunned silence as Deor agreed to Parliament's terms.

The water stilled, and all that was left to see was the stoneware bottom of the bowl.

"Here?" Rafe shouted. Aelfburga winced and Rafe lowered his voice. "They are coming here for the Proving?"

"It is the traditional location," Caedmon sighed. "We are the most neutral of neutral ground. Blasted faerie politics. They couldn't have selected a worse time." He let out another exasperated sigh and turned to Monjoie. "What or who would you like to see?"

Monjoie looked suspiciously at Rafe, doubt and longing fighting in his face, before he said, "My family and my...Juliette. I don't know where she might be at the moment though."

"You don't have to," Caedmon said, his voice kind. "Just focus your attention." He struck the bowl again, and the clear note sounded, sending ripples across the water.

Unwilling to contain his curiosity, Rafe peered into the bowl as well. The ripples became a parlor, warm and inviting. Dark wood beams crossed the ceiling, and a low fire burned in the fireplace, though the diamond-paned windows stood open to let in the evening breeze. On the mantelpiece, a magnificent fan coral stood. A blonde woman with skin the color of the ocean on a sunny day sat on one of the two couches, a grim look on her face. A man who could only be Monjoie's father paced in front of the fire.

"Juliette," Monjoie breathed. "Mon amour."

That was new information. Rafe had not considered that Monjoie might have a lover somewhere.

"How is your wife?" Juliette said, her voice tight.

"She fears the worst," Monjoie's father said. "She asked our healer to give her something to help her sleep."

Juliette nodded. "I wish we had the sort of connection the poets write about," she said. "Then I would know for sure. But I don't know and so I won't give up. He's not dead. He's missing. All sorts of things could be happening we don't know about."

"All sorts of things most likely are."

"Besides," Juliette said. "The duchess sent me a very kind note yesterday. She says not to give up hope and that she is confident Luc will return. I trust her."

"As do I," Monjoie's father said. "She has always been a kind patron to our family. She would not lie to us now."

Rafe clapped a hand over his mouth to keep from snorting in derision.

"Are you going home tonight after supper?" Monjoie's father said.

"Of course, I don't want to impose on you." Juliette got to her feet, her voice cheerful.

"No, no! You misunderstand me," Monjoie's father said. "It is we who are imposing on you." He crossed the parlor rug and took her hands. "Cherie, you are like a daughter in this house. I thought you might want to be home, not waiting here with two anxious parents. It can't be easy on you."

"It is easy on me," she said. "Easier than going home and pretending I'm not thinking of him every second. I…" Her voice cracked a touch, and she straightened her back even further. "I want to sleep in his bed and wake up with his belongings around me. It helps me believe he will be back soon."

"Of course! Anything you want!" Monjoie's father threw his arms around Juliette and hugged her.

A tear dropped into the bowl, breaking the image, and the scene disappeared. Rafe looked up to see Monjoie gritting his teeth and swiping an arm across his eyes. "Please," he said. "I have to go home to them. I don't care if I can't walk. Let me go."

"In good time," Caedmon said, "if that is what you wish." He squeezed Monjoie's shoulder. For a second, Rafe saw Monjoie not as an enemy and a traitor, but as a man of Wellhall, just a country fellow longing for his home and the people he loved. Rafe shook his head. Monjoie was a snake, a practiced liar, and a spy. For all Rafe knew, this display of emotion was just another ploy to lull the monastery into doing what he wanted.

Turning on his heel, Rafe deliberately walked away from Caedmon and Monjoie to ask Aelfburga what she needed him to do.

"Nothing but sit and eat, dear boy," she said. "The others will be here in a moment."

Even as she said it, Evelyn and Aaliyah came tramping into the kitchen, laughing at some joke between them and declaring that everything smelled wonderful.

"You both made it!" Evelyn shouted at Rafe. "We were just about to send a search party for you."

Happily taking the chance to get as far from Monjoie as possible, Rafe took a seat at the far end of the table with Evelyn. He ignored Aaliyah's disappointed look.

As the rest of the cloister took their seats, Caedmon stood at the head of the table and raised his hands. "Let us each give thanks according to our way."

Again Rafe closed his eyes and said, "Thank you," quietly. And again he felt better for having said it.

The thanks concluded, everyone dug into their meals without further ceremony. Rafe ate his meat and potatoes with all the relish of a good workout and helped himself to a huge second helping. He settled into conversation with Evelyn and Lachar and let himself forget that Monjoie was even at the table.

Shortly before dawn, Evelyn woke Rafe for their watch. Together they climbed the winding stairs that led to the highest vantage point on the island. Only the towering church spire extended further, and that was too narrow for them to get up. Up here in the chill wind blowing inland off the sea, even Rafe felt the cold. He pulled on the brown wool robe he'd been provided and tucked his hands into his sleeves. He shifted his weight back onto his heels ever so slightly, keeping his knees unlocked.

Evelyn eyed him up and down before perching on the stone lip of the tower and pulling a rectangular packet out of his pocket. "I can see you've stood watch plenty of times before. The sergeant won't catch you napping."

Rafe laughed and relaxed his stance a bit. "Force of habit," he admitted. "I came up through the Palace Guard."

Evelyn nodded appreciatively and lit a cigarette, pulling in the smoke as he looked out toward the dawn. After a few puffs, he regarded his cigarette fondly and said, "We used to call these coffin nails in the trenches. Now they tell me they can kill you. Too bad I'm already dead." He chuckled to himself and inhaled again.

Trying to keep his eyes on the surrounding area while making conversation, Rafe let a beat pass.

"You're dead?" he asked. He held off from the next most obvious question—did that mean he was dead too?

"Oh well, I suppose it's a bit of a technicality," Evelyn said. "I'm dead out there. Or just as good as. It's not easy to say really. But I'd find out right quick if I set foot off this island. Aaliyah and Aelfburga have made that clear enough."

"I don't understand…"

Evelyn waved his cigarette toward the land side where the sun was cresting the horizon. "Over there, at least on the human side of things," he said, "we call that France. We had a jolly big war in my day. The Great War, they were calling it by the time I got conscripted. I made it through the first day, but we went over the top on the second. Got the order and up we went. Last thing I heard was a whistling sound." He paused to see if Rafe understood the significance of this detail.

"Ballista?" Rafe said.

"Gas canister. Silly bugger that I was, I'd lent my mask to my mate the night before. His had a crack in it. Went down drowning in my own lungs," Evelyn nodded. "Next thing I know, I'm here. Thought I'd died and gone to heaven at first. Now I know better, but I'm not sure I'd trade it. Don't know what I'd do with myself in heaven. Here the food and drink's good, the company's good, and I can keep an eye peeled for any bastard that wants to wreck the calm of it all."

They sat together a long while that way, each man looking past the other's shoulder, watching each other's back as the sun rose.

"Does that mean I'll die if I leave?" Rafe asked. He wasn't sure how he felt about that, no matter what the answer was. But it was always good to have the facts. A sneaking, suspicious thought came to him that Caedmon's invitation to leave might have been a trap, a half-truth. Free to leave, but not free of the consequences if he tried.

"No." Evelyn spat over the parapet. "You came here on your own two feet. You were on the edge there for a bit, but not over it. Some, like you, come here from need. Some get the call and find the road. Some, the others have to go out and get. Joan and me, we're in the last category, you understand. She'd burst right into flames if she set foot in the world again."

Horrified, Rafe stared at him. "Why?"

"Cause a bunch of English tied her to a stake and set fire to her, that's why. If you die out there and go back, you don't get a second chance."

9

Deor slammed Roger's petition down on the conference room table and flung herself into the seat at the head. "That pompous..."

"Ass?" Genevieve finished for her. She settled in her normal place along the table. Victor and Stephen, both looking equal parts angry and exhausted, sat as well.

"That works," Deor nodded. "So, the Proving?" She looked around the table.

"I've read about them," Victor said. "There hasn't been one in a long time."

"In the Faerie Courts," Genevieve said. "There was a Proving not that long ago. Remember, the Goblin Parliament challenged Gregory and his wife."

"Oh, right," Victor nodded. "I remember hearing about that from my parents. They made Geoff's mother put her hands on him and on the throne and swear his legitimacy. If she'd been lying, it would have killed them both."

"Sounds humiliating," Deor said.

"And more dangerous, at least physically, than the Proving you'll deal with." Genevieve shook her head. "I cannot believe Roger is being such a horrible tit."

"I can," Victor said. "He's always been a bit that way."

"The Aethelwings have had a long relationship with Northfalls," Genevieve said. "Roger was dear friends with Finn's mother. It makes sense he would take Finn's side."

"He has to know what a monster that man is!" Stephen insisted. He snatched the scroll from parliament and opened it, scanning it. He finished and dropped it back on the table. "It doesn't look too horrible, though we are apparently responsible for catering the event."

"Oh good. Crudites for everyone." Deor propped her elbows on the table and rested her head in her hands. "We can put off dealing with the specifics of the event until tomorrow." She looked back up at her people. "Wait for the monks to call, I guess?"

"They will," Victor said. "They've been a neutral space for as long as there have been courts. At least that's what I learned from my tutor. They've often been used as a place for treaty meetings. Violating that space is bad, possibly fatal, and not by the monks. The space itself."

"Joy." Deor pushed back from the table.

The mirror on the wall blurred, waiting to be acknowledged. The house crest of Northfalls gleamed.

"There's no way Roger got back to Northfalls that fast. Even if he portalled." Stephen rolled his eyes. "So that means it's the King."

"Everyone out of sight of the mirror," Deor said.

"You could just not answer it," Victor suggested as he switched seats.

"If I don't, it will only be worse when I do." When everyone was settled out of the mirror's sight, Deor sighed. "Answer Northfalls." She didn't even bother to put on a bright, or even non-hostile face, and she didn't try to un-silver her eyes either.

"Daughter," the King said, smiling. He sat in a wing-back chair, Arthur at his side, sporting his thousand-yard stare. "How was your Petition Day?" He was smirking, like the cat that ate the canary. "Anything interesting?" He softened his face, trying for an expression of sympathy, perhaps. "I know that dealing with people can be difficult."

He knew difficult, that was certain.

"For the most part, it was delightful," Deor said, trying to remember the smile on the youngest Jaccob's face. "There were a couple of unhappy people, but up until the end, it was exhausting but good. I liked having the chance to talk to ordinary people. I learned a lot today."

"You know nothing about the country," Finn said. "It's a miracle you haven't caused a war."

"Me?" Deor shrugged. "I'm not particularly warlike. Though we did hear from the werewolves. They've officially left the Winter Court and denied the protectorate. Thanks for that."

Finn's eyes flashed silver. "Those ungrateful animals!" He rose from his chair and paced. "You cannot let this insult stand!" He glared at her. "Send troops immediately! Show them what it is to insult the Winter Court!"

"No." Deor shook her head. "For so many reasons. Number one, it is the fault of the Winter Court—the fault of the King—that this happened. You banned them. They left and won't come back. Now you want to go to war over it? That's a waste of troops. War is coming with the Summer Court—"

"And you think you can survive that? You can't handle a few unruly, barely civilized beasts, and you think you can take on D'nath, the Summer Court Sword, one of the best generals in history?" He laughed, cruel and sharp.

"I don't know." Deor shook her head. "But you ignored the signs long enough, with the help of your toadie there." She waved at Arthur who winced slightly. "I've read the reports. There's been a massive increase in Summer Court military exercises along the border. They're not doing that for nothing."

"Nonsense!" The King waved her comment away, sounding as sure as ever. How nice it would be to have that kind of conviction in one's opinions. "If they do, it will be because the Winter Court is destabilized by your little stunt. Keeping me in exile!"

Exhaustion rendered her incapable of anger. All she could do was sigh. "As soon as you can open the portals, as soon as the palace says you're fit to come back, open the portals and come back. I'll gladly hand everything back to you." She stared at him. "So?" she said. "Open them."

"Disrespectful, treasonous wench!" He pointed at her. "You sit on a stolen throne!"

"I'm Regent, not Queen," she said softly. "I haven't taken your throne." Besides, the throne hadn't objected, not even a little bit. "But if all you wanted is to call and yell at me, I'm going to end the call. I'm tired. And hungry. It's been a long day."

"The Proving!" Finn pointed a finger at her. "You'll fail miserably! I know it!"

Deor nodded. "Okay, sure."

"I'm sure of it! You will fail!"

"Okay," Deor repeated. She wasn't going to fight about it. "When that happens, you'll be all set to come back. Roger can lead you to the throne and drop your favorite crown on your head."

"And you—"

"I'll be back in the Tower, or at the block. I know, Finn. We've been over your homicidal fantasies about me." She had to learn to hold her tongue. Now she'd increased the length of the call by several minutes. A vein in his temple throbbed.

Maybe he'd have a stroke. She shook her head. She had to stop being so unkind. It wasn't that he deserved better, but she should not make a joke of someone's death. That's how bad rulers were made. First, they thought it: *why shouldn't I do what I want? I know what's best.* Then they said it out loud: *I'll handle this my way.* Then they did it: *The Tower is full of people, and the block is soaked in blood.*

"You will fail," he hissed. "I promise you that." He turned on his heel and strode out of the room, leaving Arthur staring at her.

"Arthur?" Deor asked. "Do you have something to say to me? Have you heard from Rafe?"

"What?" Arthur blinked. Clearly, he'd been miles away through Finn's little diatribe. A skill he'd likely mastered decades ago. "No." He shook his head as if to clear it. "Not at all. You?"

"No." She didn't state the obvious. Rafe must be dead. She changed the topic. "Is everything at Northfalls good? At least as good as it can be?"

Arthur stared at her for a long moment. "No." He crossed his arms. "Roger needs to come home. Now."

"There's nothing I can do about that," Deor said. "He delivered his petition in person. I don't know that there's anything else keeping him here." Arthur's frown unsettled her. "If I see him again, I'll tell him."

"Do." He looked about to speak.

"Arthur!" Finn shouted from somewhere off-screen. "To me! Now!"

Arthur winced at every syllable. He glanced back over his shoulder, then returned his gaze to her. "Prepare well for the Proving," Arthur said, his voice a whisper. "The King must not be allowed back in the palace."

The mirror went black before Deor could respond.

"Did the rest of you hear that?"

They all nodded.

"Arthur—Mr. Don't You Dare Break a Rule; Mr. I'm Sure Some Time in the Tower Will Fix Her—suggested that the King not be allowed back." Stephen said.

"That's one hell of a rule to break." Victor mused.

"This is bad," Genevieve said softly.

"What do you mean?" Deor asked. "Seems good for us, if Arthur wants to keep him there."

"What could possibly make him think that?" Genevieve asked. "It must be something truly awful. Something that would violate Arthur's unbreakable legalism."

"The King broke an inviolable law," Victor said. "But I can't even begin to think what that would be to Arthur. I mean, he saw nothing wrong with arresting kids, jailing the innocent, and torturing the heir, so where, exactly, is his line in the sand?"

Deor shook her head. "I've got no idea. But whatever is going on up there, it can't be good. And I'm sure it will be our problem sooner rather than later." Deor pushed away from the table and stood. "But we can't do anything about it tonight. Let's go get some food, then get some sleep. Tomorrow we've got to figure out the Proving." She nodded at Genevieve. "What, exactly, does one wear to justify one's rule as Regent?"

"I don't think there's a *Noble Babbies Noble Book* rule," Genevieve said with a smile. "But I'll come up with something."

10

After Rafe and Monjoie had done their usual circuit around the
inner cloister the next morning, Monjoie declared he was going
back to bed to nap whether Aaliyah approved or not. Since Rafe
was glad of the excuse not to spend any more time with him, he cheerfully helped Monjoie to his room. Afterward, Rafe spent some time in the
kitchen, awkwardly helping Aelfburga as best he could with his non-
dominant hand. Little pains shot through his left hand from time to time,
and he hoped Aaliyah was right that it meant healing.

It turned out that Aelfburga was not much of a talker even when she
wasn't communing, but her company was more soothing than disturbing.
From time to time, she paused with her face upturned and eyes closed,
bathed in the sunlight from a high window, as if listening to distant
music.

When Rafe offered to turn the spit for her, she fixed him with a
suddenly piercing look, laying her hand on his shoulder and looking up
into his eyes as if she could see every fiber of his being all at once. He
shivered as she looked at him, the immensity of being so sharply and fully
known unsettling him, but she only patted him on the cheek and drifted
away, her eyes focused on the unseen again. Rafe stood where she had left
him, turning the spit, but the sweat running down his back had nothing
to do with the heat of the fire.

Lunch was an ad hoc affair. Around noon, Aelfburga set out cold leftovers, cheeses, and meats, along with some vegetables, and members of the community drifted through, taking a plate with them or eating in pairs and leaving again. They all greeted Rafe as if he were one of them, but all seemed absorbed in their tasks.

Eventually, Aaliyah came from healing Monjoie and told him it was his turn. She had him sit at the long wooden table with her where she could examine his hand. First, she rubbed a sharp-smelling green ointment into it, massaging his hand and arm all over up to the elbow. Then she cradled his hand in both of hers, closing her eyes and humming in discordant notes as she pressed her fingers into his bones and flesh. She spent the most time on his wrist and palm, her face contorted as if with struggle. At last she heaved a sigh and let go.

"Whew," she said. "That bone did not want to heal. Stubborn thing. Try flexing your hand now."

With a little bit of concentration, Rafe was able to slowly close and open his hand. His thumb remained awkward and unhelpful, but his fingers curled inward almost enough to touch his palm.

Aaliyah brushed her hands together. "A good day's work, if I do say so myself. And now as your healer, I want you to go outside and get some sunlight. Breathe the fresh air. Get the blood flowing in your veins. We'll do some more tomorrow. In the meantime, keep your hand moving. Find something like an apple to squeeze so your muscles and sinews don't forget what they're for."

Rafe padded out of the kitchen through the wide-open doorway at the far end, seeking the open sky and the smell of the sea. He passed a turn or two that seemed to lead deeper into the monastery but chose to follow his nose to the outside. Eventually, his feet led him to a wide space paved with flagstones and ringed with a broken wall of stone that looked out over the open sea. In the center of the space, a tanned woman with short dark hair stood with her back to him. Her brown monk's robe was cast aside over the stone wall, and she wore a similar pair of linen trousers and shirt to the ones Aelfburga had supplied Rafe to wear under his robes.

As Rafe watched, she balanced on one foot, raising her arms high over her head so that the sword in her hand formed a continuous line with her body. She continued to move through each pose so slowly that her individual movements were invisible to the eye, and yet she undeniably shifted form. Fascinated, Rafe realized he was seeing the Swan Blade discipline performed with a level of grace and control he'd only heard about in books. He held his breath, not wanting to disturb the Sword Master in front of him.

Finally, she settled into the last posture, Repose, and gave him a bright smile. "Welcome!" she said, coming toward him with a hand outheld. "I knew the minute I saw your hands you were a swordsman. Good to have you in the cloister."

"Maitresse," he said, bowing. "I would be honored if you would teach me." As he said it, he wondered if he was asking for a useless gift. He held up his sword hand. "Perhaps I spoke too soon."

"Self-pity won't get you very far," she said. "If your left hand is no good for the blade, use the other one." She eyed him up and down, as he had seen Arthur eyeing horses for sale, and prodded his biceps. "You have the balance for Swan Blade, but you're a bit tight and bulky."

Rafe nodded. "I am." He ducked his head. "I tend to look more like a lumbering ox than a swan when I attempt it."

She laughed and shook her head. "False modesty is no virtue. Though if you want any other lessons in virtue, you'll have to talk to Aelfburga. My name is Joan. Care to sweat with me?" She indicated a rack of weapons against the wall.

"I'd be honored," Rafe said.

As he examined the weapons, Joan sheathed her own blade and selected a long bamboo staff.

"Here," she said. "It's light, and you can use it in two hands or one."

Rafe took the staff, weighing it and trying to hold down the weight of his own disappointment. Here he was faced with a Sword Master better than perhaps even D'nath of the Summer Court, and she was handing him a foot soldier's tool. A blunt object to hit people with. "I haven't spent much time with this weapon. I'll give it a try if you think it's worth it."

Joan stepped back, her mouth pursed and her eyes narrowed. "You think it's beneath you."

Rafe couldn't deny the accusation so he said nothing, biting his lip as he stared at the bamboo, hating the weakness in his hand.

"When I led the armies of France against the English, there were plenty of knights who thought it was beneath them to listen to a mere girl."

"Forgive me," Rafe said. "I'm not denying your worthiness. It's just..." He thrust out his broken hand at her. "Look at it. I can't hold a kitchen knife, let alone a real blade. I'm useless. Reduced to a peasant's stick. I might as well use this...this...rod to drive cattle."

Her stance softened, but there was no leeway in her tone as she said, "My body was damaged when I came here too. I couldn't walk from bed to chamber pot for weeks. And when I could, every step hurt. But even then, I wasn't useless. No one is useless. No body is useless."

With one motion she stripped off her linen shirt and stood before him naked from the waist up. Her skin flamed red in the light of the westering sun, and Rafe gasped. Every inch of her torso was scarred as if she had been dipped in fire. Ropes of shiny scars etched patterns across her chest and down her arms.

"I earned every one of these scars, every inch of pain. And I work every day, not to overcome my body, but to care for it. Do you understand?" She came closer, pulling her shirt back on and tucking it into her pants. Taking his sword hand in hers, Joan said, "Did this hand do all it could?"

Rafe nodded, unable to speak.

"Then you dishonor it, by calling it useless." Gently, with calloused fingers, she closed Rafe's wounded hand around the bamboo staff. This close, Rafe saw that she was smaller than Deor, stockier in build, but a head shorter. Still holding his hand, she looked up at him, deep into his eyes. Girl might be the most ridiculous term he could have called her, and his ear tips blushed at the thought.

"Let me teach you to understand your body again," Joan said. "Whether you ever pick up another blade or not."

"I would be honored."

She stepped back, smiled, and offered him a small bow. "Let's begin."

Under Joan's watchful eye, Rafe went through the standard swordsman's warm up that he'd practiced a thousand times in his life. His left hand slipped off the bamboo staff, and he panted a bit, trying to keep both arms even.

"Slower," Joan said as he finished.

He gave her an inquiring look, but she just shook her blade at him and took a perch on a nearby stone. He repeated the warm up, pushing himself to slow each motion without getting sloppy.

"Slower!" Joan shouted. She hopped off her rock circling him, blade held loose at her side. "Eyes on me. Don't lose control."

His heart beat harder, lungs burning with expansion as he maintained the drill while keeping pace with his circling teacher-opponent. This was getting genuinely difficult, and he hadn't even begun something complicated. By the time he was thirty, he could do the warm ups hungover and half asleep and still be complimented by the drill master as an example to the squad. This small woman with her darting motions was making him work.

A fierce grin was growing on her face as he spun into the last motion. "Ready? En garde!" She darted inside his defense and smacked his staff with hers. That was the only warning he got before she was dancing faster than a needle, in and out of his reach, landing hits as delicate as a blown kiss on his torso.

Rafe struck back, lunging to the full extent of his legs and right arm, but Joan shifted her rib cage a hair's breadth to the left, and he missed. She tapped him on the wrist and ducked under his riposte. He charged, and she stepped into his range, throwing off his movement and forcing him to throw his weight backward to avoid a crash. Her blade skimmed across his midsection.

"What was that?" she shouted, sounding disappointed. "Are you going easy on me?"

Panting, he managed "Don't want...a tangle."

She laughed. "You watch your own footwork. I'll watch mine." She rapped his staff again with her blade, and it echoed with a hollow sound. But he was cannier this time. He shifted his weight into a defensive posture, studying her as he parried. There was no time limit on this match. Time to get a feel for his opponent.

He flexed his shoulders, adjusting his grip a hair's breadth and shifted into an Agrippa defense. Joan saw what he was doing and gave him a satisfied nod before redoubling her attack. Rafe responded with a Cat's Cradle, and she whooped before bouncing off the monastery wall to leap twisting over his head.

"Use your wings!" she said.

"I don't need them yet," he said back, laughing.

"Oh, you will by the time we're done!" she laughed in return.

Back and forth their battle raged over the flagstones as the sun dipped into the west and the monastery's shadow covered the courtyard. Every so often the two opponents would pause to breathe. As the shadows grew, so did their pauses.

"I yield," Rafe gasped finally. Every muscle felt like jelly. His wings quivered with exhaustion. He dropped his staff and staggered over to the sea wall, sitting and panting. Joan joined him. He took some satisfaction in noticing that she also took a long while to pant before she could speak again.

"I have not had a bout like that in, oh, fifty years, I should think," she said. "You're a marvel."

Rafe shook his head. "I'm knackered. I barely landed a hit on you."

"You'll learn. Besides, you only just came out of the sea a few days ago. I should have called a halt."

A chuckle from the doorway turned both their heads. Caedmon stood there smiling. He came and joined them at the wall. "Yes, please don't wear our new brother to a frazzle before he's even gotten the sea water out of his lungs."

Joan waved off the caution. "He's a water faerie. He probably prefers to be damp."

Rafe smiled as she said it, taking deep breaths of the wet sea air. The wind cooled the sweat in his hair. The sound of the gulls and the waves crashing below soothed his soul in a way nothing had for a long, long time. When was the last time he had been at sea? Not since Deor arrived in the Winter Court. It seemed years gone. He watched the waves and remembered the dread he had felt as the *Duke's Pride* had sailed under the Tower bridge. It had felt less like a homecoming than a return from parole. Even after Finn had his girl back and Rafe was free to simply be Sword and not the Heir, he had not felt free. "I am a water faerie," he said out loud. "I'm not sure what else I am. Or ever was. Perhaps, I don't exist at all."

The other two did not seem startled or embarrassed by such a personal declaration. They nodded and looked out to sea with him. The sun's lower edge touched the horizon, and a sense of unease grew in Rafe's innards. He squinted into the middle distance, holding up a hand to shield his eyes.

"Something is out there."

Joan and Caedmon nodded. "The Enemy. Our one-time prisoner. Now it is our duty to keep him out until either we fail or some opponent comes to stop him for good."

Joan muttered something about Saint Denis and made a sign.

Rafe leaned farther over the broken parapets. The person, whoever they were, was coming closer, though not swimming or in a boat. They seemed more to be fading in and out of reality, never fully coming into focus but getting nearer each time and progressing along the borders of the monastery. At each approach his sense of unease grew, along with a sense of familiarity.

"Are they testing the wards?" he guessed.

"Always," Joan said. She glared at the figure, now within shouting distance. "Be off with you! Do you think we are asleep? Get gone, or we'll put you in a cell you'll like even less than the last one!"

Caedmon made a soothing noise and patted Joan's shoulder. Rafe couldn't have described the creature in any specific detail—the harder he tried the more his mind refused to give it a shape—but he was certain that the thing made an obscene gesture in response to Joan's shout.

"Am I insane to think I've met this enemy before?" Mont Saint-Michel seemed to be a good place for asking strange questions.

"Not at all," Caedmon said. "He is drawn to power and powerful people he can exploit to his own ends. If you grew up in the court, I expect you met him more than once, though he may have worn different faces. You most likely found him overwhelmingly charming, almost painfully so. People who meet him in Fae feel a strong compulsion to gain his approval. Humans generally find him terrifying and seductive in equal measure."

Rafe shivered, a sense of revulsion running down his body as if he had just been handed a live leech and told to give it a kiss. "Why can't I recognize him now?"

Joan dismissed the figure with a disgusted wave of her hand. "He's closer to his true self here. This place makes it hard to hold on to false forms. In the Winter Court, he only would have shown you whatever form you found delightful or trustworthy."

"I see," Rafe said, though he didn't. "Yes, I think... I think I've seen him before. I don't remember his name though."

The sun sank lower, and the figure began to retreat into the shadowy east, avoiding the last light of the day. Behind them a bell rang, a cheerful, homely clang.

"Dinner time," Caedmon said. "Let's get in before the damp gives us all the arthritis."

"Is it safe? Shouldn't we keep watch with...him so close?"

Joan stretched and yawned. "Evelyn and Lachar are on watch tonight, yes?"

Caedmon nodded. "We can go in," he assured Rafe. Rafe went with them, but he wondered how tight a watch could be set by a cloister only six strong, one of whom seemed unaware of her own surroundings.

Overhead, the bell rang again, and the three of them picked up their pace, hurrying to join the rest of the cloister in the kitchen where a large roast, surrounded by gorgeously browned potatoes and carrots, waited to be carved.

As Rafe settled into the rhythm of life in the monastery, he took up daily sword lessons with Joan and a regular turn on watch. But his primary duty was helping Monjoie perform his exercises. Monjoie in turn was required to massage Rafe's hand for him and help him squeeze a tightly wound wool ball. It was no joy for either of them.

After their therapy regimen ended each day, Caedmon assigned them each to different tasks in tandem and always a task that neither could complete on his own. Today, they had been sent to help Aaliyah in the gardens.

The gardens were sheltered within the monastery's inner walls, protected from the constant wind off the ocean. Here spring was in full bloom, tiny flowers poking through the soil in shades of pink, yellow, and white. Raised beds were separated by lawns of springy, low-growing aromatic herbs, and all around the walls grew fruit trees and vines, carefully trimmed and pinned to the stonework in a living lattice.

Their first task was to shred huge baskets of dried seaweed, then dig it into the soil. Aaliyah explained the process to them, showed them where the tools were stored, then went about her business in the garden.

Rafe looked at Monjoie who returned the look. They regarded the baskets of stinking seaweed, the trowels and hoes. "Another team-building exercise," Monjoie said. "It's boot camp all over again."

"At least we're not being told we don't eat until everyone on the team finishes the course."

Monjoie harrumphed. "I wouldn't put it past them."

"Right," Rafe said. "Let's divide and conquer. You sit on the bench and shred seaweed. I'll turn the dirt."

"Fine with me, but you can't manage a spade with one hand," Monjoie said.

"Then I'll stoop and use a trowel." Rafe dumped Monjoie onto a stone bench.

"Jackass," Monjoie said.

Rafe flipped him off with his right hand and grabbed a trowel.

As they worked, Aaliyah moved back and forth in the garden. She brought around a watering can full of "worm tea" and anointed the garden with it while lecturing on the virtues of soil and mineral balances. Rafe got the impression that if they hadn't been there she might still have delivered the lesson for the sheer delight she took in her work.

At the last bed, full of tiny two-leaved sprouts and dark, crumbly loam, Aaliyah knelt and dug her hands into the soil. She pulled out a double handful, inviting Rafe and Monjoie to join her. "Smell that," she said. "Delightful. It's coming along beautifully."

Dutifully, Rafe sniffed the soil. To his surprise it didn't smell like garbage or seaweed. It smelled wet and rich, almost appetizing. But still certainly dirt. Monjoie took a pinch of the soil in his fingers and crumbled it, looking like he might be about to taste it.

"It's the worms that do it," Aaliyah said. "Don't you, my dears?" She sifted over the soil in her hands until a few fat and wriggling night-crawlers emerged. "Just keep these fellows well fed and they'll turn your garden over for you better than any spade. Be careful not to chop into them when you lift a spadeful of soil."

Rafe couldn't share her enthusiasm for the eyeless worms, but he nodded along. He certainly wouldn't deny the tastiness of the garden's produce. He stooped and dug, stooped and dug. It was good, rhythmic work, and he enjoyed the simplicity of it.

After the seaweed fertilizer had been distributed, Aaliyah made Rafe sit on the bench beside Monjoie. She brought a chair over for herself and settled into it next to them. "So, what questions do you have for me?"

"Who or what is the Enemy?" Rafe said. "He feels familiar to me. Like a faerie I've met, but not quite. I need more information."

Aaliyah grimaced. "It's difficult to describe him. You probably feel we're all being very mystical and obscure."

"I do, yes," Rafe said.

She laughed a bit. The little gold rings in her ears and woven through her hair shone as she tilted her face toward the summer sun. "It's not intentional. I suppose we've all gotten so used to dealing with him we speak in shorthand. And he's slippery, very difficult to pin down or describe unless he wants you to see him. If that happens, you'll see the face he thinks will most get your compliance."

Rafe frowned. This was sounding like one of Dell's more religious moments. But Aaliyah went on, "the Enemy is just what we call him because it's a description we can all agree on. He's not exactly a faerie, but he's closer to being a faerie than anything else. Sort of what came before there were faeries, before there was a Winter or Summer Court. In a way, he's your ancestor."

Monjoie frowned deeper at that and shook his head, as if denying that anything as creepy as the thing they had seen earlier was his ancestor, and asked, "Why does he want to get in here? Aside from the fact that you all kept him prisoner once."

"Power. The same old reason anyone causes chaos and destruction, I suppose," Aaliyah said. "He wants power over the world, and we keep him from it."

Rafe tapped the trowel thoughtfully against his boot with his free hand. "Why not use that power yourselves? Kill him once and for all if he's so dangerous."

"We can't." The dark-skinned woman held up a hand as Rafe opened his mouth to object. "Believe me, I would kill him in a heartbeat if I had a way. The power we guard is not anything we can use or control. Monks have tried. So we do what we can until the world can be healed. Or destroyed." She looked around her garden with fond sadness. "Some people say they are the same thing. I hope they are wrong."

Rafe wondered what this gentle woman who coaxed green shoots out of the soil and thanked the fish she used for fertilizer could really do against an enemy of any kind. What could any of them do, for that matter, besides Joan and possibly Evelyn? A cloister of the elderly and the dead.

11

Deor swept her gaze across all the people at the table with her. She had a full house now, or at least a fuller one. Victor and Stephen, one on each side of her, had always been there for her. Now she had Bill, Genevieve, and Astarte. Brand sat at her side, chin on the arm of her chair, and Jake and Sam were a few feet away. All of them looked to her. They were there for her, to help her, but she had to do the leading.

"So," Deor said, clearing her throat. "The Proving is in a few days, and I believe I'll actually get to speak to the HMIC—the head monk in charge —today. If he calls." She gave a tight smile. "But we have a more pressing problem. I need a consort, and I need one soon." She looked at Astarte.

"A consort is as critical as any of the other offices, perhaps more so in circumstances like the Proving," Astarte said. "The King, or Regent's, magic isn't a faucet you can turn off," she said. "It's more like a rushing river. The Consort acts as a dam with an overflow area for safety. Without a consort, the magic pours in, sometimes without warning or permission, and it drowns the monarch, often exploding outward. For example," she pointed at the handful of sparks spiraling away from Deor and caught one in her hand. "Ouch!" She laughed. "I should have known they'd be sharp."

"Sorry!" Deor said. "I don't mean them to be."

"Exactly." Astarte nodded. "The Proving is all about demonstrating control. Spiky missiles shooting off you at unknown intervals are the opposite of that."

"Can clothing help?" Genevieve asked. "Could we bundle her up in something that would hold them in?"

Astarte shrugged. "Maybe a suit of iron."

"No." Victor shook his head. "She isn't bothered by iron at all. It didn't hurt her in the Tower, and it didn't dampen her magic, not even a little."

"That's a state secret we need to keep." Astarte said. "So, no, fashion is out."

"I have to have somewhere to put it all," Deor said. "That's the only solution. I need a consort." She scanned the people around the table. She'd already settled on it being Stephen or Victor. Stephen she trusted completely, but he was the only one with any knowledge of how the Palace Guard operated. There was no one to be Shield but him.

"Could it be me?" Bill asked.

"No." Deor shook her head. "It isn't that I haven't thought about it. I have. You're a human, bard or no, and that means the magic is different." She looked at Victor. "Will you do it?"

"Me? But I'm already the Sword." Victor jolted, surprise on his face.

"I need a Consort more than I need a Sword," she said. "And we're at peace. I trust you. You aren't afraid to say no to me. You are comfortable at things like the Proving, and comfortable at court. You were there for me in the Tower. You're a child of the Winter Court—and of Wellhall too. And," she sighed, "you know how to fight. You can physically protect me."

"Good reasons," Victor said, but he sounded unsure. "People might not trust me. I am Madeline's child, after all. That could hurt you."

"I suppose," Deor shrugged. "But I trust you. Please?"

"Yes," he said softly. "I will be your Consort." He looked to Astarte. "So, what do we do to make it so?"

"That's it. You've done it. She's offered the position, and you've accepted it. It will take a while for you to attune, and it will take practice. I suggest spending some time with the Consort Book in the library and with the Regent."

Victor nodded. "Good thing I've got lots of spare time on my hands for reading," he said, sarcasm dripping from every word.

The mirror lit up with an incoming call.

"Open," Deor said.

The mirror cleared. A monk smiled at her. He had white hair and was

71

clean shaven, clothed in worn brown robes over a round frame. "Good day, Your Majesty." He nodded at her.

"Good day," Deor said, smiling. "You are from Mont Saint-Michel, correct?"

"I am Caedmon. I am the Abbot of the monastery and in charge of the Proving." The smile didn't quite reach his eyes, and his annoyance at the entire proceeding was clear.

"I've never done anything like this before," Deor said. "I want it to be as painless as possible for everyone involved. Except perhaps Roger of Northfalls. He can be inconvenienced as much as you like."

The monk's smile vanished as he peered at her. "You are the Regent?" He sniffed. "I don't want to waste time talking to some lackey."

Deor frowned. "What, exactly, makes you think I'm not the Regent?"

Caedmon ignored, or didn't notice, her sharp tone. "Monarchs are not usually good at making things painless for other people, or making that any kind of priority."

"I'm not a typical monarch. I'm a regent. And if you would prefer me to be haughty, aloof, bitchy, snide, inconsiderate, or a right pain in the ass, I am quite sure I could accommodate you."

Caedmon gaped for a moment as around Deor's table her people looked down at their hands, trying not to laugh. After a moment, he recovered. "'A right pain in the ass, eh?"

"She's exceptional at it," Bill chimed in.

Caedmon's gaze flicked to Bill and a flash of confusion crossed his face. He seemed about to speak but paused and refocused on Deor.

"I could provide you with several references, some even in this room, if you need proof," Deor added.

"No." He shook his head, unamused. "It's quite clear you are proficient." He cleared his throat. "As painless as possible will be sufficient." When Deor nodded, he continued. "The abbey is strongly guarded. We open portals rarely. We will open one for you the night before the event. Everyone else will arrive the next morning." He glared at her as if she would challenge him.

"Sounds good."

"Those in attendance include the Summer Court, the Goblin Court, and the Vampire Court. The rest of those invited declined to attend."

"Fewer people to feed," Deor said with a smile.

His frown grew. "There are rules."

"Of course." Deor continued to smile. After a moment she added, "Are you going to share them with us?"

She thought the monk might lecture her on sass, but he didn't. "The names of all of the people who will be coming with you must be in my hands by an hour after this call. No one else will be permitted through the portal. This includes any servants you need to bring. The portal will open twice. Once when you arrive. Once when you leave. It will be opened inside your palace, where you can guarantee the security of the area. Everyone will be scanned for unallowed magic upon arrival. Weapons, physical, magical, or otherwise, are prohibited."

Deor considered it and scanned the table. "Any objections?" Her colleagues shook their heads. "That works," she said to Caedmon. "I'll have my Shield work out the details of the portals with you, or whoever you choose. Is that all?"

"No." He crossed his arms. "You must provide your own meals, and you are expected to provide refreshment of some kind to the others who witness the Proving. Your staff will be granted the use of our kitchen, which is plain and suited for an abbey, not a royal fete. Your staff will be allowed into the sanctuary—the location of the Proving—two hours before. Decoration is strongly discouraged, and anything that might damage or disrespect the space or anything in it is forbidden." He leaned in. "I will personally boot anyone who even hints at doing something that might damage this sacred space."

"Got it." Deor nodded again.

"Do you?" He arched an eyebrow.

"Look," Deor said. "I get that my father is an asshole. It seems that faeries have been, in the past, assholes to you in some way. I've got no desire to be a pain in your ass. I'd be happy if this thing took twenty minutes—in, do some magic, out. However, I'm told these things require some ceremony. So crudites and crap on crackers it will be. My retinue will be small—the minimum number of people I need to feel safe and to get the job done." She smiled brightly. "Thank you for your hospitality!"

"You," he paused and seconds ticked by as he stared at her. "You are not what I expected."

"Get in line," Victor said, rolling his eyes.

Caedmon glanced at Victor and back to Deor. "We will open the portal for you two nights hence, and the ceremony will take place at noon the following day." A small smile crept onto his face. "I look forward to trying crap on crackers. I don't believe I've had that before. Good day." He nodded, and the mirror went black.

"This is the way it's going to be, isn't it? From here on out? No matter what I do, Finn was an asshole, so people will default assume I am too." Deor shook her head. "It's exhausting."

"Indeed." Astarte smiled at her. "It will change over time. I assumed many things about you that were not true. I learned. Others will, too. If it helps, most of it is self-protection."

"I know." Deor sighed. "People being afraid of me just makes it worse."

Astarte stood. "With your leave, I shall go speak to the cook about the meals and staff. I'll have a very short list of servants going with us to you within the hour."

"Thank you." Deor nodded as Astarte left. "Will you come?" Deor turned to Genevieve. "Melanie is wonderful, but I'd like you there too."

"I'd be honored." Genevieve smiled. "I don't think you'll need more than Melanie and me. You'll need Gordie, who can be a valet for Victor and Stephen." She looked at Bill. "Are you planning on coming?"

Bill glanced at Deor. "I don't think I'm quite ready to be in a room with vampires again—I think I'm better off here."

"I understand." She smiled at Bill, then scanned the table. "Alright, folks. We've got two days to make sure everything is ready for the trip." She paused and frowned. There was one more thing she needed to do, and she didn't need anyone in the room. "So," she said, "off you go! I'll follow in a few minutes."

Stephen and Victor eyed her as the rest of the people gathered their things and headed for the door. As he reached the door, Stephen glanced back at her. "Try to keep out of trouble."

She laughed. "I'll try."

What she had to do wasn't trouble, per se, but it was hard.

Deor straightened her shoulders and focused on the mirror. She had a promise to keep.

She cleared her throat and spoke to the mirror. "Lady Juliette du Chanson." The mirror fogged over, and Lady Julliette stared at her.

"Good day, Lady Juliette," Deor said. "I'm sorry to call out of the blue, but I have some news about Lord Farringdon and Monjoie."

The woman pressed a hand to her mouth.

"The Lady Astarte woke from her coma and was able to tell me more about what happened that evening. She saw the two men fighting—Monjoie had Rafe pinned to the ground and was standing over him. A wave crashed over the both of them, and when it retreated they were both gone—swept out to the river."

Juliette nodded and cleared her throat. "Thank you," she said. "At best, I expected a generic letter when either the body was found or you gave up looking for him."

"Yeah. Not surprised that was your expectation. I would want to know, and you made it clear you wanted to know. This isn't public knowledge, at least not yet. Of course tell Monjoie's family, but please try not to let a rumor start."

"I won't," she said. "Do you think there's a chance...?"

"Yes." Deor nodded. "I will believe there's a chance until I see the body."

"Me too." Juliette wiped at her eyes. "Thank you again, Your Majesty."

"You're welcome." Deor ended the call. She tilted her head back and tried not to let the tears fall. There was no sense in worrying about it now. She had work to do.

The next morning, Deor frowned at herself in the 180-degree mirror set up in front of her. She stood on a stool in her sitting room, and there were altogether too many people in there with her. Her underwear covered more than bathing suits she'd loved, but still, there was something vulnerable about being in her skivvies while everyone else was fully clothed.

"Hold your arms out, please, Your Majesty." Melanie, Deor's personal maid, spun a whirl of magic around her waist, then her underbust, and then her bust. She took measurements of her hips, too, and right below her hips, her upper arm and then her wrist. "All done." Melanie said to the trio on the sofa. She handed Deor her robe.

"Thank you." Deor hopped off the dais and wrapped herself in her robe.

"I sent the measurements to your tablet," Melanie said. With a little bob of a bow, she excused herself.

"Thank you, dear." Wham!, the pixie half of Wham! And Thorsen, the chicest designer in all the Winter Court, didn't even look up. She was dressed in sleek fuchsia leggings and a light pink, off-the-shoulder sweater. Her hair, also colored pink today, swirled like a cotton candy cloud around her head. Thorsen, an older faerie with graying hair, was as conservatively dressed as his partner was eye-catching in an impeccable, gray suit. Between them sat Genevieve, a tablet in her hand. She scribbled and scratched, a slight frown of concentration wrinkling the spot between her eyes.

"There!" Genevieve said. "What do you think?"

"It is bold," Wham! said.

Thorsen shook his head. "It will make a statement." The three of them looked up at Deor.

"She needs to make a statement," Genevieve said. Her own dress today was made of delicate flowing silk in a soft peach color. Her blond hair, as always, was swept up in an elegant updo, giving off the feel that she'd simply piled it that way to get it out of her face.

"Does it have to be black?" Wham! asked. "I know that it is the Aethelwing house color, but maybe a flash of red here or there, a sparkle of green or blue?"

"Or gems lining the bodice or hem?" Thorsen added.

"No." Genevieve shook her head. "No adornments. But we can discuss other things if you don't think you can get it done in time." Genevieve smiled at both of them, full of kindness, with a touch of disappointment.

"Of course, we can do it in time!" Thorsen said, puffing his chest out.

"Excellent."

"But—" He frowned and looked up at Deor. "We need the approval of the Regent."

"Of course," Genevieve beckoned Deor. "Come see my idea for your dress."

Genevieve stood and handed Deor the tablet. The dress was plain to the point of severity. Fitted in a way that followed her curves, but not overdoing it. The neckline was straight, cutting across to off-the-shoulder sleeves, fitted down to her wrists. No plunging necklines or high slits. What could they possibly object to?

"It's lovely," Deor said. "It is plain."

"Look at the back," Genevieve said, and flicked her finger across the screen, bringing up the back of the dress.

Deor gasped. The entire back of the dress was nothing. A single, fine chain connected the sleeves in the back, and that was it. Backless was an understatement. The fabric didn't begin again until the very base of her lower back. A couple of centimeters more, and she'd be getting plumber jokes all night.

"What do you think?" Genevieve watched Deor's face. "If it is too much…"

"No." Deor handed back the tablet. "It's fantastic. A dress that covers the lashes would suggest I was ashamed. I'm not. This will show off every single one."

"You like it then?" Genevieve smiled.

"I love it." Deor looked toward Wham! and Thorsen. "You can make this?"

"Of course, we can!" Wham! insisted. "It will be perfect. We'll have a fitting for you tomorrow, and we'll have it finished the morning of your departure."

"Works for me. Thank you so much!"

The two designers immediately started speaking to each other in soft, but emphatic tones, as they made their way out.

"Let's sit." Deor sat on the couch, and Genevieve joined her. "I appreciate everything you've done. It feels weird, though, like Rafe is hovering between us."

"I know." Genevieve shrugged. "It's awkward, and I understand if you aren't comfortable with me."

"That's not it at all!" Deor insisted. "In fact, I like you a lot. I've always admired you, you seem so perfect, and sometimes that was reflected in my bad behavior." Deor wrinkled her nose. "I am sorry about Roger. And I don't think I can ever repay your kindness since I went into the Tower."

"You don't have to!" Genevieve insisted. "I admire you too. You are fascinating. And that admiration wasn't always expressed in the friendliest way either." Genevieve took Deor's hand. "Perhaps if we hadn't met in the way we did, with Rafe in the middle, we'd have been easier friends."

"I think so," Deor put her hand on top of Genevieve's. "Listen. I don't know how to ask this, and it's going to be awkward because nobility never talks about money, but I want you to be my…my go-to person. The one in charge of everything. Not a Lady-in-Waiting."

"I would be honored to be your Lady-in-Waiting," Genevieve said.

Deor grimaced. "Would you? It feels…not quite right. You deserve a title that honors all that you do." Perhaps it was a cultural difference, but to Deor Lady-in-Waiting sent up echoes of Versailles, useless women kept around for their skills in flattery and thinking up petty amusements. Genevieve was far more than the ornamental toy she had once mistaken her for.

Genevieve laughed. "I refuse to be your Lady of the Stool, no matter how close we become. You can wipe your own backside."

Deor's eyes widened in alarm, and she burst out laughing. "No! Absolutely not." She was already feeling hemmed in by her entourage as it was. "What describes what you already do? You know so much and handle everything so well. I have no idea how to navigate the court rules. That's one thing Finn is right about—my absolute lack of experience. If I don't have someone to help me, I'll make some mistake that's too big to ignore. Stephen is no help, and Victor, he knows a lot..."

"But he doesn't know enough. This isn't his area of expertise." Genevieve brightened. "What you want me to be is your Majordomo—the official in charge of the ruler's private household. I would be honored. It is an official, long-standing position, you know. One the King didn't use —he used Astarte for that." A kind of sharp bitterness filled her voice. "Used being the operative word." She frowned for a moment but then looked at Deor with affection. "I believe in you, Deor. Really. You are perfectly capable of being Regent, and, what's more, you're someone I want as a friend."

A giddy flutter danced in Deor's stomach—the popular girl liked her! A blush crept up her face as she thought about how silly it was to think that way. "I feel the same way about you. I'd love to have you as my Majordomo and my friend."

"Excellent!" Genevieve stood. "I'd like to say we should take the day off and go shopping, but we need to go over the reception menu and the logistics of bringing literally everything we need for it to the monastery."

"Fun!" Deor said, letting the sarcasm fill her voice as she stood. "Let's go."

12

On the mainland of France, summer was in full bloom, but an unseasonable squall was blowing off the ocean, pelting Rafe and Monjoie with stinging droplets as they continued their daily walk around the cloister.

"Feels good, doesn't it?" Monjoie said as they paused in the lee of a buttress. He turned his face up toward the rain.

Rafe grunted in agreement. "I could do with a bit less velocity in my water." But still, it had been days since he'd had a good soaking dip. The combined rain and ocean spray called to the magic in him, and made him feel more alive. "Ready to go on?"

Monjoie gritted his teeth, jaw clenched against the pain, but he nodded and held out one arm to Rafe. In tandem, they resumed their shuffle. Monjoie's breathing became more pained, huffing through gritted teeth. They managed another hundred yards around the building before Rafe said, "You need another rest. Let's step inside here." He gestured to a side door.

"I can do it," Monjoie gasped. "Let's get this over with."

"You're going gray," Rafe said. Using the wool sleeve of his robe as a buffer, he grabbed the door's iron ring and pulled the door open. "Let's get inside at least. I'm getting cold."

"Liar," Monjoie said.

"Fine. You're worn out. I can tell by your breathing it's time to stop. Come on."

Practically carrying Monjoie, Rafe got both of them inside the shelter of the building. Water dripped out of their robes onto the stone floor. Against Rafe's torso, Monjoie's limbs shook.

The corridor where they stood had no alcoves, no benches or other seating. They were on the far side of the cloister from the kitchen and sleeping cells. Carrying Monjoie all the way back with only one functional hand would be a strain. Rafe's head throbbed, a reminder that Aaliyah had warned him his skull still had its own healing to do. He could do with a rest himself.

Down the hallway, one door stood partially open. The archive! There were benches and seats in there.

"Come on! Few more steps." Rafe hitched Monjoie up against his hip, pushing away the thought that the last time he'd held anyone like that it had been a fellow knight, wounded in battle. Monjoie was no ally of his. Certainly not his brother, no matter how Caedmon said it.

They managed to shuffle down the corridor and stumble through the archive door where Rafe dropped Monjoie onto the nearest seat. Monjoie leaned on the work table, panting. Rafe pushed his damp hair out of his eyes.

"Wet! No, no, no, no! No water in the archive!" Lachar rushed toward them. "Out! You'll ruin the books!"

Rolling his eyes, Rafe gathered all the water from his and Monjoie's clothes into a rippling ball and sent it rolling down the corridor toward the outdoors. Lachar heaved a sigh of relief. "Thank you. You have no idea what the damp does to paper and parchment."

Rafe chuckled. "Oh, I do. I heard that lecture more than once from my tutor."

"Me too," Monjoie said. "My father loves his books. Woe betide the child who gets them damp."

Lachar laughed uncomfortably. "Heh heh. Water faerie children. I can only imagine." His smile was betrayed by the nervous way he petted the scroll nearest him, like a cat owner reassuring his baby that the nasty wet water faeries wouldn't do it harm.

"We only stopped in for a breather," Rafe said. "We'll be on our way shortly."

"Oh good," Lachar said. He blushed. "I mean, um, while you're here, are there any questions I can answer for you?"

"I have a question," Rafe said. "What is all this? What does this group exist to do? You all talk about an enemy and a source, but despite what all of you have said, I have no idea what it all means."

From his seat, Monjoie nodded. "Let's have some straightforward explanations."

Lachar looked back and forth between them. "I thought Caedmon must have explained all that by now, but perhaps not. Here. Just give me one moment." Lachar went to a nearby shelf, running his fingers over the book spines and pulling volumes until he had a pile in his arms. He laid out the books, flipping through them until he found illustrated pages.

One page showed a diagram of the buildings that crowned the island. Lachar pointed out their location as well as a few other features before pointing to the open space that dominated the center of the drawing. "This is where the Source is housed. It is the center, literally and metaphorically, of everything we do."

He turned to a neatly-drafted ink drawing of a wide-open space, the arched roof held up with columns. At one end stood a stone block that might have been a high seat or perhaps a low table. "This is what the sanctuary room looks like. And here is the Source," Lachar said, tapping the block in the picture. "It was once open to the sky, but the buildings grew up around it once humans came to inhabit the island on their side of things. The roof, fluting and columns and such were added at a later date, perhaps as much as a disguise to fool the eyes of the unwitting as to honor what the Source is. It is sometimes called an altar. Humans have used it as a place of worship from time immemorial."

Rafe and Monjoie looked at Lachar, waiting for more explanation. "No doubt you can feel its power even here. The stone is, of course, only a vessel within which the Source resides, not the Source itself. Others have likened the Source to a well and the altar stone to its lid, but that's a flawed analogy as well. One or two of the documents I have here refer to it as a seat, even a throne, though I'm inclined to think they are being fanciful. It's absurd to think of the Source as merely a chair for a king or queen to sit on."

Rafe and Monjoie exchanged skeptical glances. Lachar tapped the page in frustration.

"So..." Rafe said. "When you say it's the Source, what does that mean exactly? The source of what?"

"Everything," Lachar said, blinking in surprise.

Monjoie snorted and rolled his eyes. Rafe pressed on, "You mean it is the Creator?"

Rafe had often sworn by the Creator, more out of pure habit than anything else. John Dell had always winced at that, saying it was unwise to blaspheme in the name of one who made you, but Rafe hadn't been much bothered by it. The bards had whole rooms full of stories about where the world came from and all sorts of ideas about who, if anyone, might have made it.

"No," Lachar said, as if the two of them hadn't been listening to a word he said. "It's the Source... it is that which sustains the life of the world and everything in it."

This got a chuckle from Monjoie. "I thought that was the sun."

"That's science!" Lachar said. "This is..."

"Mysticism?" Rafe ventured. He tried, but failed, to keep the condescension out of his voice.

Lachar sighed heavily and pinched the bridge of his nose. "Creator help me. You warrior types think there's nothing in the world but what you can stick a sword in."

"That's hardly fair," Monjoie objected. "I can't stick a sword in magic, but I know it exists. But you have to admit that all of you are being more than a little vague. It's suspicious."

"My...friend here has a point," Rafe said. "If we're supposed to become part of this order of yours, we need to understand what we're actually getting ourselves into. What are we doing here, besides drinking good beer and eating Aelfburga's excellent food? Not that I object to those things, but..."

"Yes, yes, I see your meaning," Lachar said. "Though I don't understand why at least one of you doesn't simply know that he's meant to be here. I knew it the second I entered the place. Nearly every single new member feels the same way when they arrived whether they came looking for us, were drawn here, or were brought. And on top of that, Aelfburga saw you coming. She spoke about it! Described you even—a tall man, blue and black, coming with a great wound out of combat to make our order whole. I mean look at you two!" He threw out his hands at Rafe and Monjoie. "I don't know how much more literal a seeing could get."

Again, Rafe and Monjoie exchanged glances. Rafe straightened up, reaching for Monjoie, who pushed himself upright against the table.

"We should leave you to your work," Rafe said.

"Aaliyah will have our hides if we don't complete our exercises," Monjoie said.

"Tchah." Lachar threw up his hands. "Alright, go about your business. Talk to Evelyn. He was a soldier once. Perhaps he can explain it to you in a way that you'll understand."

Rafe and Monjoie shuffled off on their path through the half-ruined building and grounds once more. When they were safely out of earshot and paused for another breather, Monjoie said, "Did any of that make sense to you?"

"Not really," Rafe admitted. "Though there is something about this place. Something good that makes me feel that we can trust...not just the people, but the place itself."

Monjoie grunted. "Maybe."

Rafe bit back the impulse to point out that someone who spent decades lying about everything to act as a traitor in the King's own household was probably a poor judge of how trustworthy anyone could be. But then again, he'd trusted Monjoie and the rest of the House Boys, so who was he to claim good judgment? Hell, he'd followed Finn blindly all these years, and look where that had led.

"We should go see it for ourselves," Rafe said aloud.

"Finally, something you and I can agree on," Monjoie said. "Let's go." He hauled himself into a standing position. Rafe wrapped one arm around Monjoie's torso and they set off together, their steps falling into a half-pace march as they headed deeper into the maze of corridors.

Rafe shook his head at himself as they set off. Was he really about to go on an impromptu reconnaissance mission with the same person who had infiltrated the House Boys, aided Madeline's coup, and tried to drown him? Mad. Completely mad. But also, his only option if he didn't want to go alone. He had to trust someone. At least he knew for certain what Monjoie was. The members of the cloister were too unknown to trust, at least until he assessed this Source of theirs for himself.

"Let's go," he said. "Before someone comes looking for us. If we meet anyone, we'll tell them it's too cold and wet for our exercises outside."

Monjoie laughed. "Yes, they'll believe that. We Winter Court water faeries are known for not liking the damp and cold. During a summer shower." He held out an arm for Rafe to support him.

"Then what do you suggest we say, oh master spy?" Rafe said, hitching Monjoie's arm over his shoulders so less weight rested on his still mending hip.

"We say nothing," Monjoie said. "Never volunteer an explanation where one isn't needed. It makes you look suspicious. If anyone questions us, we politely ask if these corridors are a restricted area and promise not to do it again. The less you actually lie, the less you have to remember later."

"Ah. Yes."

Together they hobbled their way into the interior until they came to the central hall Lachar had called a Sanctuary. High glass windows intricately fitted into colored mosaics lit the interior. Pale beige stone columns held up a many-arched roof that soared overhead. At the far end stood the altar, cut from the same stone as the surrounding room. Nearest the door where they had entered, a stone bowl carved into a plinth held a pool of water. As they passed it, Monjoie reached out his fingers, gathering some of the water in his free hand.

The Sanctuary was not as grand or imposing as Finn's throne room, but the comparison grew in Rafe's mind the closer they approached the altar. The rough-cut stone would easily hold two faeries sitting side by side. A strange thought. Thrones were not meant to be shared.

Monjoie's snort broke into Rafe's thoughts. "Some Sanctuary," he said. "This place is virtually defenseless."

"It's not meant to be defended," Rafe said, his eyes still focused on the altar throne. "Sanctuaries like this are sacred to humans. Only the most depraved person would shed blood in one. They used to believe that Faeries and Goblins couldn't even set foot across the threshold without losing all our magic and having our glamours stripped away. Dell told me about it when I was a boy."

"Nice of you to warn me," Monjoie said. He looked down at the hand with which he held the ball of water, rolling with magic. "So good so far."

Rafe nodded, his attention fixed on the altar. The closer they came, the more he could feel its presence. A cold sweat trickled down his back. He couldn't shake the image of a throne from his mind. What if this piece of rock held similar magic? Would it draw him in, as Finn's throne had done at the adoption, perhaps trapping him inside it?

"Let's not touch anything just yet," he said.

"You don't have to tell me twice," Monjoie said. "This thing is powerful. I can feel it. It's…It's like standing near the ocean."

"Yes. It is." Thrones. Oceans. Great and powerful and beautiful and terrible all at once. Things you could get lost in forever. Even a water faerie like himself couldn't control the ocean.

He and Monjoie stood before the altar, arms around one another. Monjoie cleared his throat, and Rafe started.

"Put me down," Monjoie said. "I'll sit, you walk. Cover more ground that way."

"Right." He eased Monjoie to the floor near enough to touch the altar, but not in danger of falling on it. As Monjoie sent little droplets of water into the stone, testing its defenses, Rafe began circling it. He gestured, a simple dispelling to clear any glamours, but nothing changed. He tried richer, more complex magics, probing the stone as best he could, but got nothing in return. His magic didn't bounce off the altar so much as it simply disappeared into it. A droplet in an ocean.

What he wouldn't give for Arthur and his earth magic right now. Arthur could move earth and shape stone with the best of them. Even as he thought it, Rafe felt a stab in his ribs. Arthur. His oldest friend. Who had turned him over to Finn without a second thought.

He wanted to touch the altar. Yes, the more he looked the more he wanted to touch it. He stopped and examined himself, checking for any will magic, anything that would trap his mind. But there seemed to be nothing.

"Are you getting anything?" he called softly to Monjoie.

"Nothing. It's a big rock. It's a lot more than a rock. That's the best I can tell you."

Rafe circled back to where Monjoie sat. Together they regarded the Source.

"I'd give an eye tooth for a good earth faerie right about now," Monjoie said.

A laugh bubbled up in Rafe's chest. "I was thinking the same thing." He paused. "I'm going to touch it."

To his surprise, Monjoie didn't object. "Me too," he said. "I can't really explain, but...I don't think it means us any harm."

"Neither does the ocean," Rafe pointed out. And like the ocean, he wanted to plunge into this thing's depths as deep as his lungs would allow. Which was absurd, since it was a solid rock and he was a water faerie.

Monjoie held out his hand and placed it on the altar's side. Following suit, Rafe pressed his hands to the altar's top, mentally crossing his fingers that he wouldn't be sucked into it, lost in claustrophobic darkness.

Instead, he felt as sure of his location in space as he ever had before. He stood on his own two feet and felt the cool stone under his hand. He heard the gulls crying outside, the constant wash of the waves against the island walls. He took a deep breath, trying to shut out the sounds and focus on the task at hand, but the waves and the gulls and the sea wind only seemed more present. He was awash in them, cradled in them. If he closed his eyes, he was buoyed up by the vast power of the ocean, weightless, cradled in air and water.

He listened more carefully, letting the waves and gulls and the wind fill him. *I am a water faerie and this stone is the ocean.* When he thought of it like that, the sense of all the life in the ocean joined his awareness. Life upon life, spreading out all around and above and below him until it merged with the land and the air in all their abundance and the fiery, sustaining power of the sun that permeated every fiber of it all.

He drew his hands back and turned to Monjoie. "Is this what they're guarding?"

Monjoie, tears streaming down his face, nodded. Rafe collapsed onto the stone floor beside him, sobbing, joyful.

Afterward, when they had mopped their faces with their rough wool sleeves, they sat a little way from the altar, their backs against the nearest column.

"It was like I was home again," Monjoie said. "But it was home as a child playing in the salt marshes. I heard the sandpipers and the wind in the grasses and the whole world was alive."

"Yes," Rafe said. He didn't have the words yet to describe what touching the altar had been like. *Yes* would have to do.

Two sets of footsteps approached them from a side door.

"Here you are at last," Lachar said, sounding like a proud uncle. "You've found your brotherhood."

"Yes," Evelyn said. "And all it took was sending up a great, bright signal flare to the Enemy." But he sounded more amused than angry. "Come on, you truants. Aelfburga sent us to fetch you. She's calming Caedmon down as we speak. He's in a right pet. Says if the altar hasn't burned you both to a crisp, he'll have you singing penitent songs and eating dry bread for the next three weeks." He held out a hand to Rafe as Lachar helped Monjoie to his feet.

"He can't do that!" Monjoie snapped. "It's abuse of prisoners!" Lachar tutted and looped Monjoie's arm over his shoulder and led him away.

"It would be a small price to pay," Rafe said, his eyes still on the altar. Beside him, Evelyn nodded.

"I had to touch it too," the young man said. "Before I could really understand." He patted Rafe on the shoulder. "Come on. Let's get our dinner before it's cold."

"Yes," Rafe said, turning away slowly. "Of course. You'll want your dinner hot."

Evelyn chuckled. "Never mind Caedmon. He gets terribly old-fashioned when he's frightened, but he won't actually follow it through. Besides, you'll need your strength when the Enemy gets here."

"What? Is he coming?"

"You more or less called out to him that our doors were wide open," Evelyn said. "So, I expect he'll be along shortly."

"Oh." Rafe supposed he should feel sorry for that. But he found he could not. If he went down fighting this Enemy, it would still be a price well paid for what he had just been through.

13

As planned, Deor and her tiny entourage arrived at Mont Saint-Michel the day before the Proving. Caedmon and two other cowl-shrouded monks greeted them without ceremony and led them to their rooms—a plain, self-contained living space set aside for their use that reminded Deor of a college dorm. The rooms were bright with whitewash, clean, and, as night was falling, lit with small balls of light. The window of Deor's room looked out toward the water—not hard since the monastery was more or less on an island. The thin strip of land that connected to the mainland was underwater except at the lowest of tides.

She and her retinue had a shared bathroom space and a larger room for gathering. Genevieve immediately commandeered that space as Deor's dressing room and began setting it up, including the full-length mirror she had thought to pack. Stephen went on a security walkthrough with a monk named Evelyn, while the palace cook and his two helpers had hurried off to the kitchen.

Deor looked around her room. The bed was comfortable, even if it was small, like the room itself. She should rest. The next day would be a trial, even if everything went smoothly. There was something about the place, though, that got under her skin. Not a foreboding, but a weight. Whatever this place was, there was power here, not unlike her own.

A walk would do her good. None of the monks had told her she couldn't leave her area.

"C'mon, Brand," she said as she headed for the door. She'd left Jake and Sam behind in the Winter Court.

The dog fell into step next to her, and they made their way out of their quarters. Her retinue's quarters were one of four, which formed a square around a lovely green space. The stonework, arches, and decorations were medieval. She even saw a Green Man's face peeking out from behind a decorative centerpiece of leaves at the peak of the ceiling.

She crossed the green space and went down a corridor, following the sense of power through empty stone hallways and open porticos until it led her through a side door to the chapel itself. Lights, dimmer than those in her room but otherwise the same, glowed from their places on pillars. The room had no pews and was filled with a heavy emptiness. At the far end of the chapel, a larger light glowed above the altar. It was a plain stone block, with no candles, no carvings, not even an altar cloth on it.

The sense of power was definitely coming from the altar itself. She stepped forward and rested her hand on the altar. A warmth spread into her fingers and up her arm. Gentle, soothing, like nothing she'd ever felt before. The power hovered here, beneath her touch, waiting. Compared to the palace, it was absolutely placid. The palace tugged at her or crashed its magic over her. This simply waited.

"It would be best if you stepped away from the altar now," a voice called.

Deor turned but didn't remove her hand. A monk approached, his footsteps slow, but not hesitant. Robed like the others, he was taller and blonde. He was also a faerie. He strolled up to her like they were at some kind of garden party, but she could see the tension in his body, the sharpness of his gaze.

"Oh?" Deor asked, not pulling her arm back.

He stopped a little more than arm's reach away and Brand moved between them. He wagged his tail, but he didn't take his eyes off this new faerie. "I'm Lachar."

"I'm Deor." She smiled.

"The Winter Court Regent. Yes. I know." He raised a hand slowly and pointed at hers. "Please take your hand off that."

Deor didn't need to ask why. This place, this altar, was ancient. The power here was vast. She could take it, she knew. She could pull it toward herself, into herself, but what would happen then? She had no idea. She considered it for a moment and lifted her hand. "That's… I felt it all the way in my room, which is about as far away from the chapel as a person could be and still be in the building." She looked at the altar and back to Lachar. "I don't have words for what that is."

A small bit of tension released from Lachar's shoulders. "I don't know that anyone does."

Deor moved toward him, away from the altar, and he relaxed even more. She opened her mouth to respond, but she was cut off.

"There you are!" Victor strode up to her. "I've been looking for you." He nodded at Lachar who stared back and blinked at him. "I'm Victor Farringdon, Her Majesty's Consort."

Lachar forced his mouth shut, saying, "It is a pleasure to meet you."

"Do you need me?" Deor frowned. Hopefully, no one was causing trouble, on purpose or not.

"I couldn't find you, so I came looking." He smiled. "You find trouble."

"It finds me," Deor insisted. She glanced at Lachar who studied his toes, hands folded together, a courtly pretense of not having overheard. "Lachar, this is a medieval church, right? Built by humans?"

"It is," he said, surprised. "How did you know?"

"I studied medieval literature in the human world. I think I've taken up enough of your time." She looked around the room. "It really is a beautiful church. We'll see you tomorrow."

"Tomorrow," Lachar agreed. He gave a small nod to Victor, who returned it.

Victor offered Deor his arm, and she took it. Together, they left the sanctuary and headed for their quarters.

"So, what is it really?" Deor asked.

"You did vanish. But I came to talk to you about your magic. My magic. The whole consort thing. I want to help you, but you won't let me in."

"I don't know what you mean," Deor lied. Since she had made him Consort only a few days before, she could feel him. Wherever he was in the palace, she knew. She could find him, bring to mind a picture of his location, with barely a thought. She imagined he could do the same. More distressing was the tug on her magic. When she was near him, like now, her magic seemed to lunge at him, to try to reach him, and he seemed to respond, taking it in. She couldn't tell if he was pulling deliberately, or if it was simply occurring, but the lack of control worried her.

"You know what I mean." He sounded tired. He opened the door to her room. "We need to talk about it. Tonight." He gestured at the door.

Deor went in and sat down on the bed. She scooted so that her back was to the wall and waved him over. "Have a seat."

Victor closed the door and sat. Brand laid down on a rug on the floor and watched them both. "I've been reading the Consort book."

"I see." He should have been doing that, she knew, so why did the thought of it make her nervous? Several sparkles spun off her toward him. He reached up and caught them. "Careful!" Deor insisted. "They're sharp."

"Not to me they're not." He opened his hand, and there sat the sparkles, glittering like platinum-covered jacks in his hand. "Watch." He closed his hand and opened it. The sparkles were gone.

"Where?"

"Into me," he said. "This is what a consort does. All that excess magic you've got. The rush of power the palace keeps throwing at you? The Consort is the solution. You dump it into me when it is too much."

"How?"

"I'm not sure. But I have an idea." Victor held out his hand "Give me your hand."

Deor rested her hand in his.

"Now," he said. "Push your magic into me."

"I don't know how to do that!" she insisted.

"Close your eyes and try." He squeezed her hand gently.

Deor closed her eyes. She imagined her magic, a whirling mass inside her, and focused on pushing it outward. Making knives now was second nature and swords she could make, but they took concentration and effort, outside of being in a panic. So she used those experiences. She eased the magic through her, down her arm, into her hand, and out. She waited a few seconds. "Well? Did it work?"

"Yes." He sounded smug.

Deor opened her eyes and screamed. It had worked alright. Worked right through his hand. She jerked her hand out of his, but the blade remained behind, spearing straight through. "Oh my God! I am so sorry!" She flailed and grabbed the tip of the blade.

"Easy now." He caught her wrist with his other hand. "Take a breath. There's no blood."

Deor let go of her blade. "Right. I shouldn't just yank it out, then. It might make it worse." He let go of her wrist. "What do we do?"

"Nothing, I think." The blade wasn't that long, sticking out about an inch on either side of his hand. "It doesn't hurt."

"Do you think I severed nerves?" Was that his dagger hand? She couldn't remember.

"No. Look at me. Listen to me." When she focused on his face, he continued. "This doesn't hurt, and there's no blood. But I can feel it in my hand. It's pure magic, existing in me right alongside my flesh and blood and bone, but not interfering with it. It is the weirdest thing I've ever felt. And my magic feels it too. Your magic is foreign, but not invasive. Like it is supposed to be there. And I think it is." He grabbed the tip of the blade and pulled it out.

Deor squeaked, waiting for the blood to flow. It didn't.

Victor turned his skewered hand palm up and pushed her blade into it. This time the blade melted into him.

Deor jerked her gaze to his and gasped. "Your eyes. They're glowing blue. And there are flecks, like tiny snowflakes."

"That's your magic. Wait." He held up a finger. "Let me try something." He closed his hand around a newly forming icicle. It was clear as water, except for the tiny flecks, like platinum glitter, suspended in it. "That's your magic too."

Deor gave a shaky laugh, relief washing through her. "That is cool." He held out the icicle to her and she grasped it, the magic flowing into and up her arm, cold and sharp like winter air. She gasped as silver haloed her vision. She blinked, and it faded, the returned magic coalescing with the rest.

"It worked!" She laughed. "Let me try it without stabbing you." She pressed her hand to his chest and concentrated, willing her own magic into him. No spikes. No sparkles. But it moved from her to him, dancing along her skin. She shifted, bringing one knee up on the bed so that she could more easily face him. She laid her other hand on his chest and pushed more magic in.

He gasped.

"Too much?" She asked.

"No." He focused on her. "It's exhilarating." He laid a cool hand on her cheek.

Deor's heart fluttered in her chest. She could feel his magic and hers, intertwined, touching, existing together, but never blending into something else. She slid her hands up his chest to his shoulders, pushing his shirt out of the way as she went, and he cupped her face in both hands.

His lips met hers, and she ran her fingers through his hair. He let go and stood, hauling his shirt off.

They froze, staring at each other. He moved toward her again and stopped, a question in his eyes. Her heart pounded, each beat building her desire, her need, to touch him and be touched by him.

She stood. "Help me get this dress off."

"Do you care if it stays in one piece?" He grinned at her.

"Not even a little." She slid her fingers into his hair again and brought his face down to hers. She kissed him, and he kissed her, slipping his tongue past her lips, and she tasted magic, his and hers both. He slid both his hands up her back. There was a jolt and the sound of buttons scattering onto the floor.

Deor paused the kiss long enough to laugh and let him strip the remains of the dress off her. She reached for the laces of his pants as he kicked off his shoes. He pulled her close again and lifted her up, easing her legs around his waist, and lowered them both to the bed.

14

On the battlements, Rafe yawned and stretched, stamping his feet against the pre-dawn cold. Caedmon had been furious, but as Evelyn predicted, there had been no bread and water punishment. What had stung more than the long lecture on brotherhood, caution, and the sacredness of their duty to protect the Source, was the look Aelfburga gave him. Not angry, just disappointed. That look had left him drooping at the table until Caedmon wore out, concluding, "The two of you can atone for the trouble you've caused by taking the dark watch. We all have a long enough day ahead of us with the Proving tomorrow. We're vulnerable enough with so many outsiders coming back and forth. We don't need you causing any more havoc."

So far, the predicted havoc had not arrived. Stars still twinkled in the dark overhead. Beside him, Monjoie yawned in sympathy. Another uneventful watch against the Enemy.

Privately, Rafe was beginning to doubt how much of a threat this "enemy" represented. Whatever he was, he seemed more like a slightly ominous annoyance than anything else. Still, he'd stand his watch like everyone else. It gave him time to think of all the things he wanted to say to Deor when he saw her tomorrow, things both public and private. As he watched the horizon, he debated whether it would be better to tell her he was there before the Proving or wait until it was done? Better to wait. Much as he cherished the fantasy of standing beside her at the Proving, he knew the reality was more complex. She didn't need the distraction before facing down Caedmon and the Summer Court Queen.

Rafe cast his eyes at the stars, measuring their progress across the sky. Not long before the sun peeked above the horizon. Even as he thought it, Evelyn and Joan emerged through the trap door in the floor carrying a flask of hot tea and four cups.

"Warm drink before you go?" Evelyn said.

They shared the tea between the group. Joan shook her head and mock-grimaced, "I can tell who brewed this," she said looking at Evelyn.

"Taint proper soldier's tea if you can see the bottom of the mug.," Evelyn said.

Monjoie sniffed his mug suspiciously, then tasted it. "Tastes like boiled leaves," he said. "Where I come from we don't usually drink tisanes unless they're medicinal."

Joan laughed. "It's the closest Mr. Roast Beef here will come to eating a salad."

"I'll take my hot salad water over your frog legs any day," Evelyn said.

Rafe smiled as he wrapped his cold fingers around the hot stoneware cup. Unlike Evelyn and Joan, who had shivered a touch under their robes, he enjoyed the brisk cold. But the warmth seeping into his hands echoed the warmth of the three others genially teasing each other about their preferences in food and drink.

The others were debating the flavor of various mushrooms when the battlements beneath them shook. Joan drew her sword while Monjoie leaned over the edge to look.

Evelyn tossed back his tea. "He's at it again. Come on then." He beckoned to Rafe and disappeared down the tower stairs. The stone steps shook as they hustled down the tight spiral.

Rafe stooped for Monjoie. "Get on my back. It's faster."

Monjoie grimaced but clambered aboard like a long-legged child getting a piggyback ride.

Hunched double, Rafe carried Monjoie down the tightly spiraling stairs. Unlike a proper tower stair at home that would spiral left to give the defender the advantage, this one spiraled right. He wanted to be well off them before any fighting broke out. Why couldn't humans be left-handed like normal folk?

At the bottom of the watchtower, Rafe let Monjoie slide to the ground. The rest of the cloister was assembled and arming themselves from Joan's supplies.

"How do we fight him?" Rafe said.

"With whatever you've got," Evelyn answered, slinging a crossbow over each shoulder.

Rafe grimaced. If Mont Saint-Michel needed him for anything it might be for battle strategy.

Caedmon was tuning his harp. Rafe had known enough bards in his time not to question it, but he did wonder what, if anything, Aaliyah, Lachar, and Aelfburga could do. A gentle gardener, an archivist, and a dreamy monastery cook were not the defensive army he would have chosen. Monjoie was arming himself with a longbow and sword, while Lachar had picked up a spear. Aelfburga simply stood facing the horizon, her eyes closed and her hands clasped. Aaliyah stood beside her.

Joan handed Rafe a broadsword and helmet. "If you faeries take to the air, the rest of us will hold the ground." Rafe nodded and put out his wings. As he wrapped his fingers around the handle, he felt the weakness in his grip. It was a vast improvement over the total numbness he had felt when he first arrived, but still not his old strength or agility. He swung the sword around through a few warm-up motions, grimacing at the clumsiness. He could manage two-handedly, but handling the sword with his left alone was still out of the question. Frustrated, he put the sword back and picked up the quarterstaff. It might not be as elegant a weapon, but today was the wrong day to die from his own stupid pride. Or get others killed.

"Needs must," he said to Joan, saluting her with the quarterstaff and a wry smile.

She smiled back at him and nodded approvingly. She armed herself with a bastard sword and a small shield.

"Here he comes!" Aaliyah called. "Brace!" As she spoke, the ground under Rafe's feet shook and rippled. Only his wings kept him from being knocked down by the force of it. He hopped up into the air, wings beating.

Aaliyah knelt, pressing her hands to the stones and the rumbling subsided, the ground settling back into place. Caedmon struck a chord on his harp and a rush of courage buoyed Rafe up, lifting him higher into the air.

Rafe raced toward Lachar and Monjoie, now also airborne. "Where is he?" he shouted. Everyone around him seemed to know exactly what to do, but aside from the sudden earthquakes, Rafe could see no evidence of attack. No army loomed on the horizon. No great monster lifted its head out of the sea.

In answer, Lachar beat his wings, lifting himself out beyond the monastery wall. He pointed downward with his spear. "There. On the strand. He shouldn't ever have gotten this close. He's breached the outer defenses."

Flying up to hover beside Lachar, Rafe looked down at the thin strip of rocky strand between the wall and the waves. A single figure stood there, hands pressed against the monastery walls. Another wave of magic shook the monastery.

"I'll hit him from above," Lachar said. "Can you two command enough of the waves to use them against him?"

"I can try," Rafe said. Using water magic on the ocean was a bit like trying to eat a live elephant in one bite. The faerie who tried it risked being crushed. At the same time, whatever this enemy was doing, he wasn't as weak as his size implied.

Even as Rafe answered, Evelyn shot a crossbow bolt down at the Enemy. It lit up with golden fire as it flew straight toward the Enemy's head. But the bolt sprang back, shattered against an invisible barrier yards above the Enemy. He didn't even look up.

"You see?" Lachar said. Rafe nodded and slammed his helmet down over his head. Whatever creature the Enemy was, its power had no correlation to its size.

"Let's get him!" Monjoie shouted.

As Lachar dove down toward the Enemy, his spear out before him, Rafe and Monjoie split left and right, putting the Enemy between themselves and the monastery. Rafe hovered low over the water, using the staff as a focus for his hands as he reached out with his magic to the waves. The wind whipped the sea spray up to meet him, wetting him from the waist down. He drew the foaming droplets into missiles and sent them at the Enemy's back. A thousand tiny daggers of ice hurled themselves at the Enemy. None of them reached him. Shattered against the Enemy's magical defenses, they fell back into the surging ocean.

Rafe's own magic bounced back at him as his icicles failed. The backlash caught him by surprise and sent him tumbling. The chaos of unleashed magic and wind nearly knocked him into the water before he could right himself again. Beating his wings feverishly, he managed to hover just above the water and steady himself.

Above the Enemy, Lachar was darting back and forth, stinging the invisible barrier with his spear like an enraged hornet. Evelyn fired crossbow bolts. Opposite him, Monjoie wrestled with the waves, trying to send them up and over the Enemy. Like Rafe, his magic rebounded on him. A wave sloshed up and pulled him under, but he resurfaced, spluttering and furious.

"You alright?" Rafe shouted to him.

Monjoie nodded and began swimming toward the Enemy.

Rafe couldn't see the others, but he trusted they were doing whatever lay in their power. Little cracks and lighting bolts of golden light appeared above and around the Enemy. Rafe hoped those were a sign his defenses were breaking, but as Rafe watched, the Enemy began to rise up the wall of the monastery, pulling himself hand over hand.

"Oh no, you don't," Rafe said. He reached out with his hands, gathering as much of the ocean water to himself as he could, pushing his control to its limit, and hurled it all in a single wave at the Enemy.

The wave rushed forward gathering stones and ocean debris as it went. It thundered into the back of the Enemy's shield. The water crackled and danced with golden lightning. The figure climbing the wall paused for the first time and looked behind him. Rafe couldn't see the Enemy's face, but a sense of bemused fury washed over him. Whatever the Enemy was, he now had its attention.

Rafe gathered as much of the ocean together as he could again, preparing to send another wave. He beat his wings furiously, keeping himself out of the water. It wasn't that he minded the wet, but once immersed in the sea's depths he'd have no more control over its behavior than a minnow.

He hurled all the gathered water he could and watched it dash against the Enemy's defenses. Yes! There were definite faults and cracks in the shield surrounding him. Slowly, with a motion between amusement and rage, the Enemy reached up one hand and wiped a single drop of water off his face.

Rafe whooped and punched the air. Even as he did so, the Enemy left the monastery wall and launched himself at Rafe. Wings made of blinding light erupted from the Enemy's back. Rafe raised his staff and flew to meet the assault.

A wave of power struck Rafe, knocking the wind out of him. Then the Enemy was on top of him, grappling him to itself, strangling the life out of him. Rafe hammered at the Enemy with his staff and his magic, but it did no good. The pressure on his throat closed tighter and tighter. Red stars exploded behind his eyes.

They fell to the rocky strand with Rafe's wings crunched painfully beneath him. The Enemy was kneeling on his chest, choking the life out of him. But not just choking him. His life force, the stream of life inside him that was just a trickle compared to the great well of life hidden inside the altar flowed out of him into the Enemy with every second.

And even as he knew this creature, this Enemy, would gladly kill him, was killing him this very moment, Rafe felt an overwhelming need to give in, to embrace his death at the Enemy's hands if only it would win him a smile from the creature causing his death. It would all be worth it, if only the Enemy thought fondly of him. His grip on his staff slackened. Black edges closed in on his eyes.

Screaming, Monjoie hit the Enemy in the head with a rock. The grip on Rafe's neck eased a fraction, as did the grip on his mind. Monjoie hit the Enemy again and was backhanded out of the way for his trouble. But it was enough to break the Enemy's hold on Rafe's mind. Rafe shoved hard with his staff and pummeled the Enemy.

Golden crossbow bolts fell onto the Enemy's head and Lachar dove out of the sky above them. He drove his spear into the Enemy, wrestling him free of Rafe. Air rushed back into Rafe's lungs. Lachar stabbed the Enemy again and kicked him square in the chest.

And just like that, the Enemy vanished. Rafe looked around desperately, trying to find where the next attack would come from, but the Enemy was gone. Lifting himself up on one elbow, Rafe called to Monjoie. "You alive?"

"Yes." A long pause. "Ow."

Rafe scrambled and slipped on the wet pebbles until he could unkink his wings and pull them back in. He hobbled over to Monjoie and offered him a hand. "How's your hip? Can you stand?"

Monjoie lay on his back. "If that bastard broke my hip again, I'll hunt him down, so help me."

"That bad?"

Monjoie nodded. Rafe could see that his teeth were gritted in pain, lips pressed tight. Rafe looked up at the walls, assessing his options. His wings were aching and crumpled, but not broken. His limbs shook, and his heart seemed to have an unhealthy flutter to it. He could probably fly himself up the wall, but he doubted he could carry himself and Monjoie. Maybe with Lachar's help.

"Hey! Down here!" he shouted up at the other defenders.

Evelyn's head appeared over the wall. "Oy!"

"Oy yourself," Rafe said. "Is Lachar alright?"

"He will be. Taking a wee little nap at the moment though. You two able to sit tight while we get the fishing boat out?"

"I'm fine. Monjoie's not in great shape. We won't die before you get here."

Evelyn raised a thumb in approval, and his head disappeared. With his staff for support, Rafe lowered himself down beside Monjoie. The rocks were no picnic to sit on, even if they had been worn smooth by the waves. "Hang in there. Aaliyah will set you right."

Monjoie gestured at Rafe, a shooing motion. "I'm not getting up any time soon. You might as well get back in the air."

Rafe shook his head. "I'm in no hurry."

Beside him, Monjoie clenched and unclenched his fist, breathing shallowly against the pain. Reaching out his hand, Rafe took Monjoie's hand and squeezed it. Monjoie squeezed back, a bone-crushing grip. But it was Rafe's left, so he figured the lingering numbness was finally good for something. Rafe tried to make a wry joke, but his throat burned, and the words wouldn't form. Perhaps after breakfast. Together, they waited for help to arrive.

15

With no time to recover from the Enemy's attack, the members of the monastery who were able gathered in the kitchen to eat a hasty breakfast of porridge and tea. Aaliyah's hands trembled as she came in from healing Lachar. A grayish pallor tinged her dark skin as she supported Monjoie to the table. "Who's next?" she said. "Rafe?"

"I'm fine," Rafe assured her.

"Sit down and eat, dear," Aelfburga said. "You can't kill yourself putting the rest of us to rights." She pressed Aaliyah into a seat then placed her hands on her shoulders, humming a gentle tune. Aaliyah yawned hugely, but the strain on her face eased.

As Rafe watched he wondered again where the difference lay between magic power and simple kindness in this place. Or were they the same thing?

Caedmon rapped on the table for attention and cleared his throat loudly for good measure.

"We're listening!" Evelyn yelled back cheerfully at him. "Give us our marching orders."

"Good. We have fought off one attack already, but I would not be surprised if the Enemy tried again. Every time outsiders enter this space they may inadvertently create an opening for the Enemy, or even bring him in with them. Especially since these particular outsiders are Faeries who inevitably find him overwhelmingly charming." Caedmon paused to fix Rafe and Monjoie with a gimlet eye. "So, Rafe and Luc, you will remain here. Keep the hearth lit, keep watch, and make sure there's a hot meal ready when the rest of us get back. Everyone else will be circulating through our guests, manning the battlements, and keeping watch for signs of the Enemy."

Rafe opened his mouth to object, to protest that whatever his ultimate decision about the monastery was, he ought to at least tell Deor that he was still alive. But Aaliyah cut in before he could gather his arguments.

"Not Lachar," Aaliyah said. "He's too vulnerable right now. I left him asleep."

Caedmon grimaced. "All the more reason for you to stay alert, Rafe. The Enemy is cunning and subtle. If he catches you unawares, he will try to make you trust him, to let him in. Taking you to the Proving itself would be a liability."

Everyone else around the table nodded, not in the least surprised by this order of business. Monjoie heaved a sigh of relief. "Nice to know I won't be arrested as a traitor today."

Rafe rolled his eyes and half stood up from his seat. "Caedmon, Abbot... sir. These are my people, and I need to speak to my Regent. I need to at least let her know I am alive."

Caedmon fixed Rafe with an irritated stare. "The Regent will have more than enough on her plate today, Rafe. Why do you feel that you simply *must* speak to her?"

Rafe paused. He wanted to say that he needed to speak to her because he was still in love with her, and he needed to tell her so many things, apologize for so many things, but it seemed such notions wouldn't impress the Abbot. "It's my duty, sir, as the Sword of the Winter Court"

"That isn't suffic–" Caedmon stopped mid-word. "Did you say you are the *Sword of the Winter Court?*" His face flushed.

"Yes. Though she might have chosen a new one now."

Caedmon scrubbed a hand across his face. "You cannot speak to her before the ceremony." He held up a hand to silence Rafe before he could protest. "The discovery that Mont Saint-Michel was giving sanctuary to a major political person would shatter the appearance of neutrality. It is imperative that you," he glanced at Monjoie, "*both* of you not be seen before the ceremony. But—" he continued, steamrolling over Rafe's second attempt to talk, "after the ceremony, I will make sure you can speak to your Regent. Before that, you are to remain unknown and unseen to them. Do you understand me?"

Rafe nodded. "I do. Thank you." He relaxed back into his seat with a glance at Monjoie. "There's no need for Monjoie to be seen or mentioned at all unless he wants to."

"Fine, fine," said Caedmon, shoving away from the table. "Let's be on our way."

The others left as soon as they had finished eating. Rafe and Monjoie stared at one another across the littered table.

"It's not the actual washing I hate," Rafe said as he looked at the dirty dishes. "It's the knowledge that five minutes after the work is done, some wanker will come along and undo it all. Over and over. Endlessly. Until we die."

Monjoie conceded the point with a laugh. "I don't know what kitchen servants are paid, but I doubt it's enough."

It occurred to Rafe that Deor probably did know what her kitchen servants were paid. And how often they were given holidays. Back in the first days of her arrival at the Palace, she had been embarrassed at the idea of having servants. She had even scolded him once for leaving his socks lying on the floor for Jameson to pick up when he could have easily gotten them into the hamper. When he had protested that picking up socks was Jameson's job, she had been genuinely offended. "Only assholes deliberately make work harder for other people!" she had snapped at him before cocooning herself in the bedsheets, her back radiating offense until he crept out of bed and gathered up the clothes he had tossed on the floor.

"Hey!" Monjoie tossed a toast crust at him. "Are you trying to take Aelfburga's place now? Wake up."

Rafe sank back into the present and glared at Monjoie. He flicked the crumbs off his robe and said, "What?"

"I'll sit at the dish sink and scrub if you clear the table for me. Deal?"

"Sure. That's fine. Do you want help getting there?"

"No. I think I can manage now. I need the practice anyway. I'm getting positively doughy in this place. Not like you with your morning routine."

Rafe rose from the table and began gathering dishes, dumping food scraps into a single bowl for the compost heap. As he did so, Monjoie gingerly pushed a chair across the flagstone floor until he reached the sink. Rafe pretended he couldn't hear the quiet grunts of effort. Monjoie did not respond well to pity.

It occurred to Rafe that there was one additional thing they had in common. Stiff-necked and proud, Caedmon called both of them. It had taken Rafe a minute to realize that wasn't a compliment. Farringdons prided themselves on their unbending will.

"This is a far cry from being a pampered son," Monjoie said as he picked up a dishrag.

Rafe snorted and sloshed the dishes down into the water more forcefully than necessary.

"What's biting your behind?" Monjoie said.

"I'm not in the mood for your sarcasm today."

"What sarcasm? I was talking about me. You think I grew up scrubbing pots and tending the fire while the great folk went about their affairs? I may not have a title, but I was born into the gentry. And that was before Madeline and Edgar agreed to foster me."

Rafe forced himself to lower his shoulders from their defensive posture. "My apologies. I thought it was another crack at me for being the Prince."

"Not this time," Monjoie said.

They worked in silence. Monjoie scrubbed. Rafe carried. When the dishes were all cleared and the fire tended, Rafe joined Monjoie at the sink and took up a drying towel.

"How's your hip?" he asked.

"Not bad. It hurt like fire lying on those rocks, but once Aaliyah rubbed her green goo on me, I felt fine. She said it's not rebroken. Moving helps." Monjoie passed Rafe a bowl to dry. "How's the hand?"

"Clumsy." A beat passed. "I hate it."

"I hear you. My body is supposed to work, dammit."

"Exactly."

Monjoie chuckled. "My fiancée is not going to be happy if I can't hold up my end of things in the bedroom. Sorry, sweetheart, from now on you do all the work. I'll just lie here and look sexy."

Rafe nearly dropped the bowl he was drying. "I was wondering about the woman I saw in Caedmon's bowl. That's your fiancée? That didn't come up in your background check. I went over your file with a fine-toothed comb after Michael was discovered."

Monjoie turned and rolled his eyes at Rafe. "I lied. About all of it. Arthur's not the only one in the Winter Court with spycraft. Even

Michael didn't know about me beyond that I was Madeline's fosterling. I was there to keep an eye on him for Madeline."

"Ugh." Though he had to admire Monjoie's prowess if he'd managed to evade Arthur's information network.

As if understanding his thoughts, Monjoie shrugged. "It helped that I'm on good terms with my parents. They took me back after Madeline made a show of kicking me out in disgrace so it looked like I applied for the Palace Guard to get away from Wellhall."

"How lucky for you then." Rafe dried a few more dishes and began putting things away. Finally, he turned to Monjoie and said, "Why do you like Madeline? Personally, I mean."

Monjoie paused his drying and turned to look at Rafe in surprise. "I told you. She's an excellent duchess."

"I heard you. But Victor would say the same thing, and he isn't on the best terms with her. She uses people for her own ends. You either serve her purposes, or she'll toss you aside the same way she did him."

Monjoie glared. "Madeline didn't toss Victor aside. He betrayed her."

"By disagreeing with her? By refusing to assassinate an innocent changeling? Whatever you think of Finn, Deor never did Wellhall any harm. She didn't know the place existed until six months ago."

Monjoie tried to shrug, but he didn't meet Rafe's eyes. "Innocent people…"

"Don't tell me innocent people get hurt in wars. I know about war. I've fought them. I've led them. I've been a prisoner of one."

Monjoie studied his feet, frowning, though at what Rafe couldn't be sure. "The truth is, I never thought about her one way or another. I did what I was asked to do because that was the side I was on."

"And Victor?"

At that, Monjoie could look him in the eye. "Him? He deserved what he got."

Something in the cold way Monjoie said it made Rafe sure that worse had happened to Victor than just being imprisoned in the Tower. But wherever Victor was and whatever condition he was in, Rafe couldn't do anything about it now.

Monjoie shook the water from his hands and continued, "You keep insisting I'm a traitor, but I'm not. I'm just loyal in a different way. Finn is a danger to everything he touches. He's slowly sucking the life out of the Winter Court and especially the parts he hates, which you know includes Wellhall. He was never a good and faithful lord to any of us. You think

Madeline poisoned me against the King and you, but I grew up hearing my parents and their friends talking about the latest boneheaded move the King had made. About capricious taxes and failed fishing seasons. About crops withering in the field. Madeline was never a traitor to *us*. She was the epitome of what a duke should be—a liege who fought tooth and nail to protect her people. Wellhall isn't rich and prosperous just because we have resources, but because Madeline and her husband have been stewarding the land and the sea and the people for centuries. Our biggest threat isn't the Summer Court or the Goblins, it's the Aethelwings! It was an honor to serve my homeland against them. From where I stand, you're the traitor."

For a few moments, Rafe blinked, his head spinning as he finally understood. So many people had seen Finn for who he was long before Rafe had seen it himself. For months he had nursed his private hurt, his sense of betrayal at how Finn had treated him. But it was no different than the way Finn treated everyone in the kingdom. You were either on Finn's side, which meant you could be used until you were used up, or you were his enemy and deserved to be destroyed. Either way, the end was destruction. So many people he had failed to help over the decades because he had failed to stand up to the man he thought of as his father. What little he had done, he had done in secret, bits and pieces here and there while Astarte and Robbie and the whole country had suffered. And then Deor had come along and told Finn to his face what Rafe should have said.

Rafe stepped up to Monjoie. "Help you to the table?"

"Yeah." Monjoie let Rafe support some of his weight, and Rafe settled him in and took a seat across from him. "Are you staying here and becoming a monk or not?"

"Are you?"

"I don't know."

"I don't know either. The Source..."

Rafe waited for Monjoie to finish the sentence. When he didn't, Rafe said, "When I touched it, I felt connected to every living thing at once. Not just the animals and people. Everything."

Monjoie nodded slowly. "For me... it was everyone and everything I care about. My parents. My fiancée. Edgar and Madeline. The woods and fields around my family's home. The exact tide pools where Juliette and I splashed around as kids. Protect the Source, and I would be protecting them." He heaved a huge sigh. "Except if I stay, I'll never see them again."

They sat together, each looking in a different direction. As time stretched, Rafe marked the progress of the hearth fire. "I wish I had been raised in Wellhall," he said aloud. He hadn't forgotten that Monjoie sat with him listening, but he said it more to himself than anyone else.

"Why?" Monjoie said. "You hate Madeline."

"Madeline isn't Wellhall anymore than Finn is the Winter Court," Rafe said. "I've been there from time to time, you know. And I've sailed up and down the coast. That's where I went the last time I took out the Duke's Pride, when Finn decided to make me an Aethelwing. I've never felt more like an exile."

He was glad he didn't have to look Monjoie in the eye after saying something so deeply personal. Monjoie snorted, rubbed his nose, and cleared his throat in embarrassment.

"I'm an asshead and a fool," Rafe muttered.

16

Deor opened her eyes and blinked at the sunlight coming in the window. She drew a deep breath and snuggled back against Victor, who spooned her. She felt the rise and fall of his chest against her back. She had to smile—this room, this small bed, reminded her of college and learning to sleep with someone in a twin bed. Her knees hung over the edge of the bed, and Victor's feet dangled off the foot.

A knock came at the door, and it opened. "Deor?" Genevieve asked. "I'm sorry to bother you, but," she pushed the door open, "Victor seems to be missing." She froze in the doorway. "Oh. I see." She backed up. "Not missing, then. Sorry!" She stepped back and started to close the door. She pushed it open a fraction again but stayed facing the other way. "You'll want to be up in not too long," she said. "We've got about three hours before the reception is to start."

"Is she awake?" Stephen's voice carried past Genevieve. "Did you tell her?"

"It's fine," Genevieve said and tried to shut the door.

"No, it's not." Stephen pushed past, looked at Deor, and froze.

Behind Deor, Victor stretched. "Good morning, Stephen. It seems that Deor is both aware that I am missing and has found me."

"Yep." Stephen nodded. "Good." He looked down, frowned, and picked up a stray button. He glanced at Deor. "Oh." He dropped it. "Brand! Need to go out? Come on boy!" Brand gleefully bounced to his feet and trotted outside. Stephen nodded at both of them and closed the door.

Deor raised herself gently and swung her legs to the floor, careful not to fall off the bed and keeping the sheet over her, more for protection against the slight chill in the air than worry about being naked. She scooted up toward the head of the bed so Victor could sit up too without the danger of knocking her to the floor.

"How are you?" he said once he was sitting next to her.

"I'm good." She was, now that she thought about it. She glanced at him and caught him eyeing her, a look of concern on his face. "Now we don't have to keep it a secret. Which is for the best. I've got a bad track record with secrets like this."

"Yeah." He ran a hand through his hair and smiled sheepishly. She hadn't pegged him as shy. "That was... I mean, last night... I've never... I mean, I have, but not like that.... Ugh."

Deor laughed. "The magic was something else." She reached out and ran her hand down his arm. His magic stretched itself toward hers. As she moved her hand away, their magics reached for each other before settling back. "I've never felt anything like this before either. Astarte said that lovers and consorts don't mix, but this doesn't feel wrong," Deor said.

"No, it doesn't," he agreed.

She sighed. "Right now I need to feel safe, and you make me feel safe. Touching you, being near you, I don't feel isolated and alone as the Regent. Whatever problems come out of this, we'll deal with later."

"You're right." He cast back the sheet and stood. "We need to get ready for today." He grabbed his pants and pulled them on. "I'll head back to my room. I'll see you in a little bit?"

Deor climbed out of bed, wrapped a sheet around her, and followed him to the door.

He stepped out into the corridor and turned to face her. "We should talk about Rafe..." He swallowed.

"Someday, yes." Deor agreed. She leaned into him. "I miss him. So do you."

Victor looked at her, tears in his eyes. "We never spoke again after Roger's." He wiped away the tears. "We were so close to having a real relationship."

"I know." Deor had started to cry, too. A few tears trickled down her cheeks. She blinked several times, holding them back. "There were no goodbyes or anything for me either. But we don't know anything for sure. Maybe…"

"We'll keep hoping." He leaned in and rested his forehead against hers, sending the magic ebbing back and forth between them.

"Right. Focus on the problem in front of us."

"Mmhmm." Victor cupped her face gently in one hand and kissed her. "See you in a bit." He turned and walked down the hallway toward his room.

Deor stared after him, only returning to her room when he rounded the corner out of sight. She could still feel their magic connection. It didn't break as he moved away, but expanded, stretching between them.

Rafe knew he wasn't supposed to get anywhere near Deor or any of the visiting faeries, but, he reasoned, that so long as he wasn't seen or recognized, he wasn't causing any problems. He just wanted to know she was well before the Proving started. He made an excuse to leave Monjoie in the kitchen and drew his monk's hood over his face, hiding his blue hands in his sleeves, and made his way to the Winter Court's chambers.

He heard the commotion before rounding the corner, so he leaned around. Genevieve and Stephen were at the door to Deor's room. Genevieve tried to close it, but Stephen stopped her. He couldn't quite make out what they were saying, but Stephen backed out quickly, taking Brand with him, and closing the door behind him. He watched Genevieve, Stephen, and Brand leave, and waited a few breaths. He was about to gather the courage to walk down the hall and knock, Caedmon's neutrality be damned, when the door opened again.

Victor stepped out, wearing his pants and jacket, and carrying everything else. He turned back and Deor stepped out, wrapped in a sheet. They leaned into each other, whispering softly. Finally, Victor touched her face and kissed her before turning to go.

Rafe pulled back from the corner and listened as the door closed and Victor's footsteps faded. Rafe leaned against the wall, drawing deep breaths, and trying not to freeze everything around him. He spun away from the wall and stalked back to his quarters.

"Good morning again!" Genevieve smiled at Deor when she came into the dressing room. There was a small dais surrounded by mirrors on three sides. On a mannequin was Deor's dress. She gasped. She hadn't had a chance to see the finished project.

"It's perfect!" She walked over to it and ran her fingers down the bodice. The velvet was soft and pliant under her fingers. She gently turned it around to look at the back. The fine platinum chain at the top glittered, but what drew the eye was the lack of fabric. She'd had on the muslin pattern and approved of it, but now she wondered if the back was too low, if the dress was too much.

Genevieve stepped up next to her and slipped her arm around Deor's waist. "It's not too much."

Deor glanced at her. "You read my mind."

"It's not hard with this," she said, giving Deor a squeeze before letting go. "I know you're not fond of fashion."

"It's not that I'm not fond of it." She turned to Genevieve. Might as well be honest. "If I looked like you, I'd love fashion." She grinned. "But I'm short, and...not lithe."

"We are what we are," Genevieve acknowledged. "And that should never, ever keep us from having fabulous clothes."

Deor laughed. "You win. I'll wear this and be fabulous."

17

Deor and Genevieve met up with Victor and Stephen outside the entrance to the chapel. The monks couldn't be thrilled that a place of worship had been turned into a party room, but it was apparently important that this ceremony happen in a sacred space, so there they were.

"Ready?" Victor said, offering her his arm.

"As I'll ever be." She took it. "Let's go."

Two monks, Evelyn and the young woman who had led them to their rooms before, waited by the doors.

Deor tried for cheerful conversation. "That was quite the storm we had early this morning, wasn't it? The thunder really shook the walls."

"Yes," Victor said. "I didn't realize you get weather that strong here!"

"We do get things like that on occasion," the man said flatly. "I'm sorry if it disturbed you."

"Not at all!" Deor insisted. "Just making conversation."

"We'll open the doors, and you'll be announced," the young woman said. "You're the last one in, on account of ceremony." The woman carried a slight French accent and a heavy dose of disdain. The Proving was a bunch of faerie nonsense, it seemed, nothing but an inconvenience for the monastery.

"We'll follow your lead," Deor said.

The woman nodded, satisfied, and she and the other monk opened the doors.

The chapel had been serene when she had visited it before, when she was the only one there. Now it was brightly lit and filled with fae in frills. And wings. The room was a rainbow of colors flitting and fluttering. Deor spotted her servants circulating around the gathering with trays.

As she stepped into the hall proper, another monk announced her presence. The whole room turned to look. Across the church, near the altar, the Summer Court Queen stood, tall, proud, and beautiful. Deor swallowed and held her head high. Near the Queen were Geoff and two other goblins she assumed were Geoff's parents, Gregory and Ipomoea. All were impeccably dressed in faux military style, and all three smiled, looking both condescending and smug.

"Where's Roger?" Deor whispered to Victor. "I don't see him."

"Who knows?" he whispered back. "Maybe he decided to boycott?"

"Maybe," Deor said, frowning. That didn't seem like Roger.

"To the Queen?" Victor said, gently nudging her forward.

"Yes. Wait, no." Something—someone—caught her eye. At the side of the room, red wine in hand, stood a tall, lanky man with spiky brown hair, pale skin, and devilish brown eyes.

"I want to talk to him first."

Victor said nothing but shifted course. As they made their way through the crowd, Deor could hear the gasps and whispers of conversation as people saw the back of her dress.

"That's Ivan," Victor whispered to her. "So much for a vampire show of allegiance. Not sending Donovan and Chloe is a slight in itself. But in their place, they've sent the Vlad's personal assassin. The rest of the vampires cheerfully call him 'the one the Vlad keeps chained to a wall underground.'"

"Is that true?" They arrived at the man before Victor could answer. Deor nodded in acknowledgment but not deference—again quietly thanking Genevieve for hours of training. "Hello." She dropped Victor's arm and held out her hand. "You're Ivan from the Rodzevrah court, yes?"

He looked at her hand for a moment and up at her before taking it in his own and bending over to kiss it with lips cold as ice. "I am. And you are Her Majesty, Deor Aethelwing, Regent of the Winter Court, no?"

His Eastern European accent was thick, and Deor wondered if that, like the clothing choice, was exaggerated. "I am. It is a pleasure to meet you. I didn't realize that anyone outside of Faerie gave a damn about this."

He laughed. "Donovan told me you were entertaining. I am here because the Vlad asked that I be here to support you."

"How delightful!" Deor meant it, too. There was something off about the vampire in front of her, no doubt about that. He had a dreamy look that suggested he was somewhere else, but his gaze could sharpen in an instant. She had so many questions.

"Your Majesty," Victor said softly. "We should not delay meeting the Queen. We've already arrived late, and she may take it as a slight."

"You're right." Deor smiled at Ivan. "Do send Donovan and Chloe my best, and thank the Vlad for sending you. I appreciate the support."

"I will." Ivan said. "Have fun with the Queen." He nodded politely as they walked away.

The crowd parted in front of them as they made their way toward the Queen, and Deor nodded and smiled at Geoff as she passed him. The Queen wasn't on a raised dais, yet Deor felt like she towered over everyone. Her skin was a deep golden color, and her eyes matched. Her blond hair fell in waves. She had fine, sharp features that reminded Deor of Astarte. They were siblings, after all. But her wings were translucent gold, casting the beautiful glow of a warm summer sunset whenever light hit them. Where Astarte's power was subtle and gentle, this woman's was overt. Even across the room, the magic was palpable.

"Steady," Victor said. "You can feel her magic—it's not deliberate will magic. She is just like that—you'll want her to like you, and that can make you say things you might not want to say."

As Victor said it, Deor recognized it was true. There was a teasing sense in the air around them as they approached that this woman's approval was everything. That Deor should behave appropriately, defer to her, and bend at the knees. "She reminds me of your mother."

"Not surprising. If anyone in the Winter Court can take on the Summer Court Queen in a battle of wills and win, it is my mother."

"You know that when your mother made me feel this way, I punched her in the face, right?"

"Yes. Let's not do that here."

They arrived in front of her and, once again, Deor gave a Genevieve-trained non-bow. "Your Majesty, Eura, Queen of the Summer Court, it is an honor to meet you."

The woman smiled, benevolence in her features. "I am glad to finally meet you as well, Regent. This is my brother, D'nath, Sword of the Summer Court." She bent her head toward the man next to her.

"It's a pleasure," Deor said. He was both darker in his golden skin and lighter in his blond hair—it was almost white. He had green eyes that were sharp and calculating, but he stood with easy grace, one hand at his side and the other arm bent to support his sister's hand. His wings were a soft, delicate pink. Not quite translucent, but close, like a lovely chiffon. "This is my Consort, Victor Farringdon."

D'nath and the Queen nodded in his direction. "Well met, Lord Consort," D'nath said.

"Well met," Victor echoed. Though neither man was frowning, or looking the least bit like he cared about the situation at all, Deor could still sense the tension between them.

"I have wanted to meet you—the greatest swordsman in all of Fae." Deor said.

For a moment D'nath looked startled. "You flatter me, my Lady."

"Oh, no." Deor shook her head. "I'm notoriously bad at flattering people. I have heard about your reputation from several reliable sources. The Sword..." Deor stumbled a moment, "the former Sword of the Winter Court himself told me of your skill."

"Indeed?" He inclined his head. "That is quite a compliment then, as great a swordsman as he is...was." He frowned slightly. "I am sorry for your loss."

Deor's stomach knotted, and she forced herself to breathe slowly. Tears were threatening in her eyes. It had been a stupid thing to do, to bring up Rafe. The two Summer Court faeries watched her, and Deor stared back. Eura ran her hand down D'nath's shoulder, brushing past his long hair. A gesture she had repeated more than a few times since Deor had started watching her. "Why," Deor spat out, "are you petting him?"

The Queen's eyes widened. "I'm not," she said, pulling her hand away. She cleared her throat. "My brother and I are close. He is a comfort to me."

It was still weird, Deor thought, but let it go. The quip had done its job, and she no longer teetered on the edge of tears. Victor gently touched her elbow, and his magic surged through her, comforting and strengthening in equal measure, bringing to mind the rush that happened when Finn left the palace and the magic reached out to her. An idea struck her.

"Forgive me the impertinence," Deor said in a tone that suggested she wasn't all that apologetic, "but when your sister Astarte left the court with Finn, did you feel her leaving?"

"What?" Eura jolted slightly. "That is an... unusual question. It happened a long time ago."

"I know." She drew a deep breath. The woman standing in front of her was literally the only person who had even a remote idea of what she was going through with the palace. After all, she'd probably been just as shocked at her sister's abandonment of the Summer Court as Deor was of Finn's leaving. "When Finn left the palace," Deor paused and weighed her words. How dangerous was her admitting that the palace had no interest in his return? She started again. "When he fled, the palace turned to me— all of its magic, its power, came at me. The palace talks to me. Does yours talk to you?"

Eura stared at Deor for a long minute—long enough that Deor was certain the Queen wasn't going to answer. "Yes." She finally said. "To both." She cocked her head to the side and looked Deor up and down. "It hadn't occurred to me that you would have felt the same thing."

Deor let out a breath. "Was the palace angry with Astarte?"

"It was hurt. So was I." She frowned, her eyes narrowing. A glint of magic and malice lit in them, and Deor knew that if Eura ever stood near Astarte again, it would be a fight to end all fights. "Abdicating wasn't step-ping away for someone else. It broke a chain of rulers going back for ages." She pursed her lips. "I didn't know whether or not I could ever control it."

Behind Eura stood a lovely but plain woman with brown hair, eyes, and wings, but a complexion that matched the Queen. She reached out and took Eura's free hand, squeezing it gently. Eura drew a deep breath and let it out slowly. "If it weren't for my Consort, my cousin Madge," she glanced back at the woman holding her hand, "I think it might have destroyed me." Her gaze flicked to Victor for a split second. "Consort is the most important relationship you will ever have."

Deor nodded—it certainly felt that way to her. Now she had a million more questions, and, politics be damned, she'd ask them, right here and right now. This woman was a fount of knowledge that could save Deor dozens, if not hundreds, of lessons learned the hard way. Perhaps after this whole thing was over, they could talk?

Before she could ask, a monk's voice rang out.

"People of Fae," Caedmon said. "It is time for the Proving. If the Regent and Queen will come forward..." As she had noticed then, he was the kind of shape that could denote a cheerful Friar Tuck, but his expression killed any similarity. This event was central to Deor having any chance to be a ruler at all, and he looked like she'd spoiled his day.

She let go of Victor's arm, taking his hand and twining her fingers in his instead, and dutifully complied. Eura and D'nath followed, and they walked side by side to the altar together. The power she had felt the previous night from the altar was still there, thrumming away. She stole a glance at Eura but couldn't tell if she felt it too. *She must,* Deor thought. *How could she not?* But the woman's face was a placid, elegant blank.

They reached the altar, and Caedmon stepped behind it. "We will begin," he said, "with the Summer Court."

"That wasn't what I understood was going to happen," Deor said

He looked down at her. "The Queen has asked for a chance to prove—" He stopped and cleared his throat, "to once again display her lineage and power."

If Eura could do this, and Deor couldn't, that would be an even grander mark against her. Hooray for politics.

"Do you object?" Caedmon asked.

"No." Deor shook her head.

"Then we shall commence." He turned to Eura. "Your Majesty, please step—"

The door from the fellowship hall slammed open, and in hurried Roger, with Bard Ama Nefasta right on his heels. Both looked a bit frazzled, but Roger, impeccably dressed, looked like he'd just finished crying, or screaming.

Caedmon's eyes narrowed.

"My apologies," Ama said. She carried her scythe, her symbol of office —definitely NOT a weapon—and wore academic robes. "We were delayed by an issue at home."

Caedmon snorted. "Let's get this over with." He waved at Eura as if to say *off you go now.*

Eura stepped up to the altar, and the crowd, including Deor, backed away slightly. Behind the altar, the head monk glared at the Summer Court Queen impatiently, but Eura took her time. She gazed at the altar for a moment then reached out to it, laying her palm flat against the stone. She closed her eyes and drew a deep breath, seeming to savor the feeling for a moment. She blinked open her eyes and exchanged glances with the monk.

"Whenever you are ready," the monk said, though his tone was softer.

Eura nodded. She cupped her hands and rested them on the table; she spread them like she was gently setting down a delicate cup. Between her hands, a small green plant appeared. As she spread her hands out and drew them up, the plant grew from a tiny sprig of green to a stalk branching out in several stems. On the stems, leaves uncurled and buds formed. Within moments, the plant had grown so that it took up half the altar, was nearly as high as the Queen, and burst with buds. In unison the buds bloomed in huge pink roses, their scent flooding the room.

Deor glanced at the crowd around them. Everyone, even the monks, even Victor and Stephen stood rapt. She wondered if there was more magic going on, another kind of will spell. She stared hard at Eura and her beautiful pink roses and had to admit that, no, there was no sinister spell at work. The magic of the Summer Court Queen was that amazing.

After another moment and a few more bursts of roses, Eura stepped back. She scanned the crowd, catching Deor's gaze for a moment, with a satisfied smile. She turned to the monk and waited.

"Nicely done," the monk said, nodding. "Beautiful." He looked to Deor. "Your turn, Your Majesty."

Deor stared at the rose bush. It showed no sign of wilting now that the Queen had turned her attention from it. Finally, she dragged her gaze from the flowers to the monk. "My magic isn't... I mean..." She waved her hands at the beautiful plant. "That's not the kind of thing I do."

"Of course not," the monk sounded irritated. "You're not a Summer Court faerie. Now come on." He waved her forward.

Deor stepped to the altar as Eura moved away, putting out her wings. Then, as the Queen had done, Deor touched the stone. It was cool under her hand, like any other stone at first. But then, as it had the night before, magic, deep in the stone, reached for her, called to her, like the palace throne. Older. Much older. Pure. This magic was not one divided into courts; it was a touchstone for the magic of the whole of the world. Deor was surer than ever that if she could reach a bit farther, she could touch it, hold it, use it.

"Ahem." The monk cleared his throat, and Deor blinked.

She looked at the room full of people, all staring at her. Eura looked self-satisfied, while Victor and Stephen tried to project confidence, but she could see the worry on their faces. Roger's and Ama's too. She glanced down, and next to her Brand wagged his tail dutifully. She reached down and patted his head.

Deor flicked her wrist, and a flurry of sparkles coalesced into a solid piece of metal, a magic sword. With a single swing, she sliced through the main stem at the base of the rosebush, severing it clean. Black rot shot up the stem and into the flowers, and a shower of rose petals fell, disintegrating into black dust. Seconds later, the remaining stem crumbled as well.

Deor spun to face the crowd, sword still glowing in her hand. She smiled at Eura. "Any more doubts?"

"No." The head monk said. "That is sufficient."

Deor glanced behind her and met the monk's gaze. "We're done?"

"Yes," he said, eyes on the sword. "You can put... that," he waved a hand at her, "away."

"Of course." She nodded in his direction. She could drive the sword back into her body, but she didn't need to prove that her own weapons couldn't hurt her. Even though the magic loss would make her unsteady, she risked it, dissipating the sword back into a shower of sparkles that swirled in the air and floated to the ground, landing on the hem of her dress. She held out her hand to Victor, and he took it, tucking it into his arm.

"This way," he said softly.

"Thank you," Deor said, leaning on him a bit. The world spun around her enough to unsteady her, but leaning on him, with his magic seeping into her, cleared her head. As they stood at the base of the altar, the crowd around them erupted into movement. The Summer Court Queen and her Sword sauntered out, followed by her retinue. Across the room, Ivan smiled a fangy grin at her, nodded, and turned to leave. Within seconds, the chapel itself emptied, leaving Caedmon, who eyed her carefully, and Deor's retinue.

18

Rafe had walked a full circuit around the monastery, cowl up, avoiding any faeries he saw, finally arriving at the training space where he and Joan would spar. Monjoie sat on the low stone wall.

"You're back," he said. "Getting ready to speak to your Regent?"

"Not really." Rafe joined him on the wall.

Monjoie frowned but didn't follow up. He smiled and drew a small mirror out of his pocket. He leaned in and whispered, "Want to watch the Proving?"

"Absolutely! How did you manage to keep that?"

"I'm sneaky," Monjoie said. "I've been holding off using it in case Caedmon decided mirrors were an avenue for the Enemy or something. But there's no one else here, so…"

"Mine was smashed before I got here." As Monjoie flipped open the mirror, Rafe caught his wrist. "You may not get another chance to use it. Don't you want to call your fiancée or parents? Tell them you're still alive?"

Monjoie shook his head a little. "I want to know how the wind is blowing back home first. I can't risk them being monitored. If I call and tell them I'm okay, it might put them in danger." He tapped the mirror's surface, fiddling with it a moment before he found what he was looking for. "There we go. Just lock in on the altar and then outward a bit. Aha, there's Evelyn, eating finger food. And there's Joan, looking like she's got ants crawling up her leg just at the thought of someone approaching the altar. Got it. Here, look." He held the mirror so they could both see.

Rafe leaned close, shoulder to shoulder with his enemy as the mirror focused on Deor. She looked well. Whole and confident, if a bit tense. Her smile did not quite reach her eyes, but that was not too surprising given the circumstances. From the front, her plain black dress had no ornamentation, only a few artfully draped folds.

She was talking to Caedmon, with Stephen just a few feet behind and Victor close by her side. Too close. Rafe peered at them. Yes, Victor was holding Deor's hand, her fingers twined in his. As his brother shifted his stance, Rafe saw the badge pinned to his chest—the Royal Consort.

"Fuck." Rafe stood up from the bench and stormed a short way away, circling angrily back as he paced.

"Rafe?" Monjoie called. "There's more. I think you want to see this."

He returned to Monjoie and gasped at what he saw. Deor's back. Her entire back was revealed by the dress from neck to just above the last line of decency. But it wasn't the amount of exposed skin that made Rafe swear again. Laid across her back in white cross-hatches like the slices of a knife, scars. From neck to buttocks Deor carried the marks of Finn's wrath openly for all to see. As her foot touched the first step up to the altar, her shoulder blades moved, and she put out her wings. Blood red unfurled from under her scars, like a reminder of the blood she must have shed in the Tower. Rafe buried his face in his hands.

Monjoie smacked him in the arm. "You're missing the best part. Look."

Rafe looked. A giant rose bush, its leaves glossy and dark, full of full-blown pink roses grew from the altar. Deor's hands rested on the altar. From the tilt of her head, she seemed to be listening or thinking. Then she stepped back and drew a sword out of thin air. With one sweep of her hand, she sliced clean through the rose bush, silver sparks like snowflakes trailing after her blade. Blackness spread up through the stem, invading every bud and branch. In seconds the bush vanished into black powder that disappeared as it fell. Sword still in hand, Deor turned to face the crowd, surveying their awed faces. Her own face was impassive. She regarded the glimmering sword in her hand and let it go with a careless gesture, as if throwing away so much power meant nothing to her. It vanished in a shower of sparks that settled like snow on the hem of her black gown.

She took a step down from the dais, and Victor caught her hand, pulling her in close to himself. Rafe saw the look of deep gratitude and affection on her face, all of it directed at Victor. Monjoie tucked the mirror away, muttering, "Well, that's enough of that. Pompous folk with their court ceremonies."

Rafe sat on the bench, his elbows on his knees. Monjoie watched him carefully until Rafe finally spoke. "I tried to go see her this morning," Rafe said. "But when I got to the hall, I saw Victor leaving her room." Rafe stared down at his hands. "Victor was in his coat and pants, carrying everything else. She was wrapped in a sheet." Rafe tried to keep the emotion out of his words, but the cold pouring off him no doubt gave his anger, his hurt, away.

"Yikes," Monjoie said. "I'm sorry."

Rafe flicked his gaze to meet Monjoie's. "Are you now?"

"Yes," Monjoie said. "I thought your reunion with Lady Genevieve was a little too convenient at the time. Smart ploy to use with Finn, though."

"It clearly didn't help her," Rafe said through gritted teeth.

"I don't know that anything could have," Monjoie said. "Finn was terrible. Frighteningly so. He opened her wounds again, and then they couldn't heal. That's how she ended up with those scars." He shuddered.

Evelyn and Joan entered. "Well, that's done." Evelyn shook his head. "Quite a show from your Regent." He nodded to Rafe. "Come on, now. Caedmon's with her, and you can come speak to her now."

"No." Rafe shook his head. "I think that would be a bad idea."

Evelyn frowned. "You seemed about ready to jump out of your skin to see her."

When Rafe said nothing, Monjoie spoke. "Feelings have changed."

"She has her new Consort. She doesn't need me,"

"I thought—" Joan said.

"They were lovers," Monjoie said. "And now she's with his brother, Victor." Rafe thought about punching Monjoie in the stomach but clenched his fist inside his sleeve instead.

"Oh," Joan nodded. "I'll let Caedmon know Rafe doesn't need to speak to her." She huffed and patted Rafe on the shoulder before leaving.

Evelyn nodded and took a seat next to Rafe. He dug into a pocket and pulled out a pack of cigarettes. "Want one?"

"Yes." Rafe took the proffered one, and Monjoie took one too. Evelyn lit them. The three of them sat in silence. For the first time, Rafe considered that maybe Mont Saint-Michel was where he was supposed to be.

19

Deor waited until the room was empty, save Victor, Caedmon and herself, and then spoke. "Can I ask you a question?"

"What kind of question?" Caedmon said, raising an eyebrow at her.

"An academic one, I suppose." She waited.

"Go on then," he said with a put-upon sigh.

"Are you Caedmon who wrote Caedmon's Hymn? The one that Bede wrote down, and included in his *History*?"

Caedmon gaped. "I wrote that over a thousand years ago!"

"So it is you!" Deor clapped her hands. "I wondered. I mean this is clearly a magical place. You've been here since you were a monk in England?"

"I have," he nodded, looking a bit lost. "That wasn't my only poem, you know. I wrote several and about things other than God." He crossed himself. "Songs about life and love. How did you hear about me?"

"Oh, I studied medieval literature in graduate school. I studied the later Middle Ages, mostly, but I took some classes on Old English, though I probably couldn't make heads or tails of it now."

"She's a doctor in the human world," Victor added.

"A PhD," Deor said. "Not like a medical degree. I was a college professor before finding out I was a princess."

Caedmon's frown briefly returned. "I think I'll need to learn more about your history at some point. Thank you for asking about my poetry. It made my day."

"I'd love to hear more about that time period. I mean, to actually speak to someone who lived through it…" She shook her head in disbelief.

"Maybe someday," Caedmon said as he glanced behind her.

The small, dark-haired woman appeared again. "The portal is ready whenever you are."

"I thought—" Caedmon started. The woman shook her head. "I see…" He frowned. "Very well." He returned his attention to Deor. "Lady Regent Doctor Professor Aethelwing Smithfield," he said with a twinkle in his eye, "it has been an adventure." A door opened. "Ah, I see your people are ready to join you." He put a hand on her arm. "Take care."

"Thank you," Deor said and watched as he left.

Genevieve, Stephen, Roger, and Ama walked toward her.

"I'm sorry, for our tardiness, Your Majesty," Ama said.

"It was my fault." Roger bowed.

"How did you get in? I thought the monks closed everything." Deor asked.

"I was able to contact them through the bards. They permitted us to come through." Ama glanced at Roger. "It is important, Your Majesty, that he was here. And that you listen to what he has to say."

Deor eyed Ama—she was as polite as Deor had ever seen her. She turned to Roger. "Are you satisfied that I can be Regent? Or are you going to parade around proclaiming I'm stealing the throne and Finn should be brought back as soon as possible?"

Roger grimaced. "Your Majesty, I will never, ever again suggest that you should not be Regent. Nor will I persist in arguing that the King should return."

"What?" Victor said. "That's a fast change of heart."

"It certainly can't be from this performance," Deor said, gesturing toward the ashes on the altar.

"No." Roger shook his head. "Arthur reached out to me."

"I see." Deor crossed her arms. "After I spoke to my father about the Proving, Arthur asked for a word. He told me to tell you to return to Northfalls. Then he told me never to let my father back in."

"Yes." He seemed relieved. "Arthur didn't say he had spoken to you. Then again, he was never out of the presence of the King when he spoke to me. Your Majesty, I apologize."

"Roger." Deor reached for him and laid her hand on his arm. "What happened?"

"When I arrived home to Northfalls, I found the house in chaos. The King was angry, irrational, demanding. When servants didn't move fast enough, or, in his mind, treated him poorly, he would fly off the handle. At one point, Pookie could not stand it anymore and intervened." He stopped, dropping his gaze to the floor. "I should have seen this coming," he said, mostly to himself.

Deor thought back to Arthur's bruises. "He hurt Pookie."

Roger's gaze snapped up to hers. "Yes." He shook his head. "I've loved the King his whole life. His mother was among my closest friends. He raised a hand to my husband, in my own house."

Deor thought about the lashes on her back. "Is Pookie okay?"

"Yes, thank God. Finn backhanded him, sent him sprawling. He would have done more, but Arthur, bless him, intervened. He stopped the King. And for his troubles—"

"Got a horrid beating himself," Victor finished.

"Yes." Roger nodded. "From here on out, I support you one hundred percent, my Lady Regent. I will return to Parliament, with Ama, and declare publicly that I support you. Even if he hadn't raised a hand to Pookie, I could not deny what I saw here. You are fit to rule—more fit than Finn, even on your worst day."

"Thank you for your support, Roger." Deor squeezed his shoulder and took her hand away.

That evening, home after the Proving, Deor sat in her bed, along with Brand. Jake and Sam sat dutifully at the foot. They all stared at Victor, who stood, hands on his hips, frowning, wearing nothing but dark blue lounging pants. For the third time, Victor started to take a step forward toward her, and stopped, scowl deepening.

"Oh, fuck it!" He threw his hands in the air and came around to the far side of the bed, where Deor had already pulled back the covers. He stared at the empty spot.

"Sit down," Deor said gently.

Victor sat but didn't get into bed.

She rested her hand on his back. "You don't have to sleep in here."

"I want to." His shoulders slumped, and he didn't turn back to face her. "But I don't know if it is the right thing to do."

"I get it." Deor got out of bed and came around to his side where she sat down next to him. She leaned her shoulder against his. "I've got no idea what the right thing to do is. I know that I feel safer, more stable, when you're close to me." She sighed, and it shook her whole being. "We can't change anything that happened. We can only do what we can do right now."

"I know." He leaned in toward her, too. "And I feel the same when I'm with you. It's like I'm supposed to be here." He stared straight ahead. "I've never quite felt like I was where I was supposed to be. Not back at Well-hall when I was the favored son, or in London, or anywhere. But here? This feels close." He turned to look at her. "But a romance? I don't think..." he trailed off.

"I agree," Deor said. "The sex was," she stopped. "It was good, but it wasn't..." She reached out and laid her hand on his arm. Their magics swirled together. "It wasn't this. And this is what's important."

Victor took her hand in his. "Yes. Exactly." He drew a bit of her magic toward him and released it back to her. "It's my job to keep the Winter Court—to keep you—safe. I know that in my soul."

Deor squeezed his hand. "I do too. There is something about this touch, our touch, that is vital. I want you to stay. I need you to stay. But staying doesn't mean sex."

He laughed. "You're right, but that sounds insane. 'No, no, we really were just *sleeping* together.'"

She chuckled. "Nothing about me since I've come to the Winter Court has been normal. Why would this be any different?"

"Fair point." He shooed her out of the way, and when she stood he swung his legs into bed and slid them under the blankets.

Deor climbed into bed on the other side. After a few moments of futzing around, they settled in, her back to his chest and his arm around her. As soon as the lights went out, the weight on the bed shifted as Sam and Jake both climbed up as well. As she drifted off to sleep, Victor's magic ebbed and flowed, mingling with hers, like the tide.

20

I n the weeks following the Proving, Rafe and Monjoie did not speak much about the future or their part in it. Except once, after a particularly long round of stretching and exercising their hurt parts, where both of them grimaced and cursed in pain more than once. Sweating and exhausted, they both slumped on a parapet, looking out over the water that separated them from the land.

"You ever think about just heading east and seeing where it takes you?" Monjoie said.

"Of course," Rafe said. "But in my case, I know where I'd end up." Monjoie waited patiently for him to finish the thought. Rafe pointed. "Romania's that way. Roughly. I could probably show up on the Vlad's doorstep, and he'd take me in for a few decades, or at least a couple years as long as the Winter Court didn't demand me back. He likes me well enough, and Donovan is my friend."

Monjoie nodded. "I've never been to the human world. Is it still full of cold iron?"

"A lot, yeah. Though they use something called plastics now. It helps. You still want to make sure you have a glove on before reaching for anything that might be metal. And a lot of their buildings have steel mesh embedded in the walls now. They're like cages for magic."

Monjoie shuddered. "When was the last time you were there?"

Rafe considered. "About forty, fifty years ago. I went on a vacation with Donovan and Chloe. We started in a city called Paris then wandered down to the southern coast."

Monjoie laughed a bit uncomfortably. "A vampire weekend? Sounds horrifying. What did you do, hunt humans for sport?"

"Sort of? Though not the way you mean." Rafe blushed a little, his cheeks flushing hot. "We did play a few too many rounds of 'who can seduce more humans,' but... um... that's a sport Donovan and Chloe take way more seriously than I do. Mostly we gambled and went to clubs. Chloe wanted to sunbathe on the beach, if you can believe it." Rafe chuckled. "You do not want to be in a room with a couple of high-powered vampires having a marital spat over which one of them is being 'fucking stupid'." He mock shuddered. "At one point, I thought about just opening a window and flying away, but the hotel we were in didn't have windows that opened wide enough."

Whistling low and shaking his head, Monjoie laughed. "You have lived a charmed life."

"You're hardly a starving orphan yourself."

"Yup. And now here we both are standing watch with dishpan hands like a couple of thirty-year-old enlistees."

Rafe looked down at his hands. It was true—he had plenty of callouses from the sword, but the dish soap did something to his skin that wasn't entirely pleasant. "I like it here though," he said.

"Me too."

A long pause stretched between them, both pondering where their future lay and with whom.

"Why did you stay?" Monjoie said. "When I was hurt."

"Leave no man behind," Rafe quoted.

"They were coming to get me," Monjoie pressed. "I wasn't in any danger of dying. You could have easily flown up the wall."

"It would have been churlish." As he said the word, Rafe's mind connected to something Deor had said. Finn had accused her of being churlish. She had snapped back that she got it from her mother. Later she had told Rafe that churl was an old English word for a commoner. "You fought with me. Not under my command, but on the same side. Neither of us wants the altar to fall into the Enemy's hands. Whatever quarrels we have... or had... here we're on the same side."

"And if we go back home?"

"I don't know." Rafe looked at Monjoie. "I don't have a personal grudge against you if that's what you mean. We ended up on different sides of a slow-boiling civil war, caused by Finn and Madeline, but I don't blame you anymore. When I go back…*if* I go back, I don't know if I'll still be Sword, or how long the Regency will last. I don't really know what comes after that." Internally he shuddered at the thought of Finn coming back and declaring war on his own daughter. If that happened, Rafe knew which side he would fight on, but it tore at him to think of fighting against the King's banner instead of under it.

"My fiancée's name is Juliette," Monjoie said.

"It's a lovely name," Rafe said. "Thank you for trusting me with it."

Monjoie nodded. After their sweat had cooled they went to find Caedmon and be assigned various tasks for the day. He and Monjoie didn't speak again that day, but they sat next to each other when supper time came.

21

Deor?" Deor started, jerking awake to find Stephen standing at the foot of her bed. Jake and Sam were already on the floor, standing at high alert, but Brand merely raised his head, tail thumping at the sight of his friend.

Deor sat up, "What do you need?"

"What is it?" Victor sat up, too.

"The Summer Court attacked Northfalls."

"What?" Deor swung her legs to the floor, dragging the sheet with her. "When?"

"They invaded at dawn. Roger called as soon as he was able. For now, everyone is safe inside Northfalls."

"Go get the rest of my council. I'll put on clothes. We'll be in the conference room in ten minutes."

Ten minutes later, Deor stared at Roger in the mirror. He looked fine. Arthur was with him, also looking fine. Everyone else around the conference table looked as worried as she felt, but there was a calm that surprised her. It felt like someone should be shouting orders, people should be scurrying around. But the only person there to shout was her, and she had little to say.

"We're safe for now," Roger said. "They are mostly testing defenses which are all holding fine. We got those nearest the castle inside, and the rest have fled to Mirrovere, where Tess is taking them in."

"You seem really blasé, Roger." Deor frowned. "You're not trying to be positive, or keeping something from me?"

"Not at all. I've been through this before with the Summer Court. Northfalls is a fortress as much as a castle."

"So what do we do?" Deor asked. "Evacuate?"

"The palace?" Roger frowned. "Where would you go? And why?"

"Not the palace!" Deor insisted. "Northfalls. We could open a portal and bring you all in here."

Roger laughed. "No. That would hand this place to D'nath. If they take Northfalls, they've got an easy march straight down to the capitol. They also take a major shipping route that could be used to bring up troops. We're fine." He glanced behind him. "Arthur?"

"He's right," Arthur confirmed. "No one has been hurt. There is plenty of food and drink. We can wait out a siege for months." He shrugged. "Will it be fun? No."

"What does the Summer Court want?" Victor asked. "Are they trying to get to Finn?"

"Maybe." Arthur thought about it. "It certainly would make the nation unstable to take away the monarch, even with the Regent ruling well."

"If they want him, they could have just asked," Deor said, rolling her eyes. "I'd have handed him over in a heartbeat."

Arthur shrugged and changed the subject. "Rafe and I thought this invasion might happen. We'd been running troop training exercises up here, so we've got a pretty good standing group of soldiers for now. It might not hurt to send more. I can do a quick run-through and give you specific numbers."

Deor looked at Roger. "Is there anything else?"

"No, that's it," Roger said. He stared at her for a long minute. "You can do this," he said softly. "You've already asked for and taken more advice than Finn ever would. The Summer Court is just testing you. I don't think they are serious about invading."

"What about the border with Wellhall?" Deor asked.

Roger snorted. "Wellhall is harder to get through than Northfalls, and Madeline is there. They could slam armies into the walls of that place for centuries and it wouldn't crack."

"Good to know." Deor sighed, relieved. It made sense, about Madeline. That woman hated Finn and probably hated Deor too. But she didn't hate the Winter Court. She wanted to rule it, not see it destroyed, and the

131

Summer Court would surely destroy it. "You take care up there," Deor said. "And let us know the moment anything changes."

Roger gave her a salute, and the mirror went black.

"So," Deor said to everyone around the table. "We know what we're doing with Northfalls. Does anyone else have anything?"

"Yes." Astarte spoke up. "I don't like this. D'nath is smart. I don't know why he'd be banging his head, or his army, against Northfalls,"

"Could this just be a test like Roger suggested?" Stephen asked. "Since it is a siege, and Roger's not sending out troops, it seems pretty low risk in terms of danger to Summer Court soldiers."

"No." Astarte shook her head. "I've not been there in a long, long time, but my sister has never been the kind of person to play at war. She's a lot of things, but she's not someone who risks lives—who starts wars—for no reason. Whatever their goals, they are certain they have a good chance of achieving them."

"And figuring those goals out?" Genevieve asked.

"That's the problem," Astarte said.

A knock came at the door.

"Your Majesty?" Gordie stepped into the room. "There is a mirror call for you, from Wellhall."

"Thank you, Gordie. We'll take it in here." She flicked her wrist at the massive mirror at the end of the room. "Open."

The mirror blurred a bit and cleared. Madeline Farringdon stood at a table much like Deor's own. On her right stood her husband Edgar. Behind her was a group of Wellhall soldiers, a few of whom looked uncomfortable enough that Deor noticed.

"Duchess Farringdon," Deor said, inclining her head and reminding herself to be polite. For now, against the Summer Court, they were on the same side. Getting along could be the difference between winning and losing. "What news does Wellhall have for the Palace today?"

"Your Majesty," Madeline smiled. "I have called to negotiate the terms of your surrender."

Deor blinked. "My surrender?"

"Well," Madeline conceded, "the surrender of the Winter Court."

"To what?" Deor's stomach lurched. The ground seemed to shift under her feet like an earthquake, and she rested her hand on Victor's arm to steady herself.

Madeline waved her hand and the mirror zoomed out, like a camera, showing the full table.

D'nath stood next to Edgar, a small smile on his face. "To the Summer Court, of course."

"You can't be serious!" Deor said, knowing the words were cliché and stupid as she said them. Of course, Madeline was serious.

"The era of the Aethelwings is over. Your family is nothing but a plague on this land. It is time for one Court, one rule."

Deor pressed a hand to her mouth, suppressing the need to wretch. Nausea overwhelmed her. Next to her, Victor took her hand in his, and his magic eased into her, calming her senses. She drew a deep breath. "No. The Winter Court will not cease to be. It will not become some protectorate of the Summer Court, and no matter what happens to it, it will not be ruled by you. Not now, not tomorrow, not ever."

"She's right, Madeline!" Edgar burst out. "I have followed you for too long. Against Finn, I would follow you to the ends of the earth, but against the Winter Court? I will not betray my home." He stepped away and drew a sword, leveling it at D'nath. His eyes flashed blue, and Deor could see Rafe in his father's features.

D'nath stepped back a few paces but made no move for a weapon. "Don't be a fool, Edgar. It's done. The wards are down. The gates are open. As we speak, a regiment of the Summer Court's finest is taking possession of Wellhall and the surrounding area. None of your people will be harmed."

"Damn you, Madeline," Edgar snarled. "And damn you as well!" He lunged at D'nath who simply darted out of the way. "I'll cut you to pieces even if your army is at the door! You'll—" Edgar gasped and looked down, a bloody icicle poking from his chest. He dropped his sword and turned, slowly, catching the edge of the table. "Mad—"

Madeline stood triumphant. "Stupid man." She flicked out her hand, the same gesture Deor used, and created another weapon, a perfect sword of solid ice, transparent as glass. She stepped back and swung the blade. Edgar's head dropped, landing on the table as his body crumpled to the floor.

"Father!" Victor screamed.

Madeline spun to face Deor again, her sword dripping bloody icicles. "Surrender and you might escape the same fate."

Deor gaped. Next to her, Victor trembled, and she could feel the rage and despair at war with one another.

"You're a monster," Victor managed.

"Monster or not," D'nath interjected, "she is right." He locked eyes with

Deor. "If you surrender, you'll spare the lives of thousands of your people, including yourself." He smiled benevolently. "We do not wish to hurt you, Lady Deor Smithfield Aethelwing. Our quarrel is not now, nor has it ever been, with you. There is no reason why you may not live out your life in the borders of the Winter Court, even in the palace in London. You'll find my sister to be a generous and merciful queen." He shot a look at Madeline and returned his gaze to Deor. "Others are not so."

When D'nath settled his gaze on Deor again, she shuddered but remained silent. Surrender seemed unthinkable, but what other choice was there?

D'nath's eyes filled with pity. "You have some time to think, young Princess. But not much. The assault on Northfalls will continue, and once the fortress falls, there is no negotiation, no surrender. I will march my armies from the North and the South, I will hack through the capital city to your gate, and I will pile the bodies of your people on your very doorstep. You know where to contact me."

The mirror went black.

Deor stared at the faces of the people around the table, each one mirroring her horror, her rising panic. Tears tumbled from her eyes. "I'm sorry," she said, her voice a whisper. "I don't know what to do."

Victor bolted to his feet, knocking over his chair behind him. He let out a wrenching scream. "Damn her!" He stormed to the far side of the room and back again. Tears ran down his cheeks. "I don't know what to do either," he said softly. He righted his seat and sat.

Deor took his hand. "I'm so sorry, Victor, that you had to see that, that your father—" Deor choked, and the tears came faster.

He squeezed her hand. "I can't dwell on it, not now. Not when we have to do something."

"I can't imagine the people of Wellhall are happy with this!" Genevieve insisted. "Everyone there is proud—proud to be a part of the Winter Court. They may hate Finn, but they love their home. Aiding and abetting the Summer Court? Handing the duchy over to D'nath? No."

"If she's let them into the palace, there's not much they can do," Victor said.

"So what do we do?" Deor said. "What do I do?" She rubbed her hands up and down her arms as though the room had suddenly grown cold. She glanced at Victor whose gaze was far away, a frown frozen on his face, even as tears continued to roll down his cheeks. "Can we move troops there?"

"No." Victor said, gaze still distant. "It would be a slaughter if we tried."

"Can we defend the capital?" Deor waved her hands at the conference table. "Winter Court map!" she snapped. The Winter Court appeared on the table. "Northfalls, London, Wellhall." The three named places increased in size and glowed red. There was a straight line connecting them. One end of the nation to the other. In between, the mass of the Winter Court itself. Most of its people lived around that corridor. "Do I surrender?" When no one answered her, she reached for Victor. "Victor? You're the Sword. Do we surrender?"

"I can't do this," Victor said, voice low. "I can't be Sword." He clutched Deor's hand. "I was not trained for this. Rafe was Sword, so I deliberately specialized in other things. I'm more Arthur than Rafe. In peacetime it didn't matter, but now? You have to find someone else!"

"Okay," Deor said in a calming tone. "We can do that." She turned to Astarte. "Who else is there?"

"I would have said Roger or Edgar, but neither is possible." Astarte's gaze wandered over the room, finally, she sighed like she had reached a decision. "There is one person. Bartholomew."

"The former Sword?" Genevieve said. "I thought he disappeared."

"He did when he quit about thirty years ago."

"Ah. So he quit because of me." Deor shook her head.

Astarte said, "That does seem reasonable. Bartholomew is a man of supreme integrity. He always hated Finn's intrigues. But I am good friends with his wife, so I can reach him." Astarte looked in the mirror. "Mirror, call Claire."

The mirror cleared, revealing a stately, pale yellow woman with broad shoulders and a short bob of silver hair. She reminded Deor of the women in her grandmother's bridge club. "Astarte, it is good to hear from you." She scanned the table, her gaze lingering on Deor. "I see you're in the war room."

"Hello, Claire. We're in a bit of a situation here and were wondering if we might ask Barty for help."

Claire's smile turned solemn. "Of course. I'll fetch him." She disappeared from view, and a few moments later, they heard Barty before they saw him.

"My answer to the palace is always no. I don't know why you think this would change," his voice boomed. Bartholomew burst onto the mirror. A large man with purple skin and a shock of white hair filled the mirror with his body and the room with his personality. He had broad shoulders and a round belly, but he absolutely looked like he could still swing a sword.

Deor nodded at him. "Hello," she said. "I'm Deor Smithfield Aethelwing. It's nice to meet you."

The man froze in his tracks and stared at her, mouth open. "Finn's daughter," he said, shock palpable. "You died."

"I am Finn's daughter. I did not die. That was a lie made up by his then-Shield Michael."

"Dear," his wife said, coming to stand next to him, "I've told you that you should be reading the papers. She's been back for some time now. She's the Regent."

"Regent, eh? Huh." He sat down and took each person in. "You're the younger Farringdon boy, right?"

"Victor, yes." Victor nodded.

"Your parents?"

"Traitors hiding in Wellhall."

He looked at Stephen. "You, I don't know."

"Stephen Bolton, sir. I recently came to the Houseboys."

"Victor is my Consort, and Stephen is my Shield," Deor said.

Bartholomew glared. "Where's your Sword?"

Deor pursed her lips. "That's why we've contacted you. I need a Sword. I was hoping you'd take up your old position."

"I retired from that long ago!" He shook his head. "I'm sure young Rafe will do fine."

Deor drew a deep breath, but Victor spoke first. "He's missing. He fell defending the King against Wellhall soldiers. Finn left him and Astarte behind."

"Oh, no. Poor lad. Damn Finn. I knew he'd ruin that boy, but I didn't think he'd get him killed. Not this young."

"Please," Deor said, voice cracking. "The Summer Court is besieging Northfalls and Madeline allied herself with D'nath, opening Wellhall to the Summer Court. She murdered Edgar. They demanded my unconditional surrender, or," her voice caught and tears began to fall, "D'nath said he'll carve a path to the palace and dump thousands of bodies on my doorstep." She wiped her eyes. "I—we—need someone who knows what the hell they're doing, or the Winter Court is lost. Please, Bartholomew."

Bartholomew softened "You know, your father never asked for help. He'd demand it. Never heard the man say please." He stood. "I'll do it. I'll portal straight there, right now." Within a few minutes, he was striding into the war room.

Deor rose. "Thank you, Bartholomew."

"Call me Barty. All my friends do." He smiled at her.

Deor darted in and hugged him. He froze and then softened, returning the hug.

"It's okay, lass," he said. "It's going to be okay."

Deor nodded against his chest and clung just a bit longer before stepping away and returning to her seat. Barty took the Sword's seat, and everyone else settled back in. "So, we have some time to think, but not much. Who are our allies?"

"The vampires support me, but won't do so openly—even if they had the armies to send. The werewolves of Ireland have formally left the protectorate. The Goblins are our only official allies, but I don't know how far we can trust that."

"Then it is to them we turn," Bartholomew said. "I don't trust them either, but they're what we've got."

"So I call them up and ask for an army?" Deor asked. "That seems like a lot."

"No," Genevieve shook her head. "It's far more political than that. You'll have to meet with them—with the King and Queen, and Geoff, of course. We could invite them here?"

"Yes." Bartholomew nodded. "A political and social affair." He looked at Astarte. "You can do that, I'm sure?"

"Of course. Just name the date and time and give me five—no, four—hours' notice, and I can put it together."

"You'll have to give concessions, Deor," Bartholomew said. "But right now their aid is more important than our dignity. It won't be pleasant. Agree to just about anything to save the Winter Court, and we'll deal with it later."

22

Rafe found himself more and more sure that he would not return to the Winter Court. No one in the chapter mentioned his relationship with Deor, but as days went by the monks spoke more and more as if a decision had been made. Only Caedmon and Aelfburga reminded the other chapter members from time to time that Rafe had not yet taken any vow or voiced a decision. Life went back to its rhythm.

Once or twice, Rafe caught Aelfburga and Caedmon whispering to one another outside the kitchen, but Rafe intentionally stopped his ears and walked the other way. If it was news of the Winter Court, he didn't need it. If it was news of the Enemy, they would tell the chapter soon enough. He grabbed Evelyn and Lachar and suggested they fish for their lunch while Monjoie was with Aaliyah getting his hip worked on.

The three of them were returning in triumph with their catch to the kitchen, laughing and teasing each other, when a pain shot through Rafe from the top of his head down through his spine. He dropped the kreel and doubled over, clutching his face and panting with the pain of it. Cold poured off him as unrestrained rage flooded his soul and body.

Dimly he knew that Lachar was leading him to a chair, urging him to not lose consciousness. He'd never felt more conscious in his life. Every fiber of his being twanged with painful awareness.

"Everyone give him room," Aaliyah commanded. She put her fingers to his wrist and laid her ear against his back, listening. Rafe tried to tell her he was fine, but he couldn't manage the words. He felt as if his body were trying to be in two places at once.

Aaliyah put a vial to his lips, saying, "You don't have to drink this. Just let it trickle in if you can't swallow." Slowly she dripped the herbal mix into his mouth, letting it ease between his clenched teeth. As the medicine worked, she laid her hands on either side of his head, her forehead pressed against his, humming a dissonant tune in a minor key. She swayed a bit, rocking Rafe gently. The tune and the liquid and the rocking found their way into his brain. His breathing eased. The pain shrank down, burying itself deep in his core where he could hold it under control.

He looked up into Aaliyah's deep brown eyes, so full of compassion. Around them the entire chapter stood in a circle, watching.

"Can you tell us what is happening?" Aaliyah said. "Does this feel like an attack of the Enemy?"

Rafe shook his head slowly. "I feel torn. Like I'm being pulled. I don't know why. It hurts, but it doesn't feel like an attack. There's no hostility behind it. Anger, maybe. But it's more like pleading."

"You're exhausted," she said. "Whatever this is, I can see it is wearing you down. You should try to sleep."

Rafe accepted her ruling. In his old life, he would have protested that he was a grown man and didn't need to be put to bed in the middle of the day like a child with a cold. But here at the monastery, things were different. He was different. The community cared for its own, including him. So he let them care for him.

Lachar and Evelyn walked him to his room. While Aaliyah hung a bundle of healing herbs in the open window, Aelfburga brought him a hot stone for his feet. Monjoie poked his head in the room, a look of worry on his face, and was shooed away after being allowed to give Rafe a "feel better." Caedmon sat in the chair, strumming soft, tuneless notes that wrapped themselves around Rafe's mind, cushioning it from the pain.

"I dropped the fish," Rafe said. "It's a shame to waste them."

"Close your eyes," Aaliyah said. She laid her hand over his forehead, covering his eyes. He obeyed her. He wasn't sure when she took her hand away, but he followed the notes Caedmon played down inside himself to where the pain resided.

At first, he felt as if he might be sinking infinitely downward through the bed into the floor. Eventually, the sensation changed. He found his feet and his balance, walking deeper through the darkness. It reminded him of the darkness of the throne during his adoption, and he shuddered.

There were no knives here though, no voices screaming "thief" at him. Maybe this was the throne darkness again, and she was trying to reach him. "Deor?" he called. She didn't answer.

There was no center to the pain. The closer he got to it, the more it felt like thousands of hooks set into his flesh, tearing him. Or thousands of voices crying out. One voice made up of many voices. But what they were saying was dim and jumbled like voices heard through a wall. The more he tried to listen, the less the hooks hurt. So he sat in the dark inside himself and listened.

When he woke, or came back to himself, he wasn't sure which, Evelyn was there, an unlit cigarette in his mouth and his feet propped on the bed as he read a book. Rafe shifted, wriggling the stiffness out of his shoulders and hips. The light had changed. It was dark outside, and the room was lit by the overhead light.

He pulled the covers up around his neck and watched Evelyn read. "Good book?" Rafe said. "Something deep and spiritual from Lachar's library?"

Evelyn grinned and held up the book so Rafe could see the cover. On it, a man in a strange plaid hat held up a magnifying glass to one eye while a fellow in a bowler hat and mustache stood behind him with a raised weapon. *"Hound of the Baskervilles,"* Evelyn said. "Cracking good read. Feeling better?"

Rafe considered. Even in his dreams, he had done nothing but sit and listen. Still, he felt deeply tired and disinclined to move from the bed. The pain was still there, spreading, diffused through his limbs. Something about it was different though. Less sharp, perhaps? No. Simply less novel. Pain like anger. And grief.

"I feel like someone is yelling at me," he said.

Evelyn raised his eyebrows. "You know what Dr. Freud would say. If it's not one thing, it's your mother."

Rafe laughed, though he had no idea who Dr. Freud was. He wriggled about on the bed until he lay on his side. "You know," he said. "Now that you mention it, that sounds right. This pain does seem to be connected to her in some way."

"Perhaps she's working with the Enemy to attack you. Stranger things have happened. The Enemy does like to use proxies."

Rafe continued to lie in bed, trying to hear the distant, intermittent voice of the pain inside him and decipher what it was saying. Evelyn read on.

23

Deor's invitation to the Goblins to come to the palace had been refused on the issue of safety. They had, however, countered with an invitation for her to come visit Barizan in order to "renew the ties so lately strained between our kingdoms." After some tense discussion with her council, Deor had agreed to the visit. Only Victor had raised any real objection, but when pressed on why he had only said that the Goblins couldn't be trusted.

"Of course they can't be trusted, lad," Bartholomew had said. "But they can be negotiated with. And that's better than we can ask from anyone else these days."

Victor had subsided into a tight-mouthed silence after that, his eyes fixed on the table. If Deor hadn't known him better she would have thought he was sulking.

"If you don't want to go, you don't have to," she said. "It might be better for you to stay here while I'm gone."

"No!" Victor snapped. "I'm not letting you go there alone. Absolutely not."

"I won't be alone," Deor said gently.

"You know what I mean," he insisted. Deor looked around the table in confusion, but no one else at the table seemed to understand him any better than she did.

"Alright. That's settled then." Deor stood. "Let's get on to other business."

By supper time, Victor seemed less angry though still subdued. In bed that night, he clung tightly to Deor in his sleep. She stroked his back, her forehead pressed against his head until his muscles eased and his breathing became less ragged.

On the morning of their journey, Deor and her retinue gathered in the great hall. Deor smoothed her skirts. Her skirts needed no smoothing, of course. Melanie would rather suffer the lash than send Deor out in something ill-pressed. Victor and Stephen were in finery, not uniform, though she knew full well they had weapons hidden somewhere. Of her council, only Barty and Astarte were staying behind.

Then there was Bill, who hadn't so much as insisted on coming along as assumed, like a true bard, that no one would tell him no. Hopefully, he wouldn't cause a diplomatic incident by asking "innocent questions." Bill wore jeans and a "nice" shirt—meaning the image on the tee shirt hadn't faded to near oblivion. In fact, the cluster of white philosopher's heads on a black shirt was near pristine. She had no idea who any of them were—there were no names—but that, she assumed, was the point.

"Okay," Deor said to the two soldiers waiting to open the portal. "Let's do this. Are they ready?"

"Yes, Your Majesty," the one on the right said. "The Goblin side of the portal is open."

Briefly, Victor reached out a hand and laid it on her shoulder. "I'm with you," he whispered. The sense of his presence eased the tension in Deor's own back. She took a deep breath and patted Victor's fingers. Geoff was a murderous weasel, but he wouldn't assassinate her on a public diplomatic visit, surely?

Doer nodded at the waiting soldiers, and they whispered their words of command. The doors swirled away, revealing an opening into a room like a Rococo cave painted in acid-trip colors.

A line of people waited. Geoff, of course, and his parents, King Geoffrey and Queen Ipomoea; the Sword and the Shield were there too. Genevieve's crash course in Goblin court life included the fact that the Goblins had no consort, which made her wonder how else Goblin magic differed from faerie magic. Deor led the way and her people followed.

143

As the portal closed behind them, Deor heard Bill mutter something about his insides flipping about. She had hardly noticed this time, another sign of her growing comfort with the Winter Court as home. She swallowed and fixed a smile on her face.

"Welcome!" Geoffrey said as he stepped forward. "We are so thrilled to have you." His soft smile and bright eyes seemed genuinely inviting.

"Thank you for having us," Deor said, smiling. She moved forward, meeting Geoff halfway between their two groups and accepted the hug that he gave her. It was quick and gentle—one might even call it appropriate. Perhaps this wouldn't be a total clusterfuck after all. Next to her, Brand whined softly. Jake and Sam were back next to Victor and Stephen.

Geoff looked down at the dog. "Hello there," he said, crouching down. "You're a good boy, aren't you?" He gently patted Brand on the head and then stood. "Malossian purebred. He's gorgeous."

"Thank you," Deor said, resting her hand on Brand's head. "He was a gift from Rafe."

At the name, Geoff frowned. "I'm so sorry he's... missing?"

"Me too," Deor said. "So," she changed the subject, "please introduce me to your family and court!"

Geoff held out his hand to Deor, and she took it, allowing herself to be led to the row of Goblins. "This is my father, Gregory."

She curtsied as Genevieve had made her practice several dozen times. Enough of a bow to show courtesy, but not to defer her place as equal in monarchy. "Thank you, King Gregory, for your gracious offer to come visit. Ever since Geoff told me of the beauty of Barizan, I have wanted to see it for myself. It is stunning."

Gregory laughed. "Thank you. This is my wife Ipomoea, my Sword Heinrich, and my Shield Ernst." All three nodded and smiled at her. Gregory himself looked like Geoff, only older, with a bit more bulk and darker green skin. Gregory's Queen was a petite woman, small and delicate, with light green skin and bright green eyes. Heinrich was a man of medium height, his eyes and face soft and innocuous. He reminded Deor of a high school math teacher. Ernst was the oldest, with white hair and wrinkles, and a few age spots on his brownish-green skin. All three of them smiled in what felt like a genuine welcome.

"Thank you all," Deor said and gave another of Genevieve's curtsies. She glanced back at her own group. "You know my Consort, Victor Farringdon, and the Lady Genevieve. My Shield Stephen Bolton and my dear friend Bill." She left out Melanie and Gordie, which annoyed her, but Gregory hadn't introduced anyone who seemed to be staff.

Gregory glanced at Victor and Stephen. "You, too, Consort and Shield, are welcome." He nodded graciously at them before returning his attention to Deor. "Come, Little Lady Regent," he waved her forward. "We shall have lunch, and then a tour of our fine city!"

Deor winced at the *Little Lady* but kept her smile frozen in place as she had been trained. If she could keep this up for the entire trip, she'd buy Genevieve a house or something to say thank you. As Deor allowed Gregory to take her arm, his Sword headed straight for Victor. "Good afternoon to you, Victor!" he said cheerfully. "It has been a long time since we have seen each other."

"Indeed, it has," Victor said, a tight smile on his face.

"I look forward to catching up!" Heinrich smiled broadly as he slapped Victor on the back.

Deor held her hand out to Victor and, with a relieved look, he quickened his pace and reached her, offering her his arm. She took it and followed the royal family further into the palace.

As promised, Geoffrey took Deor and her companions in an open carriage through the underground city and Barizan was indeed beautiful in a surreal way. It was as if someone had taken an aboveground city and rolled it in on itself so that there was no longer an up or down. The Goblin palace stood at the center of a vast cavern, built on and into a giant stalagmite. The walls, floor, and even ceiling of the cavern contained the Goblin buildings. Deor could look up and see people walking around, going about their business, their heads pointed down at her. She turned, looking for a reference point, and realized they were now at a right angle to the Goblin palace.

"If you get dizzy, look down at your feet," Victor whispered. "Whatever you're standing on is down. Don't look for a horizon."

Deor suppressed the nausea she felt and squeezed his hand. His fingertips were cold in hers. By the time they had eaten lunch and returned to the palace, evening was beginning to fall. The cavern reflected this, with fading light filling it and street lights coming on. They followed the main road through the city center, passing near a market where Deor could see people wandering among the stalls selling wyvern meat and spiced cave crickets along with clothes and kitchen goods.

They made a circle through the city and returned via the main road, a wide parkway lined with stately homes that gave way to large buildings, including a Winter and Summer Court embassy, lining the way to the palace. A grand fountain greeted them as they passed through the gates onto the palace grounds. She looked up at the goblin palace and shook her head in wonder.

For the rest of the day, Geoff and Gregory had relentlessly resisted any hint of politics. That night, Deor lingered in the shower, letting the hot water release a bit of the tension in her shoulders. She let her mind wander, wondering what help the Goblins would be, what D'nath's next move would be, how Roger was holding up at Northfalls. Finally, she gave up and got out. As she dried off and put on her robe, she heard Victor shouting, screaming really, at someone in the outer parlor. She rushed in, a knife ready in her hand, and stopped short.

Melanie and Bill were huddled near each other in front of the fire-place. In front of them, by about a yard, stood Gordie, red-faced and at attention, looking as though he was about to cry. To the side stood Stephen and Genevieve, faces stern with worry. Even the dogs cowered. Brand huddled behind Deor the moment she stepped into the room.

Her entrance did nothing to slow Victor's tirade. He was flushed, and cold poured off him in waves.

"Do you understand me?" Victor demanded.

"Yes, sir." Gordie's voice was quiet and full of shame. "I'm sorry, sir."

"Sorry isn't good enough!" Victor snapped. "I gave you an order, dammit! You do not ever go anywhere alone with a goblin. Ever."

"It was the Goblin Sword…" Gordie whispered. "He said—"

"I don't care if he said the city was burning and he knew the only way out!" Victor strode up to Gordie and pushed a finger into his chest. "If you can't follow a simple order like that you can forget about becoming a knight. You are a disgrace!"

"Okay!" Deor called. "I think that's enough, Victor. I can tell from his expression that Gordie has taken your point, and the others too. No one will make that mistake again."

Victor turned on her, livid, his eyes filled with an anger she had never seen before. She actually took a small step back before regaining her composure.

"Can I speak to you in my room?" She didn't wait for an answer but walked away, hoping he would follow.

He did.

Deor sat on the small settee at the foot of her bed and patted the space next to her. "Come and sit."

He stalked over and sat.

"Why don't you tell me what that was about?"

He glared at her for a moment. "I told them, all of them, to never, ever go anywhere alone with a goblin. Period." He met her gaze and fumbled. "I mean, it is politically dangerous for them to engage in conversation and not have anyone there who could verify what was said. It could lead to all sorts of accusations."

"That seems wise," she said cautiously. "And Gordie broke that rule?"

"Yes." Victor shook his head. "I came back to the suite from tea, and I saw him heading down the hall, alone, away from our suite, with the Goblin Sword."

"Okay." Deor nodded. "And you're sure he was going away and not just chatting?"

"Yes!" Victor shouted. "The only thing in that direction is a portal to the private quarters in the palace!"

"You are very angry," she said, reaching out and taking his hand. "I've never seen you this angry, not even in the Tower. So I feel like there is more going on here than social protocol. Do you want to tell me what that is?"

For a split second, Victor looked like he might cry. "The private quarters of the palace aren't safe," he said. He wasn't looking at her at all. He'd picked a spot in the middle distance between them. "The goblin would say something like he had news or information. He'd tell Gordie that he knew the squire was important to the Regent, and he had some information that had to get to her, but he couldn't give it directly. Gordie, being the good kid he is, would go with him. And then we wouldn't see Gordie for a while, and someone at dinner would notice, or maybe no one would notice until the next morning. And then we'd start asking where he was, and who saw him last. And maybe we would find him, and maybe we wouldn't. But if we did, he wouldn't be able to tell us much about what happened, or how long he'd been gone. His story would start with how the goblin offered to share his favorite drink with him, as peers. Gordie would know that something bad had happened, but the details, all of it would be vague, except for goblin laughter. That, nothing can wipe away."

Deor put one hand over her mouth even as she kept hold of Victor's hand with her other. Her chest was tight, and she was almost trembling. A rage had built in her through the story. Victor's gaze was still distant, and she knew he was miles away, decades away, too, very likely in a horrible memory. She cleared her throat, forcing the words out. "You're saying they would drug him and then he'd be raped."

He looked at her then, blinking. "I... I hadn't thought of it like that, but yes."

Deor turned to face him and spoke gently. "This is why you hated coming here. Because it happened to you."

"Yes," he said, his voice a whisper. "I'd been warned too. Some friends and I went on tour. We wanted to see the world outside the Winter Court. My father told me to be careful. He told me not to take a drink that I didn't see poured, not to eat something that no one else was eating.

"We saw... lots of places. When we got to the Goblin court we were invited to a party at the palace. The Sword's personal guests. I felt so grown up...I drank something, and..." He closed his eyes. "I couldn't find my friends, but the Goblin Sword was there. I remember him laughing..." He shuddered. Tears flowed down his cheeks. "The Sword... he was laughing as he led Gordie away."

"Oh Victor," Deor said. "I am so sorry."

"My friends thought I'd been out having fun." He shook his head. "I cut my trip short after that. Went to the Winter Court embassy and said I was needed at home. They portalled me." He shook his head. "I was so dumb. It was my fault."

"NO!" Deor snapped. She took a breath and softened her tone. "It was not your fault. That man, those people, chose to do you harm. No matter what you did, you did not deserve that. You don't think Gordie deserved it, do you?"

Victor stared at her, and she could see the conflict in his eyes. Rage boiled in her again, and she bit her tongue, trying to keep from going silver. A few sparkles spiraled off of her.

"No." Victor finally said. "He didn't deserve that. He couldn't."

"And that means?" Deor prompted.

"Neither did I." He shook his head. "I don't know if you understand, if in the human world—"

"I get it," she cut him off. "I got the same talk from my grandmother because unfortunately where I'm from, there's about a one-in-three chance that I know all too well."

"That's terrible," he said, but he seemed to relax. "I told my parents when I got home. My mother raged. My father just looked sad. There was nothing else they could do. Even the Duchess of Wellhall couldn't touch the Sword of the Goblin court."

"I'm glad your parents supported you."

He nodded. "They wanted me to talk to someone, but I didn't... I just wanted to forget it. I thought I was over it, but, then we got here..."

Deor leaned in conspiratorially. "We could kill him."

"What?"

"Heinrich. We could ask him to our suite, and stab him a bunch of times, and then we could stuff him in one of our trunks and leave his body in the Winter Court wilderness for wildcats and unicorns to eat."

He stared at her for a moment and then laughed weakly.

"I'm not kidding," she said. She wasn't. For once in her life it seemed like she had the chance to pay back someone who had hurt someone she loved. He might have gotten away with it for a while, but not forever.

"Thank you." He smiled at her. "Thank you, but I think right now our alliance with the Goblin Court is more important."

"You're right. We'll kill him another day." She squeezed his hand. "Why don't you get ready for bed, and I'll let people know everything is fine. Okay?"

"Yes." He nodded and stood. "I'm going to take a shower." He headed for the bathroom.

When he was gone, Deor allowed herself to feel the full weight of her anger. She was Regent of the Winter Court, and she couldn't get her own Consort justice. She let her vision go silver and she savored the wicked sharpness of her nails as she curled her hand around an imaginary sword's pommel, and magic coalesced. She shook her hands out, dissipating it before it could become solid. She drew in deep breaths and blinked away the silver in her eyes, curled in her fingers, and ran them along her thumbs to soften the sharpness. Someday there would be a place to let her free the rage she felt both for Victor and for the damned helplessness she felt. But today she needed the Goblins.

24

After some time had passed, Rafe was able to get up. Aaliyah had ruled out any sort of physical ailment. He went back to his usual routine about the monastery, but he was slower and needed to pause frequently. Joan reassured him that he didn't need to join her for sword practice, but he found that picking up a sword and practicing raised his spirits and reduced the pain. His hand was nearly healed. He could wield the sword one-handed now, though using both hands gave him just that much more stability. With a sword in his hand, he felt closer to understanding the message in the pain.

He went to Caedmon one afternoon with these thoughts. "I feel like I need to get away," Rafe said. "Usually when I feel that way I dream about taking my yacht and sailing out to sea. Now I want to go toward the land."

"You don't need my permission, dear man," Caedmon said. "I am the Abbot here, not your commanding officer." He peered at Rafe. "Do you feel you are being called to leave us for good?"

Rafe nodded. "I might be. After the Proving, I was sure I wanted to stay. Maybe I was right not to go back to being the Sword, but wrong about not going back at all. I don't want to go back to the way things were, that's certain. But when I listen to the pain or I dream before falling asleep, my mind is full of Wellhall. I see its shores and its hills, its people."

Caedmon leaned back in his chair, stroking his beard. "Perhaps this is a problem of language."

That made Rafe smile. "You sound like my old tutor, John Dell. The right word in the right place was one of his favorite mottos."

"If anyone knows the value of a right word, it's a bard," Caedmon agreed. "I am thinking of the word 'back.' You do not wish to go back. Very well. How can you go forward?"

"I'm not sure if that's a riddle or not," Rafe said.

Caedmon's eyes twinkled. "What consumes words all day long, but is none the wiser by nightfall?"

"A poor scholar?"

"A bookworm!" Caedmon slapped his knee and laughed at his own joke. "That was a riddle. As for going forward, I meant it as literally as possible. You are restless, unfixed in this place, but unwilling to go back to the place you left. It seems you must move forward then, but in what direction? I think it is time for the chapter to meet for discernment. Perhaps we can help you better that way."

Rafe shuddered, but he clenched his jaw. If that's what it took, he would endure whatever arcane ritual Caedmon had in mind. He wondered what it would involve, and if it would tear at him as the adoption had done, sifting him down to the atoms to find out what he truly was.

But Caedmon patted him one more time on the shoulder. "We'll argue it all out at supper. Food and debate go well together."

To ease his mind, Rafe went back to the practice space and selected a sword. He moved through the warm-up motions slowly, with deliberation and attention as Joan had taught him.

"Want a sparring partner?" Monjoie stepped out of the doorway into the late afternoon light. Rafe lowered his sword and stepped back, giving Monjoie space to choose his own weapon.

Instead of the broadsword Rafe favored, Monjoie took up a short sword and knife like Victor favored.

"Ready?" Monjoie asked, and Rafe nodded, raising his own weapon. They closed, circling and feeling for an opening. Rafe made a half-hearted feint at Monjoie, and Monjoie parried it but didn't follow up the opening Rafe left him. They moved again, and Monjoie ducked under Rafe's arm, darting to tag his sleeve. Rafe sidestepped the attack, but he brought his sword down too slowly to strike Monjoie as he passed.

They separated, not exercised enough to breathe hard, and Rafe lowered his sword. "Truce," he said. "I don't want to fight you."

Monjoie sheathed his weapon and approached. "Still feeling sick?"

Rafe shook his head. "Not sick. Torn." He walked his sword over to the weapons rack, and Monjoie followed. "I don't know where I'm meant to be. I love this place. What they—we—do here is vital, and a part of me would be content to stay forever guarding the altar. But I long for Well-hall. I feel like my guts are being dragged out of me in different directions. I'm needed. I'm just not sure where."

Monjoie looked up at the sky, then fixed Rafe's eyes with his own. "You are a son of Wellhall and the heir. If something is attacking Wellhall, it makes sense you would feel it."

Something about Monjoie's words rang true. "Thank you," Rafe said. "I am of Wellhall, even if I've spent most of my time away from it." He looked at Monjoie. "What about you? Where will you go when you're healed?"

"Home," Monjoie said. "I'm not you. I'm not the knight looking for a cause. I want to go home to my fiancée, my family, the land where I grew up. Whether they need me or not, that's where I want to be."

"Nothing wrong with that," Rafe said. "I wish I had your clarity. And Wellhall does need you. More than ever, I think."

Monjoie shrugged, but a hint of a blush crept into his cheeks at the compliment. "Let's go to dinner," he said. "We soldiers can let the spiritual people talk it out."

The debate began as soon as the evening thanks had been given. At Caedmon's invitation, Rafe described all his thoughts and misgivings, the pain and the darkness in his dreams in as much detail as he could. When he finished, Evelyn said, "That's the most words I've heard you speak all together since you got here."

"It seems clear to me," Lachar said, "that you have unfinished business. You won't be content here until it is done."

Aaliyah grimaced. "Rafe, my brother, we may have been mistaken. Perhaps you will never be content here."

Lachar and Evelyn both turned to her in shock as Joan protested, "But we need him! A new member always appears to fill up the complement and keep the Source safe. We lost Sasha years ago and have been searching ever since. Rafe is clearly the one."

"Is it clear though?" Aaliyah pushed back. "Rafe arrived still living. He has a life in the world. How many of the rest of us can say that?"

Monjoie raised a hand. The others turned to look at him, and he put his hand back down. "I don't have anything to say. I just meant I have a life to go back to at Wellhall. I'm going back as soon as it's safe."

The rest of the chapter slumped. Lachar pointed mutely at Aelfburga, as if appealing to her for support. At the far end of the table, she pursed her lips and swirled her fork through the gravy on her plate. "Perhaps my vision was wrong."

This was met with universal derision. Aelfburga's visions were not up for debate.

"Visions require interpretation," Caedmon said. "Interpretations may be incorrect."

All around the table, the mood deflated even further. The chapter members slumped glumly over their plates, poking at their food. Joan slammed her knife into the table and got up to pace between the table and fireplace.

Aaliyah broke the silence. "No one who comes here is meant to stay against their will. Our service must be voluntary."

"No one's forcing him!" Lachar shouted back. Aelfburga reached out a hand and laid it on Lachar's. "I apologize, sister."

Aaliyah nodded, silently accepting his apology.

"Voluntary and without reservation," Evelyn said, his normally devil-may-care voice more sober than Rafe had ever heard it. "When I first came here I felt like I had been drafted into a second war with no end in sight. After all, 'leave and you'll die horribly' isn't much of a choice."

"I remember," Aelfburga said. "You were angry with us for many years afterward."

"Not with you, mother," Evelyn said. The older woman smiled at him like a teacher with an erring student, and a smile quirked his own mouth. "Alright, I may have thrown a few dishes against the wall and called you an old witch. But it wasn't you I was truly angry at." Evelyn turned to Rafe. "Don't go. I'll miss you."

"I'll miss you too," Rafe said. "All of you, more than I can possibly say." He looked around the table, his companions' faces warmed by the fire-light. "This is the first and only place where I was simply and only myself, not the Prince, not the King's boy, not the royal hostage, not the Sword, just Rafe." As he spoke the reality of what he was saying fully dawned on him. "You have given me a place to be myself first, regardless of role or title. I can't express how precious a gift that is."

Caedmon leaned back in his chair, hands folded over his stomach. "Thank you, Rafe."

Silence settled over the table, each chapter member lost in their thoughts. Some ate another slice of bread or drank their beer. The rest sat, hands folded, as the silence grew. Rafe sat still, understanding that the silence was also part of the discernment.

As he sat, he thought about his own words. Who was he with his roles and titles stripped away, with no uniform? He traced a bead of water that ran down his mug. He rolled it between his fingers, forming the liquid into a perfect sphere. He thought about obligation and duty. He had never been released from his service as the Sword, but what duty could he possibly owe to Finn that Finn had not wasted a thousand times over? No, he had no more duty to Finn. And his mother could get bent if she thought he owed her and the Farringdon house anything.

But as he rolled the ball of water between his fingers, turning it to ice and back to liquid again and again, Rafe revisited that last thought. Madeline. Somehow the pain, the hook set into his mind, agreed with him about Madeline. The anger at his mother was his own, yes. Old and deep, it had been a part of him for so very long that he had not recognized he was not the only one angry with her. Wellhall itself felt betrayed by her.

And he did have a duty. Finn was not the Winter Court any more than Madeline was Wellhall. What he might owe Deor he couldn't sort out yet, but he had sworn to protect the Winter Court, and now a part of it was calling to him for help.

He looked around the table, re-finding his focus on his friends' faces. "Wellhall needs me. That's the forward. I will go to Wellhall."

All around the table, the chapter members nodded, their faces solemn. Beside him, Evelyn and Lachar reached out their hands to squeeze Rafe's shoulders. One by one the other chapter members got up from their seats. They crowded closer to him, stretching out their hands to embrace him and speak a word in their native language, of blessing or encouragement, of farewell.

"I'll get your favorite sword from the armory," Joan said. "You'll need it." She patted him too hard on the back and turned away, wiping her eyes.

Only Monjoie was left. "I'm going with you," Monjoie said. "If Wellhall needs you, then it needs all the help it can get."

"You son of a bitch. Thank you." They stood there awkwardly for a moment, not yet close enough to hug. Rafe cleared his throat. "We'd better get some sleep. Who knows what we'll find tomorrow?"

25

Deor's time at the Goblin Court was filled with meals and meetings. A brunch with the Goblin Queen. Lunch with the Shield. Tea with Geoffrey. Dinner with the entirety of both parties. At no point during any of the meetings was there any mention of the attacks on the Winter Court. By the last night, Deor knew the Goblins had no intention of helping them.

Dinner was a small affair. Deor felt overdressed in a sleek, strapless black sheath dress and a sable wrap. She also wore glittering emeralds, a set that she liked, given that they reminded her of her grandmother, who loved emeralds. Genevieve, too, seemed overdressed in a pale green silk dress and pearls. Victor and Stephen were in their dress uniforms. Bill happily remained in the suite with the dogs.

The goblins were much more casual, with no uniforms. It was another quiet, pointed slight. They ate in a small dining room at a table for eight. Gregory and his wife, Geoff, Heinrich the Sword, and Genevieve, Victor, Stephen, and Deor.

As the last of the dessert plates were finally swept away, Deor cleared her throat. "Gregory, thank you so much for having us. It has been delightful. I'm sorry to drag business into what's been a very pleasant meal, but you must know that the Winter Court—that I—need your help."

"Of course, my girl," Gregory said, setting down his after-dinner tea. "We have always been allies, the Winter and Goblin courts. That has not changed with the absence of your father. I promise that we will keep you and your people here safe."

A chill rolled down Deor's spine. The sentiment seemed supportive, but the language felt like wordplay. "Thank you," she said cautiously.

"So," Gregory said, standing up, "I have heard that you enjoy card games?"

"I do," Deor said, reeling from the change of subject.

"I thought we might play. A bit of fun in a rather dreary situation. We goblins do love games, and if you feel like a little wager, well..." He winked at her. "Come along into the card room."

"That sounds fun," Deor lied. Whatever this final charade was, they'd get through it, and tomorrow, they'd go home.

In the card room, a lush fire crackled in the fireplace behind a beautifully carved gaming table. Overstuffed couches and chairs sat on a raised level behind the table, allowing spectators to watch.

"How many people will play?" Deor asked.

"Four. It's simple and easy to learn." Geoff smiled at her. "I imagine you don't know any goblin card games."

"I played cards in the human world. When I was little, my grandmother taught me to play her favorite games." Deor smiled at the memory. "She'd even let me cheat."

"How delightful," Gregory's wife said, with a glance at her husband.

"I'll be playing," Geoff said. "Heinrich will be my partner." He gestured to the Sword.

The man took a drag of his cigar and blew out a plume of blue smoke. "Of course, Your Majesty."

Deor reached out and took Victor's hand. "You don't have to be my partner if you don't want to play," Deor said. "I'm sure Stephen could."

Stephen shrugged. "I played some in basic training, and me and some guys would play sometimes to pass the time."

"No." Victor squeezed her hand. "I'm happy to play."

Genevieve swept up and gently re-secured an emerald in Deor's hair. "They will cheat," she whispered, a quiet smile on her face. "It's normal for goblin rules. You won't be able to catch them. You'll lose."

"That's the point," Deor whispered back. "It will make them more pleased with us." Out loud Deor thanked Genevieve for fixing her jewels. "So," she turned to Geoff. "Where shall I sit?"

Victor took a seat and gestured for her to sit across from him. She noted that this meant it was impossible for anyone in the gallery to see either of their cards. Geoffrey and his Sword took the other seats. Everyone else made their way to the gallery to watch.

"So," Geoff said, taking a deck of cards from the table and shuffling them. "Do you understand tricks and bidding?"

"If it is like cards in the human world. Thirteen cards in each suit, four suits. The person with the highest card in the suit played first takes the trick."

"Exactly!" He grinned at her. "You're dealt a hand, and then you and your partner bid on the number of tricks above six. So, if you bid one fire, you'd be saying that you think you can take seven tricks with the fire as trump."

Deor frowned in faux concentration since he was explaining how to play bridge. "I think I get it. What are the four suits? I've never heard of fire."

Geoff flipped the deck over and fanned them out. "This," he pointed at a card with a bouquet of seven flowers, "is the seven of earth. This," he pointed at a card with a man in uniform holding a pennant blowing in the wind, "is the Duke of Air."

"This," he pointed at a card with three fountains on it, "is water. And this," he pointed at a card with a single, dagger-shaped green flame, "is the ace of fire." He gathered the cards back into a deck. "Lowest to highest, earth, air, water, fire."

"Got it." Deor nodded.

"Shall we play a hand?" Geoff shuffled the cards and moved to deal.

"You're not going to explain goblin rules?" Victor interrupted Geoff's task.

Geoff laughed.

"Goblin rules is a euphemism for cheating," Victor said.

"It's only cheating if you get caught." Geoff arced the cards from one hand to another. "You must catch the person in the act for them to lose. If they get away with it, even if you know it happened, they still win."

"What constitutes cheating?" Deor asked.

"Not cheating," Geoff insisted. "Goblin rules. Any use of magic on the cards."

"Got it." She nodded. "Let's get started."

Geoff passed out the cards in a flash, like he'd been playing all his life. He probably had. Deor gathered up hers and arranged them by suit. Not a great hand, not horrible, either. Not that it mattered. She was going to let him win. Not too obviously, of course, because Geoff wasn't stupid, and he might notice and be insulted, or feign insult.

After the first half a dozen hands, of which Deor and Victor had won one, Geoff brightened. "Why don't we make this more interesting?" He opened up a panel in the table and took out a box of chips. "We'll bet." He passed out the gold, silver, and bronze disks.

"Real money, or just chips for fun?" Deor asked.

"What's the fun if it's not real money?" He smiled. "Gold are worth two thousand, silver one thousand, and bronze five hundred." He took out another small box. "These," he opened it up revealing a dozen platinum disks, "are worth ten thousand each."

"Why not?" Deor said, flashing a smile at Victor. "I mean, it is my dad's money." Deor could hear Gregory and the other goblins laughing from the gallery. A few moments later, she had her own stack. Six platinum disks, each with the mark of the Goblin royal family (only she and Geoff were given those), and twenty each of the rest to everyone.

Round and round they went, and more than a few times, Deor saw a flash of magic on the cards but said nothing. Because she could count cards, she knew that there were several glamoured cards she didn't catch. Until one moment, when Heinrich was so obvious that Victor looked like he might scream if the card passed unnoticed.

"Hey!" Deor caught the card. "There's magic all over this." She wiped it away. "Shame on you," she scolded the Sword. "Getting caught like that."

A flash of irritation danced across the Shield's face, but Geoff laughed, and so he joined in, too. "Fair enough, little Lady Regent." He bowed slightly and shoved the pot in her direction.

The game went on, and on, Geoff always winning, but never enough to call it quits. As Deor's stack dwindled, and Geoff's glee grew, the game was more tedious than ever. Finally, when the clock struck eleven, Deor had had enough.

"I don't know about the rest of you," she said, "but I have to get up early. Let's call it a night."

"But you still have coins!" Geoff said. "One more hand?"

Deor looked at her stack. Victor was out entirely, and Heinrich was down to a few. All that remained for Deor were her six platinum coins. "All of this?"

"All of it." Geoff shoved his stacks forward.

"I don't know," Deor said. She'd lost enough money to him already. She should have done the math before they started, but the total in chips was well over five hundred thousand dollars. Not chump change even for a regent. She steeled herself to say no.

"Come on now, Victor," Heinrich said. Victor started and looked the man in the eye. He had barely done that the whole of the game. "I remember when you were younger. You loved to gamble." His orange cat eyes glittered, black pupils dancing with mischievous excitement.

"I—" Victor started.

"I'm all in," Deor cut him off.

Geoff jerked in surprise. "Really?" He grinned. "Delightful." He watched Deor push her remaining disks into the center. "Though that seems hardly fair." He stroked his chin like a villain in a Tex Avery cartoon. "I know." He pulled his ring off. "Let's add jewelry to the mix. Your emeralds are lovely and will even the pot. And I'll even throw in this." He let the ring drop onto his pile of chips and pushed the whole stack forward.

Deor picked up the ring and examined it. The Royal Goblin Family crest, with a special symbol. She'd seen the ring before, at Roger's party. His purity ring. Proof of his promise to never sully his body with carnal lust. Of course, that meant he could fuck any fairy, human, pixie, or whatever came across his path, just not another goblin. The asshole.

"You don't have to do this," Victor said, pleading in his eyes. He was right. This was an extraordinarily bad idea. They should lose and go.

"Fine," Deor said. Victor sagged with relief. She dropped the ring back in the pile. She reached behind her neck and unfastened the clasp of her necklace. She dropped it on the stack. Her earrings followed next, and then the dozen gems in her hair. "All or nothing."

She stared at the hand she'd been dealt. Geoff had won the bidding, stating he was certain he could take at least ten of the thirteen tricks. From Victor's bids, Deor guessed that his hand was as bad as hers. Fire was the trump suit.

Deor, to Geoff's left, was the first to play. She took three tricks, with her highest cards, an ace, King, and Duke of Earth. Everything else was worthless. She led with a low air and watched Geoff take his first. Deor had exactly two flames, the two and the three.

He was smug, laughing and making jokes as he tossed out card after card. Heinrich, too, laughed gleefully. Neither seemed to be gracious winners.

She had planned to lose, and she had cheated at cards when she was little, and her grandmother had let her, but she soon learned winning that way wasn't nearly as fun as doing it right. A small part of her abhorred the idea of cheating, but the rest of her abhorred the idea of losing to this jackass more.

On the third-to-last hand, Geoff dropped the second-to-last fire—a five. The last one was in her hand—the two. Deor ran her hand over the two of earth, the lowest in the deck. She pushed a little magic in and reshaped the pretty daisies into wicked flames, and with a dejected look on her face, cast the fake two of fire.

"Ha!" Heinrich barked out a laugh that he tried to cover as a cough. "All that's left is for Geoff to run out the rest of the tricks." He cast a side-long look at Victor. "Unless you'd like to concede?"

"Not a chance," Victor said, his voice low and angry.

Geoff played the second to last card, a fountain, which was higher than the one Deor had. She held her breath.

"I win," Geoff said, flicking the Queen of earth onto the table.

Heinrich set his ten of water on Geoff's Queen. Victor slammed down his final Jack of air in disgust. Deor flicked her *real* two of fire out onto the pile of cards.

Gasps came up from the gallery.

"What? No." Geoff shook his head. "You played that card already." His dismay turned to a grin. "Oh, trying goblin rules? You have to not get caught!"

Deor said nothing as he inspected her two of fire. He muttered spells under his breath, trying to disenchant the card. "It's the two of fire, Geoff. No matter how much magic you spend on it, it's always going to be the two of fire."

"You played this earlier!" he insisted.

"Check then," Deor said. "Maybe there are two in the deck?"

Geoff grabbed the stack of tricks and went through them. "Here!" He insisted. "This is the last round of trumps I played and—" He broke off mid-sentence as he flipped the four cards over. Fire, fire, fire. On the last card, a small flurry of silver sparks flitted into the air, revealing the two of earth.

Deor gathered up the platinum coins, her jewelry, and Geoff's ring. "It's only cheating if you get caught, right?" She batted her eyes at him and stood. "That was a delightful game, wasn't it Victor?"

Victor, still gaping, pulled himself together and stood. "Indeed. Thank you so much, Your Majesty. I learned a lot tonight."

"But, wait," Geoff gestured at the remaining pile of disks.

161

Deor patted him on the shoulder as she walked past him toward the door. Stephen was already there, opening it for her. "Don't worry about the rest of the five hundred thousand. You can send it around whenever you like." She looked at Gregory and his wife. "Thank you so much for your hospitality! Tomorrow we'll discuss our alliance in detail."

Gregory recovered first, though his face was flushed with anger. "Of course, Lady Regent," he said stiffly.

"Goodnight to you all," she said and left the room, Victor and Stephen close after her. Genevieve had already made it into the hall.

"Here!" She shoved the jewelry at Stephen. "I don't have pockets." He slipped them into his jacket.

Deor kicked off her heels and scooped them up. When they all stared at her, she added. "We've got to get out of here. Now. Run." She took off back to their suite and they followed.

26

In the old stories Rafe loved, great heroes always rode out on their quests at dawn, their armor shining in the sun. In Rafe and Monjoie's case, they left Mont Saint-Michel not long after sunset, on foot, and wearing plain brown woolen robes. As Rafe stepped into a wooded area below Wellhall Castle, he turned and caught a last glimpse of Caedmon and Evelyn waving. He raised his hand in a silent goodbye before the portal snapped shut.

Caedmon had assured them again that the way back would remain available. "You are leaving us, but you are not cut off," Caedmon said. "I will check in on you from time to time with my scrying bowl. Just to be sure you are well."

The entire chapter had hugged both him and Monjoie goodbye. Aaliyah stuffed their packs with salve and advised them not to neglect their exercises. Joan loaded them with weapons. Evelyn gave them both a pack of coffin nails and reminded them to keep their feet dry. Aelfburga had spent the day before baking waybread for them, fire-hardened rusks packed with nuts and dried fruit that would keep fresh for weeks and could be gnawed cold or softened up with hot water.

Aelfburga also pressed a cloth-wrapped piece of cold iron into Rafe's hand before she embraced him. It was shaped like a scallop shell, pierced at the top with a small hole, and threaded on a leather string. "I carried this on my wrist when I set out on my last pilgrimage," she said. "May it see you safely through your travels, wherever they take you."

Too touched by the gesture to answer, Rafe had hugged her close, her bird-like bones fragile under the soft comfort of her embrace.

Together he and Monjoie crept to the edge of the wood and surveyed the situation. To his right, the road veered upward to the high cliff of Wellhall Castle, an impregnable fortress. Lights showed in some of the windows, as did the guards on the battlements. Even if he could force his way in just by the sheer power of being the heir, that wouldn't stop Madeline's people from filling them with arrows.

On his left, the town sloped gently downward toward the seashore. It offered a maze of alleys and streets to hide in, as well as the possibility of eavesdropping for information.

Turning to Monjoie he said, "Town?"

Monjoie nodded. They pulled their hoods low over their faces and set off toward the town. If anyone saw them they would, he hoped, mistake them for itinerant bards.

With Monjoie leading, they headed through the quieter streets and empty markets for the docks, figuring that taverns full of fisher folk and merchant sailors would be more likely to open at this hour. As they walked, Rafe leaned on the quarterstaff he had first scorned, Aelfburga's pilgrim badge tied to around the top and his sword strapped to his back. Appearing shorter and feebler than he was seemed like a good idea, just in case he was seen, so he leaned on the staff as he went. Monjoie's slight limp was no fake, but he insisted it didn't matter.

Even as they came close enough to the docks that he could hear the waves sloshing against the piers, the streets stayed dark and empty. They spotted a trio of men staggering drunkenly against each other, but they soon entered a house. The taverns were shuttered and their lights were out.

"Is this normal?" Rafe asked. No seaside town he'd ever been in rolled up the sidewalks at sundown.

"Absolutely not. This place should be humming," Monjoie said. "The market square farmers are usually cleared out by now, but people come out in good weather just to stroll. Some of the taverns never close."

They circled back through the town, making a rough spiral toward the town center, looking for any sort of movement or information. Twice they dodged pairs of Civil Patrol guards wearing the Wellhall insignia.

When they reached the central plaza, Rafe's anger flared upward, drawing heat in and freezing the air around him. He tapped Monjoie who was watching in the opposite direction. When Monjoie turned, he drew in a hiss of angry breath.

A pillory had been set up in the town square. Two prisoners stood in them, drooping from exhaustion, their bodies locked in a painful ninety-degree angle with their heads and hands clamped in wooden stocks. By the way one sagged, he was unconscious. In the center of the plaza, the town fountain splashed and rippled merrily.

"Is this how you treat criminals in Wellhall?" Rafe whispered, his voice harsh.

"Of course not," Monjoie snapped. He peered closer. "That one's a baker. I doubt he's got a criminal bone in his body."

Rafe reined in his anger and held himself to the shadows with Monjoie. He'd learned the value of slowness over the last months. As the moon progressed across the sky, he counted the number and direction of the Civil Patrols that came through. One pair every twenty minutes, give or take.

Overhead the spring wind blew clouds over the moon, dimming the square. Rafe caught the groan of a prisoner as a patrol passed him. "Water. For pity's sake, water."

The Patrol ignored his pleas and passed on. Rafe gripped his staff harder. Monjoie poked Rafe with one finger and pointed. He held up three fingers and pointed at the Civil Patrol again. Rafe looked closer at the third person in the trio. In the dim light, it was hard to see, but her uniform was lighter than the other two and on her shoulder, she wore the insignia of a rose.

"Summer Court?" Rafe breathed when they had passed. "Why?"

Monjoie shrugged.

Once the patrol had passed, Rafe considered using his magic to send water from the fountain to the prisoner, but that would leave magical traces. This close to Madeline, that might be a fatal mistake. Simpler might be better. He was about to step into the open plaza to scoop up water from the fountain when he heard footsteps too light to be the tramp of soldiers' boots.

Two women darted out of the shadows of a nearby alley. Wings out, they flitted silently across the plaza to the prisoners. One had curly hair piled on her head and seemed to be in charge.

She set down the bag she was carrying and bent over the sagging prisoner, dabbing at his face. As quickly as the two women could manage, each prisoner was given water, food, and basic medical aid.

The slightly shorter woman who had fetched the water embraced the one on the end. Curly tugged at the other one, urgently.

In the alley, Rafe made eye contact with Monjoie and jerked his head at the women, a question on his face. Monjoie took one more look around the plaza and nodded. "You go. I've got your back."

Rafe waited until the women had gathered their things and were halfway back to the safety of the side streets before he coughed and stepped forward. Both women gasped, and Curly pushed the shorter one behind her.

"Please don't be frightened," Rafe said, his face hidden by his hood. "I want to help. Who are these prisoners? What did they do?"

Curly settled to the pavement, her wings still out and ready to fly. "What kind of question is that? Have you been living on the moon?"

Behind her, the shorter woman whispered, "Is he a bard?"

"Please," Rafe said. "Tell me what has been happening the last few days. Why are the streets so empty? It isn't even midnight yet."

"It's curfew," Curly said. "People weren't happy when she let the Summer Court in. Now no one is allowed out after sunset."

"She?" Rafe asked.

Curly jerked her head toward the castle that loomed over the town. "The duchess. That bitch betrayed us all. She let the Summer Court in and when her poor husband objected she gutted him like a fish. Now the place is crawling with Summer Court soldiers."

"What?" Rafe shouted. "Why would she do that?"

Curly seized the front of his robe, as she and the shorter woman hissed at him to be quiet.

He quickly lowered his voice. "Has she gone insane? Is it a will spell?" Madeline was famous for her skill with spells of that kind. It was virtually unthinkable that someone else could compel her to betray Wellhall and her beloved Edgar like that.

The smaller woman peeked out from behind her friend. "She says she's going to be Queen. That the Summer Court are our allies against the Aethelwings and it will all be well if we just go along." Both she and her friend looked behind them at the two prisoners.

"And you're sure it was deliberate? Madeline let the Summer Court in on purpose?" Whatever this was, it was not all well.

Curly shook her head. "I don't know what to think. The duchess hates

the Aethelwings; everyone knows that. Most of us do too. But Farringdons have always taken good care of their people, no matter what the
King did to the rest of the country. Maybe it was a will spell or maybe
she's dead and it's all an illusion to keep us under. But the Summer Court
and the Wellhall guard are working together now. They patrol together.
Word is they've killed the garrison of king's soldiers up the coast and all
the borders are watched. We can't leave."

The girl nodded again. "They said on the mirror anyone found more
than a mile from their home had to show a pass! Even the fisherfolk aren't
allowed out on their boats because they might be giving help to the
Aethelwings."

Before Rafe could ask more questions a voice across the plaza shouted,
"You there! Put your hands where I can see them." The accent carried the
southern lilt of the Summer Court.

The woman gasped. Curly shoved the younger woman back behind
her again and put up her hands, but there was no surrender in her face.

"Easy, easy," Rafe said. "I'll handle this. Be ready to run when I tell
you." He slid his free hand into his robe's pocket. Between his shoulder
blades his spine tingled. Now would be a spectacularly bad time to find
out that Monjoie did not have his back, or worse, was about to stick a
blade in it. But he did not glance back to betray his companion's position.
Either Monjoie was good to his word or not.

Behind him, the march of boots came closer. The soldier's voice
shouted, "You! I said freeze! Put the weapon down!"

"How many are there?" Rafe breathed.

"Five," Curly whispered back. "Three Summer, two Wellhall. You can't
take that many."

"Trust me," Rafe said. He smiled, though he knew his hood covered his
face still. The boots broke into a jog. "Run!"

Rafe whirled. The dagger in his hand flew straight, burying itself in a
Summer Court soldier's throat. The short girl screamed, not a terrified
wail, but a high-pitched keen that cut straight across every nerve in Rafe's
body and made the soldiers in front of him flinch and clutch their heads.
Ah, she was an air faerie. Convenient.

Monjoie's hands reached out from the shadows and the soldier at the
back of the group disappeared with a gurgle. Rafe caught the nearest
soldier across the head with his staff. The man went down, skull cracking
against the pavement. Rafe's backswing knocked the half-drawn sword

SARAH JOY ADAMS & EMILY LAVIN LEVERETT

from the nearest Summer Court man's hand. By the sound of it, his wrist was broken.

The man spoke a word and a jolt of pain magic caught Rafe in the center of his body, lighting his lungs on fire. He breathed deep and slow as Caedmon had taught him and broke the man's knee before he could gather another spell. The pain faded.

Ice slicked the ground under Rafe's feet as the Wellhall soldier sent magic to freeze the fountain's spray.

But Rafe laughed and spun, skating across the frictionless surface to crack the head of the Summer Court soldier who was cradling his wrist and gathering magic for the next assault. A scream to his left was cut short as Monjoie stepped from the shadows and stabbed the Wellhall soldier who had used ice magic. As the man went down, Monjoie spat on him.

"Friend of yours?" Rafe said.

"He was."

Rafe nodded and leaned down to rip the Wellhall badge from his uniform. "This is what happens to traitors."

He retrieved his knife from the throat of the first soldier and turned to inspect the Summer Court faerie. The man lay on the ground, his throat slit and his life ebbing away. Rafe took his badge too. The first soldier he had hit with the staff showed the print of the scallop-shaped iron badge burned into his forehead. Curly and the short girl stared at him, mouths open. Curly clutched a short kitchen knife in one hand. Wordlessly she pointed to the prisoners in the stocks. Rafe beckoned to the women and raced ahead of them. Monjoie stood guard, his knife out.

A simple but sturdy sealing spell was all that held the stocks together. Rafe considered for a moment, then pressed the iron badge into the spell. It shattered. Rafe allowed himself a little chuckle at that.

He helped the women lift the prisoners out of the stocks. One could stand, but the older man's knees buckled. Curly dug her fingers into the stocks and dry rot spread through the wood. She kicked it and the pieces shattered across the pavement.

Rafe leaned near her, his voice low. "If I help you with a little magic, will you promise to dispel it as soon as you get home? And tell no one who might try to find my identity?"

"Of course."

Rafe laid a hand on the unconscious man, whispering. His body rose off the ground, hovering. "It won't last long and you'll have to shove him, but this should allow you to get home."

"Thank you!" The girl threw her arms around Rafe. "You're a hero."

He shook his head and pushed her gently toward her companions. "Get him home. The next patrol will be here soon if someone hasn't reported this already." He pointed toward the windows of the buildings surrounding the plaza. Any one of them could hide watching eyes. Curly nodded and herded her little group into the nearest side street.

Rafe took one last look around the plaza for signs of life and ducked down the alley to Monjoie They wove through the shadows, putting as much space between themselves and the bodies as possible.

As they passed a signboard near the outskirts of town, Rafe paused to tear down a curfew notice. It had been signed with Madeline's name and counter-signed by D'nath. So he might be up there in the castle at this very moment. While Rafe nailed the torn badges to the boards with a splinter of wood, Monjoie set fire to the signed notice and scattered the remnants to the wind.

27

Deor followed as Victor led the charge back to their suite, slamming the door and locking it once everyone was in. Stephen and Victor hauled the massive couch over to barricade it.

"It won't keep folks out for long, but it will slow them down," Stephen said, crossing his arms.

Jake, Sam, and Brand all stood at attention, ears perked. Melanie, Bill, and Gordie appeared from their quarters, confused.

"Get dressed," Victor said. "Fast. We've got to get out of here."

"What happened?" Melanie said, but Gordie grabbed her arm and hauled her back toward their rooms before anyone could answer.

"Now what do we do?" Genevieve asked.

"We've got to get out of here, but I don't know how. If we could get to a portal, I might be able to make it work..." Deor said.

"We can't fight our way there though to the main portal," Victor said.

Deor cursed under her breath. "Should I just surrender? They might let the rest of you go if I do."

"No. They never had any intention of letting us go back to the Winter Court." Victor scowled. "We never should have come."

"We didn't have much choice," Genevieve said softly. "We had to try to find allies."

Deor looked at the couch against the door. "Brave last stand?"

Stephen snorted. "They're not going to kill you. The rest of us, sure." He paused. "Well, maybe not Genevieve and Melanie. But you're going to be held for ransom until you surrender to the Summer Court."

Gordie, Bill, and Melanie returned in practical clothes.

"What do you need?" Gordie asked, back straight.

"Another way out of this suite," Victor said.

"Oh, that's easy. There's a back exit from here into the servant's stairs. I followed it after your lecture."

"Sorry about that, lad," Victor said. "I was worried for you, but I shouldn't have behaved that way."

Gordie shrugged like he didn't know what to say. "The stairs go all the way down to the main floor. I snuck down and watched a bit. There's a portal there. It's how they bring in supplies."

Deor and Victor exchanged glances. "Think it will work?" She asked.

"I don't know, but it's the only choice we've got."

Stephen headed for the fireplace, picked up a poker, and handed it to Bill. "Here. Hit people other than us with it."

Bill wrapped his hand around the pommel and stared at it. "Do you really think they'll try to kill us?" It was the first he'd spoken.

"Yes." Deor crossed the room to him and laid a hand on his arm. "I'm so sorry I brought you. I should have known better."

"No." Bill said. He took a couple practice swings with the poker. "I want to be here with you. Besides, they deserve some whacks for all the insults. I'm not the only one who noticed, right?"

"Of course not," Genevieve said. "They weren't subtle."

"I'll be right back." Victor headed into the bedroom. After a few moments everyone heard, "Fuck!" Victor stormed back out. "They've been through our things. They found the weapons I had stashed."

Deor strolled over to the table, still set with the remains of their lunch. "The servants took our weapons, but they couldn't be bothered to clear the table." She picked up one of the knives—a simple dinner knife, not even a steak knife. The metal thrummed in her hand. It wasn't iron, she could tell that, but it was still metal. "I wonder," she said softly. She ran her finger along the blade of the knife, back and forth, concentrating.

"What are you thinking?" Victor asked.

Deor turned to him and smiled. She flung the knife, just as he had taught her to do in the Tower, and buried it nearly half an inch into one of the wooden chairs.

"How?" Victor asked.

Deor picked up a fork and sharpened its tines. "I'm my father's daughter. I can sharpen pretty much anything metal. Knives, certainly, but forks, spoons too. We don't have swords and daggers, but we aren't unarmed." She gathered the rest of the silverware, including a butter knife and sugar spoon, and sharpened them all, distributing them among her friends. She even gave the fire poker an edge and did the same to the ash shovel as well.

"Alright." Victor said, "let's—"

Someone pounded on the door and then tried the handle, finding it locked. "Your Majesty?" It was Heinrich. "Open the door. There's no need for this farce. We have a key. You and yours will be treated well if you surrender now. If not..." He trailed off.

"Why does everyone say that?" Deor frowned.

Victor took command. "Gordie, lead the way with Melanie and Genevieve. Deor, you follow them with Bill, Stephen and I will take up the back, and fight them off. Keep the dogs with you."

"Go," Deor said to them. "You too, Bill."

"But—" Bill started.

"Help them. I'll be along soon, I promise."

Bill frowned but nodded. He waved at Gordie. The four of them headed out the door and down the stairs.

A key slid into the lock and clicked. The handle turned, and the door opened, banging into the sofa.

"Fine," Heinrich muttered.

"Get back!" Victor said.

They scurried toward the servants' door as the fireball hit, blasting through the sofa and into the room. Luckily the sofa took the brunt of it, and the flames didn't reach them.

Heinrich stepped through the smoke, a cadre of soldiers looming behind him. "Come now," he said. "Be sensible."

Before Deor could say a word, Victor let out a cry and flung the butter knife.

Deor gasped at his accuracy. The blade hit Heinrich in the eye, burying itself in his brain. The man crumpled to the floor.

"Nice shot," Deor grabbed Victor's hand. "Let's go."

He resisted for a moment, staring at the corpse in front of him.

"Now, Victor." Stephen shoved him toward Deor. Victor stumbled but recovered. They made their way down the dark staircase, Brand, Jake, and

Sam in front and behind. They reached the bottom and paused. A struggle was happening on the other side.

"Let me go!" Deor heard Melanie cry. There was a *thunk*.

Stephen flung open the door. A group of soldiers had Melanie and Gordie cornered. The one that had grabbed Melanie lay on the floor. Everyone, goblin soldiers and faeries alike, gaped at Bill, who clutched the now-bloody poker.

"I said unhand her," he whispered. "All he had to do was let go…"

"Bill!" Stephen snapped. Bill spun around. "Good show."

"The portal is through there," Gordie pointed to a door. In between them and the door were three soldiers.

"You don't think we didn't know about the servant's route? Heinrich was just there to flush you out, send you down here. There will be a dozen more of us along any moment." The soldier gloated.

Everyone moved at once. Jake and Sam leapt at one of the soldiers. A few sparks of flame burst from his hand, but not enough to get through their thick coats, and they knocked him to the floor. Genevieve screamed.

Gordie stooped to grab the sword from the fallen soldier and charged to join Victor and Stephen, already engaged with the other two soldiers. The space was small— ten feet across at most. Victor, Stephen, and Gordie handled the other soldiers easily, shoving their bodies out of Deor's way.

"Get to opening it," Victor said as they heard the sound of footsteps heading their way.

Deor hurried to the door, dragging Genevieve as she went. She opened the door itself. On the other side was a small space, no bigger than an elevator. Goblin markings, in a language Deor didn't recognize, lined the doorframe on both sides. She touched one and pushed her magic into it. It flared to life, and Deor yanked her hand back. "Ouch!" She shook her fingers out, trying to ease the sting. Still, the marking had responded to her magic. The pain would suck, but it was better than being captured.

She rested both her hands against the largest markings on either side, drew a deep breath, and explored them. They flared to life again but only warmed, didn't burn.

"Hurry!" Melanie called, clearly trying not to sound panicked.

Genevieve huddled against the pantry wall, her eyes big as dollar coins, her face pale.

"It's okay, Genevieve," Deor said. "We'll get out of this."

Genevieve didn't even blink.

Deor focused again and tried to find her own palace door, on the other side. She could feel it far away, but layers of Goblin magic lay between her and those portals. So she searched for others, any place that wasn't here. They flashed in her mind, gone as soon as she'd seen them. She had no way to stop them moving, to control them. Her heart raced. "Easy," she said to herself. She had to find a way to hold on to each door, at least long enough to see it and try to open it. *Imagine*, she thought to herself, *that this is a series of pictures on a phone. Look at one, and then flick it aside.* The chaos flashing across her vision slowed. Place after place flashed by, other rooms in the palace, courtyards full of Goblin guards. Nowhere safe.

At last, one gave her pause. At first, she couldn't quite tell what she was seeing. She concentrated. There were stone pillars of some kind. It was dim, and there was a rushing noise. Something flashed into her vision, a snake, perhaps. No. Not a snake. A train. An honest to God, human world train. She shoved hard with her magic, forcing the portal open despite the pain.

Deor leaned through, feeling the iron all around her. Why have a portal to the human world? Perhaps they liked to play with the humans. All that mattered was a way out.

"Come on!" She called. She whistled for the dogs. Brand appeared immediately and stayed by her. "Go on!" Deor waved at Melanie as Bill and Gordie appeared in the doorway.

"Where is that?" Gordie said, coming toward the portal.

"Does it matter?" Melanie snapped. She grabbed Gordie's hand and dragged him through, stepping easily to the other side.

Jake and Sam rushed after them. Victor grabbed a set of pantry shelves and hauled it down across the door he and Stephen had been defending. Goblin soldiers battered at the door from the other side.

"Go!" Deor shouted at them. The portal was getting heavy.

Bill went, dragging Brand along.

"You go," Victor said. "I can hold it."

"You can't," Deor said through clenched teeth. "It's full of iron. This is the human world. Go!"

Victor stepped through.

Stephen caught Genevieve by the arm and hauled her forward from the corner. She let herself be dragged a few steps, but then stopped and jerked herself free from his grasp. "No. No no no."

"Come on," Stephen said gently. "Just a few more steps."

"No." She planted her feet, fighting his grip.

Voices on the other side of the door grew louder. The wooden door and shelves wouldn't keep out the fire magic at all. Deor pulled one hand from the doorframe and grabbed Stephen's hand. "Go, please."

Stephen frowned and glanced at Genevieve.

"I've got her," Deor said. He let go and leaped through the portal.

"Come on, Genevieve!" Deor said as gently as she could muster. She reached her hand out and took the trembling woman's. "We've got to go. You can make it."

Genevieve shook her head. "I can't. I can't move. I can't."

"You can." Deor let go of Genevieve's hand and grabbed her arm. With all her strength she dragged the woman forward—she was light enough. When Genevieve stood in front of her, Deor grabbed her by the front of the dress and half hauled, half flung Genevieve through the portal. As she moved to step through, an explosion blew through the door and shelf behind her. Deor shrieked as pieces of shrapnel were buried in her left shoulder. The portal flickered.

"Get her!" she heard.

Deor stumbled through the portal and let go. She was on the other side of a heavily graffitied human door, the Goblin magic symbols hidden under layers of paint. "Deor!" Victor was next to her, trying to move her away from the door.

"No!" she shoved him back. The Goblin markings glowed. Someone was about to come through the portal after them. She forced the nails of her right hand to go silver and sharp, ignoring the pain in her shoulder. With what was left of her strength she dragged her nails through the markings, clawing the magic away. With a flash, the other markings vanished and the glow stopped. The door was just a door.

"Come on!" Deor heard Bill and tried to turn to face him.

"Fuck," Victor said, eyeing her wounds. He stripped off his coat and wrapped it around her. He scooped her up and headed toward Bill.

A rush of wind and a roar. Deor's eyes were already drooping closed.

"In here!" Bill hollered.

"Make sure everyone makes it out," she mumbled.

"Everyone's fine. Except you," Victor muttered under his breath. He stepped forward into a train. Another whoosh of sound and air, and Victor lurched forward. They were moving. She leaned her head against his shoulder.

"Deor?"

She blinked her eyes open to see Bill. "We're on the Berlin U-Bahn. We'll get off soon."

A few jerky stops later, at Bill's command, Victor carried her out into the open air.

"Follow me!" Bill said. He sounded confident and in charge. She sighed, relieved. Around her, she heard voices, but couldn't make out what they were saying. A language that sounded familiar, but not recognizable.

They walked and then went up, a turn, and up again. The space opened up and above her, far above her, was a dome made of glass, interconnecting panels that let her see the night sky. A rainbow of colored lights glowed through the glass.

"Alright," Bill said. "Let's pause here."

The group gathered around their de facto leader.

"Where are we?" Deor asked.

Bill smiled at her. "We're at the Hauptbahnhof station, Grand Central in Berlin. Man, this place brings back memories from my dissertation. There's a hospital nearby. We need to get you help."

A hospital sounded good, but then it didn't. "No!" Deor shook her head trying to force the fuzziness away.

"You need medical care," Victor said.

"Yes, please." Genevieve was a few steps away from everyone else, staring at her. Tears were running down her cheeks. She had bits of dirt and some wooden shrapnel from the exploding shelf in her hair, and a small cut on her cheek.

"No." She cleared her throat. "It isn't bad or deep. It just hurts."

"Medical care," Bill said.

"No." She shook her head. "The goblins had a portal to a subway station in Berlin. They must come here often. They know the area. They'll be looking for us, and they'll know they hurt me."

"Dammit." Victor resettled Deor in his arms. "You're right. And we don't know what connections they have here in the human world. Who knows what they can do? So where to? Back on the U-Bahn thingy?" He grimaced and the other faeries murmured their agreement. Riding in a steel tube wouldn't just be uncomfortable for them. It would sap their strength and cloud their minds.

"A hotel." Bill said. "There are a couple just outside the station down the street. We get some rooms, and I'll go find a pharmacy, and get a first aid kit. I can still manage conversational German and I'll blend in better than the rest of you."

"That's smart," Stephen said, sarcasm tingeing his voice. "Except we don't have any human money."

"You may not," Bill said, reaching behind him, "but I don't leave home without my wallet." He pulled out a faded and creased brown leather wallet and flashed a credit card. "As they say, never leave home without it."

Stephen slapped Bill on the back. "Who says bards are useless?"

Their short journey was a blur as Bill led them out of the station into the cool evening air. People around them sometimes paused to stare and point at the bloody crew and their unleashed dogs. After half a block, Victor and Stephen risked casting a glamour over their group. The three dogs became rolling suitcases. Bill led the way through a revolving door of a nice, but not too nice, hotel. He greeted the man behind the front desk in perfect German. Deor had no idea what he said, but the credit card worked and soon they were on the elevator, on their way up to a series of two connected rooms. "One has bunk beds that will hold four, and the other has a queen and they'll bring a cot up."

"Perfect," Stephen said. "It'll be just like basic, right, Gordie?"

The kid smiled weakly. The elevator ride was clearly getting to him, and to the others, too. Genevieve hadn't spoken since the station, and Deor could sense Victor's exhaustion. Victor set Deor down gently on the bed.

"So we're safe for now," Victor said. "How do we get home?"

"Do you have a mirror?" Deor asked.

"I do." Victor dug a small mirror out of his pocket. It looked a bit like a Lady's compact, and a protective magical glow surrounded it.

"Let's phone a friend." She held the mirror in both hands and concentrated. "Donovan Rhodzevrah?" The mirror swirled and Deor wondered how long it would take him to answer, if he ever did, but the mirror cleared in a matter of seconds.

"Your Majesty," Donovan smiled at her, all fangs. "I've been expecting your call."

"What?" Deor frowned.

"His Majesty King Gregory contacted me less than an hour ago. He said you made quite the scene, killing guards, murdering his Sword, and fleeing through a portal into Berlin."

Deor's shoulders sagged.

"He asked that I and my family help to find you. He offered a very generous reward. He offered an alliance, assuring my father a seat at the table in the new Fae order as a favored friend of the Goblin and the Summer Courts."

It occurred to her that he was chatty because he was tracing the call. No doubt any moment a small strike force of vampires would appear. She sighed. They could run, again, but what good would that do? They had no allies in a city full of goblins, all looking for her.

"Of course he did," Deor said bitterly. "So, now what?"

"Now?" Donovan seemed genuinely startled. "You don't have a counteroffer?"

Deor pinched the bridge of her nose. "No. I've got a shoulder full of wood. We're exhausted, and most of the folks are getting iron-sick." She met his gaze. "I'll come quietly if you'll let everyone else go. None of them deserve to suffer for my poor diplomacy." Victor and Bill shouted at her not to say that, but she waved them to silence.

Donovan sat back and stared at her. "You're serious."

"If you want me to beg, I can. I can promise you all sorts of things, but I wouldn't know if I could actually give them to you. I have nothing to bargain with, and I've had enough bluffing for the night. You want to hand me back to Geoff? There's nothing I can do to stop you."

Donovan drummed his fingers on his desk. "Why did you go to the Goblins in the first place?"

"Because they were the last ally we had. You made it very clear that you'd not make any public moves to help us. Rufus's people are suitably furious and see no benefit to joining a losing war against the Summer Court. Both the Summer Court Queen and Madeline want Finn to suffer, and it looks like they're going to get it." Hot tears burned in her eyes, and she held Donovan's gaze, refusing to blink, in the hopes of keeping them from spilling down her cheeks.

Donovan smiled, his fangs showing over his red lips. "Did you really murder Heinrich?"

"It wasn't murder, it was self-defense," she snapped, not caring that the tears fell. "And long overdue justice. But yes, we killed him. He took a butter knife through the eye. Don't expect me to pretend I'm sorry. He had it coming."

"I'm sure he did." Donovan's smile grew wider, hungrier. He glanced to one side as another vampire handed him a piece of paper. "You're in the Hotel Schulerin, I see. Berlin has a truly fantastic system of closed-circuit cameras, though your glamours confused my people for a minute. Stay where you are. We'll be along shortly."

Deor nodded. Perhaps the others could flee separately, in groups of two or three while she waited for the vampires to collect her. Glamoured and split up they might make it. Some of them.

A servant brought Donovan a glass of blood and he sipped it, talking in a conversational tone. "My father listened to Gregory's terms. Thought about them carefully, along with Geoff's recent decision to involve me, without my consent, in his attempt on Finn's life. That was quite embarrassing for me, not realizing I was being used as a Goblin stooge. So, my father has left it up to me. Catch you and renew our alliance with the Goblins, or...not."

"Or not?" Deor wiped her eyes.

"I like you more than I like him," Donovan said flatly. "The Summer Court 'giving us a seat at the table' is utter bullshit. You, though, have never been anything but honest. Your dad's an asshole, but that's not on you. So, I choose to help you and to let Geoff and Gregory learn what it feels like to be betrayed." He grinned.

"Okay..."

"When my people arrive, I'll need you to glamour a few of them to look like faeries. Ivan will escort you and your retinue to me in Romania. I've already sent a couple of old friends to treat any wounds and make sure you and yours are safe."

Relief flooded through Deor, almost too good to be trusted. "What about your vampires? Won't the goblins hurt them when they realize they've been tricked?"

Donovan snorted. "I imagine they'll try."

"Donovan," Deor said, the tears welling again, "I don't know what to say, except thank you."

His face softened into a gentle smile. "Thank me when you arrive safely here."

The mirror returned to her reflection. She looked over the top of it at Stephen and Victor who had been sitting across from the bed, in two chairs. "Did you get all that?"

"Yep," Victor said.

"Do you trust him?" Stephen asked.

"Yes," Deor said. "At least as far as getting us to Romania. What happens then, who knows? But I'd rather be there than here."

28

After their escapade with the men in the stocks, Monjoie led Rafe far into the woods, following trails he had learned as a boy with the Wellhall foresters. They bedded down for the night in a grass-floored grove. It was too dark to gather firewood, so they ate cold provender and wrapped themselves in the oil cloth tarps the cloister had given them.

"Not a bad night's work," Monjoie said. "Not enough to drive out the Summer Court, but it's a start."

Rafe agreed. He swallowed a mouthful of apple. "Just the two of us can cause a fair bit of mischief, but to do more we'll need allies. We can't be the only ones fighting back. We need to find the others and join forces."

"Obviously."

"Let's not allow the general population to know there are two of us. We're both blue—hard enough to tell apart in the dark. If we keep our wings in and our hoods up, no one will be able to tell the difference. We could spread a lot of fear and uncertainty if a single hooded figure bent on violence starts popping up at unpredictable and disparate locations."

"Get inside their heads," Monjoie said. "I like it." He tore a chunk of bread and chewed it thoughtfully. "You should burn that scallop shell into a few more faces. Make them think that the sea itself is out for revenge against the enemies of Wellhall."

"Madeline won't be fooled."

"No, but she'll be angry. And it won't matter if she's not fooled if everyone around her is spooked. You know how superstitious sailors are."

Rafe laughed. "I can't throw stones there. I'm superstitious when I'm on a boat too. There's something about the sea that brings it out in a person. Besides, if the entire crew tells you wearing yellow stockings brings bad luck, you listen. Better to lose your stockings than the entire vessel."

"You never wore yellow stockings in your life!"

"No, but one of Genevieve's friends did. I took a mess of them out on a pleasure cruise a few summers ago, and the Captain pulled me aside to inform me that either the stockings went or the crew did. Genevieve and I had quite the spat over that one."

Now it was Monjoie's turn to chuckle. "Did you wrestle her friend to the deck and rip his stockings off bodily?"

"No, but I did tell him they were going overboard with or without him in them. She felt that was unnecessarily harsh." Rafe threw his apple core into the brush. "Proposing to her has to rank among my stupidest decisions. She's a good woman, but we were never suited to each other."

Monjoie said nothing, but somehow he managed to radiate smugness from where he lay on the ground in his bedroll.

"Yeah, yeah," Rafe said. "Milord Happily-Engaged."

"That's Milord Secretly Happily-Engaged," Monjoie said, yawning. "No one knows except our parents. Safer that way." He wriggled and scrunched around like a dog finding a spot to lie down. Soon he was breathing softly.

Rafe leaned back against an oak tree and breathed deeply, taking in the summer air, the smell of new leaves and old leaf mold. The anger and pain inside him still throbbed, but the pull was gone, replaced by a sense of anchor. Here he was in Wellhall, and here he was meant to be. Soon he too scrunched down into the grass, pillowing his head on his pack and letting the summer frogs sing him to sleep.

Rafe crouched behind a stack of crates and watched Summer Court faeries unloading goods from the boat that had just anchored in the harbor. The girls they had met in the square had taken to leaving food outside the town limits every other day and the most recent drop had included a brief note that a merchant vessel was due to dock that night when the tide came in, despite the embargo.

Monjoie was hidden in an alley opposite his position. The man was almost as good at subterfuge as Arthur. The thought gave Rafe a pang of grief for his lost friendship, but he shoved it away and concentrated on the scene before him.

The ship had docked with no trouble, but the minute the captain signed her name to the Harbor Master's tablet, a troop of soldiers in Summer Court armor, led by a man wearing Wellhall insignia, had stepped out of glamours and arrested the entire crew. The captain cold-cocked the harbor master before she was tackled and subdued. Now she knelt on the dock with her first mate, while the crew unloaded the ship's hold and debated what to do about the situation.

"A lot of fine wines," one of the soldiers called as he carried a box up the dock. "Rangley stock! It will make for lovely drinking tonight with the lads."

"Box six of twelve," the customs official said quietly, marking it down.

Rafe focused on him, peering across the darkness. He whispered a few words under his breath, and magic swirled around him, letting him see the man's face more clearly. Though his voice was steady, his eyes were not. He stared at the tablet in front of him, one hand clutching it with white knuckles. It seemed the man was not a happy collaborator.

"Don't worry." Another soldier slapped him on the back. "You'll get your reward."

The man nodded but didn't speak.

Rafe let the magnification spell go. Magic was so easy for him here. It swirled in the air around him, trembled in the earth beneath him, and radiated from every living thing. He could even feel the magic of the seas. It had taken him some time to realize that the richness of magic here wasn't only a product of Wellhall's strength and vitality. The magic responded to him, the heir.

"We're all set, sir," one of the soldiers said. The man in charge nodded. "Burn it," he said, nodding toward the ship.

"Aye!" Another of the soldiers grabbed a torch from a pile and lit it with a burst of magic; her eyes sparkled in the flames as she reached for more, lighting nearly a dozen and handing them to other soldiers.

"You can't do that!" A young woman lunged forward from the crowd of huddled sailors. "That's our livelihood! All our belongings…"

The ship's captain shouted at her, "Nerida, stop. It's not worth it."

The young woman lunged for the arm of a soldier holding a torch, wrestling him for it before being dragged down and spellbound. When she tried to rise, the Wellhall official shoved a foot into her stomach. "Stay," he commanded.

This had gone on long enough. Rafe stretched his magic out, running along the ground out from him and into the sea. A few of the soldiers looked puzzled for a second, but that was all he needed to send a huge wave crashing over the people, Winter and Summer court alike, dousing all the flames. At the same moment, Monjoie erupted from the shadow of a toolshed, slit the throat of the nearest Summer Court soldier, and faded back into the shadows.

The Wellhall official turned on the captain.

"You little..." He raised his sword.

Rafe bull-rushed the man, knocking him sideways. He swung his staff before the man could recover, first knocking the sword out of his hands, then bringing the scallop shell down onto the man's skull. He sagged, his eyes open and blank.

Rafe spun to see Nerida already on her feet, the guard's sword in her hand. The ship's captain leapt to her feet, shouting for her crew, and every one of them sprang into action, hurling themselves on the Summer Court and Wellhall traitors alike.

Rafe gave no quarter. Rafe slicked the ground under him and leaped forward, sliding across the ice. Every few seconds or so another Summer Court soldier would cry out and fall into the water, Monjoie doing his unseen work. Within moments it was over and the ground was littered with fallen Summer Court soldiers and Wellhall traitors.

The captain charged toward the customs official, grabbing him by the collar. "I'll hang you from my mast and use your carcass for my figurehead. We trusted you, you traitor!" she spat at the man.

The small man struggled in the woman's grip. "Please. I had no choice."

"Let him down, captain," Rafe said.

The captain, keeping her grip, turned on Rafe, a snarl on her face. "This rat must have told them we'd be comin' in tonight!"

"If that's true, we will make an example of him," Rafe said quietly. "He is a citizen of Wellhall, so at least hear him out."

All around him, the ship's crew gathered in a circle, weapons at the ready.

Rafe stepped forward, looming over the smaller man. "Did you tell the Summer Court guard that this ship came in tonight? Did you help them?"

"Yes." Tears streamed down his face. "They came this afternoon and tied up my wife and daughter. If I hadn't helped the Summer Court, they said they'd kill them." He gazed in terror at the custom house windows then dropped to the ground, hands over his face. "If their guards saw, they're probably already dead."

"Sad story," Rafe said. He looked at the captain, "I suggest you send a few of your best to see if it's true."

"You talk like you've got the run of the place," the captain observed. But she pointed to her first mate and daughter. "You two go and see. Take as many as you need."

"Wait! Please, don't kill him!" A woman's voice shouted. The customs officer's wife, a small child clutched in her arms, ran toward them. "Please! Please don't hurt him." She had a black eye and rope burns on her wrists. Rafe stepped back, pulling his hood up, as others lifted lights to see her better.

"Where did you come from?" the ship's captain said.

"A man broke in. He wore a hooded robe, but his hands were blue. He killed the two guarding us and said I should run if I wanted to save my man's life."

"Daddy!" the little girl screamed, reaching for her father.

"Let him live," Rafe said. The captain glared at him for a moment, her knife still at the customs officer's throat.

"And who are you to tell me so?"

"A son of Wellhall, once lost at sea. I have come back to help my people." A slightly confused cheer went up from the ship's crew. The captain let the man down and he collapsed into his wife's arms.

The captain turned to her crew, "Right, look lively all of you! We've got to get this stuff under cover and be ready to sail out before the tide turns. Nerida, you're in charge." She stepped closer to Rafe, suspicion on her face. "Are you a ghost that you can be in two places at once?"

"You could think of me that way," Rafe said.

"Hmm. And what kind of payment would a ghost want?"

Rafe tucked his hands into the sleeves of his robe. "I didn't come for payment. If you wish to thank me, tell me how to find others doing the same work as you."

"I don't know that," the captain answered. "It's harder to betray names if you don't have them. But I can tell you where to look for a contact."

"That's more than enough."

"Cote," she said.

Rafe thanked her and slipped away, trusting Monjoie to catch up to him under the shadow of the close-packed houses. Unlike Rafe, Monjoie had seized a bundle of food from the customs official's house, along with a couple of bottles of Rangley Red.

"I did not come for payment, my sky blue rear end," Monjoie laughed when they were back at their hidden grove. He carved a hunk of cheese for himself and drank from his bottle. "We have to eat too, you know. You melodramatic asshole."

Rafe laughed and accepted a piece of cheese. "Call me melodramatic? You certainly stole the show, saving the harbormaster's wife and child."

Monjoie smiled and dusted off his knuckles on his robe.

Rafe pulled the cork on one of the bottles, took a swig, and passed it to Monjoie. "If this is the way ghosts live, I think I'm going to enjoy the afterlife."

29

Deor sat on the bed, wincing slightly as Melanie continued to treat her wounds. The splinters weren't deep, Melanie confirmed, but they hurt like hell.

Room service had been delivered, and Deor sat next to Genevieve on the queen bed, a plate of schnitzel on her lap. "Are you okay, Genevieve?" The answer was obviously no. Genevieve had suffered a few cuts and bruises, a couple bits of wood stuck here and there, but Melanie had pulled them out and treated her wounds. She wasn't quite as good as new, but close. Whatever troubled Genevieve was in her head, not her body. "Talk to me."

Genevieve pivoted quickly, shifting her weight so that she was facing Deor. "I froze." Tears tumbled out of her eyes. "I couldn't move, couldn't do anything." Genevieve wasn't even looking at Deor—her gaze was somewhere else. She wrung her hands and shivered.

Deor reached out and took one of her hands. "It's okay," Deor said softly. "You've never been in a situation like this before."

"And your lady's maid has?" Genevieve's gaze was suddenly sharp, piercing, as she met Deor's.

"She has been trained," Deor said.

Genevieve's shoulders relaxed a bit, but she seemed unconvinced. "If you hadn't thrown me through the portal, I'd never have moved." Genevieve stood and paced, rubbing her hands up and down her arms as though she was cold. She stopped at the window and stared out. "You got hurt because I couldn't make myself move."

"Genevieve." Deor got up, suppressing a wince at the pain, and joined Genevieve at the window. The train station glowed in the distance, the glass dome sparkling with light. "It isn't your fault. It's the goblins' fault. They attacked us."

Genevieve sniffed but said nothing.

"Really," Deor said, putting an arm around her shoulder, "I'm fine."

A full body shudder rattled through Genevieve, and the tears got worse. She pressed a hand to her mouth. "Please," she whispered. "Leave me alone." Her tone was desperate, not harsh, and so Deor dropped her arm and stepped away. Genevieve glanced at her for a split second and turned and fled to the bathroom, gently closing the door behind her. Seconds later, Deor heard the shower running.

Victor came in. "Everyone's settled."

Deor moved away from the window. "Except Genevieve. She's..." Deor shrugged "She's having a hard time of it. She feels guilty."

"I'm not surprised," he said, keeping his voice down. "She's always poised, always on, always capable, and here she wasn't. And you got hurt *helping her.*"

"It wasn't her fault!" Deor insisted.

"Of course, it wasn't." Victor took her hand, and the tension in her shoulders eased. "But she still feels responsible. You understand that, right?"

"Yes." Deor would feel the same way. "But I wish I could help her."

"When we get home, we'll find a good healer. Someone who knows how to deal with trauma."

"God," Deor sat on the bed. "I hadn't even thought of that. But you're right. Genevieve, Melanie, Bill, Gordie—they're all traumatized by this. They didn't sign up for it." She smiled softly. "You and Stephen and I, we enlisted."

Victor chuckled. "That doesn't make it much better. You should talk to someone when we get home as well."

A massive, thundering knock came at the door, interrupting their conversation. "What the hell?" Victor drew his knife and Stephen bolted in from the other room.

Deor glanced through the peephole. Two huge men stood at the door. Even the fisheye lens couldn't take in their full height, but the one closest to the door held up the Rodzevrah insignia. Deor stepped back, hoped she was making the right decision, and opened the door.

"Hello, professor." The large man smiled down at her warmly.

"Bernie!" Deor flung herself into the werebear's arms. She hadn't seen him since she had been at Eisteddfod, but she knew that he and his brother, Bob, left the Winter Court after Finn banned werecreatures.

"Easy there," he said, gently pulling her away. "That shoulder looks bad."

Deor stepped back. "It hurts," she admitted. "But it isn't deep. Donovan said you'd have a medical kit?"

"We do." Bob smiled and held up a backpack. He was slightly taller than his brother. Both had near-black hair and dark brown eyes. They passed as human, barely, since they were both over seven feet tall.

"Please come in," Deor said, stepping out of the way. "It's good to see both of you." She bit her lip. "I'm sorry about the werecreature ban," she said softly. "I reversed it…"

"Yes, you did." Bernie said, stepping into the room. "It's likely that we'll go back to Eisteddfod one day, but not while things are so unstable."

Deor shut and locked the door behind them.

The rest of Deor's crew came into the room.

"This is Bernie and Bob," Deor said. "They're werebears." She introduced each of her friends. Jake, Sam, and Brand had formed a loose circle around her. "Down, boys," Deor said. "These are friends." Jake and Sam backed off, but Brand, at the word *friends,* darted forward and sniffed both Bernie and Bob cheerfully, wagging his tail all the while.

"Those are Lord Farringdon's dogs, aren't they?" Bernie rumbled. His voice sounded much rougher than his brother's, and Deor wondered how much time he spent as a bear.

"Yes," Deor said softly. "He fell fighting for Finn's escape. Jake and Sam were left behind. I'm watching them until…"

"I see," Bernie said. He reached out and laid a dinner-plate-sized hand on her unhurt shoulder. "Let's get your shoulder fixed."

Deor nodded. "Where do you want me to sit?"

"The bed will be fine." Bernie followed Deor to the bed.

Deor sat.

Bernie pulled a pair of wire-rimmed glasses from the backpack and settled them on his nose. "Hmmm." He gently pulled on the piece of wood. "You're right that it isn't serious, as in life-threatening. But it's in there pretty good. And pulling it out will leave splinters. First, before I do anything, I'm going to numb it up. Is that okay with you?"

"Definitely." Deor braced herself for a needle. Instead, Bernie pulled a piece of cloth out of the med kit and laid it over her wound, pressing down gently. As he did so, magic flowed out of the cloth into her shoulder, sending blessed numbness all along her nerves. She breathed a sigh of relief.

"Bob," Bernie said, "why don't you show everyone else what you brought while I work on this here."

"Got it," the quiet werebear said. He dropped the large duffle bag he carried on the floor with a thud.

"Now," Bob said as he opened it, "this isn't the height, or even the middle, of faerie fashion, but you don't need fashionable right now. You need practical and, if possible, discreet." He pulled out various pairs of jeans and shirts in a range of sizes. "I think we've got something that'll fit everyone—and don't worry, there isn't iron on any of it." He smiled. "Now, don't all of you rush over at once to take your pick..."

Melanie was the first to come forward. Bob looked her up and down and pulled a pair of jeans from the stack. "These ought to fit you," he said. "There's a belt if they are a bit too big." He waved at a stack of t-shirts. "Take your pick—but leave the bigger ones for the gentlemen."

As the rest of the folks gathered, Genevieve emerged from the bathroom.

"Oh good," Bernie said. "You're a plant faerie, right?"

Genevieve blinked. "Yes. I am."

Bernie waved her over. "Come help me find all the bits of wood. I don't want to leave any behind." He glanced at the people pulling clothes from the pile. "And you'll want to pick some human attire."

"I'll help you first," Genevieve said as Melanie came out of the other room dressed in black jeans and a "99 Luftballoons" t-shirt.

Genevieve made her way over to Deor. She had gotten herself together in the bathroom and was wearing magical makeup. Not much, Deor noted. Just enough to smooth out the blotchy skin and puffy post-ugly-cry eyes. "What do you need me to do?"

"Her shoulder's all numbed up. I've got the big chunk out, and I'm working on getting the little bits. Can you put your hand on her shoulder and tell me where they are?"

"I can do that." Her words came out as assured and confident, but

Deor could tell from her expression that Genevieve was anything but. Bernie set back to work. Using tweezers from his medical backpack, he tugged the small pieces of wooden shrapnel out.

30

As Rafe and Monjoie made their way out of the city, Rafe hummed a little tune that Evelyn had taught him: "The Bells of Hell go ting-a-ling-a-ling, for you but not for me. And the little devils have a sing-a-ling-a-ling, for you but not for me."

Monjoie chuckled softly and joined in.

They walked that way for a bit, in companionable time, until they were well out of the city and into the dense woods that surrounded it. If they walked all night, they could camp and sleep during the day, and they'd be in Cote by nightfall tomorrow.

Rafe was footsore—full body sore, to tell the truth of it—by the time he and Monjoie reached the latter's ancestral home. The forest had grown more and more dense until they were following barely visible deer paths traversable only because Monjoie had wandered through them since he was a child.

"Hold here," Monjoie said quietly, crouching down behind a tree.

Rafe followed suit. "What is it?"

Monjoie jerked his chin in the direction he was staring. "Take a look."

They were at the edge of the trees. A hundred yards in front of him was a stone manor house, lovely and weathered. Beyond it by a few hundred yards was the sea.

"It's beautiful," Rafe said.

"It is." Monjoie nodded. "My ancestors, who were here before the

Farringdons, carved this space out of the forest." Monjoie started to rise from his crouch. "Come with me."

"Wait." Rafe ducked down and tugged Monjoie with him.

"What?" Monjoie flailed, almost falling backward.

"The front door. It's opening."

"I'm sure it's—" Monjoie froze. "Who the ever-loving fuck is that with my fiancée?!"

Rafe grabbed Monjoie's shoulders and held him in place, though he agreed with his sentiment. A lovely blonde woman had strolled out the front door—Juliette—on the arm of a man who, at least from where they were, was the spitting image of Monjoie.

The man leaned down toward Juliette and kissed her.

Rafe pinned the struggling Monjoie and sat on him. "Stop it!" he hissed.

"I've got to get to Juliette!"

"She seems fine." Rafe said. At that Monjoie surged again, struggling. Rafe shifted his weight, putting it all on Monjoie's shoulders, and grabbed the hair on the back of his head. He brought his mouth close to Monjoie's ear. "Whatever that is, it's clearly fucked up, no question, but if we go rushing down there without knowing what's going on, we're likely to get ourselves, or possibly her, killed."

Monjoie stopped his struggle and drew a deep breath. "You're right," he relented. "Let me up."

Rafe eased off carefully and when Monjoie showed no sign of sprinting to Juliette's rescue, he let him up.

The lovely couple chatted for a few more moments when a carriage rumbled up the driveway to the house. The driver wore a Wellhall uniform, but the people who emerged wore Summer Court clothes. The first of the Summer Court soldiers approached Monjoie's father, hand out. They shook hands and chatted, both cheerful. Monjoie's father made a sweeping gesture, welcoming the three other soldiers who emerged from the carriage. The man with Juliette, whom Rafe had dubbed Monjoie Two, embraced the soldier in a hug and led everyone inside.

Monjoie dropped back from his crouch with a thud. "What the hell was that?"

"A glamour?" Rafe suggested.

"Obviously. Except I've never known a glamour to be good enough to fool a lover." He blanched. "If that man has touched my fiancée…."

"Right," Rafe agreed. He knew how Monjoie felt, and his own spike of anger flared for a moment as he thought of Victor and Deor at the Proving. "But we've got a bigger problem. If the Summer Court has infiltrated your family, they can have free and easy reign of the coast, right?"

"Yes," Monjoie nodded. "We have ships that are..." He paused and stared at Rafe for a moment. "I trust you," he reminded Rafe. "We have warships. They all look like merchant ships, fishing boats, whatever, but we've got some in case the king ever decided to send the Admiral from Northfalls."

Rafe pinched the bridge of his nose. Caedmon was right, Monjoie and Rafe were brothers, and they had been pawns all along. "What a bloody mess."

"What are we going to do?"

"Break in, I suppose. Get a hold of that imposter and shake the glamour free." He watched Monjoie carefully. "Or we can head back to the capital city and keep disrupting the Summer Court soldiers there. Maybe we'll find allies."

"No." Monjoie shook his head. "Number one, I can't let my family think that's me. Number two, if the Summer Court hasn't already invaded Northfalls, it will soon. How much faster would a siege be broken if the Cote fleet came in support of the Summer Court?"

"Do you think your parents will be willing to betray Madeline?" Rafe said. "Harboring you is one thing. Fighting their own duchess is another."

"For bringing in the Summer Court? Probably. Though it's likely the death of Edgar that will send them over the edge. Edgar was far closer to our family than Madeline ever was. He came here a lot when I was younger, while I was being fostered and after. We did a lot of hunting in these woods."

"My father was like family to you." Rafe hadn't considered the emotional connection to Edgar that Monjoie and his family might have. A thrill of jealousy ran through him, followed hard by anger. How much love had Rafe lost? He barely knew who he was, even as he stood on his own duchy, the land's rage and indignation a constant hum in the back of his mind. Without Monjoie as a guide, Rafe would be lost—literally. He had no idea of the geography or the people. "Alright." He shook his head, clearing it. "I'll follow you. You know a way to sneak in?"

"Nope." Monjoie cast a glamour over himself so that he looked like an old man—rather like Caedmon. "We'll go in through the front door."

Rafe followed suit and cast a glamour, too, patterning it off Evelyn, minus the eye patch. It was easier to glamour what you knew. "Good enough?"

Monjoie put his hood up. "I think Evelyn would be insulted. He's much better looking."

Rafe laughed. "You make Caedmon look better." He put his hood up, too. "So, we're traveling bards?"

"Yep. Believe it or not, my dad studied at the University in Wellhall. He loves bardic stuff."

"Huh. Your family is a wealth of curiosities." Rafe sounded like he was cheerfully teasing, and he was. Except for the acute pang of guilt and stupidity for not bothering to find out about his soldiers' families. Monjoie had been in the guard for decades, like so many others, and he knew nothing beyond the dossiers Arthur produced. He followed Monjoie as they cut through the woods to the road leading up to the house.

31

Shortly after dawn, Deor woke from a fitful sleep to someone knocking at the door. Bernie, who had slept in bear form in case the Goblins had tried anything, raised up on his back legs and glanced through the peephole. He gave a nod and dropped back to the ground with a huff. Victor, clad in jeans and t-shirt from a band called Poets of the Fall, answered the door.

"Good morning," Deor heard Ivan's voice.

"Good morning, Ivan," Victor said as he stepped out of the way.

Ivan looked the same as he had when Deor met him at the Proving. He was lanky and tallish, with brown hair and sharp features. Seven vampires followed him into their room, crowding the space. They moved with quick grace, as predatory as they were casual, regardless of size or shape. They made no move at all to seem harmless, and Deor wondered how they could move through the human world unnoticed.

"Alright," Ivan said. "Come. Pair up with your new twin."

Everyone paired off like drawing straws. The vampires then hustled into the other room, eveningwear in hand, to change clothes.

"Once they are ready," Ivan said, "we will be heading out the back, through the staff entrance. As soon as we get out of here, I'll contact our people who are with the goblin crew, and they'll storm the building. I believe they've even got local police uniforms on."

The vampires reappeared dressed in the faerie formalwear.

"It is time for you faeries to go to work," Ivan said. "They are in the clothes, but now you must do the glamours."

"I can do that," Genevieve stepped forward. "I'm excellent at fashion glamours."

Once the vampires had been transformed, more or less, into faerie doppelgangers, Deor and her group were ready to go.

The werebears peered into the hall. "Clear," one of them called.

"Let's go." Ivan stepped into the hall and waved for them to follow.

Deor and the dogs were first out of the room, and Victor and Stephen were last. The whole thing felt like one of those action comedies where the main characters bumbled their way to success, more Inspector Gadget than James Bond.

They spilled out into the underground staff parking area, and Ivan clicked a button. A few feet away a large Cadillac Escalade beeped in response. Its twin sat next to it. They were black with windows tinted so heavily that Deor wondered how anyone saw out of them.

Ivan handed a second key to Bernie and waved them into the cars. "Lady Regent, you are with me. Sit in the back with your gentlemen and your dogs." He glanced at Bill—the only one who hadn't needed to change his clothes. "You are the least known to the goblins, so in front with me."

Deor touched Bill's shoulder and whispered, "Are you okay with that? Sitting so close to a vampire?"

"I'll be fine." Bill's face was a mask of stoicism.

"Someone else can sit in front—"

"No," Bill insisted and got in the car.

With much shifting and struggling, they managed to get everyone, including the dogs, into the cars. As they made their way out of the city, Ivan said, "It is about four hours to Prague. We'll stop there and then push on through Slovakia and Hungary." Deor knew enough modern geography to know that what he said was accurate. Vampire territory was roughly synonymous with Romania, though its borders had little to do with modern nations.

Victor slipped his arm around her shoulder as Bill and Ivan struck up a conversation in the front seat. "Why don't you lean on me and sleep?"

She fell asleep to the surrealism that was Bill and Ivan discussing nihilism.

Deor blinked and opened her eyes at Victor's nudging her.

"We're here," he said, and opened his door.

"Where is here?" Deor asked, following Victor as he climbed out.

"Somewhere outside Timisoara. Which is a city, I think."

They were in a small clearing in the woods. After they were all out of the cars, Bernie waved and he and Bob drove back the way they came. Ivan drove a bit further up the road, making a sharp left turn.

"What the hell?" Deor gasped. The car vanished. After a moment, she heard the engine cut out and the door open and close. Ivan stepped out from nothing.

"Vampire illusion," Ivan said. He spoke a few words in a language Deor didn't know, and a building appeared behind him. "Come," he said, waving them forward. "It is not much further, but we go on foot. Maybe thirty yards." He turned and continued into the woods. The dirt road big enough for a car dwindled to a path that two people could barely walk abreast.

Deor twined her fingers with Victor's. Was this the part in the story where they walked into an even worse trap? Deeper in the woods, they came to another clearing. "Here we are!" Ivan said. He barked something in Romanian, and a doorway appeared in the air. "Come, step through to my home. There are carriages waiting to carry us to the castle."

Deor stepped through first. The world swirled, as it so often did through a portal, and she was in a Gothic novel. The bright woods had turned dark, with swirling fog despite the midday. The trees were laden with dark green leaves on branches that twisted and jutted, draped in creepy moss and spiderwebs.

"Someone bought everything in the Halloween store," Bill whispered next to her.

Deor snickered.

Ahead of them, on a narrow road canopied with tree branches, two carriages waited, each led by two horses and topped with a driver in smart, black livery.

Ivan opened a carriage door. "My Lady Regent?" He bowed. Deor let him help her into the carriage, followed by Stephen, Victor, and the dogs. "I will see the others into their carriage," he said. Moments later he joined them again, shutting the door behind him.

The carriages jerked into motion, and Deor peered out the window as they wound their way up the mountainside to a large stone castle looming on the peak. Its towers pushed into swirling gray clouds, parting every now and again to give a glimpse of pale blue skies.

They rolled through the massive entrance, the sharp spikes of the portcullis overhead, and into a courtyard. Ivan hopped out and spun to face her, hand extended. "Shall we?" He helped her out of the carriage and up to the front door, which opened as they approached.

Deor stepped into the foyer expecting dim light and long shadows. Instead, she found a room filled with candelabra. A massive chandelier of crystals reflected its candles in dazzling brightness.

Waiting at the foot of a sweeping staircase were Donovan and Chloe. They were both dressed casually—him in leather pants and a t-shirt, her in jeans and the same. His brown hair was back in a long braid, and his eyes were bright. Chloe's brown eyes and dark skin glowed with warmth. Both Donovan and Chloe's fangs, white as alabaster, glinted in the light.

"Vlad Drogos," Deor nodded at Donovan, "and Lady Chloe, it is so good to see you again."

"Please, Lady Regent," Donovan said, stepping forward to embrace her, "call me Donovan." He let her go and Chloe stepped in for a hug.

"I love the fashion choice," Chloe said, nodding at Deor's t-shirt and jeans. "It suits you."

"Thank you."

"All of you are welcome in our home," Donovan said, bowing formally to her and to her Consort and Shield beside her.

"Thank you," Victor said, stepping forward and extending his hand. Donovan took it. Victor pulled him forward into a brief embrace. "We are in your debt."

Donovan patted Victor's shoulder with his free hand before letting go. "We are glad to help." He snapped his fingers, and servants appeared. "They will see you to your rooms," he said. "We have fresh clothes for you there," Chloe said. "And if you'll allow me, I'll do what I can to heal your wounds."

Deor would count the ensuing experience as one of the strangest in her life. Once in Deor's room, Chloe sat her down in a chair at a vanity. "Take off your shirt and bra," she said, standing behind her.

Deor did as she was told, watching Chloe in the mirror.

Chloe poked gently at the wound. "This isn't bad," she said. "I can fix it." She frowned slightly. "I don't think I can do anything about the lashes, though. Those are..." She shook her head. "I can't quite tell..."

"They're magic wounds," Deor said. "An angry king's magic is hard to undo."

"Right." Chloe met Deor's eyes in the mirror. "This won't hurt, but it will be weird. I'm going to lick your wounds."

Deor's jaw dropped, but she couldn't quite make words come out. She wanted to say *oh hell no*, but couldn't find a way to say that politely. So she managed a small, "Oh."

"Vampire saliva has healing properties. It's how we can bite through someone's jugular and they not bleed out."

Deor nodded.

Chloe rested her hands on Deor's shoulders. Faster than Deor could follow with her gaze, Chloe leaned down and traced her tongue across the wounds on Deor's back. Deor winced at the sensation and closed her eyes.

"All finished. You can open your eyes now."

Deor did. In the mirror, she saw Chloe wiping her mouth with the back of her hand and making a face. "Are you okay?"

"Yes," Chloe said. "You taste like faerie, which is gross. It isn't great for vampires. It makes us woozy."

"I didn't know."

Chloe shrugged. "No big deal. I didn't get a lot, and the human in you tempers it some." She patted Deor's shoulders. "You're all healed up. There are clothes in the closet. It's been a long few days, so get some rest. We'd like you and your friends to come to a reception and meal tomorrow."

"That would be lovely," Deor said, and mostly meant it.

"Good. The reception is at 3 pm. The servants will see to anything you need tonight or tomorrow morning." She smiled once more and left.

Moments later, Victor came in.

"Are you alright?" She asked.

"That was the weirdest, most..." He shuddered. "I've never been licked by a vampire before."

"Yeah. That wasn't on my bucket list either. We've got time to rest before the reception tomorrow. We need to call the palace and let them know we're safe."

"Good idea." Victor handed her his mirror.

Deor tapped the mirror. It swirled a moment before Bartholomew's face came into view, more purple than usual, and nearly filling the screen. Behind him, Deor could just see Astarte, looking equally distressed.

"Where are you?" Bartholomew demanded without even so much as a hello. "King Gregory mirrored and said you went on some kind of murderous rampage and fled into the night. I knew it was hogwash, but I was afraid he had you killed."

"They were planning on holding us prisoner and turning me over to the Summer Court. We escaped."

"Where are you now?" Astarte insisted.

"We're safe." Deor assured them. "I asked Donovan for help, and he gave it. We're at the Vlad's home now."

Bartholomew's shoulders slumped in relief. "They might be scary as hell, but they've always proven to be trustworthy. When can you come home?"

"Whenever I like, I think. They're having a reception and dinner for us tomorrow. I feel like we've got an opportunity here. Gregory contacted Donovan before I could and asked him to capture us. The vampires double-crossed Geoff to help us. They may be willing to stand with us now."

"It's worth a shot," Bartholomew said.

"I'll call you tomorrow, after I've had a chance to speak with the Vlad." Deor ended the call.

32

R afe and Monjoie made their way to the front door. "You're sure you don't have some kind of long-lost twin, right?" Rafe asked.

"I'm sure. Ready?" Monjoie didn't wait for an answer, just pushed the bell.

A few moments later the door opened. The butler smiled when he saw them. "Bards at our doorstep? What a day it has been." He sounded bitter.

"I was wondering if I could speak to Henri," Monjoie said smoothly. "I hope we aren't intruding."

"Not at all!" The middle-aged man, lean and wiry, shook his head.

Even if Rafe hadn't known there was something wrong, he'd have figured it out from this guy's behavior. He was twitchy and shaky, clearly pretending to be okay. Rafe caught Monjoie's eye—he saw it too. The butler stepped back and waved them in.

"They are in the parlor." He closed the door and moved to guide them.

The inside of the manor house was lovely, soft, and warm. A staircase led upward, while the entrances to the two wings of the house were on either side. The butler led them to the right, down a hallway with a stone floor made plush with rugs. He rapped once on the door of the parlor and opened it. "Pardon me, sir," he said, sticking his head in the doorway. "Two bards have come to speak to you."

Rafe and Monjoie exchanged glances as they were ushered into the room Rafe had seen in Caedmon's scrying bowl. In person, the room was brighter, the dark wood lit by the warm crackling fire. The windows were open, too, letting in the cool evening air.

Monjoie Two sat on the smaller of two couches with Juliette, holding her hand. Henri stood by the fire while his wife sat on another sofa. Two faeries were sitting with her, while the other two stood chatting with Henri by the fireplace. All of them were in the dressed-down version of the uniforms.

"Welcome!" Henri said brightly. "It's been a long while since we've had visitors from the university!"

"Thank you for your hospitality," Rafe said after Monjoie hesitated a moment too long.

"What brings you here?" Monjoie Two stood, smiling. There was an unfriendly glint in his eye, and he still held Juliette's hand. Even knowing the man wasn't Monjoie, Rafe was almost fooled. Something hummed in his mind, suggesting that the real Monjoie—the fake bard next to him—wasn't real. The magic was so subtle that it didn't feel like magic at all, more like an obvious truth. Rafe swallowed hard and forced himself to try to see beyond the glamour. He couldn't pierce it, and trying was drawing beads of sweat along his scalp.

"We know that Master Henri has always been a friend to bards from the university. We were heading for the capital city, but we traveled more slowly than we had hoped."

"Are you looking to stay the night?" The Summer Court soldier in charge stepped away from the fireplace toward them.

"No, no," Rafe said. "We were hoping for a bite of food. The weather is lovely for walking, even in the evening, and we had planned to camp."

"I see." The Summer Court soldier came to face him. "I am Velasco," he said with a nod. "And you are?"

"Caedmon," Monjoie said cheerfully.

"Evelyn," Rafe said.

"My," Velasco said, coming closer to Rafe. He was tall with olive skin, black hair, and copper eyes. He had the inquisitive, untrusting look of a soldier who had sussed out more than one lie, or one spy. "That is an interesting walking stick." He reached for the shell dangling from the top of the stick.

"Careful!" Rafe jerked it back right as Velasco was about to touch it. "It's iron." It would be silly to lie. "A pilgrim's badge," he said, repeating the lesson Aelfburga had given him. "From the human world—it's quite old. A totem for good luck on the road."

"Iron as good luck?" Velasco raised an eyebrow.

"Strange, I know," Rafe admitted with a chuckle. "But what better way to warn off any danger than with a bit of iron?"

"What kind of bard are you?" Velasco asked.

"Old manuscripts," Rafe blurted out. "I study old fae and human manuscripts."

"Human?" He raised an eyebrow.

"That's a more recent study, I admit." Rafe inclined his head. "What with the new heir, I thought it might be wise to study up."

Velasco laughed. "She might not be a problem much longer."

Rafe flinched slightly. "Oh?" He looked around the room. "I'm not much of a follower of politics." He dropped his gaze as if embarrassed.

"I remember being at uni," Henri interrupted. "It was very easy to forget the world outside its walls." He came up to Rafe, giving a sidelong glance to Velasco. "You are welcome here, friend." He glanced at Monjoie. "Both of you." He looked back to Monjoie Two. "Come over here, my boy!"

Monjoie Two let go of Juliette's hand and crossed the room to Henri. "Welcome," he said to Rafe and the real Monjoie. "My father often spoke about his time at the university. He even took me to visit once when I was in my teens."

"Is that so?" Rafe smiled. He glanced at Monjoie, who stared at the statement but recovered quickly. Monjoie Two must have told the truth. The question then became, how did he know?

"What building are you both in?" Monjoie Two asked.

"Featherwave Hall," Monjoie said. "Near the library."

"Oh, that's my favorite building on campus!" Henri said, beaming. "It's the one that's got a pub in the basement." He chuckled. "I spent a bit too much time there, I think."

Rafe and Monjoie dutifully laughed, but Rafe couldn't take his eyes off what looked like a perfect clone of Monjoie. And now, up close, the sense that Rafe should believe this imposter was Monjoie was strong enough that the dissonance made his head ache.

"So," Monjoie Two continued, "what do you at the university think of the duchess's political move of late?"

Velasco raised an eyebrow and the three other soldiers shifted in their seats, readying themselves to stand. Rafe was sure he and Monjoie could take them, even if they weren't buying the bard schtick.

"I believe the duchess has never wavered in her care for Wellhall," Monjoie said. "Truth be told, I am a child of this area," he went on. "I grew up near the city of Cote."

"Oh?" Henri said. "Do we know your family?"

"No." Monjoie shook his head. "My family didn't run in your circles, sir." He smiled genially.

Henri nodded. "Alas, I don't know every family that lives here."

"So," Rafe said, watching Monjoie Two, "how was growing up here on the coast?"

"Delightful," the impostor said. "I spent a lot of time playing in the surf." He glanced lovingly over his shoulder at Juliette. "We'd play in the tide pools for hours."

Juliette laughed. "Yes. We both came home a mess of sand and seaweed. I think that's where..." She trailed off, her eyes becoming distant. "Where..."

"We fell in love," Monjoie Two finished for her. He returned to her side and took her hand. "Are you feeling well, *bécasseau?*"

Monjoie stiffened and jerked forward a tiny bit. Rafe caught his arm. Thankfully, with eyes on the loving couple, no one seemed to notice.

Juliette frowned. "I must be tired. Perhaps I should go to bed."

"That sounds like a good idea." Monjoie Two helped her to her feet. He kissed her gently on the lips and hugged her. He whispered something no one else could hear in her ear as he held her. She shivered briefly—a flash of movement. From the tension in Monjoie's body, Rafe knew he saw it too. When she was released from the hug, Juliette beamed at Monjoie Two, all concern, even signs of fatigue, wiped away.

"That's it," Monjoie muttered.

Rafe didn't bother trying to stop him. He brought his staff round, ready for the fight.

Monjoie shook himself, sending the magic of the glamour off him in pieces. "I don't know who the hell you are," he said striding across the room, "but get your hands off my fiancée!"

Monjoie Two gaped and pushed Juliette behind him. "Who the hell are you?" he said. He looked to Henri. "See?! Madeline was right to warn you about spies trying to take advantage of me being missing." He uttered a few words under his breath and a burst of magic hit Rafe and Monjoie.

Rafe's glamour shattered like glass. The rest of the Summer Court soldiers leapt to their feet.

"The Sword himself," Velasco sneered at Rafe. "Quite the prize. I'll take your head back to the duchess and my Sword."

"You can try," Rafe said.

"He looks the spitting image of my son!" Henri said, staring at the man who was in fact his son.

"Stay back, father," Monjoie said. He raised his weapon toward the imposter. "I'm the real Luc Monjoie!" Monjoie cried. "I don't know what kind of magic you're using, but you are not me!"

Monjoie Two drew a dagger and waved it at Monjoie. "Pretender. Traitor! Aligning with the King's pampered boy." He charged Monjoie and the two met. Monjoie struck back, knocking the dagger away, but not disarming him. At the same time, Velasco and two others came for Rafe. He threw magic at them, a spray of ice shards that caught the two soldiers in the eyes, sending them flailing. Velasco, though, produced a puff of red-hot flame, dissolving the shards into steam. "Great," Rafe muttered. "A fire faerie."

Rafe swung his staff low, knocking Velasco's feet from under him. He held the sharp tip over the man's throat. The three other Summer Court soldiers froze. "That's right," Rafe said quietly. "We're all going to stand here and let those two figure out who's who." He pointed his chin at the two Monjoies, both with daggers, swinging at each other.

As the two of them lunged and parried, punched and dodged, Rafe saw faint trails of magic coming off the fake one, wisps of iridescent sheen. The two men's fight brought them closer to Rafe, and soon Monjoie Two was within arm's reach.

Rafe gasped as he was hit with the magic aura that surrounded the double. Once again, his mind reeled as his brain tried to hold on to what he knew to be true though the very fiber of his being wanted to believe the imposter was real. He drew a deep breath. The magic that wrapped Monjoie Two was not just a glamour, it was will magic. He'd never heard of a glamour being a conduit for such power. Then again, if anyone would figure out how to do it, it would be his mother. But underneath the magic demanding that he believe his eyes, not his brain, he felt something else, too. This man before him was powerful, respectable, worthy of leading. In fact, not only should Rafe believe him, but he should defer to him, too.

"The Enemy," Rafe whispered, a light dawning. That desire to succumb was a shadow of what he felt when the Enemy was choking the life out of him.

Monjoie Two swiped at Monjoie's midsection with his dagger, and Monjoie barely dodged.

Rafe looked at the man pinned on the ground.

He smirked up at him. "You're not going to win," he said, voice soft. "No one can resist that magic. Even his fiancée believes."

Rafe snorted and drove his sword into the man's throat. Warm blood fountained up, spattering across his robe as he withdrew the blade and spun on the fake Monjoie. But he did not swing his sword. Instead, he lashed out with his staff.

The iron scallop bound to the staff's tip caught the imposter across the face. The blow was hard enough to knock a man back, and the fake stumbled, doubling over and clutching the side of his head. He righted himself and glared at Rafe. A scallop-shaped hole in the glamour marred his features.

Monjoie hollered and flung himself forward, grabbing the man by the head and digging his fingers into the edges of the broken magic.

Rafe spun to face the three Summer Court soldiers. He swung the staff again, connecting with the scallop and knocking one to the floor. He slicked the ground under the other two, sending them tumbling. Behind him, Monjoie and the fake struggled.

"Take that!" A woman's voice cried out, followed by a heavy thud. Rafe turned.

Juliette stood over the prone body of the fake, fireplace poker in hand. The magic was dripping off him now, revealing a man that looked in passing like Monjoie, but not much more—certainly not enough to be mistaken for Monjoie by those who knew him.

Rafe readied his staff as the two conscious Summer Court faeries came at him. They exchanged glances and bolted for the door.

"Oh no," Monjoie said, flinging his dagger and catching one in the back of the neck. The man dropped.

Rafe sprinted and caught the last of the fleeing men in the head with the staff. His skull cracked and he fell in a heap.

Monjoie turned to Juliette. *"Bécasseau?"*

She dropped the poker and ran to him, flinging herself into his arms. *"Huîtrier!"* After a few moments clinging to him, she stepped back. "What happened to you?" She looked at Rafe. "Why are you with him? Is that really the Sword?"

"Father, Mother, Juliette, let me present to you Rafael Lord Farringdon, heir to Wellhall." Monjoie said, glancing at Rafe. "And Rafe," he paused a moment after using his first name, "these are my parents, Henri and Cossette, and my fiancée, Juliette."

"It is an honor to meet you," Rafe said, bowing slightly.

Cossette hurried to Monjoie, laying a hand on his face. "You're home safe." She hugged him. She turned to Rafe. "Thank you, Lord Farringdon, for bringing our son to us."

Rafe laughed. "I didn't bring him here. We came together." He caught Monjoie's eye. "Brothers-in-arms."

The man on the floor stirred and Juliette snatched up the poker ready to swing.

"Woah, woah!" Rafe said.

Monjoie gently caught her arm before she could pummel the guy. Rafe didn't doubt for a moment that she'd kill him, given the chance. He did not blame her. "He might be worth talking to," Monjoie said. "Since we dispatched the others." Monjoie knelt next to the man and uttered a few words. The man fell unconscious again.

He stood and turned to his parents. "Mother? Father?"

Henri embraced his son. "I don't know why we believed he was you. Looking at him now, I don't see how we possibly could!"

"What ugly magic," Juliette said softly. "If Madeline can do that, I don't know how anyone stands against her."

"We'll find a way," Rafe said darkly.

"I must ask, Lord Farringdon," Cossette said plainly, "why are you here? Why now? And why are you in the company of my son?"

"Both of us were washed into the Thames when Finn—I mean the King—escaped from the palace at Madeline's attempted coup. We both fell from Faerie into an in-between kind of place." He looked to Monjoie.

"It's hard to put into words," Monjoie said. "We were both badly wounded, and the monks healed us. While there Rafe and I found common ground. There are things more important than the fight between our foster parents."

"Both of whom are terrible," Rafe said with more anger than he meant to let out. "My mother, the King, they kept me away from my family, from my brother. Neither of them are fit to rule."

"The duchess has always done well by us!" Henri insisted. "Even when the rest of the Winter Court—"

"Was failing. I know." Rafe nodded. "But as far as I understand it, she made some sort of deal with the Summer Court and now allows them to occupy Wellhall. We freed three men from the stocks in the city square. D'nath himself is in the palace with her."

"She murdered Edgar," Monjoie said.

"What?" Monjoie's mother gasped.

"That's what one of the people in the city said," Monjoie added. "I've got no reason to disbelieve her. I cannot imagine that Edgar would stand for this invasion. He, like most of us, hates the King, but I can't ever see him helping the Winter Court become a Summer Court puppet. Even if it meant his wife was on the throne."

"I agree," Henri said. "Edgar loved Wellhall and the Winter Court. Madeline loves power."

"Have you told the Regent you're here?" Juliette asked.

"No," Rafe said.

"Don't you think you should?" Juliette asked. "She notified me when she found out that you and Monjoie had been washed into the Thames."

Rafe managed not to snort in derision. The last time he'd seen the Regent, she'd looked like she was faring just fine without him. "I think," he said slowly, "that I can do more good here in secret than in the spotlight back in the palace."

Monjoie nodded. "I agree. No one can know that he's here—or that the man who showed up here wasn't me."

The door opened, and the butler came in. "The evening paper—" He froze, staring at the bodies. He looked up at Rafe and then to Henri.

"Come in, Valois. That man," he pointed to the slumbering faux Monjoie, "was an imposter. My real son is home. And he's brought a friend."

Valois stepped into the room and closed the door behind him. "The evening paper, sir." He handed it to Henri. "There's a very interesting front page." He bowed to Rafe. "Your Lordship." He looked to Monjoie. "That man didn't feel like you, Luc, not a bit. But every time I was close to him…"

"It felt like doubting him was stupid," Juliette finished, kicking the man for good measure.

"Like I was failing at my job," Valois said, nodding.

"So, were you boys busy before you got here?" Henri said with a smile as he held up the evening paper. *Ghost frees loyalists from stocks, slays Summer Court soldiers.*

"That was us," Monjoie said, taking the paper from his father. "Huh," he said as he skimmed the page. "It appears that the rumor is that there is only one figure—a ghost." He looked up at Rafe with a wicked grin. "Who knows where the Ghost will strike next?"

"Do you think that there are people here who object to the Summer Court occupation? Who would be willing to participate in some guerilla warfare, perhaps?" Rafe asked.

"Oh, I know it, Your Lordship," Valois said. He then cringed. "Begging your pardon for interrupting."

Rafe had to put a stop to this, and fast. "Please," he said to all of them, "call me Rafe." When he saw the wide-eyed stares from all but Monjoie, he sighed. "I'm not the Sword anymore. I'm certainly not the King's boy." He grimaced. "The truth is, I don't know who I am. But when my mother let the Summer Court into Wellhall I felt it. And it hurt. It still hurts."

"The land hates it," Henri nodded.

"That's good to know," Rafe said. "So please, right now, all that matters is saving Wellhall, right here, right now. If that means the Winter Court, too, then that's great."

"The Winter Court needs saving," Juliette said. "The invasion didn't just happen here. There's an attack on Northfalls too."

"Don't tell me Roger let the Summer Court in?" Rafe said, a wave of despair flooding him.

"Heavens no!" Henri said. "That man may be a King's loyalist, but he's no traitor to the Winter Court. Northfalls is under siege. Apparently, the Summer Court Sword has suggested to the Regent that she surrender."

Rafe snorted. "She's not the surrendering type."

"I'm not so sure," Monjoie said softly.

"What?" Rafe turned on him.

Monjoie held up his hands. "I don't mean that she'd give in or sell out the Winter Court. In the Tower, when the King had Victor tortured in front of her, when he... you know..." He glanced at his parents and fiancée and then continued. "He told her that being the monarch was important, and sometimes other people had to die for them. Victor told her that too. Arthur scolded her, warning her that people were getting hurt because of her."

"And?" Rafe felt his temperature rise.

"She doesn't want people to suffer because of her. Even after she was hurt by Finn the second time, she insisted that Asphodel tend to her dog before she'd let Asphodel touch her."

"And?" Rafe repeated. The image of Deor, bleeding, insisting that the dog got help first was unsurprising.

"I imagine D'nath's threats were pretty frightening and unlikely to be empty. She might surrender if she thinks it is the only way to keep people from dying."

"You're right," Rafe conceded. "So, we've got to give her reason to think we can win." He chuckled darkly. "It's just like Evelyn's song—time to bring hell for them, so it won't be for us."

33

The next afternoon, servants escorted Deor and her companions to the reception. The obsequious and fawning nature of the servants made Deor twitch, but that wasn't a problem for now. Deor, Victor, Stephen, and Genevieve were going to the reception. Bill, Gordie, and Melanie remained behind with the dogs.

The clothes Deor had been given fit well, both in size and style. Dark gray slacks, a black sweater, and a nice pair of three-inch black heels to make her not feel like she was in a world of giants. Donovan was dressed as he had been the first time she met him. Black leather pants and boots and a linen shirt strikingly similar to Ivan's. Chloe, on the other hand, looked like a femme fatale from a noir novel. She stood almost as tall as Donovan, and she wore a tight, deep green velvet dress that clung to her every curve, with a deep vee neckline and off-the-shoulder long sleeves. At her throat was a choker of rubies the size of dimes with a huge one set in gold in the center. Earrings matched. Her hair was free in spirals around her face.

The faeries followed Donovan and Chloe through the foyer and into a medium-sized hall. There, a number of vampires had gathered. They watched her closely as she came in, still as the dead. Deor had a similar sensation once, in a natural history museum, walking through a display of predators. A single hall led through the gallery, each side lined with apex predators, each seemingly eyeing the museum's guests.

At the end of the crowd stood the Vlad himself and his wife. As Deor and her companions reached them, they each gave a small bow.

The Vlad wore a rich, deep red kaftan that fell below his knees. Gold brocade in elaborate vines decorated the rich fabric. Onyx clasps held the kaftan closed from the neck down to the waist. He wore loose-fitting black pants and fine black shoes.

He, like Donovan, was built like a brick. Broad shoulders with a slightly narrower waist, square jaw, and hands the size of dinner plates made him look like a boxer. Fangs, the longest she'd seen yet, reminded her that he was far from human.

Next to him, his wife Yessina was the picture of opposites. She was petite, with pale skin and long red hair. She had been a commoner, according to Victor's recounting of the vampire history as they dressed. A girl who lived in the village at the base of the castle, a human part of the magical realm of the vampires, who stole the Vlad's heart when he was a young man, not yet Vlad and not even heir. Yessina was pretty, vibrant, but not soft or beautiful. Her thinness was rangy, like she spent a child-hood on a farm, or running through the tight woods that surrounded the castle. Her dress was deep blue, elegant, and playful. It fit perfectly, but was in the style of a simple peasant dress, with long sleeves, a sweetheart neckline, and a lightly flowing skirt. What was neither simple nor plain was her jewelry. There was enough to drown a horse. Strings of gems around her neck and wrists, dazzling diamonds in her ears, and rings of precious metals and jewels around her fingers.

"It is an honor to meet you, Your Majesties," Deor said with another curtsy.

"We are not majesties," the Vlad scolded playfully. "You may call me Vlad and my wife Yessina. We are delighted to have you as guests."

"I am so excited to be here," Deor said, and meant it. Vampires had fascinated her as a child, and more than once she'd read the kind of novel that young women read about the kind of vampires that are nine parts monster and one part hero, once they meet the right girl, of course. Terri-fying and seductive, dangerous to everyone but the heroine. Bill had chided her more than once about her taste for dashing, trouble-making men. In his defense, she had yet to break the pattern. So despite the current mess, that teenage girl inside her was as thrilled as could be.

"One moment," Vlad said. "Vashti!" He yelled, voice booming with both volume and power enough to make the faeries wince in unison. "Now!"

A woman sauntered through the parting crowd.

"That's Vlad's youngest," Victor whispered to her.

"Ah." Deor could see that well enough. Red hair, though darker than her mother's, but the same square jaw as her father in feminine form. She dressed like Donovan in leather pants and a more fitted, but still piratey white shirt. The laces were open allowing sight of her cleavage. Like Donovan she broadcast killer. Unlike anyone else there, she smoked. A thin white cigarette, its tip alternatingly flared to bright orange or faded to ash, dangled from her lips. She casually took it out and blew smoke into the air.

"I am here, Father. There is no need to shout." Her voice was sharp like shattered glass and a small *pop* of power filled the air as she spoke, clearly directed at her father. To his credit, Vlad's smile didn't break, but Deor did notice the vein in his left temple throb a bit. "I would never miss a chance to meet the Princess."

"Regent," Vlad corrected, voice low. Any teenager, and that's what Vashti resembled more than anything, would read that as a distinct warning to tread very lightly, to get into line, immediately.

"My apologies," Vashti said to her father with no apology whatsoever in her voice. Before he could respond she slipped the cigarette back into her mouth, turned to Deor, and held out her hand. "I am Vashti, daughter of Vlad."

Deor shook it. "I'm Deor," she said. "Daughter of Fionnleigh." Something about the young woman made Deor smile. Whatever it was, it was the same thing that told her that Vashti, no matter her numerical age, was still a young woman, old enough to chafe under her father's eye and to do whatever she could to annoy him.

They stood for a moment, hands clasped, sizing each other up. Finally, Vashti broke into a huge grin. She dropped Deor's hand and looped her arm through Deor's. "I'm so glad you're here! We're going to be best friends!" she trilled. "Dinner's on. Shall we?" She caught her cigarette in her free hand, took another drag, and dropped it on the beautiful Turkish rug, crushing it out with the toe of her shiny leather boot.

Deor glanced at Vlad, who was frowning sternly in the way only a long-suffering father could. He met her gaze and sighed, relenting. "Yes," he said. "Please to dinner." He gestured at a doorway in the direction that Vashti was pulling.

Deor nodded and let Vashti lead her into the dining room.

The dining room was filled with light, like the foyer, Deor realized, despite the lack of windows. A long deep brown table was set with fine china and silver. There were small cards with names on them at each place. Vlad sat at one end, with his wife on his right. Victor had been placed on his left. Donovan sat at the other end of the table, with Chloe at his right, Genevieve next to her, and then Stephen between her and Yessina. On his left sat Vashti, and then Deor. On Deor's other side was Ivan, between her and Victor.

The first course came, a soup, and only four bowls were presented— for the faeries. The rest of the vampires were served thick red liquid from decanters. Blood. Deor looked down at her soup. Chunks of sad gray meat floated among pale vegetables. She could tell by looking it would have no flavor whatsoever. She glanced up to see all of the people at the table staring at her. She smiled brightly, took up her spoon, and ate a bite. "Lovely!" she managed.

The food wasn't bad, though it seemed the only technique their chef had mastered was boiling. They had boiled soup. Boiled steak and pota- toes, and some kind of boiled pudding.

The conversation was delightful. It wasn't awkward, as she feared, though Deor spent most of her time talking to Vashti about the human world. She apparently had always wanted to visit California. Donovan had, and it was only fair that she get to as well.

"When you're older," Yessina said, overhearing Vashti. "Your aunt can be," she cast a sidelong glance at Chloe, "difficult."

Chloe laughed. "Yes, my mother can be quite frightening. But Vashti is a young woman, and my mother reserves her ire primarily for men. And she's even grown to like Donovan." She smiled, full-fanged, at her husband.

Donovan nodded. "I met Chloe in San Francisco. I was traveling with Geoff, he thought for his amusement, but I was there to try to meet my aunt, who hadn't seen anyone in our family for over a century. Chloe found me and took me to meet her."

"He couldn't take his eyes off me," Chloe said with a smirk.

"It's true. So I convinced her to come home with me, just to see the land where her mother came from, and she did. We married here." He took her hand and kissed it. "Alas, her mother has not quite forgiven me."

"You married your cousin?" Deor said, attempting nonchalant. Cousin marriages weren't uncommon in the past century, and maybe they didn't matter with vampires.

"Of a sort," Donovan said. "My mother and aunt are made vampires.

My father and I, most all the vampires here, are born. Chloe's mother didn't give birth to her, she made her. So, not cousins in the way you mean."

Deor nodded. "That's very sweet."

Vlad arched an eyebrow. "I think you are the first faerie to describe our breeding as *sweet*."

"Everyone else has kids that way," Deor said with a shrug. "Why shouldn't vampires?"

The vampires nodded, and the conversation moved along to some of the ways that the vampires lived. Deor noticed that Genevieve was in a particularly involved and quiet conversation with Chloe and didn't interrupt.

Suddenly, Deor felt a hand on her thigh. She glanced at Ivan, who was eyeing her with the most smoldering gaze she'd ever seen. She gently took his hand from her thigh and set it in his lap. After a few minutes, the situation recurred. This time, Deor not only moved his hand but said, "Ivan, please don't do that." She spoke quietly, and no one else seemed to hear.

"Are you sure?" he replied, his voice equally low. She shivered at the promise in it. His voice didn't hold any kind of compulsion or will magic, only the low purr that warmed her cheeks and dared her to give him a try. He placed his hand on her thigh again.

Deor stilled. No one around the table noticed. They were all merrily chatting away. She glanced again at Ivan, who watched her, a small smile on his lips. "These are not my pants, Ivan. I'd rather not ruin them."

He frowned, confused. "My hand won't soil them."

"I know," she conceded. "But blood will." She concentrated on her thigh, on the spot where his hand touched her. She pushed a pulse of magic, and a spike shot out, through his hand.

Ivan gasped and his eyes widened.

Deor set down her dessert spoon and slid her hand under the table. She grabbed the blade where it stuck out of his hand, and gently curved it, so that the tip now pointed toward his hand. He could yank his hand up, but he'd lose a lot of flesh and bone doing it.

As the meal came to a close some thirty minutes later, Deor looked at Vlad. "Thank you so much for your hospitality." She set her napkin on the table. "I hope it wouldn't offend you if we retired for the evening. I hope I'll get a chance to talk to you more tomorrow?"

"No offense at all!" Vlad's eyes sparkled as he said it. "Of course, we'll have time to chat tomorrow."

"Thank you," Deor said. She drew in a deep breath and with it the magic flowing through the spike in her leg, shrinking the blade and drawing it back into herself. Ivan let out a small sigh and jerked his hand back to his own lap, not raising it above the table. Deor pushed back from the table and stood.

Vashti rose and gave Deor another hug. "I'll see you tomorrow!" She let go, glanced at the blood on Deor's pants, smirked, and walked away.

The rest rose as well, and Victor, Stephen, and Genevieve joined her.

"Don't say anything!" Deor whispered when the three saw the blood on her. "It isn't mine. I'll tell you once we're out of here."

They nodded. They bade the vampires goodnight and followed a servant to their rooms.

"What the hell is that!" Victor said, pointing at her leg.

"Ivan's blood." Deor frowned as she kicked off her heels and stripped off her pants. "I think there's no salvaging them," she said sadly.

"Good thing they gave us more than one set of clothes." Stephen pointed out. "How did you get Ivan's blood on them?"

She explained what happened, ending "I think it was a test. Vlad wanted to see how I'd react. Who knows if I passed or not."

"I noticed Ivan seemed a little stiff during dessert," Victor said.

"What were they testing?" Genevieve asked. "It couldn't possibly be manners, could it?"

"No idea," Deor said. "But I can't imagine Vlad would put me in a situation to be sexually harassed without his knowing about it. And no one said anything about it, even though they saw the blood. Vashti just smirked at me."

"We'll figure it out tomorrow," Victor said.

"Yes." Deor smiled. "And I imagine it will be just as fun as tonight!"

34

Rafe stared at Monjoie Two. He was bound, hand and foot, with iron chains. Otherwise, Henri's office, with a desk, some bookshelves, and a worn wingback chair in front of a small fireplace, was comfortable. A "place to talk" in the palace would have been far less friendly. Rafe didn't ask Monjoie where he got the iron chains, or why his family had some. Being prepared, he guessed.

Rafe sat on the desk, staring at the man a couple yards away. Monjoie was on his feet in front of the impostor, glaring down at him. "Do you have a name?"

"Of course, I do." Monjoie Two said, grinning.

Monjoie backhanded him, snapping his head to the side. "Care to share?"

The man winced, but his smirk didn't change. "I don't think you need to know it."

Rafe stood and caught Monjoie's arm before he could hit the man again. "You're right," Rafe said. "We don't need to know it. You're a Summer Court faerie. Probably from the south, judging by your complexion and accent. I'm less interested in who you are than I am in the magic you used."

"Clever trick, isn't it?"

"It is." Rafe reached out and touched the man's face. He flinched but held steady. "I'm not going to hurt you." Rafe concentrated. There wasn't an iota of magic left on him. The iron would hold down the man's abilities, but it wouldn't mask spells. "All the magic is gone."

"Yes." He nodded. "As untraceable as it is irresistible, especially among those willing to believe." He leaned to the side so he could look Monjoie in the face. "And boy, did Juliette want to believe I was you."

Rafe spun and caught Monjoie as he lunged at the man. "Easy," Rafe spoke low and calm, but without any magic. "He's needling you."

"I know," Monjoie said through gritted teeth. "But he put his hands on Juliette." Monjoie looked up at Rafe. "Think about how you felt just a few days ago."

"I wanted to punch somebody—my brother specifically. And it was clear there was consent." Rafe remembered the way that it felt, seeing Deor with Victor. They didn't know, not for sure, what had passed between this impostor and Juliette, but Rafe could imagine. "He will pay, Luc. I promise. But right now..."

Monjoie jolted at Rafe's use of his first name. "Right now, we need information," he said without meeting Rafe's gaze. He held still, staring at the man. He shifted his gaze to Rafe's. "When we've got what we need..."

"When we've got what we need," Rafe said with a nod, "you can gut him however you like."

"I'll do one worse than that," Monjoie said with a smile. "I'll let Juliette at him."

Rafe let go of Monjoie and turned to their captive. "So," he crossed his arms. "Where were we? Ah, yes. The glamour you used."

"That magic is nothing you've ever seen before!" he said with glee. "It's irresistible power, beyond your imagination."

"So you've said," Rafe shrugged. "Except we resisted."

"Well," he stammered. "I mean, he's Monjoie."

"He is. The real one." Rafe walked in a wide circle around the man. "You're wrong, by the way, that I've never seen that magic before. I have. We both have, Luc and I."

"Liar." The man spat on the floor.

"No." Rafe paused next to the man and looked at Monjoie.

"The Enemy." Monjoie said. "That's what it felt like, on a much smaller scale."

Rafe leaned down. "Whatever touched you, it's evil. Not petty hatred or political rivalry. Life-destroying evil."

"Hah," the man said, though he seemed unsure.

"You had to have known that," Rafe said. "I can't imagine what it was like, living all the time with that magic clinging to you. Could you even have taken it off if you'd wanted to?"

"Why would I want to?" he snapped. "But of course I could. I wasn't a slave." As soon as the word was out of his mouth, the man gasped.

Rafe shook his head. "You let them put it on you willingly, but you'd never have gotten it off, gotten away from the wretched stench of it, without someone else's help. Now." Rafe knelt down in front of him. "Tell me how it worked."

"I don't know," he whispered. "Really, I don't. I went into the duchess's workroom with her. Someone else was there too, but I can't remember their face. They spoke to me. I couldn't hear it, but I could feel it." The man was shaking now.

"It's alright," Rafe said, and put a hand on the man's shoulder.

"No," He shook his head. "It's not. It hurt."

"You're safe here." Rafe said.

"No." The man was trembling from head to foot now, some kind of fit. "She said this would happen." Tears poured down his face. "She said if I tried to tell anyone…"

"Tell anyone what?" Rafe kept his voice low, conversational. "No one can hurt you here. Trust me."

The man barked out a laugh. "No one is safe." He squirmed and jerked. "She's in my mind. They both are." His eyes widened. "They know I'm made." He whimpered. "She told me not to worry. She told me it wouldn't hurt." He struggled, thrashing, and Rafe scrambled away from him. "She lied." He let out a terrible scream, blood pouring from his nose, his eyes, his ears.

"Gods above," Monjoie said as he grabbed Rafe's arm, pulling him further back.

The terrible, throat-rending scream died away, and the man was dead.

"Have you ever seen this before?" Rafe asked Monjoie. "Maybe working with Arthur?"

"No." He gaped. "Never. We caught various spies. Most of them didn't know much of anything beyond the bare necessity to do their job. There have been spies that have killed themselves rather than be interrogated, but this?" He shook his head. "No. It's like there was a magic bomb in his head that triggered when he started to tell us things."

"If my mother and D'nath have the power to do this—" Rafe said.

"We're all in deep trouble."

219

"Not just us," Rafe said thoughtfully. "Not just Wellhall, or even the Winter Court. All of Fae."

"You really think it was the Enemy?" Monjoie asked.

"Yes." Rafe nodded. "My mother couldn't do that, no one can, not on their own."

"So now what?" Monjoie asked.

"Now we see what your family knows." Rafe stared at the bloody mess that was a man before him. He'd said that Madeline lied. That seemed to be the one truth about her. That, and her willingness to kill anyone who got in her way.

35

Deor sat up in bed when the first hint of sunlight filtered through the bedroom window. She'd already been awake for a while, but now that it was at least a bit light, she could get up. Next to her, Victor slept, curled up in a ball, back to her. He had fallen asleep only after he had taken something Donovan had given him. Even that had taken a long time to work.

In his sleep, his features were soft and smooth, his body taking a break from displaying the pain of the past few weeks. She knew from experience that grief was exhausting work. Eventually, a body simply couldn't cry anymore, no matter how depthless the well of tears felt. Sleep was a collapse. In the dim light, she could see movement under Victor's eyelids. REM sleep meant dreams, and she didn't envy him his.

She had wept with him, often silently, with tears running down her cheeks. After he slept, her tears continued. Did she weep for the loss she had suffered? Or for the ones that she knew were coming? Either way, she wept for herself. Why was she the one who had to make the choices, all bad ones, of what to do? Why had it come to her? She wasn't qualified to lead a country in a war. She wasn't qualified to lead at all. The stupidity of monarchy, she thought, was that it relied on the assumption that wisdom was genetic.

"It's not fair," she whispered to no one. Finn had made this mess. Finn and a boatload of other people enabling him. Rage sparked in her at the thought of Rafe's absence. She had admitted that he was probably dead, but probably was as close as she could get. She didn't know why she believed he was alive. Denial and self-protection? Right now, rather than missing or mourning him, she was angry, irrationally angry, that wherever he was, alive or dead, he was not here. Whether it was his choice or not, he left her, and she hated him for it.

She gently pushed back the covers and swung her feet to the floor. On the bed, Brand lifted his head and blinked at her.

"Shhh," she whispered and put a finger to her lips. It would be folly to try to get him to stay, so as she stood, she waved at him. "Come on." They slipped into her closet and she dressed in plain, comfortable clothes.

Brand followed her into the parlor. Jake and Sam were asleep by the fire but woke at her coming. She shushed again but waved them to her as well. They were happiest when they were with her, protecting her. She chuckled sadly. Like her, they managed their grief by working.

She grabbed a small mirror from the coffee table and sat on the sofa. Brand hopped up next to her, and Jake and Sam took up sentinel posts on either side. The light from the windows was faint, still, but the blue of night had faded, and pink filled the sky. It was early, but not too early. Deor had an idea of who might be awake at this hour.

She tapped the mirror. "Arthur. Northfalls."

The mirror swirled for several moments before clearing to show Arthur. He was dressed and ready, like he had been up for hours. Maybe he had. Or maybe he hadn't slept at all. "Your Majesty?" He frowned. "Are you alright?" He spoke softly.

"Am I interrupting something?" she asked, equally softly.

"No. Just a moment." The image swung as Arthur moved from wherever he was to somewhere else. She heard doors open and close, and finally, he sat and set the mirror in front of him. "I'm in Duke's office," he said, voice normal. "I had been in the household of the King."

Deor frowned at the mention of him. She didn't want to talk about him and didn't really care how he was. Still, she had to ask. "How is His Majesty?"

Arthur rolled his eyes. "He's stopped beating people, which is nice. Mostly he skulks around his rooms. Occasionally he comes out to give impassioned speeches about how horrible you are and how this is all your fault." Arthur shook his head. "He's a useless lump of whiney, self-absorbed asshole."

"How are you holding up?"

Arthur blinked at her. "Pretty much the same as always. Has something changed?" He frowned, worried. "Is there an invasion elsewhere? Did D'nath tell you something?" Suddenly his gaze darted around her, sharp and piercing. "I don't recognize where you are. Are you still with the Goblins?"

"No." She shook her head. "We went to try to get help, and well." She shrugged and gave him the rundown of past events.

"Fucking hell," Arthur whispered and shoved his hands through his hair. "Not like I thought they'd help, but kidnapping? Ugh. At least Victor killed their Sword. I never liked that guy."

"You're a good judge of character for that," she said. She hadn't mentioned Victor's experiences and didn't plan on it.

"So, you're with the vampires? I visited there a few times with Rafe. Are you afraid you're in danger there?"

"No, nothing like that. They're being great hosts, actually." Deor sighed. "I just couldn't sleep and didn't know what to do."

"Ah." Arthur smiled softly. "I understand. You've never been through a war."

"Not like this, no. My country went to war, or was at war, a lot, but not recently on our own soil. It was always a handful of troops in a faraway land. More like a story than something real. It makes me feel sick to say that now."

"War is not what most people expect. It's mostly boredom. That's the hardest part. The flashes of battle are all adrenaline and muscle memory. It's waiting for those moments to come—hours, days, weeks, that is the killer. D'nath will keep his word—he's not a liar. He's not going to start marching to London for a while yet. My guess is that Wellhall will prove slightly harder to pacify than they thought. We do have some time."

"What about the siege?"

"What about it?" Arthur shrugged. "We spend our days playing cards when not on duty. When on duty, we run a circuit, repairing and reinforcing the wards. We listen to the sounds of the magic they're launching at it. After a while, the booming and shaking stops being startling."

"I am so sorry." Tears threatened again, but she held them back.

"I know." Arthur pursed his lips, thinking. Finally, he said, 'This isn't your fault. I know you're the one dealing with it, but I also know you didn't make this happen."

"Thank you," she said. "I know you don't flatter."

He laughed. "True."

"Good morning, Arthur," Roger's voice rang out. "Oh!" he said when he came into view of the mirror. "Your Majesty. Has something happened?" He sat next to Arthur.

"No." Deor shook her head. "I just couldn't sleep. Arthur was telling me that boredom is a fundamental part of war."

"That it is," Roger agreed. "I've lived a long time and participated in a lot of wars. The worst is the waiting to kill or be killed." He cocked his head. "This is the first time I've been in the group waiting to be killed."

Deor shuddered. "Is there anything that can be done?" She rested her forehead in her hands. "I know the answer is no. I know we've been over it a thousand times." She looked up. "I'm sorry. I shouldn't be bothering you. I'll let you go."

"Nonsense," Roger said. "We've got nothing else to do either, right, Arthur?"

"Right." He thought for a moment. "Why don't we try this from a different angle? What would it take to win, regardless of what we can do?"

"That's an interesting question." Roger drummed his fingers on the table. "We've got the two-border problem. We can't solve Northfalls without solving Wellhall at the same time. Otherwise, even if we win one back, the other will be the source of invasion and will get to London before Winter Court regiments can make it there. So, it would have to be coordinated."

"Right," Arthur confirmed. "And it isn't going to be an army. Not at Wellhall. It's better fortified than even Northfalls. It could withstand a siege easily."

"So, it would have to be an inside job," Deor said, shaking her head. "I don't think there's anyone inside any more willing to help. They're either all in with her, or they're too frightened to do anything about it. Though, we are hearing that not everything is smooth sailing down there. Before I left for Geoff's, Bartholomew had reports there might be a small band of resistance. Though we lost contact with the garrison. We don't know if they're fighting on our side or Madeline's. But the locals don't seem to appreciate the Summer Court presence."

"That's unsurprising," Arthur confirmed. "The people in Wellhall have long hated, or at least distrusted, the Aethelwings. That doesn't mean they'd capitulate to the Summer Court. I doubt they were thrilled with Madeline's choice. They might have followed her to some sort of liberation of Wellhall from the Winter Court, some sort of autonomy, but I can't see any of the folks I met there happy to be a part of the Summer Court."

"True." Roger settled in on the couch next to Arthur. "But even the scrappiest of scrappy Wellhall citizens can't get into the palace there. And I doubt they have the weapons to fight armed soldiers."

"Don't be so sure," Arthur said shaking his head. "They're fishermen and farmers. Pretty much every 'tool of the trade' can be made into a dangerous weapon. Scythes and harpoons can stick in people as easily as they can cut wheat or spear fish."

"Fair." Roger said. "That still doesn't get anyone inside the palace. And even if we could, they'd find the best fighters with D'nath and Madeline. D'nath would have come prepared. I've watched him for a long time. He doesn't underestimate anyone."

Deor sagged in her chair. "So we'd need a small group of folks with an 'in' to the palace who were elite fighters to sneak in and kill all of the Summer Court faeries in charge?"

"Yes." Roger said.

"That would be perfect!" Arthur agreed. "And since we're in fantasy land we'd need something similar here in Northfalls. There isn't the 'who will let them in' problem, of course. Because we'd happily open the portals to let in allies. Except—"

"Except," Roger cut in, "if we open a portal, that weakens the wards, and the army waiting at our doorstep would come pouring in. Unless the group was ultra small, like a couple hundred, and incredibly well-trained killing machines."

"And while we're at it, I'd like ten bottles of Rangley's finest from three hundred years ago. I heard that was a near-perfect vintage!" Arthur chuckled darkly.

"Oh, well, if that's all it would take." Deor shrugged. "Easy. Why don't I just—" She stopped right before the words came out of her mouth. Trained killing machines? How about assassins? "How many people did you say you'd need?"

"If we were able to portal directly into the castles themselves, it wouldn't take much. Maybe three hundred all told." Roger concentrated.

"Yeah," Arthur agreed. "I mean, if the soldiers were able to get inside, it wouldn't be hard at all. But you'd never get into Wellhall."

"I won't. And neither will you," Deor agreed. "But Victor might. He's the heir." She looked to Roger. "Rodney can get into Northfalls, right? Even if you didn't want him to? Like I opened the doors in the Tower?"

"Yes," Roger said. "That's some of the deepest, oldest magic there is. The land has its own will. Wellhall itself might well be revolting beneath her feet." He sighed. "Of course, the land can't protect Victor from Madeline or D'nath running him through."

"Yeah," Deor said. Her mind was wandering, wheels turning.

Behind Roger and Arthur the door opened, and a feminine voice called out. "Hello! I've brought you breakfast!" Thea stepped into the room, a tray of food and water in her hands, followed by Roger's nephew Rodney. "Oh!" Thea said when she saw Deor. "I'm sorry. I didn't realize you were on a call." She set the tray down.

"We'll clear out for you," Rodney added.

"No, it's fine, both of you," Deor said. "As long as it is fine with Arthur and Roger, I don't mind you staying."

"It's fine," Arthur said, though he looked a bit miserable.

"I didn't know either of you were in Northfalls," Deor said.

"We weren't," Thea said. "When I heard that Arthur was up here with the King, I decided I would come and help. That's what friends do."

"How kind of you," Deor managed. Joining a besieged castle wasn't exactly what Deor would call friendship, and the way Arthur watched her with sorrow and longing suggested his feelings were more than just friendly as well. There was no time to do anything about it right now. "How did you get in?"

"We've got a portal between the house in London and Northfalls," Rodney said. "It's been there for centuries. It was built so that portalling from one place to the other wouldn't hurt the wards at Northfalls."

"That's convenient! Could we use it to send people?" Deor asked.

"No." Rodney shook his head. "It's an heir thing—you've got to be part of the family to activate it. Plus, it is small. You can't send more than about three people through at a time, and then you've got to wait a few hours if the wards are up."

Deor nodded. "So you two came to help?"

"Yes," Rodney said. "I'm heir to Northfalls, I should be here."

Roger frowned but said nothing. Though neither Rodney nor Thea could see the expressions on Roger and Arthur's faces, Deor could, and she recognized the fear there. Neither of them, she realized, expected to survive the siege. Losing their own lives was something they were willing to do, but they balked at risking the lives of those they loved.

"I'll let you two go," Deor said. "Take care."

"You too," Roger said. "Let us know when you're home safe."

"I will." She tapped the mirror closed and stood. She needed a walk—some time to let her mind wander. She snapped her fingers, calling the dogs to follow her as she rose. Outside her suite, a servant led her to back gardens filled with roses, a perfect place to wander and think. The sun was fully up now, a beautiful summer morning.

As she paced through the winding paths of the gardens, something needled at her. Arthur needed killing machines. And now, here she was, given safe haven by the ultimate in killing machines. Plus, vampires were assassins—murderers for hire. Getting their aid was a long shot, no doubt, but if it worked, it could mean victory rather than slow annihilation. Her family had ties to the Vlad's for centuries. She knew from the exchequer that the tournament had depleted a lot of the cash, and much of it was needed to pay soldiers and to pay for whatever damage the war caused. Still, how much would three hundred assassins cost?

Then again, if what she'd seen so far was any indication, the Vampire Court didn't lack money. What they lacked was prestige. The Summer Court treated them like monsters. The Goblin Court had humiliated them, and the vampires had certainly burned those bridges even more by helping Deor. The bards looked down their noses, and everyone else avoided them. The only place they'd found something close to acceptance was the Winter Court. Deor was sure her father had been an ass to them —he was to everyone—but they seemed to genuinely like Rafe and he them.

Money couldn't buy prestige. Sure, you needed money to join the club, but you needed sponsorship first. The faeries, like it or not, were the most exclusive club in Fae. Maybe she could come to some sort of agreement with the vampires.

She turned and headed back to the palace. Her idea was insane, but then again, so was everything about her situation. She'd never solved anything in Faerie by following the rules. The Summer Court had all its chess pieces on the board, and the Winter Court had only a few, with the King all but in checkmate. As the board stood now, she would definitely lose to D'nath.

But Deor wasn't King, or Queen for that matter, she was Regent. It was time she played her own game.

The next morning, Rafe and Monjoie returned to the parlor and explained what happened to Monjoie's parents and fiancée.

Juliette shuddered. "He didn't feel right when I got away from him. There was something else there."

"Did he…" Monjoie looked to the floor. "Did he hurt you?" He brought his gaze up to meet hers.

"No." Juliette crossed the room to him and took his hands. "He didn't lay a hand on me. Not that way. Not beyond a kiss here or there and holding hands. I don't think he had confidence that the glamour would work that well."

Monjoie's shoulders sagged with relief. "Thank the creator." He hugged her close.

"Henri," Rafe said, "do you know anything about any resistance?"

"No." He shook his head. "But I know someone who will." He pulled a cord, and a few moments later Valois appeared.

"You called, sir?"

"The resistance," Rafe said. "Where do we find it?"

Valois eyed him for a moment and looked to Henri.

"Go on, Valois," Henri said. "You won't get any trouble from me."

"Yes, sir." Valois straightened. "There is a group of people not far out of Wellhall city. They are made up of those who slipped the castle before the duchess and the Summer Court Sword could shut it all down. Not too many—maybe a dozen at most. I've heard they've gained some supporters, but the group stays small, mobile."

Rafe laughed. "What are you? In charge?"

Valois reddened. "No. But my son was seeing one of the young men in the palace guard. They made contact when he escaped."

"Great." Monjoie said. "You're our way in."

Valois eyed them for a moment. "I can take you to them, but it will be a few days."

"Why?" Monjoie asked.

"They only come back to the area once every couple weeks, to keep them from being easily found. I know when they are coming so that I can give them supplies." He glanced at Henri.

"It's fine, Valois." Henri said with a gentle smile. "Take what you need. We've got plenty of supplies and plenty of reasons to help. It's also fine that you kept it a secret."

Valois visibly relaxed. "Thank you, sir."

"Alright," Rafe said. "We'll go as soon as we can. Until then?" He raised his eyebrows and looked at Monjoie. "Is there more local mischief we can do?"

"I'm sure we can find some Summer Court faeries to harass."

"Excellent," Rafe grinned.

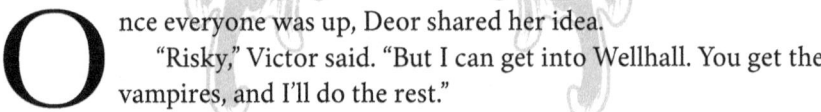

36

Once everyone was up, Deor shared her idea.

"Risky," Victor said. "But I can get into Wellhall. You get the vampires, and I'll do the rest."

"Right. I'm off to talk to Vlad."

Vlad's office was spacious, with rich rugs, a huge desk, and heavily curtained windows. Like the rest of the castle, it was lit luxuriously. He gestured for her to sit in the chair on the far side of the desk and settled into his own.

"Thank you for your hospitality," Deor said. "I appreciate you taking the time to speak to me too." She settled back in her chair. There were, she assumed, many different soft ways to lead into the requests she needed to make. She preferred direct. "I need your help."

"Of course you do!" Vlad nodded, sympathetically. "And of course, I'll give it to you."

"You will?" Deor started. "Are you—"

He waved her words away. "Of course, I am happy to grant you and your companions sanctuary. We will keep you safe from the Summer Court here."

Deor bristled. Was he suggesting the same kind of safety that Gregory had offered? "I appreciate your offer, but I haven't come to ask for sanctuary."

"Oh?" He frowned. "What then?"

"I'm not good at negotiating, Vlad," she said. "You obviously know of the situation with the Summer Court invasion and the treason of Wellhall. I cannot possibly abandon my country for sanctuary. I couldn't live with myself. I won't let my people fight and suffer and die while I watch from afar safe in a foreign castle."

He leaned forward, interested. "My estimation of you has grown." He quirked an eyebrow. "If it is not sanctuary you want, what else can I give you?"

"I need three hundred assassins."

Vlad's jaw dropped.

Deor plunged on. "A small strike force could easily deal with the Summer Court attempts on Northfalls. We can portal them in, and Arthur and Roger can lead the rest. If we can break that siege—"

"That siege, yes," Vlad said, nodding. "I can see how I might assist you there. But what of Wellhall? So long as that is held against the Winter Court, it is only a matter of time before the Winter Court falls. They could last years, maybe even decades, against an army at its gates. The Summer soldiers would merely retreat for a time. And D'nath is cunning enough to keep any army out."

"Yes," Deor said. "You're right—"

"And without both places, the war is merely longer, not won."

"I know," Deor snapped. When Vlad jolted back, she sighed. "I apologize for being short with you." She took a deep breath. "You are right that we cannot besiege Wellhall. Like Northfalls, we would need to get inside the palace."

"Unlike Northfalls, Wellhall is not manned by friends." Vlad crossed his arms.

"True. But it is manned by traitors and enemies." She paused. She didn't like "airing dirty laundry" as her grandmother would say, but her country was far more important than her embarrassing father. "When Finn left—when he escaped to Northfalls—the palace revolted against him and chose me. I believe that Wellhall will be like that with Madeline. She holds it now, but her land and her people cannot welcome it. Which means that the castle is breachable by a Farringdon. Victor can get in. He, with a small handful of people, can cross into Wellhall unnoticed—he did grow up there—and he can open the castle. They cannot keep him out. So, he will get in and open a portal. Your people will go through and take out the small Summer Court force that holds Wellhall. If possible, they will capture or kill D'nath. Without those two posts, the Summer Court cannot win."

He eyed her for a moment. "It is not a foolish thought." He rested his hands on the table. "I do not give my assassins for free. In fact, as an English professor, I believe you would know that the word 'assassin' implies pay."

"I am aware." Deor shrugged. "And now we are at another place where I do not know how to negotiate. I don't know how to pay you in money. My father spent the coffers very low for the parade of ego boosting that was his tournament."

"So we are at an impasse?" He shook his head sadly. "I still offer you sanctuary…"

"I may have some things to offer that aren't money," Deor said hurriedly.

"I am wary of faerie bargains," he said. "But I am listening."

Deor nodded and drew a deep breath. Insult first, then smooth over later. "You are not a king." She saw him bristle. "Nothing you can do can make you one. You have the money; you have power, but you are not a king."

"Yes?" His voice was low, and his eyes showed hints of black around the irises.

"I can make you a king." Before he could interrupt again, she plowed on. "I will call you a king. I will call your son a prince. Every time I speak of you. Every time anyone in the Winter Court speaks of you, your son, your people, it will be the Vampire Kingdom and their King and Prince. Over time, people will follow my lead."

He frowned. "Rhetoric."

"Yes." Deor nodded, relieved that he understood. "Exactly. We are the makers of meaning, so we'll remake the meaning."

"I am intrigued. But that promise—one that may not come to fruition after hundreds of my people are dead—is not enough."

"That's fair." Deor slipped her hands into her pockets and removed two small bundles, the Goblin platinum chips and the Prince's ring, both wrapped in handkerchiefs. "These are worth a lot of money," Deor said. "But I believe, to you, they will be worth far more than simple cash."

Deor undid the first bundle, showing the stack of platinum coins.

He studied it for a moment. "A goblin IOU?" He picked up a coin and examined it. He laughed. "I see why it is easy to give away." He glanced up at her. "You do not, I think, intend to return to the Goblin Court to collect?"

"Not a chance. I was going to keep it as a souvenir, but I think you might have fun collecting on it."

"I might. And it is a fair sum of money. It might buy you one or two assassins." He looked at the other small bundle. "I am aware that small things can be quite valuable, but what you have in there must be truly impressive if you think it is worth three hundred of my people."

Deor shrugged. "I think it is priceless."

He undid the knot at the top, and his eyebrows shot up. He took the ring and turned it this way and that, inspecting it. He looked over it at her. "Is this real?"

"It is."

"This is the Goblin Prince's purity ring!" He brought it close to his face again. "The inscription is clear." He cradled the ring in his hand. "Did you steal it?"

"No!" Deor was mildly insulted. "I won it off him in cards. I bet everything, including the jewelry I was wearing, on the last hand. He threw in the ring just to be a jerk. Then I won."

"Did you cheat?" He asked, amused.

"I played by Goblin rules." She smiled.

He slipped the ring on his pinky and held his hand out. "It does not suit me." He looked up at her. "But I think it will suit my son just fine." He winked. "You have your assassins, Regent." He slipped the ring off his finger and set it on the cloth. He held his hand out to her. "We have a deal."

"Thank you," Deor said and shook his hand. "I do have one more thing to ask."

He inclined his head toward her. "Go on."

"Can you give Astarte and her daughter Robbie sanctuary? I don't know that we'll win the war, and I can only imagine the horrors they'll face if they're taken prisoner. I'm fine risking my own life, but not theirs."

He smiled. "That is easy. I will send Chloe with Donovan and his assassins, and she can bring the former Consort and her child back."

"Thank you! I'm sure Robbie and Vashti will get on like a house on fire," she said with a smile.

Vlad rose, and Deor followed suit. "Come. We must tell those outside what has transpired. Though I believe we'll keep the full details to ourselves, no?"

"Fair enough." Deor let him open the door for her and show her out.

Donovan, Stephen, and Victor leaned against the walls on either side of the door trying to look nonchalant. They stood to attention the moment the door opened.

"Come in, Donovan, and I will explain what has transpired." Vlad smiled at Deor. "Give me some time to discuss strategy with Donovan. We'll solidify the numbers and plan with the help of you and your companions after the party this evening."

"Thank you!" Deor said. She gestured at Stephen and Victor to follow her as she walked away from Vlad's office. When she heard the door close behind her, she stopped. "We've got our vampires."

"All of them?" Victor gaped.

"All of them."

"It was the ring that did it, wasn't it? Insulting the goblins to win the vampires is a good trade, in my opinion," Stephen said.

"They're far more trustworthy," Victor confirmed.

"And I like them a lot better too." Deor said.

37

The reception after their meeting was marked by drinks—Deor and her companions never touched any red liquid—in another small ballroom, and a flurry of chatter with various family members, excepting Ivan. Deor spent most of her time with Vashti, who literally clung to her. Vashti always had an arm looped through Deor's or, on occasion, clasped her hand. As Deor scanned the room, she realized that Vashti was behaving as everyone else. Vampires were touchy-feely. Donovan and Chloe always had their hands on each other, and Vlad and Yessina as well. It was how they were. It was not how Deor was, but she was tolerating it.

Stephen and Victor stayed close enough to her to always be within reach, but far enough away to not imply that they didn't think Deor was safe. Though her opinion clearly didn't hold much sway with them, she felt as safe as she ever had. There was something about Vlad's old-school mannerisms that convinced Deor that, barring some massive insult, Vlad would never, ever break hospitality. Even if she embarrassed Donovan at cards.

A sudden hush dropped over the room, and Vashti gasped. The crowd parted as from the far end of the room, someone approached.

"He came!" Vashti squealed in Deor's ear. "I knew he would! I knew he couldn't resist meeting you!"

"What did you do?" Donovan asked, appearing at Vashti's side.

Vashti grinned, showing fangs. "He hasn't seen a princess in centuries."

"Regent," Donovan corrected, frowning. He sighed and turned to Deor. "I promise," he said, "you are safe in my home."

"Um. Thank you?" Deor said.

"Over here!" Vashti called out and waved her free hand while Donovan scowled.

"Father is going to lock you in a cell in the basement for this, little sister," he muttered.

A giant of a man was approaching. He stood two feet, at least, taller than Deor, towering over everyone in the room. He wore nothing but a pair of lace-up breeches in a deep brown that made his skin, a kind of brown-orange, seem brighter. His broad chest and arms were tightly muscled, and his hair, a reddish orange, fell down to his waist. He focused on her, meeting her gaze and not blinking, with glittering orange eyes.

He made a direct line for her, never taking his eyes off hers, and stopped a moment before she thought she would have to step back. "Hello, little Princess." His voice rumbled in a deep bass, like it echoed through him. Whatever he was, he wasn't human; he certainly wasn't a vampire, and he wasn't faerie either.

Deor shook off Vashti's arm and held the creature's gaze. "I am Deor," she said, holding out a hand. "Regent of the Winter Court."

He regarded her hand for a moment before taking it gingerly in his own. His fingernails were long, but his touch was delicate, as if he took care not to hurt her. "I am Leonidas." He drew in a breath, like he was sniffing her. He let go of her hand. "You are a royal," he said with a smile.

"I am," Deor said. He had a strange effect on her, one that troubled her. Around him, the world seemed to blur, and she wondered what magic he might have. She shook her head and blinked, her eyes stinging just slightly. She gasped. It wasn't blurring, and it wasn't magic. It was smoke. Wisps of gray and white curled off him in faint spirals.

Stephen and Victor were next to her then, the former muscling Vashti out of the way.

Leonidas glanced at them, and his mouth quirked into a smile before he returned his attention to her. "You've brought your little knights to protect you."

"I can protect myself," Deor said, perhaps a touch too quickly.

Leonidas laughed, a booming sound that filled the room. "Can you now?"

Deor's eyes flashed silver, and she made no effort to stop them, as did her nails. "Indeed."

His smile changed, shifting from condescending to delighted. "A changeling! I have not seen one of these in...," he seemed to count, "thousands of years." He snorted. "Though I have not, of late, traveled much, and even fewer travel to see me."

"I do!" Vashti insisted.

Leonidas glanced at her briefly. "Indeed you do, little one."

"What are you?" Deor asked, fascinated. Even if he was insulting her, which, now she wasn't sure was his intent, he demanded attention.

The creature laughed again. "You have never seen one of me before, I am sure, so I will not take offense. I am a dragon." He nodded benevolently.

"A dragon?" The silver vanished from Deor's eyes and fingertips. She actually clapped her hands. "A real dragon?"

"A real dragon," Leonidas said, amused. "I take this form in the Vlad's home as a gesture of respect." He looked past her and nodded at Deor's host. "We have had an agreement for some time. I live in his land in peace and unwelcome intruders never leave."

Deor nodded. Every good instinct she had told her to be polite, make nice comments, and let it go. She'd never been the best at listening to good instincts. "Can I see you as a dragon?"

"Oh, for fuck's sake!" Victor said behind her.

"Do you think that would be wise?" the dragon asked, teasing.

"Wise?" Deor shrugged. "I'm not sure. Are you impressive enough that it would be worth the risk?"

"You are a princess," he said.

Deor didn't bother to correct him. "So you'd eat me?"

"No." He shook his head. "Dragons collect expensive and shiny things, and you are both." He glanced at the men on either side of her. "Though I often have to eat knights in pursuit of princesses."

Deor laughed.

"I do not wear my true form in Vlad's house, as a matter of courtesy. Perhaps later, should the Vlad feel it is acceptable." He looked to the Vlad.

Deor turned to look behind her.

Vlad wore an expression somewhere between irritated and amused. "In the courtyard?"

"I would be happy to," Leonidas said with a smile.

"Wonderful!" Deor beamed. "I can't wait."

Shortly thereafter, Deor rocked back and forth on the heels of her boots and wrapped her arms around herself against the chill air in the courtyard. The sun was high in the sky, but still, a cold wind swirled around her. Though it was summertime back in the Winter Court, it seemed to be autumn here—she guessed there was something magic about the place that kept it always on the cusp of winter, with colored leaves swirling in the breeze.

Donovan leaned against a wall with practiced indifference. Chloe and Genevieve stood a bit apart chatting—Genevieve had spent most of her time with Donovan's wife. They seemed to be planning something. Whatever it was, Deor could wait until they got home to find out.

Vashti stood a few feet from Deor, arms crossed, a pout secured on her face. "He has never changed shape for me," she muttered not quite under her breath.

Deor considered apologizing but figured that would make it worse. She could have refused the offer, claimed that she didn't want to be an imposition on her hosts or the dragon, politely demurred. While it was true that she didn't like imposing, she would impose for this.

On either side, slightly behind her, Bill, Victor, and Stephen waited. They'd been firmly told not to bring weapons—bringing weapons would be like waving a juicy steak at an already hungry rottweiler. So Victor and Stephen stood solemnly, opening and closing their fists at their sides as they instinctively grabbed at weapons that weren't there.

Bill crossed his arms and frowned at her, but he couldn't hold the scowl.

"You're as excited as I am," Deor said.

"Yeah," he admitted. "More so than they are." He jerked his head at her protectors. Jake and Sam sat at their feet, clearly agitated too.

"Don't worry," Deor said to them in a whisper. "I'll make you swords if you need them." She reached down and patted Brand's head as he pressed himself against her legs. He let out a small bark.

From the tree line, Leonidas emerged, still in his human suit, still barely clothed. If the cold bothered him at all, he didn't show it. Then again, he could make his own fires, so why would it bother him?

The dragon stopped about ten feet from her. "You still wish to see my true form?"

"I want to see a dragon," Deor said, nodding. She'd played enough word games to know that *true form* might not mean dragon.

"As you wish."

There was a brief moment of silence and a *pop* like an airplane pressurizing. Then there was a dragon. There was no agonizing wail, no stretching of skin, no Hulk-like bursting of pants. Where there had been, an instant ago, a man, there was now a dragon. He was huge, though not quite as huge as Deor had supposed he would be. He was easily twenty feet long. His body glittered as the morning light danced across his orange scales. From the underside of his chin, down his belly, and through to the tip of the underside of his tail were red scales. He stood on four legs, each foot tipped with wickedly sharp claws. His face resembled a cat's, with a longer snout and sharp teeth protruding just slightly. His glowing orange eyes gleamed with ancient cunning.

Deor took a step forward, and then another, shaking off Victor and Stephen when they tried to stop her. "You're beautiful," she said, not taking her eyes off the dragon's.

"Thank you," he rumbled. He leaned down, bringing his face closer to her. He sniffed again. "You smell like silver and magic."

"You smell like cedarwood and smoke." She reached her hand out to touch the side of his face, but paused. "May I?"

He nodded.

Deor laid her hand on his neck and ran her hand down the smooth scales, each cool to the touch and metallic, like dozens of perfectly aligned shields. Magic ran through them too. He vibrated with it. This close she could see the rise and fall of his breathing and hear the rumbling of fire in his belly. Swirls of smoke drifted from his nostrils. "You are like nothing I have ever seen before."

"You, too, are unique among my experiences." He blinked at her. "You would, I think, be for keeping, not for eating." He cocked his head to the side. "Though I think I would pay dearly if I were to try to add you to my collection."

"I think that is true," Deor said, laughing. "Though someday, when there is time, I would like to see your collection of shiny things."

He drew back slightly, eyes narrowing. "I would not allow you to steal from me." His harsh voice emphasized the threat.

"Oh no!" Deor shook her head. "I don't want to steal from you," she insisted. "I would just like to see your home."

"Hmmmm." He pulled his head away, eyeing her carefully. "You don't smell like a liar. So perhaps someday." He sat back. "You are different from those faeries I have seen before. And I have seen so many faeries." He snorted sparks that skittered across the ground and spun off into the breeze. "I have lived a long time. I slept dozens of your lifetimes, and yet you remind me of the time before the world was civilized." He shook his head. "There is so little magic now. That, I suppose, is why you sparkle so brightly in my sight."

Deor closed her eyes and drew forth her magic, sending up a shower of silver sparkles as she opened her eyes.

The dragon laughed, delighted, and leaned forward, letting them land on his face and neck. When he turned to look at her again, his eyes were rimmed with silver. "A gift I did not expect. Thank you. I shall carry your magic home with me, and add it to my collection."

Deor gasped. She hadn't thought that her sparks were anything more than bubbles of magic, landing and bursting, dissipating into air. The idea that such magic could be collected, carried, and stored baffled her. Still, the dragon seemed pleased. "I hope you enjoy it."

He nodded. "I will." He shook his head. "I think it is time I returned to my cave. The Vlad has business with you, and he looks eager to complete it." He raised his head and looked past her, nodding at the vampires behind her. He spread his wings, tucked sleekly against his body until now, and flapped them, raising wind around her. "I have no gift for you, Princess. So I will give you this: you may come to me for a boon, and I will give it to you. Until then, farewell." With a small kick of his feet, he was in the air, spiraling upward and then sailing away through the sky toward the depths of the vampire forest.

"A boon, eh?" Vlad said, stepping up to her. "He hasn't offered one of those in a long time." He shrugged. "I'm not sure why you might need a dragon."

"I've no idea," Deor said, watching Leonidas disappear behind the trees.

The carriages for Deor's people rattled into the courtyard, laden with her things. Another followed for Chloe, Donovan, and Ivan. When they returned to the Winter Court, they would work with Bartholomew to open a portal and bring the rest of the vampires through. It would have to be done in small groups, given there was no fixed portal in the vampire kingdom and so it could be kept open only a short time.

Stephen elected to ride with Ivan and the others, allowing Chloe and Donovan to join Deor and Victor.

As everyone settled into their carriages, Deor paused before climbing in. She looked back at Vlad and Yessina who stood at the door, arm in arm, and at Vashti, who still sulked, now because she wasn't going to be one of the assassins.

"One second," Deor said to Victor. She hurried back to Vlad and flung her arms around him, holding him in a tight hug. "Thank you so much," she whispered. He returned the hug, and she stayed there, in his arms, feeling for a moment like a daughter, like a part of a family. She gave a final squeeze and let go.

He smiled down at her. "Good luck, little one."

She nodded and hurried back to the carriage.

38

A few days later, a cold spring rain drizzled steadily from the early morning sky, dripping off the hood of Rafe's robes as he waited under cover by the forest path. A few feet away in a small clearing was a lightning-blasted tree stump taller than a man and hollowed out from fire. Valois had explained that locals used the spot to leave food and other supplies for the faeries who had fled or been driven into the woods by Madeline and D'nath.

Rafe didn't particularly mind the rain. He was a water faerie after all. Even if he weren't, the brown wool robe he wore over his other clothes kept him comfortably warm. He and Monjoie had tucked themselves into the shadow of a low-hanging branch an hour before dawn to wait. Valois sat at the base of the tree, wrapped in a cloak that gave him near-perfect camouflage, so long as he sat still. Rafe knew they'd come back here to this spot, and soon, because they had made it a cache for perishable food. Even with cold spells on them, the milk and meat they had stored would only last a few days.

The smell of damp leaf mold underfoot mingled with the smell of leaves in the summer rain. Monjoie was motionless, legs bent in a forester's crouch. Rafe settled back against the tree's bark and waited. A spider ran over his chest and down his sleeve. He took that as a sign he was being sufficiently quiet.

The sun lightened the overcast sky as it rose. Rafe glanced up. Difficult to judge the time, but he'd give himself another hour before they gave up. Perhaps the rain had kept the group from going out last night. Except he had found boot marks that told a different story, and Valois was certain they would be here today. And if their marching order was any indication at least some of them were trained soldiers who knew a good rainy night with wind made excellent cover for a raid. If the fire he'd seen on the horizon was any indication, someone had been out and about last night, and up to no good. Exactly the kind of people he wanted to meet. So he waited.

Sure enough, subtle footsteps approached not long after. That and a murmur of voices told him there were at least three in the band coming toward him. One was chortling gleefully.

"Did you see that? Boom! Went up like fireworks," a younger voice said.

"Keep your voice down," another said, "we're not home free yet."

Smooth as a snake, Monjoie stood up beside Rafe. They nodded to one another and stepped out into the path.

Instantly, six other faeries pointed weapons and spells at them. Three of them wore Wellhall uniforms, or pieces of uniform, but the other three were clearly civilians. The talkative youngster was one and a broad-shouldered woman with the facial tattoos of a deep sea fisher was another. Rafe kept his hands where the group could see them, one hand holding his staff, the other out and open. Monjoie kept on hand on his knife hilt, but he kept it sheathed.

"We're friends," Rafe said.

A few in the group lowered their weapons at that, but not all the way.

"Show us your faces," the leader said.

Valois scrambled upright with a small groan and threw back his hood. "It's me."

"Father?" A third man in civilian clothes stepped forward cautiously. "What are you doing out here?" The lad couldn't have been more than thirty, possibly younger, but the resemblance was clear. He stepped toward his father.

"Wait." A man in a Wellhall uniform threw his arm out, blocking the path. "How do we know it is really your father? He could be working with Monjoie and that Summer Court bastard." He drew his sword and held it out.

Valois straightened. "Armand!" He stepped forward, his chest touching the point of the soldier's sword. "I have known you since you were a boy! Shame on you!"

Armand frowned. "Even if you're him, how can we trust you? The Monjoie family is in league with the Summer Court!"

"No, we're not." Monjoie threw back his hood and stepped forward. "That was an impostor. I'm back now. And we've handled the impostor."

Valois nodded. "It's true, sir. Some dark magic made all of us believe Master Luc was home, and now he really is."

Armand wavered slightly.

A woman in a Wellhall uniform, silent and watching, stepped forward. Armand and Valois's son fell back. So this was the person in charge. "I want to believe you," she said softly. "I want to believe that you are the real Monjoie. I spoke to you, two nights ago, with Juliette."

"That wasn't me," Monjoie's voice dropped low.

"I've known you a long time," the woman said.

"I know, Eloise. You're Juliette's best friend, and you always thought Juliette was too good for me." He smiled darkly. "I'm sure you're right."

"Monjoie at the manor would say that," she said.

"I know!" Monjoie snapped. "I know he would. He did! My parents, even Juliette, believed in him. But he's dead. When we tried to interrogate him, he... he..."

"Blew up." Rafe said quietly. "Some sort of spell to keep him from talking killed him. Painfully."

"And who might you be?" Eloise said, drawing her sword.

Rafe sighed. He had to tell them, though it might make things worse. He eased back the hood of his cloak. "I'm Rafael, heir to the duchy of Wellhall. I've come home with Monjoie to fix this mess Madeline has made."

Everyone's eyes widened. The eager youth stared at Rafe, stars in his eyes. "The Sword," he breathed. He reminded Rafe of Deor when she spotted her first unicorn. Only the solid fisherwoman remained unmoved, her billhook still over her shoulder.

"The King's boy?" Eloise snorted.

"Wellhall and the Winter Court have my loyalty," he said. "The King... is no longer my Master. And I am no longer the Sword." He frowned. "Monjoie and I fought against each other as the King escaped Madeline's coup. We were both washed out to sea and ended up...somewhere else. The invasion of Wellhall called us back. I know it sounds insane." He nodded. "Surely impostors trying to get into the resistance would have a much better story."

Eloise eyed him. She stepped up to Valois and muttered a few words, casting dispelling magic on him.

"It really is me, and this really is Master Luc and Lord Farringdon," Valois said. "I promise on my life."

"Alright," Eloise relented. "But I expect you to prove yourselves useful in a hurry."

"Yes, ma'am," Rafe said, without irony.

The starry-eyed youngster said, "Are you the Ghost?"

"I suppose," Rafe said.

The boy pulled out a mirror. He turned it to display a picture of three Summer Court faeries' heads neatly stacked at the crossroads. The top head carried a burn on its forehead in the shape of a scallop shell.

Rafe nodded. "That was us."

"But the Ghost is only one person," a soldier objected.

Monjoie gave him a look that said "are you really so stupid?"

"A faceless person in a dark robe?" Rafe asked, and the group laughed; even the fisherwoman joined the laughter.

Together the group gathered the supplies that had been left for them in the hollowed-out tree. The boy was delighted to find that fresh eggs and bacon were included in the trove this time. Valois and his son hugged as Valois left to head back to the manor. Monjoie gave the man a hug too.

As they began to move, Rafe fell in beside the fisherwoman. The smile she gave him was warmer now.

"I'm Zaya," she said, matching his stride. "It's about time you showed up."

"I agree," Rafe said. "Nice to meet you, Zaya."

After that, they marched in companionable silence while the woods dripped and the birds sang.

39

Happy to be back in the palace, Deor settled on the couch in her parlor and stared up at the mirror above her fireplace. Bartholomew and Donovan had worked out the plan to get Vlad's three hundred vampires to the Palace as discreetly as possible. Now it was time to share her plan with Roger and Arthur. Next to her, Brand curled up with his head in her lap. Jake and Sam, somewhat settled now that they were home again, watched her from their place in front of the fire. "Northfalls," she said to the mirror.

The mirror blurred for several seconds and finally cleared, revealing Roger. "Good afternoon, Your Majesty." He bowed slightly.

"Hello Roger," Deor said. "Are you and Arthur available to talk right now?"

"Of course. Arthur is right here. We were just meeting about provisions." Arthur came in view of the mirror.

"How are things?" Deor asked.

Roger shrugged. "Same as always. There is plenty of food, plenty of water, and the wards are holding well."

"Their attacks have become perfunctory," Arthur said. "Like they are going through the motions, waiting for us to run out of supplies. It's a textbook holding pattern until they are ready for their end game."

"So how long do you have? A conservative estimate," Deor said.

"Six weeks before we have to start rationing, I'd say. We'll end up in the reserves, but not in starvation danger in a few weeks. We've got fresh water and access to food in storage"

"What about you?" Arthur asked. "How did your visit with Vlad go?"

"Really well." Deor smiled. "I took your idea and ran with it."

"My idea?" Arthur asked.

"You and Roger said a small group of assassins could take on the Summer Court. So I got you some Vampires. Vlad agreed to give me three hundred of his people. Ivan will lead a group to Northfalls, and the rest, with Donovan, will go to Wellhall. As soon as we're ready, you can just open a portal, and we'll send them through."

Arthur drew a deep breath. "Not to be a killjoy, but what did you give them?"

"That's between me and Vlad, but trust me, it's not a bad exchange."

Arthur frowned but didn't respond.

"What about Wellhall?" Roger asked. "How can they get in?"

"Victor is going," Deor said. She tried to sound nonchalant and not terrified. "He can get in because he's heir. Once inside, they can open a portal to the palace and let the vampires in. Inside, they won't have as hard a time taking the palace. Besides, Bartholomew has good intel that there is a resistance force there. They'll do their best to meet up with them. From what we've heard, Wellhall is not happy with Madeline's choices."

"Sending your Consort," Arthur said, "is that really the best idea?"

Deor shrugged. "It's the only idea, so it must be the best one."

"Okay, then. It's a plan." Arthur smiled. "I've always wanted to work with Ivan. I've never had a chance to meet him, but he's supposed to be crazy as a loon and deadly as a viper."

"I'm sure you'll get along great," Deor said, leaving off that she imagined they had a lot in common, at least when it came to killing. "Bartholomew will call you tomorrow with more details. He's working right now with Donovan, Ivan, Victor, and Stephen solidifying plans. Victor and Donovan will leave for Wellhall tomorrow."

"If this works, D'nath is not going to know what hit him," Roger said. "And if it doesn't, it will still be legendary."

"If anyone lives to remember it, anyway." Deor glanced away, trying to keep her fear from showing. "Take care." She closed the mirror and blew out a deep breath, leaning down to hug Brand. She let her tears fall into his fur and held him close. She did as much of her crying in private as possible. She knew that their plan was crazy and didn't have a huge chance of success, but no one had said they shouldn't do it, and no one had any better ideas.

That night they all gathered at supper. The vampires and Deor's counselors seemed pleased with their ideas and progress. Astarte and Robbie had reluctantly agreed to slip away to sanctuary in a few days, though both seemed to want to stay. As they were about to wrap up, Genevieve cleared her throat.

"Excuse me, Your Majesty," she said, glancing at Chloe. "I've been talking some with Chloe, and we have an idea."

"What do you have in mind? Are you okay?"

"No," Genevieve said. A couple of tears ran down her cheeks. She drew a deep breath and wiped them away. "In the Goblin Court, I froze, and I almost got you killed." She held up a hand to stop Deor's protests before they could begin. "I know you said it wasn't my fault. But that doesn't matter. So when I got to the Vlad's home, and I saw Chloe, I asked her about it. She agreed to teach me how to not do that. She agreed to teach me how to defend myself." Genevieve raised her chin and scanned the table, as though she was daring people to contradict her.

"That's awesome," Deor said with a smile. "Really, Genevieve. I know I'm not safe to be around, and I want you to be as protected as possible."

Chloe laughed. "She's not going to be protected. She's going to be deadly." Chloe eyed Deor. "You should train, too, you know. Until now, you've relied on your panic response, which, to be fair, is effective. Surprise stabbings often eliminate threats, but at some point you'll encounter someone who is ready for you."

Deor had some minor self-defense training in college—the kind a school half-heartedly gave young women as if the dangers they would face were men jumping out of bushes. "You're right. I'd be happy to train with you."

"Great!" Chloe said. "I can certainly teach anyone you want to learn."

"Why don't you start as soon as Donovan and I leave?" Victor suggested. "It will give you something to do other than worry."

She wanted to argue that she'd be fine, but that was a lie. "Sounds good," was all she could muster. Any distraction would help. In a couple of days, Victor—her Consort and her friend—would be gone, very possibly for good. She swallowed her fear and smiled at the rest of the table.

40

While Monjoie had been welcomed back with open arms by the Wellhall people, Rafe's reception was more guarded. Some few welcomed him immediately as a returned captive, blaming Finn that Rafe had never been one of them. But the Farringdon name carried less weight than it had before Madeline betrayed the Winter Court and most of the resistors watched him suspiciously, not sure where Rafe's loyalties lay.

He tried not to take it personally, but it bred a certain familiar loneliness. At least here, there were no toadies. The fisherwoman who had greeted Rafe told him to his face that she'd trust him when he'd proved he was worth trusting. Then she told him to go chop some firewood. Rafe complied, not particularly offended by the chore or the honesty. Wielding an axe wore out his sword hand sooner than he would have liked, but it gave him something to do besides sit around the camp poking the fire.

Sgt. Eloise Assane was the most open about her suspicions. She only spoke to Rafe when he spoke to her and never involved him in command decisions. She was most often huddled with Monjoie and the other leaders, discussing strategies and gathering information. If Rafe joined them, Monjoie shared what they were discussing while the others looked uncomfortable and said nothing.

By keeping his ears open and his mouth shut, Rafe gathered that she and the other Wellhall guards in the camp had slipped out of the castle the same day Madeline killed Edgar with nothing more than the clothes on their backs. The ones who had hesitated were now trapped, unable to leave without being killed. Over time they had gathered a few civilians, mostly cousins and neighbors who they had gone to for food and supplies. The population seemed to be in a state of shock, locked in by Madeline's people and the Summer Court before they could decide on a response. Half the fishing fleet was under a No Sail order in the harbor, and the other half was out at sea, unable to return without also surrendering.

Rafe made no effort to wrest command away from Assane or Monjoie. Instead, he followed the habits he'd learned at Mont Saint-Michel—find out what needs doing and do it, quietly and without any fuss. If water needed carrying, he filled a bucket. If the cook fires burned low, he added wood and tended the flames until they were steady. In between, he practiced with the sword and staff.

When Assane assigned patrol rotations without giving Rafe a job, Rafe waited until she was alone and said, "May I have a word?"

She was sitting on a log at the moment, nursing a cup of soup. Her uniform jacket hung open in the summer heat. Rafe sat down on the log beside her, close enough to speak privately, but not close enough to crowd her. "I noticed you didn't assign me to a rotation."

Assane grunted and sipped her soup.

"I'm happy to do my part," Rafe said. "You don't have enough people that you can afford to have me slacking around camp."

She grunted again, a sound halfway between affirmation and rejection. Rafe opened his mouth to say more, then closed it again. He rested his arms on his knees and stared off into the distance, waiting.

"Monjoie trusts you," she said. "But I'm not convinced. You may mean well, but what happens when all this is over?"

"Assuming it ends well," Rafe said, "My mother dies a traitor's death, the Summer Court retreats back to their own borders, and I become Duke of Wellhall. We all live happily ever after. I don't really expect it to go that way."

"What do you expect?" she said. "The Summer Court wins?"

"It's a possibility." He saw the startled look on her face. "Do you want me to lie to you? I don't know how the war is going in the rest of the country, but I still know everything I learned as Sword. We weren't ready for this war, even with everything I did behind Finn's back. And I always assumed that Madeline would hold Wellhall against all comers. Not that she'd let them in by the front door. If Wellhall and Northfalls both go, we've lost. It's that simple. The Winter Court might recover its sovereignty in a few hundred years, but we'll have lost."

Rafe tossed strips of green bark into the fire where the sap hissed in the flames. He went on, "Certain pockets of the country will be harder to subdue than others, but we'll become a part of the Summer Court. Finn will die. The Regent will be held as an involuntary guest of the Summer Court Queen for the rest of her lifetime. She may or may not be permitted to have children who would become client kings of the Summer Court.

"Or more likely, one of the Summer Court Queen's sons will be given the Winter Court as a sub-king of his brother. He'll establish a new dynasty. Eventually, that line will demand equal footing with the Summer Court rulers, and a new war will break out. Of course, you and me, we'll be long gone by then."

"Aren't you a jolly ball of sunshine?" Assane said, though her tone implied she liked him better for saying all that.

Rafe pointed with his stick at the surrounding trees, the sky overhead. "This is what will remain. All this, the woods, the water, the land, the sky. And the people. Kings come and go. Nations. Titles. But maybe we can save the people who live here, no matter who they pay their taxes to." He thought of the altar back in Mont Saint-Michel. The rush and fall, as if he had plunged deep underwater, then the sense of connection, the sheer overwhelming awareness of the richness of life that filled the world.

"And what about you, Rafe, Lord Farringdon, future Duke of Wellhall?" Assane said, breaking into his memory. "Where will you be in all that?"

Rafe shrugged. "Dead eventually, though I'm in no hurry to get there. I don't expect to ever hold the title of Duke. Either I'll die in this war, or I won't. If I live, I'll do my best to protect Wellhall and its people with the skills I have, Duke or not. If, by some strange luck, I survive, and the Summer Court loses the war, and I'm not stripped of my title and my land taken by the crown for Madeline's treachery and..."

"And cats wear boots and Yule comes twice a year," Assane said laughing.

"Yes, exactly, if all that, then I'll move into my ancestral home and start learning how to govern a duchy. But I don't really expect it."

"Stranger things have happened," Assane said. "There's a changeling on the throne, and she has a Farringdon for a Consort."

If Assane saw the stab of pain that went through Rafe's guts at that, she didn't mention it.

"Yes," Rafe agreed, his voice gruffer than he wanted it to be. "We live in strange times." He shook off the thoughts of Deor leaning on Victor for support and said, "So put me to use. I can chop wood and haul water, but that only takes up so much of the day. If you don't trust me, give me a minder you do trust. We don't have enough people on our side to be wasting a trained swordsman, especially not if you want that raid on the port to go well."

Beside him, Assane sighed, threw back her head, and said, "Monjoie told you?"

"I am very good at overhearing things."

"You're right. We need all the trained fighters we can get. Farmers and fisherfolk," she waved at the camp, "they're good in a punch-up, but they're not trained for sustained combat. I don't know how well they'll keep their wits about them against Summer Court soldiers, let alone their own people in Wellhall uniforms. It's not the same, fighting your own cousins on your home ground."

"I've trained soldiers," Rafe said. "Let me drill them, get them used to fighting as a unit, not individual brawlers."

"It's not a bad idea." She finished the last of her soup and stood, brushing the damp from the seat of her trousers. "Staff meeting is in an hour at my tent. In the meantime, go find some of the civilians and teach them how to handle a sword in close combat without cutting off their own faces."

Rafe laughed and stood too. "First lesson, children. Pointy end goes in the other guy."

Assane let out a single bark of laughter and walked away shaking her head. Rafe smiled, ran his hands through his hair, and went to round up what civilians he could find for a lesson.

In the shadows of the docks, Rafe crouched beside Monjoie in the pre-dawn dark, waiting for the signal. Of all the raids they had been on, this one required the most careful timing. The tide would go out when the tide went out, and no power on earth would stop it. Either the boats would go out with it, or they weren't going out at all.

In front of them lay the fishing fleet, a forest of masts with sails furled.

From one of the boats down the line a baby cried. Rafe grimaced. Knowing that whole families lived on some of these boats just added another layer of danger to the raid. If D'nath and Madeline's people sank the boats in retaliation, a lot of innocent civilians were going to die. But if they didn't release the fleet, people would starve.

In the cabin window of the nearest boat, a red light winked three times. Up and down the docks, similar lights blinked and went out. The fisherfolk were ready.

"Ready?" Rafe whispered to Monjoie. Monjoie nodded back. The tide had just begun to turn. Monjoie pulled out his mirror from the shielded pouch where he kept it and whispered "Go. Everyone go. Go now!" He shoved the mirror back into its pouch. Hopefully, that brief use hadn't given the magical sensors a chance to lock on their position.

As Monjoie gave the order, Rafe darted forward to the nearest docked boat, racing down the dock to its anchor chain. He knelt beside the bollard where the boat was tied and laid his hands on the slender line that held the boat fixed in place. It wasn't the line's peculiar strength that kept the fishing vessel from floating away, but the magic bonded to it. Just up the dock, Monjoie was working on another line in the same way.

Rafe dug his fingers in, wrestling the magic knots under his command and shredding them. With a silent twang that he felt as a vibration all along his bones, the bond gave way. Rafe threw the line free onto the boat's deck. "Go!" he hissed. "You're free! Get out."

"Aye, sir!" a child's voice answered. Little feet pattered away into the dark, "Mum! Dad! We're away." Rafe looked up in time to see a man yank the sheets and the topsail dropped down, catching the wind as the tide pulled the boat off the dock. At the helm, a woman gave him a quick wave. Rafe sent a small current of water magic after the boat, giving an extra shove. He thought he caught a glimpse of a small face peering over the edge, waving furiously at him. He waved back once and ran to the next vessel.

All up and down the docks, fishing boats were beginning to drift quietly out to sea. Rafe freed a second boat and then a third before shouts broke out on the shore.

"We're made! To arms!"

Rafe drew his sword, racing back up the dock to meet the attack. He ran past Monjoie, still frantically trying to free one more boat, and swung his sword up to meet the attack from the Summer Court faerie about to bring a sword down on Monjoie's head.

As Monjoie cursed at the magic, Rafe twisted his sword, catching his opponent's sword by the hilt and wrenching it out of his hands. A quick thrust and he ran the soldier through. With a kick, Rafe knocked the Summer Court faerie into the water.

"Go! Go! Go!" Monjoie screamed as the boat set sail.

Flaming arrows arched overhead and landed on the boat's deck.

"Son of a bitch!" Rafe sent a spray of water lashing over the boat to put out the arrows. Monjoie screamed an inarticulate gurgle of pure rage and charged the archers. He was still screaming furiously as he cut the last one down.

"You got them!" Rafe shouted. "It's okay." He laid a hand on Monjoie's shoulder and gently turned him toward the harbor. The entire fleet was under sail and gaining speed.

"There are kids on those boats!" Monjoie shouted at him. "Bastards!"

"Yes," Rafe agreed. "Let's go kill more of them."

Monjoie smiled at him. "Let's," he said.

Rafe crossed his arms and stared at the map as the leaders discussed their options. The tent was small and a bit crowded with Rafe, Assane, and a few others.

"Our supplies are getting low, and we can't keep getting them from my family," Monjoie said. "Eventually someone will notice."

Most nodded, but Assane frowned and shook her head. "That means we'd need to do another city raid," she said, pointing to the capital city. "Every time we go all the way into the city and back out we're like rats finding our way through a maze. Sooner or later, it's going to go badly for us."

"She's right," Rafe said. "Most of us are trained for open warfare, not street-to-street combat." Sergeant Assane gave him an ungrateful look for the support.

"We need the supplies," Monjoie said.

"Then we get them from the countryside," Assane said. "An unguarded barn is a lot easier to take than a warehouse surrounded by traitors and summer court soldiers.

"No," Rafe said. "We're not looting our own people."

Assane turned on him. "They're my people, not yours, Prince. The ones that are loyal would be glad to give us food. And the ones that aren't..." She spat on the ground.

The smallest sound of movement from outside drew their attention. Zaya stepped into the tent. "I've got news. There's a supply shipment being sent from Wellhall to support the Summer Court siege at Northfalls."

"What kind of supplies?" Assane asked.

"Food, weapons, and people," Zaya said and stepped up to the map. "The Winter Court soldiers who were captured when D'Nath first arrived are being moved to the Summer Court and half the Summer Court soldiers already here are headed to Northfalls, since they feel Wellhall is under control."

"We have to stop them," Monjoie said. "If Northfalls is taken, nothing we've done here matters."

"If they go over land, we can't stop them, but we might be able to harry them enough to slow their progress," Rafe said.

Assane snorted. "Sure. That's a great idea. If they were going to move the supplies overland. But they won't. They'll go by sea, out the harbor, up through disputed waters to the Summer Court, and on to Northfalls for good measure. We won't be able to touch them."

Rafe leaned over the map, stroking his chin. It was good, but not as good as the classified maps he'd had to work with back in his Tower office.

"Do we still have contact with the fishing fleet?" Rafe asked Zaya. "If we can recruit them, I have an idea."

"Every boat is an independent entity," Zaya answered. "They don't function like a navy under a command structure. But I do have some contacts, and most of us would be happy to help if it meant killing Summer Court soldiers. What are you thinking?"

Rafe pointed to a spot about ten miles up the coast from Wellhall's harbor. "Right around here, the currents force ships to sail close to the shore. If we could put together five fishing boats we could blockade their ships. They won't expect an attack from civilian vessels."

Assane narrowed her eyes, but she looked intrigued. "For good reason. These are fisherfolk, not privateers," she reminded him.

"They don't have to be," Rafe put his finger on the map. "Right here there's a..." He paused, considering who his audience was. "There's a trap. It's a string of inert mines. You can sail back and forth over it all day in safety unless it's triggered by a member of the Admiralty command. We trigger the mines, board the Summer Court boats, and unload everything we can before they sink, including the prisoners. Then we send a garrison worth of Summer Court soldiers to the bottom."

Monjoie chuckled, a grim smile on his face. "Did you put that there or did Roger?"

"Roger and I designed it together at the King's request shortly after I was made Sword," Rafe said. "Arthur helped with the camouflage."

One of the younger lieutenants looked equal parts outraged and confused. "I don't understand," he said. "Why the hell would you plant a trap right in friendly waters like that?"

Rafe exchanged glances with Monjoie. Assane sighed. "I'm guessing the King considered Wellhall a hostile power inside the Winter Court a long time before this war ever broke out."

"Exactly," Rafe said. He raised a hand before Assane could raise the next logical question, "I don't know for certain that they haven't changed the access spells, but I'd be willing to gamble a substantial amount that Bartholomew doesn't even know it's there. He would never have agreed to it in the first place."

"What about Arthur?" Monjoie asked. "How do we know he hasn't already set it off or changed the trigger codes?"

Rafe chuckled. "Believe me, if that trap had gone off, the entire coast would have noticed. As for the triggers? As far as Arthur knows, I'm dead. Dead men aren't a security threat." He turned to Assane. "Feel up for a spot of piracy, fair lady?"

For the first time, Assane smiled at him, a wolfish smile that should have sent chills down the spine of Madeline herself, if she could have seen it. Rafe stuck out his hand and she shook it.

41

Deor snuggled herself back against Victor as he draped his arm over her. She breathed in and out, letting their shared magic settle around them. The rise and fall of his chest against her back had become a nightly comfort, a place where she could find peace and center herself. The only place, nowadays, she felt truly safe.

"I wish you didn't have to go," she whispered, a small part of her hoping he was already asleep and wouldn't hear.

"I know," he said. He gently kissed the top of her head. "I will miss you, miss this, too."

"You want to go," Deor said. It wasn't a question. She could feel the eagerness in him.

"It's my home," he said.

"I understand," she cut him off before he could once again list all the reasons he had to do this—reasons she agreed with completely. They didn't make his leaving any easier. She sighed. "I know all the reasons. They're all good reasons. You have to go."

"But you don't want me to go." She could hear the smile in his voice.

"Exactly." She blinked hard a few times, knowing that the tears would only be kept at bay for so long. She didn't fight them. She didn't want to fight anything anymore.

He tightened his grip on her. "I'll still be with you. You'll still be with me."

Deor nodded and sniffed. "I know."

He scooted down and rested his chin on her shoulder, his cheek pressed against hers. His tears mingled with hers. "I'm afraid too," he said quietly. "We all are."

"I know." Deor said.

"This will all be over soon enough," he said, though she sensed he wasn't certain. "I believe we can win. Your plan to bring in the vampires is brilliant. It will work. We'll keep the Winter Court and everyone in it safe."

"We will." She gave as much confidence to the words as she could, knowing that Victor could see right through any kind of obfuscation. She did believe it, or at least believed it was possible. She knew, too, that the cost would be high. "I don't want to lose you.".

"You won't. I am the protector of the Winter Court, of you. Always." The words weighed heavy in her ears, like he spoke a prophecy, not a platitude. Something about them ended any argument. She said nothing else, closing her eyes and letting the warmth of his body and his magic help her drift to sleep.

The next morning at the portal, she clung to him for a few extra moments, drinking in their connection, their magic, finding the place where they touched, the link between them, anchored at both ends, connected no matter how far apart they were, stretched infinitely thin, but never broken.

As he let go and she relented, releasing him, he whispered in her ear, "Always."

Before she could say anything else, he brushed his lips across her cheek and turned away, gesturing at Donovan. In the blink of an eye, they were through the portal, offering only a glimpse of the woods in Wellhall before vanishing.

42

The raid of the Summer Court ships was still a few days away, and Rafe whistled an old sea shanty to himself as he sharpened his knife by the fire, waiting for the evening conversation to begin. It was a long way from the formal morning briefings he had once held with Finn, Arthur, and Michael in the Palace, but, as far as Rafe was concerned, that was all to the good. On the other side of the fire, Sgt. Assane poked the coals and kept an eye on him.

Not too long after, Monjoie and the rest of the command team had gathered around the fire. As a group, the resistors had no official hierarchy, but they functioned. Authority was taken and given as expertise and a willingness to lead emerged. Most decisions were made by loose consensus or deference to whoever knew the issue of debate best.

When Rafe spoke, people usually listened, but they weren't hesitant to question or argue. He suspected that even if he attained the title of Duke someday, his people would maintain the same attitude. Titles were inherited. Respect had to be earned. As Monjoie stood and cleared his throat, Rafe politely stowed his knife and whetstone and folded his hands on his lap.

"Alright," Monjoie said. "We're well supplied for now and reasonably well sheltered." Most of the others nodded, although an air faerie beside Sgt. Assane muttered something about "Shelter my ass. Maybe if it would stop raining." Monjoie ignored her and went on, "And we're on track to take down that Summer Court transport ship in a few days, thanks to the information Rafe has supplied us. But we've got a new problem. Someone else is in these woods, and I think they're looking for us. It's a small party—only two people by the signs. But we've got to move camp again."

Resigned groans answered him.

Assane said, "Or we could just find them first and kill them."

"She's got a point," Rafe said.

"I don't disagree with eliminating them," Monjoie said. "But we still need to move camp. If they found us it's a sign we've been in one place for too long."

One of the others by the fire, a forester for the duchess, said "They're city folk, I'd guess. Their woodcraft isn't the best, though they aren't total blunderers. They aren't locals looking to join us either, I think. It shouldn't be too hard to lay an ambush for them."

"I'd like to be in that party," Rafe said. "If there's only two we should be able to capture and question them to find out what they're doing and who they work for."

Others blinked at him for a minute before Monjoie said, "I should think that was fairly obvious."

Rafe shook his head. "If it were Madeline and D'Nath sending out spies, they'd have sent people who knew their way around the woods. They could even be allies looking to join us."

"Unless they're trying to lure us out by looking incompetent," Sgt Assane said. "It could be they're trying to trap us."

"Fair point. But we can't run too far, or we'll lose our base of operations. And they already know we are here. So let's have a chat with them," Rafe said. That got a murmur of agreement around the fire.

Monjoie nodded. "Let's take them alive if at all possible."

True to the forester's prediction, it took only a day to track down the intruders. Crouched beside Monjoie, Rafe peered at them from a bush as one tended a small, smokeless fire and the other hung well back, wrapped in a cloak as he leaned his back on a stump. Two others from the resistance were already positioned opposite the strangers' camp, waiting for the signal.

The one by the stump said, "I understand preferring your food warm, but charred? Madness." He sipped from a flask as his companion threaded a skinned squirrel onto a stick for roasting.

Rafe gripped Monjoie's arm. "I know him," he said. "Hold back." Quietly, he drew his sword. Without waiting for Monjoie's signal he stood up and walked into the circle of firelight. "What are you doing in my lands, Donovan?"

Donovan's already pale face could hardly get paler at the sight of Rafe walking out of the shadows, but he did grip his flask to his chest. Faster than Rafe's eye could follow, he was on his feet, a knife in his hand.

"I see who you're pretending to be," he said, "but as far as I know Rafe is dead. So drop the glamour, please."

"It's no glamour," Rafe said. "Look. It's me." He pointed to his cheek. "I haven't even glamoured my scar."

This did not seem to reduce Donovan's suspicion. He glanced at his companion, who was still crouched by the fire, hand inching toward the knife on his belt. He raised an eyebrow, and Rafe heard Victor speak a word of dispelling.

The next second Victor let out a yell and threw his arms around Rafe's neck. "You're alive! You're alive!" He squeezed Rafe so hard, Rafe thought his ribs might crack. Then he stepped back, taking Rafe in, sword, staff, and monk's robe, and he punched Rafe hard in the chest.

Rafe gasped and stumbled a step back, rubbing his chest.

"Hands in the air!" Arrows nocked and knives out, Monjoie and the others stepped out of their hiding places. "Not another move or I'll drop you," Monjoie said.

Wheezing, Rafe tried to wave them off. "It's okay. I'm not hurt. Much." Cautiously, the party lowered their weapons. "What are you doing here?"

A feral smile spread across Donovan's face. "I've been hired to invade your castle and handle your little Summer Court infestation for you." He took a deep swig of the blood in his flask and saluted Rafe with it before throwing an arm around Rafe's shoulders and hugging him tight. "You have a lot of explaining to do, you truant."

That got a laugh from the rest of Rafe's group. Knives went back in their sheathes, and the forester put her arrow back in its quiver. Only Monjoie kept his hand on the hilt of his sword and a wary eye on Victor. Rafe hid his hands inside his sleeves to cover his own impulse to punch Victor in his smirking mouth.

"Hang on a moment," Victor said. "He's here?" He pointed at Monjoie with his knife.

"Yes. It's a long story."

Victor crossed the small clearing in two strides, his knife pointed at Monjoie. "I swore I'd gut you if I ever got the chance. Defend yourself, or I'll cut you down as you are."

Monjoie backed away and Victor charged after him. He lunged and slashed at Monjoie. Cloth shredded, and a line of blood oozed across Monjoie's stomach. Victor stabbed again, and Monjoie drew his sword, parrying the stab, but only barely. The others fell back in confusion, not sure who to attack. The forester nocked an arrow, but before she could fire it into Victor's back, Donovan had her in a stranglehold, one arm twisted behind her back.

Rafe lunged after Victor, grabbing him by the back of his shirt. "No!" Rafe hauled him backward, tumbling both of them to the ground. They thrashed on the ground, a mess of limbs and knees. Rafe got Victor by the wrist, fighting to force his hand away. "Let go. Let. It. Go." Rafe knelt on top of Victor, pinning his body to the damp ground.

Victor thrashed under him. "Let me kill him! You don't know what he did to me! You don't know." His voice was ragged with pain.

"Knock it off. Whatever petty quarrel you have with him can wait. He's on our side."

Victor glared up at Rafe from the ground. "Petty? You call torturing me in the Tower petty?"

Rafe lowered his voice, leaning in so that only Victor could hear him. "I'm not beating the stuffing out of you right now, much as I'd like to. So you can control yourself too. We have Summer Court enemies enough."

Surprise knocked some of the anger out of Victor's face. "Why would you be angry with me?"

"Don't be coy. I saw you coming out of her room half naked the morning of the Proving."

Victor thrashed under Rafe's knees and finally threw his knife at Donovan's feet. "I'm unarmed. Happy? Now let me up."

Slowly, Rafe did. All around them the Wellhall Resistance and Donovan held each other at knife's point, eyes locked on Victor and Rafe. Victor made no further move for a knife and Rafe did not draw his sword.

"What the hell were you doing at the Proving?" Victor hissed.

"I could ask you the same thing," Rafe said. "Now are you going to tell me what you're doing in my forest or not?"

"Your forest? I grew up here!" Victor looked around the circle of firelit Resistors and then took in Rafe's brown wool robe. "Unbelievable. You're the Ghost. My dead brother is the Wellhall Ghost." His shoulders sagged and he rubbed his hands over his face, muttering curses and half laughing to himself. Donovan dropped his grip on the forester and Monjoie cautiously resheathed his sword. "I'm the Regent's Consort. She sent Donovan and I to find a way into Wellhall Castle. Our intelligence said that Ghost was most likely an entire resistance movement, so our first plan was to find them."

"Well, you found us." Rafe sagged with relief, even as the sight of Victor's face twisted his insides with grief, jealousy, and a host of other emotions he didn't have time to sort out. "We could use all the help we can get, but I don't know if the two of you are enough to turn the tide of battle." Shaking his head, he deliberately turned his back on Victor to pick up his quarterstaff, showing the others that the danger was over. The tension in the clearing eased further.

Rafe held out his hand to Donovan and they clasped hands before Donovan pulled him into a one-armed hug. "Welcome back from the dead. How did that happen?"

"It's good to see you too," Rafe said. "Let's get back to our main camp and we can all answer each other's questions there." He looked between Victor and Monjoie. "Whatever quarrels the three of us have will wait. Understood?"

Monjoie stepped forward. "Please, Victor. I know I can't change what I did, but I promise you I am deeply ashamed of myself. I thought at the time I was doing the right thing. If you want to call me out after all this, I understand."

Victor spat on the ground. "I don't trust you. I never will. I don't care what side you're on. But as long as we're fighting the Summer Court it can wait."

Monjoie nodded, his shoulders drooping with shame. Some of the resistance members edged closer to Monjoie, throwing hostile looks at Victor, while others looked back and forth between Rafe and the other two, not sure where their loyalties lay.

Rafe couldn't bring himself to put his arm around his brother's shoulders, but he said. "That's good enough. We can sort out other things when the war is won."

As he spoke, Rafe felt again the power and connection of the land beneath his feet and all around him. This was his land. His home. Madeline might still hold the title, but it was time for him to take command. "Alright, marching orders. We're going back to camp. Tonight Victor and

Donovan will explain their mission here. Tomorrow we're going to take those Summer Court ships and all their cargo, or send them to the bottom of the ocean. Let's move out."

Without waiting for the others to debate, Rafe doused the fire with a flick of his wrist. He cast a light ahead of him and strode into the dark. The footsteps of the others fell into line behind him.

43

Deor sat in her office, chin in her hand, staring at nothing. Her mind wandered from subject to subject, flitting like a butterfly on flowers. She'd barely touch on an idea, and her mind would jump again. Anytime she tried to focus on something that stirred her emotions—which, at this point, was anything at all—she would lose focus and drift.

For now, her mind drifted to Astarte and Robbie, who she had sent to the Vampire Court this morning. An entourage of vampires had come to escort them, and many stayed in preparation for the invasion. Bartholomew had planned the exile of the former Consort and her daughter well, playing like it was some big secret, hidden poorly. They all hoped Queen Eura would hear of it and see in it a desperate resignation by the Winter Court to protect people in the face of certain defeat.

Daily reports from Northfalls had maintained the status quo. A few deaths here and there, always more on the Winter Court side than on the Summer Court side. Farms outside Northfalls burned by the invaders. She could see the worry in Roger's eyes as he tried to pretend that everything was fine. Everyone was trapped in a holding pattern until she heard from Victor.

The door to her office swung open, no knock, and Stephen strode in, followed by Genevieve. Both looked breathless and giddy, like something delightful had happened.

Deor sat up. "What is it?" Hope fluttered in her chest.

"I can't believe it," Stephen said, running a hand through his blond curls. He swept his fingers through again, like he was making sure his hair was in place. Stephen, the least vain person she knew, was worried about how he looked. He straightened his uniform.

Next to him, Genevieve bounced like a young girl. "You have a visitor. A very important visitor!"

"The most important," Stephen added.

"Oh?" Deor frowned and squinted. She couldn't see any magic on them, though she'd swear they were under some kind of spell. "Who is it?"

"Puck!" Genevieve declared like it explained everything.

"Puck?" Deor asked. Like the one from the Shakespeare play? It hadn't occurred to her that any of Shakespeare's faeries could have been real, but why wouldn't they be?

Stephen shook his head at her and hurried forward. "Stand up. He'll be here any second."

Deor stood, motivated more by surprise than compliance.

A man appeared in her doorway.

Genevieve and Stephen stepped to the side, flanking his entrance.

He was about average height for a faerie, with blond curls and brilliant golden eyes. He had fine features, perfect in symmetry. He wore Victorian style clothes, with fine-cut black slacks, a waistcoat and jacket, a crisp white shirt, and a golden cravat that matched his eyes. The man glowed— but it wasn't light that shone off him, it was magic. Bright enough that it made Deor wince. The magic around him was soft and fuzzy. Hollywood could not have done a better job of lighting. He carried a walking stick, topped with a golden butterfly, and he rested the golden tip on the floor. He stared straight at her, a small smile on his lips. He seemed utterly nonplussed by the fawning people around him.

He nodded his head ever so slightly, "Lady Regent. I am Puck."

Genevieve let out a small squeak of delight, and Stephen waved him into the room. "This way, Your Majesty."

Puck chuckled, "Thank you, young man." He crossed to Deor's desk, where she stared at him. Behind him, Genevieve and Stephen fell into step. Neither of them could take their eyes off the faerie that stood before them.

"It is nice to meet you." Deor held her hand out across the desk and waited.

Puck took it and raised it to his lips.

As she pulled her hand back, magic tingled across Deor's skin outward from where his lips brushed her hand. It raced up her arm, and soon the sensation covered her whole body. Her own magic pressed back against it, and she resisted the urge to shake like a wet dog and fling the evidence of his touch off her body. He stared expectantly, and she forced a flattered smile. She couldn't quite put a finger on the source of her caution, only that it was necessary. For a second, she wished she were in the throne room, the full weight of the Winter Court behind her.

"If you wouldn't mind, I would love the chance to speak to you alone." He subtly tilted his head in reference to Genevieve and Stephen.

"Oh, of course!" Genevieve answered before Deor could speak. "I'm sure Her Majesty would appreciate the privacy."

"Right," Stephen said, much to Deor's surprise. He was disinclined to leave her alone in a room with just about anyone, but he merrily swept out the door with Genevieve.

Deor sat and gestured at the chair across from her. "Please," she said. "Do sit."

Puck lowered himself into the chair with liquid grace, his eyes never leaving hers. "Thank you."

"So... Puck... what can I do for you?" She shook her head softly. "I'm sorry, my people seem to know who you are, but I am at a loss. Do you come from the Summer Court?"

He burst out laughing, and it rang through the room, a small part of her thrilling with delight at his mirth. "Goodness, no." He leaned toward her. "I am of no court, of no people, save the faeries. I am older than the courts, older than almost any sentient thing in this world." His voice was low, hushed, tempting and Deor had to lean forward to hear.

"Is that so?" she said. "I haven't been here long, and that must be why I had not heard of you." She paused and considered him. "Except in that play by Shakespeare."

His eyebrows shot up. "Oh, you know the play? That was so long ago. I thought you were young..."

"I am," Deor said. "But I studied Shakespeare in school. I've taught the play. So you are the Puck in the play? Robin Goodfellow?"

"I am. Puck is the name I go by now, though I've gone by others, like Goodfellow, in the past."

"How fascinating." The Puck in Shakespeare's play was a psychopath, no matter how many cheerily dressed actors tried to make him harmless. She doubted the Bard had made a mistake. "So, what can I do for you?"

"Nothing, my dear," he said. "I've come to do something for you. To help." His face turned sad. "The war with the Summer Court is a nasty thing." His face was filled with compassion, and his eyes radiated a desire to help her, to ease suffering.

Deor jolted as a memory flared in her mind. This man—this creature —sitting in front of her. She had met him, well, not met, but seen him before. The man in the corner of the dungeon. The man to whom Finn looked for guidance before he ripped the lashes on her back open again. Puck. Puck had tried to comfort her then, sending healing magic, and her whole body, faerie and human, had recoiled. Whatever he was, he was wrong. Once again, as it had that night, her whole self screamed at her *kill it.*

"Are you well, Your Majesty?" Puck said. A small glint of worry creased his brow.

"Yes," Deor said, too quickly. "I'm sorry." She was shivering now, and fear surged in her. "I realized that I recognize you. You were in the cell the night Finn tore open my wounds."

His eyes widened slightly, but then he beamed. "I thought you saw me then. Your father was out of control. I tried to talk sense into him. The relationship between the monarch and heir must not be so broken. But he did not listen." He shook his head sadly. "This result—his exile and the war with the Summer Court—are the result of his foolishness, his malice, and his narcissism."

Deor couldn't argue with that. "True."

"I've come to help you try to stop the war. You and your people need my aid. The kingdom, without a true monarch on the throne, is weak, vulnerable."

Deor nodded, unhappy that she couldn't disagree with his logic. Still, her instincts screamed at her not to trust him. "What do you suggest I do?"

"Take the seat yourself." He shrugged as if it were the easiest solution in the world. "You've already proven yourself more rational and reason-able, more fit to govern, in a matter of weeks than he proved in centuries. You will be a great queen." He leaned forward and extended his hand to her. "Come. Let us go to the throne room. I will help you."

She eyed his hand. "Alright," she said, without taking it. "Let's go to the throne room."

She stepped away from the desk and touched the lintel on the door. Whatever this was, whatever was going to happen, she didn't want

Stephen, Genevieve, or anyone there for it. Not with their irrational love of this creature. "The Throne Room." The portal opened. "Come on," she said, beckoning him to follow.

"You do not want your friends?" He stood, looking puzzled.

"No," she said. "I need to do this on my own."

"Ah, yes!" He beamed at her, and it reminded her a touch of Finn, like she was a pet that had performed some clever trick. "You are strong that way."

Deor said nothing. She gathered her skirts in her hands to hide the silver of her fingertips and stepped through the portal.

The throne room was empty. The black and white marble checkerboard floor gleamed in the light from candles always kept burning and the large windows above. At the far end the throne sat, black stone on a raised stone dais. Today it seemed a normal, if slightly large, chair. There were days it loomed, and days it beckoned.

As Deor walked toward the seat of the Winter Court's power, the feeling of Puck's power grew. He hovered barely a step behind her. In his swirling power rose a desperate hunger, a longing that made her shudder once again. Her silver fingernails grew and a silver halo framed her vision. She stepped onto the dais next to the throne and turned to face him.

Puck paused at the foot of the throne. Hunger etched each of his features and his golden eyes burned with desire—violent and insatiable. No matter what else happened, Deor knew, he must not touch the throne.

Deor rested her hand on the back of the throne, the stone cool under her fingertips. A loud roar filled the room as Boomie appeared, the feline, winged avatar of the palace. It swooped around and around in circles before settling on the back of the throne. It hissed, bearing its teeth.

"Easy now, gentle palace. I've not come to harm you or take your power, deep and ancient as it is. I am your ally."

Puck's words echoed in her ears, and she recognized them as Faerie, Old Faerie. Older than anything she had heard before, even on the throne itself. She suspected she only understood because she touched the throne.

Boomie sat back and stared at Puck but did not hiss again.

Deor drew magic from the throne into her—something she had never done before, never had known she could do, but now it waited there, in the stone itself, eager to pour itself into her. "You claim to be the oldest faerie alive," she said. The magic filled her with light, and her eyes glowed silver.

"I am." He stepped a bit closer. "I can show you power like you've never seen. You won't just stop the Summer Court, you'll conquer it, and all of the Fae, all of the world."

The magic filled her now, so much that she couldn't tell what was her and what was magic. The foundation of Fae itself trembled deep in the earth, below the throne, below the court, a well of magic itself, pure. Pure and vulnerable. And this thing, this creature, wanted it.

Kill it.

The words came from inside and outside of her at once.

The shimmering beauty, the stunning power, the demand to be adored that coated Puck cracked and fell away. He looked no different—if anything he was even more beautiful, more powerful, like an angel—but with his power laid bare, so was his essence. At his core was an abyss so dark, so vast, that it would swallow the world.

Maybe Puck had been an angel once, like Lucifer, filled with light and grace. Now, like Lucifer, the beauty remained, but the grace was gone, and Puck was hungry to get it back. Deor gazed at the power of him and wondered why he didn't take it, seize the throne, and eat his fill.

"*Let me help you, Majesty,*" he said to her. "*Through you, I can end the suffering not only here, but across the world.*"

"You cannot take it, can you? Even as close as you stand."

"*I will make you a queen incomparable.*"

Deor laughed then, and sparkles blossomed around her. "And all will love me?"

"*Yes?*" He seemed confused now, like he knew she asked a trick question.

"And despair," she said, only to herself. She lifted her hand from the throne, and magic filled her palm, coalescing into the pommel of a sword. Sparks rushed upward into a blade whose edges glittered with light and magic. She lowered the sword, pointing the tip at his chest. "No." She stepped toward him, and he backed up, nearly stumbling off the dais. She drove him back across the room to the door. "Whatever you are, the answer is no. Now," she leveled the sword at his throat, "get out of my kingdom, or I will slay you where you stand."

Puck's eyes narrowed, and all pretense of civility fell away. Before her stood one of the original faeries, whose power should have burned her eyes. His rage should have terrified her.

Under her feet, the Winter Court stood, hers. Hers to draw from, hers to defend. Beyond that, all of Fae, too, hers to protect.

"Fool," he spat. He twirled toward the door but vanished before his hand touched the knob.

Deor blew out a sigh and let the sword fall from her hand, vanishing into a fountain of sparks. Behind her, she heard Boomie jump off the throne and land with a loud stone *thud* on the marble floor. He padded up next to her. "We've not seen the last of him, have we, Boomie?" She knelt down and stroked his chin.

No. The creature purred.

The doors to the room burst open, and Deor fell back on her ass, narrowly avoiding being hit. Brand hurled himself in and flung himself at her. Behind him, Stephen, sword drawn.

"What are you doing?" she asked as she caught Brand and hugged him. He rested his paws on her shoulders and sniffed her all over.

"Brand was barking and whining in your office. I opened the door, and you were gone. Why didn't you get me? Why didn't you take Brand with you? Why are you in here?"

Deor gently shoved Brand aside and held out her hands to Stephen. He slipped his sword in its sheath and helped her up. "Our visitor is gone."

"Who?" Stephen frowned.

Deor blinked at him. "Have I had any visitors to the palace today?"

"No." He shook his head. "Were you expecting someone?"

"No." She glanced down at Boomie who stared up at her expectantly. "I just meant Boomie. I came here to think and have a chat with him. I should have told you, and not just portalled." Something about Puck, the power he wielded over Stephen and Genevieve, shook her to her core. She didn't have words to explain the danger she felt in her soul, and they had more immediate problems than some all-consuming faerie elder god that she had no idea how to kill.

"Yeah, let me know." He scanned the room. "Plus I'm jittery today—everyone is. Genevieve was short with a servant—and she's never like that. Even Chloe stalked off to beat up a punching bag."

"I think we're all out of sorts." Deor linked her arm through Stephen's. "Come on, let's go check on Genevieve and see what's on the docket for tomorrow."

44

Rafe stood on the upper deck of the fishing boat, squinting into the sun as the distant Summer Court ships tacked against the wind toward the hidden mines in the waters below. The fishing boat they were on, *The Eider Duck*, was captained by Zaya. She held the helm lightly, guiding her vessel with imperceptible twitches of the wheel. Her water magic was weak, barely enough to stir the waters of a bathtub, but it had been evident the minute they stepped aboard that she held her crew's full respect and admiration.

When Monjoie had elected to go on one of the other vessels and Donovan had gone with him, Victor had been quick to volunteer for the *Eider*. But Rafe was barely more comfortable with him there than Victor was with Monjoie. Every time Rafe looked at his brother fully, he pictured him shirtless, leaving Deor's room.

Some part of him could admit that wherever he and Deor's growing intimacy might have gone without Arthur's interference, none of that obligated Deor to keep celibate after he was gone. But the louder part of him kept repeating *my own creator damned brother! Of all the eligible men in the Winter Court she had to choose my own godforsaken brother to sleep with the minute I was gone.* Victor had tried once or twice to raise the topic between them, but Rafe had pushed the conversation off as much to keep himself from punching a needed ally in the nose as anything else. Sooner or later they would have to talk, but he preferred later. After the war was over, perhaps.

For the time being he used Zaya as a buffer between them. They could fight and work beside each other. They didn't need to talk about it. Under Rafe's feet, the deck rocked in the gentle swell, canvas half-furled and a net draped over the side as the *Eider* gave the impression of a sleepy fishing vessel gently trolling the waters.

"Never thought I'd turn pirate," Zaya said, her hand barely twitching the wheel.

Rafe laughed. "Don't lie. I'll bet you dreamed about it as a kid just like me." He gestured at the wicked billhook hanging at her belt. She laughed and cupped her hand over her eyes, shielding them from the sun.

"It's not piracy if you're acting on the Queen's warrant," Victor said with a wry grin. "We're privateers. Very respectable." He had tied a piece of cloth over his head and tucked a brace of knives into his belt.

Rafe took out a pocket mirror and flipped it open. "Ready?"

Monjoie answered. "Waiting for your signal."

Rafe turned his attention to the ships, mirror held out in front of him. Timing was everything. "Steady on." Below on the lower deck of each ship, sailors stood by the sheets and nets, ready to haul in as soon as the signal came.

Using his mirror and the position of the sun as focal points, Rafe watched the Summer Court vessels close the distance. Ten seconds. Nine. Thank the Creator Roger had insisted Rafe learn some basic navigation all those years ago when Finn had bought him his first yacht.

"You can't sail just by giving orders, Princeling," Roger had said, "not if you want your crew to have any respect for you at all. Either you're a good captain who knows how to bring the boat back safely, or you're just a spoiled lump of a passenger the sailors have to put up with to earn their bread. The sea doesn't give a damn how many shiny titles you have."

Over the course of a long summer, Roger had shown Rafe how to use every rope and sail, how to navigate by the stars and sun, and how to keep a steady hand on the rudder. The fact that he had done it all while wearing impeccable lace cuffs and embroidered silk waistcoats over his kilt had only made the lessons more impressive.

Rafe held up his hand, gathering magic power tethered to the mines that lurked under the surface. Four seconds. Three. Two. Rafe spoke the words to trigger the first mine. A geyser shot out of the water, rocking one of the Summer Court ships. For a second, Rafe thought the ship would turn turtle, but it slowly righted itself.

"Now! Now! Go now!" he shouted into the mirror. Behind him, Zaya was shouting to her crew. Sails unfurled with a thud and a snap. Sailors hauled in the empty nets even as the ship picked up speed. The blue and silver flag of Wellhall flared from the masthead.

"Give us a boost there, Consort," Zaya shouted to Victor and he complied, calling the waves to push them faster over the waters. Rafe added his magic to Victor's and was shocked to find that his brother didn't need it. He had never been weak, but now there was a power in him beyond anything Rafe would have expected. In a faint way, it reminded Rafe of what he felt when he had touched the altar.

The other four boats were coming, heading for the other ships, but the *Eider* would reach the lead ship first. Rafe shoved his mirror in his pocket and turned his attention to the mines. Timing their approach to be just outside the blast radius, he spoke the trigger word, imbuing it with his magic. A second mine erupted, and the second Summer Court ship shook, then listed heavily to the side. A third and the last of the Summer Court ships was hit. On board the Summer Court ships, air faeries scrambled to fill the sails while other crew warded the ship and sent currents against the approaching vessels.

Rafe drew his sword. "Bring us alongside, Captain," he shouted. Gripping a rope with one hand, he braced a foot on the ship's rail and hopped up onto it. On either side of him, grappling hooks flew out and thudded into the Summer Court ship's deck, biting into the wood. Arrows and crossbow bolts answered from the other side.

"Surrender in the name of the Duchy of Wellhall!" Rafe roared. "This is your only warning."

"Never!" the ship's captain shouted back. A crossbow bolt ricocheted off Rafe's shield spell right at chest height.

"Then prepare to be boarded!" Rafe leaned far out over the water, held only by his grip on the rope, as *The Eider Duck* swung alongside the Summer Court ship. At the peak of the swing, he launched himself forward, wings flaring out at the last second to slow his landing on the deck. He cut down an open-mouthed sailor where he stood and pulled his wings in a split second before another sailor could put a knife through one.

Chaos of weapons and limbs erupted across the deck as sailors poured off the *Eider*. Rafe fought his way aft, headed for the steersman. A soldier loomed across Rafe's path, and Rafe cut him down, kicking the body out of the way.

Rafe risked putting out his wings and jumped off from the deck, his wings giving him the extra lift to reach the steersman. He pulled his wings in and dropped, sword slashing downward. The man died before he could put up his hands.

Without anyone to manage it, the tiller swung wildly. The Summer Court ship groaned, its masts waving back and forth as the sinking ship floundered. Rafe grabbed the helm, fighting to straighten the tiller and keep the ship upright.

A last cry of pain and suddenly everything was deadly quiet. The writhing chaos on the deck below him came to a halt. There was no one left to fight. Rafe's people looked around in shock, weapons still raised.

"Huzzah!" Zaya bellowed.

"Huzzah!" the boarding party echoed her cry, Rafe joining in.

On either side of the ship, Rafe heard similar cries go up from the other Summer Court vessels. They'd won.

"Alright, my friends," Rafe shouted from the helm. "Let's get this tub stripped clean. Free our comrades and get whatever we can take before she sinks."

Victor, his face spattered with blood, put out his wings and drifted downward to alight next to Rafe. "My kind of battle," Victor said. "Quick, decisive, and best of all, over."

Rafe nodded, giving his brother an awkward smile. Under their feet, the ship groaned. No doubt they were taking on water fast, but there were plenty of experienced sailors aboard who could estimate just how long they had before the ship went down.

"There never seems to be a good time to say this," Victor said, "This is probably the most privacy we've had since you found us..."

Rafe put up a hand. "We don't need to discuss the Regent," he said. "You both thought I was dead when you got together."

"True," Victor said. "But that's... We should still talk. About several things." He jerked his head toward the deck, indicating Monjoie with his eyes and his frown.

"Later," Rafe said.

"When?" Victor said.

How about never? Never is good for me. Rafe knew that was foolish, but before he could give Victor an answer, Donovan arrived with a blur, putting on a pair of dark glasses and a fanged smirk. "I do so enjoy winning."

Rafe laughed, relieved. "Any battle you can walk away from… right?" he said. "What's the word below?"

"As I understand it, this ship is going down," Donovan said.

"Boat," both Victor and Rafe corrected him in unison.

"It has three masts," Victor said, pointing.

"It's a large floating thing that keeps me on the water instead of in it," Donovan said. "Everything else is trivia. More importantly, it's sinking faster than expected. Monjoie sent me to get you. Your mines put a big hole in the side."

"Right." Rafe slapped the helm affectionately. It had been a beautiful boat. Pity to send it to the bottom. "Let's get off this baby and get a safe distance away."

Donovan was already gone, leaping to the lower deck, and the fisher-folk were helping the freed soldiers onto their boats. Victor caught Rafe's sleeve. "We really should talk. About personal things. About Deor. And us. And Wellhall."

Turning, Rafe looked him in the eye. "Alright, we'll talk. But not here."

Victor opened his mouth, closed it again, and said, "Okay. But let's not wait until the war is over to have that conversation."

Under their feet, the deck groaned and warped. Rafe put out his wings and kicked off the shuddering deck. Victor followed suit.

When Rafe landed back on the *Eider,* he turned to look behind him, eyes focused on the floundering Summer Court boat. Victor landed not far from him. They watched as the Summer Court vessel creaked and groaned, its deck a tangle of spars and canvas as it tilted toward its watery grave.

Later that night, Rafe approached the two civilians on watch and gave the password to relieve them.

"Hello, Lord Farringdon!" the younger, curly-haired girl said, gleefully.

"Counter pass!" Rafe snapped at her. They had been over this again and again. Glamours existed, and the Summer Court was hunting for them. This wasn't a game of hide and seek, even if he did remember these two from rescuing the men in the stocks.

Beside the youngster, the older girl sighed, lightly clouted the younger one on the back of the head, and gave the counter pass.

"Thank you," Rafe said. "I'll take it from here." As the two returned to the main camp, Rafe positioned himself in their place, his back to a wide tree that afforded him a good view of the relatively open space around him while giving a good dapple of shade even in the light of the moon. He settled into a watchman's stance, checking that his knees were not locked and noting the position of the stars overhead so that he could mark the passage of time.

After about an hour had passed, light footsteps crackled in the underbrush, coming from the direction of the camp. Rafe pressed further back into the tree's shadow but didn't glamour himself. This close to whoever it was, the motion would give away his position more than a glamour would help.

"Rafe, it's me," Victor said. "The password is swordfish."

"Marlin," Rafe said back

Victor joined him in the tree's shadow, his own stance as practiced as Rafe's. They stood, shoulder to shoulder, but not speaking.

Finally, Rafe said, "What do you need, Victor?"

"This is a fairly secure spot," his brother said. "And Monjoie is asleep back in camp, so I know he won't overhear us. Let's have that talk."

"You can trust Monjoie," Rafe said. "We're on the same side."

Victor barked a single laugh. "Not if I had a signed affidavit from the entire bardic college."

"What he did…"

"You have no idea what he did."

Silence lapsed between them again, this time cold and angry, a silence that pushed them further and further apart the longer it lasted.

"I don't give a hang about reconciling with Monjoie," Victor said. "But you and I barely had a chance to know each other as brothers before you disappeared. Now you're back from the dead, in league with the person who tortured me in the Tower, and somehow you're angry with me. What happened?"

"It's a long story."

"And a watch shift is two hours. Talk."

Rafe took a deep breath, searching for words that wouldn't sound dismissive. What did you say when you were friends with your brother's torturer? Anything short of, "Let's go slit his throat," was too little, but he tried to explain.

"The place we were... Mont Saint-Michel, the location of the Proving. Neither of us knew if we were ever coming back here. It's a small place that makes everything else in the world feel far away and distant. There's only the community. And you're either a part of the community, or you're a dead man."

"So they forced you?"

"No. No one ever forced us to do anything. Not really. We arrived at the same time and we were healed together. At first, I hated him too, but after I touched the altar, everything was different. All the squabbles over power, between Summer and Winter, between Finn and Madeleine... They all seemed so petty. So beside the point."

Victor threw up his hands. "If it's all so 'beside the point' what the fuck are you doing here? What makes this petty squabble so worth it? Or is it not so petty when it's your title that's on the line?"

Rafe shook his head. "Wellhall matters. The people, their lives, the life of the land, those things matter. Having a Farringdon in the ducal seat— that doesn't matter nearly as much. If I die, you can take over. If we're both gone, a new family line can be appointed. We're just stewards." There it was. There was the word he had needed. "We're stewards," he repeated. "We hold the land and the power to keep the people alive. If we fail it will do harm, but we can always be replaced."

Victor rolled his eyes, shaking his head and looking out into the dark, waving branches of the trees overhead. "So now you're a mystic."

"No! I'm not Finn's boy anymore. I'm not the Sword. I'm not the Duke either. I passed up the chance to become a monk and guard the Source that's held in the altar because I'm needed here. That's all I know about myself these days. I'm needed here. So here I am."

"And you brought Monjoie back with you. Stellar choice that. You should have gutted him and sent his ears to our mother. See how well she likes her precious little tool then."

"I used to think the same thing about you," Rafe said.

"That was different!"

"Monjoie has less of a conscience than you do. He's more fanatical about Wellhall, from what I can tell. But still, it's not that different."

"I'm not a torturer," Victor said.

Rafe pointed to the scar on his face. When was the last time he'd bothered to glamour it? Never mind. It didn't matter.

"I told you!" Victor shouted. His voice rang among the trees, and he hastily lowered it to an angry whisper. "I didn't know the blade was poisoned."

"And I believe you. But listen to me. Monjoie believed in Madeline, just like you did. He hurt you because he was following her orders and, yes, because he wanted to hurt you for 'betraying' Madeline. He knows better now. Just like you do."

Victor harrumphed and turned his face away. "I'm your brother. Your only brother. And you're taking his side."

"If brotherhood means so much to you, why are you sleeping with the woman I…" Rafe broke off the sentence. There it was. The anger at Victor he'd been trying to suppress Now the dam had broken, and the words poured out. "When did that start, eh? Were you already 'comforting' her in the Tower or did you have the decency to wait until I went missing?"

"What the hell is wrong with you?" Victor didn't bother to keep his voice down anymore. "She was nothing more than a fling to you and here you are acting as if I seduced your paramour. Not to mention you were presumed dead! What was she supposed to do—cast a veil over her face and retreat into the Palace to weep? So yes, she picked me as her Consort. And then we slept together. What is it to you?"

And that was the question. Rafe stared at his brother until he couldn't meet Victor's eyes any longer. "You're right," he said. "A fling was all she offered me. I have no right to be jealous. But I am," he went on. "I miss her every day. And yes, I am angry she didn't mourn for me. Or at least wait until she knew I was dead."

Victor bit his lip and looked up at the stars as if asking them for patience. "You don't know her very well if you think she isn't mourning."

"I don't know what she's doing," Rafe said.

In the moon's light, Victor's blue skin seemed gray, rigid and distant. The new and different power that Rafe had felt in him at the sinking of the Summer Court boat vibrated in him. "That, at least, is true," Victor said. "You don't have any idea what she's dealing with as Regent. But I do. So for now, I'm not going to tell her who the Ghost is or that you were there at the Proving. She has enough to manage. Afterward, you can explain yourself. If you think any explanation would be good enough."

Sorrow weighed down on Rafe. The more he tried, the more people he lost. Everything had been so simple, so slow and clear at Mont Saint-

Michel. Back in the Winter Court, life's complications piled up more and more, even as he tried to keep his focus clear and simple. "When this is over—if I survive it—I'll tell her myself."

"When this is over," Victor agreed. He shook his head once and walked away, fading into the dark and leaving Rafe to his watch.

45

Deor sat at her desk in her office reading over intelligence reports. Three ships headed to aid the Summer Court siege of Northfalls had been taken, plundered, and sunk. The more D'nath's invading force patrolled the area, on foot or by sea, the more Summer Court soldiers died at the hands of the mysterious Ghost and his allies. She just hoped Victor would be able to find whoever it was and retake Wellhall before Northfalls was lost. Despite the Ghost's success, morale around the country was falling. The people knew that it was a war of attrition and, from their perspective, there was no help in sight. The same weariness came from Northfalls, too, and Roger and Arthur became more and more somber by the day. Deor suspected the positivity had been mostly for her benefit, but now they couldn't muster the energy to keep up appearances.

She wasn't sure how much longer she could keep a confident smile on, either. The vampires in the castle were restless—she didn't blame them—eager to fight, not to hide in a castle all day and night. Ivan visited her frequently, a kind of ambassador, who repeated information and assured her they were all still on her side. He never once brought up the hand-on-the-thigh incident, and she didn't either, as he was nothing but a complete gentleman with not even a whiff of impropriety.

The large mirror on the wall lit up in violent red, an emergency call. "Open!" she commanded it.

Arthur appeared. He looked exhausted and, for the first time ever, frightened. "They're attacking now." He drew a deep breath and looked off to the side, listened, and nodded. "Lock the doors," he said softly. He returned his attention to her. "I've never seen magic like it. It's slamming into our magic barriers, and they're cracking."

"How long?" Deor asked.

"Twenty-four hours," Arthur said. "And even if it is longer, we won't last much more than that. An enemy got in somehow." He paused, eyes on hers. "They've poisoned everything. The water, the wine, the food, it's all contaminated or rotten. Everywhere. Like I said, I've never seen magic like this."

"Christ," Deor muttered. "No way to fix it?"

"No." He shook his head. "We've got our people on it, but whatever magic did it seems to be gone. And I've never even heard of a faerie, no matter how strong, who could un-rot spoiled fruit." He rubbed his hands over his face. "This is not an occupational force, Your Majesty. They aren't going to take the people of Northfalls prisoner. They're going to slaughter them."

"Twenty-four hours?" she asked. "You can hold on that long?"

"If we're lucky."

Deor nodded. "Give me twelve to contact Victor. If I haven't by then, I'll send Ivan and his people."

"We'll lose the element of surprise against D'nath. He and Madeline will dig in at Wellhall."

"I know." Deor said. "But if we lose Northfalls, we lose everything between here and there too."

Arthur nodded. "We'll be ready in twelve hours." Lines of worry creased his face, and he glanced off to the side again. "I have to go."

"Go," Deor said as the mirror went black.

Deor called Bartholomew and Stephen into her office and explained the situation.

"Fuck," Stephen said.

"Indeed." Bartholomew dropped into a chair in front of her desk. "At least we might save Northfalls."

"I have to contact Victor," Deor said. "Mirror: Victor!"

46

Inside Monjoie's tent, Assane, Zaya, Rafe, Victor, and Monjoie each frowned at a sketch of the Wellhall central keep, looking for a way in.

Rafe pointed at the back of the sketch where short parallel lines showed a stairway. "I still say the water gate is the best option we have. It's a long, narrow route up from the water to the inside, but it's also the most vulnerable."

Monjoie growled, "Which is why she will have it guarded and trapped. We'd be walking into a gauntlet, no question."

"We can't go through the front gate!" Rafe snapped, finally giving in to the strain of the days spent looking for a way to breach an impregnable castle. "And I haven't heard anyone suggest a better way in!"

Both he and Monjoie sat back in their camp chairs, arms crossed, their eyes not meeting. The air around them chilled as both of them fought to rein in their tempers. Finally, Rafe rubbed his hands across his face. "I'm sorry," he said. "I'm out of other ideas."

Monjoie grunted, a sort of grudging, "Me too."

"What do you think, Victor?" Rafe said. "You spent your whole childhood there. Tell us there's some secret garden gate no one else but you has the key to."

"I wish," Victor laughed. Suddenly, his mirror went off, flashing red. "It's Deor." He waved at Rafe and Monjoie to stay out of the way.

Rafe crept a few steps closer to Victor and listened.

Victor answered the call. "What do you need?"

"It's Northfalls," she said. "Something has happened—some enemy got in and poisoned everything—all the food, the water, the wine, it's all lost. And something massively powerful is crashing into the barriers. They've got less than twenty-four hours before Northfalls is taken." She swallowed a sob. "Arthur is sure they mean to kill everyone inside. We have to send the vampires. But if we send them there before we send them to Wellhall—"

"D'nath may well find out and be prepared." Victor nodded. "How much time?"

"I told Arthur we'd open the portal to Northfalls in twelve hours. So, you've got less than that."

"Twelve hours it is, then." He glanced at the people beyond the mirror. "We've talked about getting into Wellhall. We've met up with people—"

"The Ghost?" Deor asked.

"Yes. The Ghost is a group of people, now including me and Donovan. Some are Wellhall soldiers who ran when Madeline betrayed them. We can do it."

"I'm so glad you're alive." Deor sniffed. "Do you think it will work?"

"Yes," he said without missing a beat. "It has to work. This isn't how the Winter Court ends, not with a Wellhall betrayal. In twelve hours, a small army of vampires will be ridding Wellhall of a Summer Court infestation." His gaze darkened. "And Madeline Farringdon will answer for her crimes."

"Perfect. We'll talk soon, then." She closed the call.

"You got all of that?" Victor asked Rafe.

"Yes. We've got less than twelve hours to get into the palace," Rafe said.

"We'll have to use the water gate," Victor said.

"We'll do it like this." Rafe leaned forward, borrowing the pencil from Monjoie's hand and drawing battle plans on their crude map.

Deor disconnected the mirror call and drew a deep breath. "Alright, now what?"

"I'll head down to talk to Ivan." Stephen stood.

Barty stood too. "I'll inform everyone else."

"Thank you." Deor stood. "I'm going to take a bit of time to myself, and then I'll join the rest of you. Say we meet back here in half an hour?"

The two men agreed and left. Deor laid her hand on the doorframe. "Throne room." She stepped through the portal and headed straight for the throne.

Looking at the hunk of carved stone, Deor shuddered. Though it had behaved itself at the Petition Day, she still worried what it might do to her. More times than not, it poked and prodded her, dumped information into her head, and lectured her. She had no idea how to control anything in it. The throne was something that happened to her.

Nevertheless, she marched up to it and sat, easing into the seat. As it had done before, the stone seemed to soften under her body, cradling her. But that was the extent of its actions. There were no visions, no void sweeping her away. She settled back and closed her eyes. Still nothing.

Deor concentrated, focusing on the stone throne and the foundation beneath. She reached her magic outward, and it ran through the land. Rocks, plants, animals, people, she felt them all.

Instantly, the room was black, and she stood, not sat, in the middle. The thrum of the Winter Court's magic pulsed around her, comforting and soft.

"Hello?" She called out.

"You've done well so far," a voice behind her said.

Deor spun to find the woman she had spoken to before when she'd proven she was the rightful Regent and sat on the throne. "It's you," Deor said. "I'd forgotten…"

The woman was tall with chestnut hair in a long braid. She wore bard's robes, though they looked ancient, and her skin had an iridescence that made it seem all the colors at once. "You told me something important. Last time." Deor frowned. She couldn't bring the memory to the surface of her mind. It was out there, hovering on the edge of consciousness, like a dream ebbing away upon waking. "Why can't I remember?"

The woman shrugged. "That you remember seeing me at all is a feat."

"So why bother to tell me anything then?" Deor snapped.

"Your waking mind may have forgotten, but your magic hasn't. You're doing well, even if you feel like you're failing."

"With the war?"

"Yes. And no." Suddenly the woman was next to her. She laid a hand on Deor's shoulder and the heavy worry in her heart lightened a bit. "The Enemy has seen you and knows you and fears you. It is your world." She leaned down, bringing her face closer to Deor's. "It is your world. The Enemy will try to convince you otherwise. Do not listen." She stepped away. "Now, back you go. With my blessing."

"It's my world," Deor whispered to herself. She had to hold onto that, to carry it with her. "It's my world," she repeated as she closed her eyes and reached for the real world.

Deor opened her eyes. As had become custom, a shower of sparkles filled the air around her. "It's my world," she echoed. "And I must protect it."

47

Deor drummed her fingers on the tablet-sized mirror she held. She stood between two sweeping staircases that led to the second-floor gallery over the ballroom. To her left and right, packed in as tightly as possible in front of the massive doors on either side were Ivan and his assassins. A path had been kept open for Deor so that she could easily reach whichever place, Northfalls or Wellhall, hailed her first. Once she allowed the portal to Northfalls to be opened, she wouldn't need to hold it. Bartholomew as Sword could manage it, with the help of Roger.

Wellhall was another story. If Victor could get inside and if he could open a portal, and if he could do all this before Northfalls was too desperate to wait any longer, they would still have next to no time before someone, perhaps Madeline herself, tried to close the portal.

Stephen came to stand next to her. "You okay?"

"Nope." She gave one shake of the head. "I'm terrified."

"Just like all of us, then, eh?" He smiled at her. "You've done everything you can. This is the best shot we've got." He glanced pointedly at the vampires. "They're all hungry for blood. I'm sure the Summer Court won't know what hit them."

"Provided we hit them both at the same time," Deor added.

As the waiting game stretched into hours, Deor breathed a small sigh of relief. The more time Northfalls gave, the more chance Victor and

Donovan would be ready. It was morning, the sun already up, when Deor's mirror lit up, violent red, with the call from Northfalls.

"Answer," she whispered.

"We need you now," Arthur said. He was out of breath.

Before he could get another word out, Deor yelled, "Northfalls now!" as she bolted through the vampires to the door. "Ready?" she breathed as Bartholomew took his place. "Ready Northfalls?"

"Ready!" she heard Roger call.

Deor took a deep breath and let the magic of the palace fill her. "Northfalls," she murmured, eyes closed. In an instant she felt someone else, someone on the other side of the door. A lock seemed to turn, as though she had been knocking on a real door, and someone answered. The huge doors shimmered and rippled like sunlight over a baked California desert highway.

"Now!" Both Deor and Roger's commands overlapped.

"Follow me!" Ivan called. He glanced back at Deor with a fanged grin. "Don't worry, my Lady Regent, we have been cooped up here too long and are ready for sport." Before Deor could reply, he was through and his vampires followed, darting through the portal and vanishing in whatever direction they were pointed.

"Thank you," Roger said and closed the portal.

Deor sat down on the bottom step of the stairs and let tears fall. Her body shook, and all she thought, over and over and over, was *please let Wellhall call soon. Before it's too late.*

48

Under cover of the early morning fog, Rafe crouched in the prow of the *Eider's* lifeboat, guiding it by magic silently over the waves toward Wellhall. They had rowed the first mile after the *Eider* set them down, but this close to the cliff walls even the sound of oars on water was too loud for safety. Fifteen people to take a castle. If any of them lived long enough to reach the main halls, it would be a story worthy of an epic.

Victor crouched next to Rafe while Monjoie, Assane and Zaya were just behind them. Donovan sat a few feet away, his legs crossed, his hands palm up on his knees. His eyes were closed, and he was drawing deep breaths in and out through his nose.

"What are you doing?" Zaya asked Donovan.

He opened his eyes. "Something I learned from Chloe, my wife. It will help me cope with the will magic without going black-eyed and psychotic." He gave a fanged grin. "I'm saving that bit for when we get inside."

She nodded. "Centering yourself. My folks taught me how to do that in storms. I'll leave you to it."

Donovan nodded and closed his eyes again.

Rafe scanned the small crew. Zaya and Assane looked stoic but tense. The rest looked worried. Especially one guy in the back—one of the Wellhall guards who escaped. He'd insisted on coming, and now he looked like he regretted it. Too late now.

Rafe returned his gaze to the watery path in front of him, took a deep, calming breath, and concentrated his mind and his magic on the water, pushing the boat forward to the base of the cliff. Somewhere high above the fog bank, Wellhall loomed. As they reached a cluster of jagged rocks, Victor gestured for a halt. Rafe held the boat as still as it could get on the choppy water. Victor leaned forward, extending his hands, and the rocks disappeared.

"Get ready. We're going in," Victor hissed. He motioned toward the solid cliff face just feet ahead. "Keep your blindfolds on and tell yourself there's an opening. See the opening in your head."

"What? That's no glamour. We'll smash ourselves on the rocks," the regretful sailor hissed.

"We've been over this. It's will magic, you oaf," Monjoie hissed back. "What do you think the duchess is known for, flower arranging? The more you look at the rocks, the harder it will be to will yourself through them."

Rafe turned to the people in the boat. "Blindfolds on. This is what we prepped for." People complied, covering their eyes with whatever they had brought with them. Even Monjoie tied a cloth over his own eyes. Another cruel reminder that he wasn't a "real" Farringdon. He may have spent his adolescence under Madeline and Edgar's care, but he had no ingrained resistance to her magic and no inherited right to enter Wellhall. Rafe looked upward at the cliff to where it faded into the fog overhead. "Ready, little brother?"

Victor swallowed hard and nodded. Together they extended their hands and their magic, willing the cliff and the castle anchored to it to recognize them as rightful entrants. The magic resisted. Here at the heart of the duchy, Madeline's will spells were rooted in the land itself.

Cold sweat rolled down Rafe's back, and his arms shook. A few feet away, Victor panted, both hands held out, his fingers digging into the rock as their boat banged into the unyielding cliff. In the choppy surf, the boat thumped, wood crunching on the rock. A few more large waves, and they would be swimming, beaten against the rocks like clothes in a washerwoman's hands.

Rafe stood up, the boat rocking wildly under him. "I am the heir!" he shouted. "The heir and firstborn. You cannot keep me out!"

Another wave surged under the boat, lifting them up and through. Rafe felt the rock part around him. The dim, fog-filtered light disappeared, swallowed in the darkness of the sea cave. A man screamed, the sound suddenly cut off. The one who had doubted was gone. Poor bastard. Rafe hoped for his sake he was merely dead and not trapped inside the wall that closed behind them.

"We did it." Victor's voice shook with exhaustion. "Blindfolds off."

Monjoie pulled his free, lit a lamp, and held it up. There were sighs of relief as the survivors, now fourteen, looked around, blinking.

Donovan opened his eyes. "That was fun." He shuddered. "Even with my eyes closed." He shook his head. "Damn, that's a lot of power."

Rafe glanced at Victor. "I certainly couldn't have done it without you."

Victor nodded but said nothing.

"Everyone row with your hands." Monjoie's light was just enough to see by. The boat bumped and jostled against the walls as the natural sea cave funneled into a narrow tunnel. Where Finn's water gate had been large enough to house a yacht and a pier, Wellhall's builders had clearly been thinking in terms of secrecy, not comfort. The tunnel overhead scraped Rafe's hair before he lowered himself back into the boat.

"How far?" he whispered to Victor.

Victor pointed ahead. Stone steps rose out of the water, their lowest levels slick with algae and crusted with barnacles. At high tide, there wouldn't be enough room for even a rowboat to slip out. The boat crunched on the bottom step.

"Check your weapons," he whispered. "We're not coming back here." Either they'd leave Wellhall by the front door that day, or not at all. As the boat emptied, Rafe moved higher up the stairs, his sword ready and his staff strapped across his back. His monk's hood was drawn down, covering his face in shadows and leaving just enough room for him to see.

The stairs spiraled upward, getting drier as they went until they reached a narrow door without a hatch. Victor and Monjoie had disagreed on whether there were two doors or one between the sea cave and the dungeon, but both remembered the dungeon door being guarded.

Rafe laid his hand on the lock, testing it. Locked, of course. The oak boards were old, warped at the bottom from damp and woodworm, but still solid. Even if he had room to swing a battering ram, getting through this door by force was unlikely. Fortunately, Rafe had known Arthur for many, many years.

He wriggled a finger into the keyhole as deep as it would go, feeling at the tumblers with tendrils of magic. Click. The next tumbler stuck, perhaps corroded into place by the salt air from below. Rafe closed his eyes and leaned against the door, centering himself as Aelfburga and

Caedmon had taught him. He turned the magic, willing it into place. Click. Click. The door swung open onto an empty landing and a further set of stairs.

Behind him, Victor let out a relieved breath. The two of them exchanged looks.

"How the mighty have fallen," Victor said in an amused hush. "First you become a monk, then a pirate, now a lock pick? What next?"

Rafe shrugged, giving Victor a wry smile. "Who knows? Perhaps I'll turn highwayman with a bunch of lace at my throat."

They shared a silent laugh and stepped into the landing. The stairs were wider here, enough for two to walk abreast, and they rose straight up to another door. Monjoie joined them on the landing.

"Dungeon?" Rafe said, barely mouthing the words and pointing upward.

Monjoie and Victor nodded. As planned, Monjoie and Victor hovered behind him, their swords drawn, and Donovan lounged against a wall with the rest of the crew as Rafe undid the lock as gently as he could. The last tumbler clicked into place with an audible *thunk*. On the other side of the door, someone swore.

Monjoie kicked in the door, bellowing as Victor leaped through the opening and cut down the Summer Court soldier on the other side. Rafe and Monjoie both swung on the Wellhall guard, but instead of parrying he dropped to his knees, covering his head. "Don't kill me!" he screamed. "I surrender."

"Miserable traitor." Monjoie kicked his sword out of the way and drew back his foot to kick the man in front of him, but Victor put out a hand.

"Why should we trust you?" Victor said to the kneeling soldier.

"Master Victor!" the man exclaimed, his voice equal parts fear and relief. "I'm no traitor! I was only following orders, sir! I swear to you, I am loyal to the Farringdons always. Just give me orders, and I'll obey you, I swear."

Victor frowned and glanced at Rafe, but Rafe kept his hood down over his face.

The cowering soldier saw where Victor had looked and shook even more. "Please. Please, don't kill me. I'll do anything."

"Until my mother orders you to do something different," Victor said. He snatched the keys off the man's belt. Monjoie drew back his sword.

"Don't kill him," Rafe said. "Take his mirror and put him in a cell. We're not here to slaughter our own."

Babbling thanks, the man immediately handed over his mirror and shut himself in the nearest cell. Monjoie tossed a silencing spell on the dungeon, just in case the man got the idea to scream for help after they were gone.

The dungeon led out into the wine and cheese cellars and up into the kitchens. "Remember," Victor whispered, "don't kill civilians unless they try to kill you first." Whatever their personal feelings on the matter, the servants were not to blame for Madeline's actions.

Assane and Zaya exchanged glances but nodded, as did the rest of their crew.

Donovan shrugged. "You point me at the people you want dead." He grinned. "All you faeries look alike to me."

Rafe rolled his eyes and laid a hand on the door between the cellars and the kitchen, prepared to work his lockpicking spell, but the handle turned for him. Convenient. The butler probably didn't see a need to keep the wine and cheese locked up during the day, and it hadn't occurred to the powers in charge to tell him otherwise.

"Ready?" The little band behind Rafe nodded, weapons raised.

With a shout, he threw open the door and charged into the kitchen. Someone screamed. A footman dropped an entire silver tray laden with breakfast and the sound of shattering china echoed through the kitchen. At the large central table, breakfasting maids, footmen, pages, and stable hands froze with spoons halfway to their mouths.

"Stay where you are!" Monjoie shouted. "We're not here to hurt you." He motioned for the others in their band to fan out and cover the exits.

Everyone obeyed except the butler, who rose from his seat at the head of the table. "Captain Monjoie," he said. "What a pleasure it is to see you alive, sir. And Master Victor, or should I say, Prince Consort. This is an unexpected surprise. I presume you are here to rid us of the Summer Court?"

Victor and Monjoie exchanged glances and then nodded at the butler.

He rubbed his gloved hands together and a perfectly villainous smile spread over his face. "Most excellent, sirs. Ever since the appearance of the Ghost, we in the servants' hall have been discussing how we might contribute in such an event. Might I suggest that we lock the younger folk up in the cheese cellar where they will be safe?" This caused an outraged squeak from the scullery maid and a page, but the butler ignored them. "We older servants are ready to assist you in any way possible."

Rafe was glad his hood hid the amused smile on his face as Victor and

Monjoie both stood blinking, trying to take in this new information. It was so easy to forget that servants had opinions of their own, not to mention access to fire and most of the sharp objects in any house.

Warping his voice with magic, Rafe said "We would be delighted if you could tell us where the duchess and the Summer Court Sword are at the moment."

"Lord D'Nath is generally in his chambers at this hour. He prefers to breakfast alone." The butler gestured toward the footman who had dropped the heavy tray. The footman blushed. "I believe her grace is in her workroom in conference with… someone." Here the butler's smooth tones faltered a bit. "Or perhaps she is speaking with herself. One cannot be sure. She… She does not sleep much these days." A ripple of discomfort went through the servants at the table. All the etiquette books in the world didn't contain a polite way to say, "I think your mother has completely lost her mind."

Victor nodded, his face a mix of anger and shame. He looked around the room. "Is everyone here trustworthy?"

"I believe so, sir. I could not speak for the members of the duchess's guard, however. I would consider them hostiles until proven otherwise."

"We're wasting time," Monjoie said. "Speed and secrecy are our only two assets here." The band behind him muttered their agreement.

"You're right," Rafe said. "Butler, Victor, Donovan, and I need access to an established portal point. Monjoie and the others need to disable the outside wards—we've got reinforcements coming. Can you get us there?"

"I'll take you to the duchess's portal myself, sir." He looked to the head footman. "He can escort Monjoie and his followers to the watchtower."

"Good. We'll do that," Rafe said. "The rest of you arm yourselves as secretly as you can and go about your normal business. We don't want anyone realizing there's anything unusual going on. Get D'Nath his breakfast before he comes looking for it. When all hell breaks loose, you'll know it. And if you see vampires running around, remember they're on our side."

As the butler led the invaders up the servants' stairs, and the head footman took Monjoie and his followers out the opposite door, the kitchen buzzed with the sound of footmen and maids filling their pockets with weapons.

Armed with a fire poker, the butler led Rafe and the others up through narrow passages and hidden doors meant to give servants quick access to the inner keep. There were two other portals elsewhere in Wellhall, but since both were attached to outer gates, there was no chance they wouldn't be heavily guarded. Unfortunately, the reason the portal in Madeline's parlor was unlikely to be guarded was that it lay near the center of the keep, close to the family bedrooms, and worse, directly across from Madeline's own workroom. The last few yards to the parlor were open hallway. The butler bowed and gestured toward the room.

"Wait here," Rafe said to him. He nodded, taking up a post at the junction of the hallway.

Victor, Donovan, and Rafe slid silently down the passageway to the parlor.

As he passed Madeline's workroom, Rafe felt more than heard his mothers' magic. It was a crackling, angry presence, but not untethered or striking out wildly. He could hear her voice too. She was definitely talking to someone, and from the pauses in her speech, they were answering her. In a way, the thought was a relief. If Madeline still had control of her senses, she was fit to be held accountable for her treachery and for murdering his father. A glance at Victor told Rafe that his brother was thinking along similar lines.

They crept into the parlor, swords sheathed. They would need all their concentration to wrest control of the portal.

"Ready?" Victor said, taking out his mirror. Once he activated the mirror, they would have a minute at most before internal alarms went off.

Rafe nodded, gathering magic. Knives out, Donovan nodded too.

49

Deor wasn't sure how long it took before her mirror rang again and she darted to the other set of doors as she answered it.

Victor smiled at her. The room he was in with Donovan and a handful of others looked like a private study. Hovering close to the door was a tall person in monk's garb—the Ghost, it would seem. "We're ready."

Deor repeated her process, drawing the magic of the land to her and willing a doorway. Unlike Northfalls, Wellhall fought her, even with Victor trying. The land itself careened back and forth between fighting to keep the portal closed and fighting to open it. Victor was mumbling something, but she couldn't quite make it out. The tone reminded her of her own conversations with Boomie, the palace avatar. Perhaps he was trying to coax Wellhall into trusting him.

Whatever words Victor spoke worked. Finally, the portal opened, wide and clear. Donovan called to his cousins and they rushed past Deor into Wellhall. The Ghost, with Donovan, led them from the room before the entire contingent could get through.

Deor and Victor stayed at the portal, straining against the magic of Wellhall, its hostility apparent. It recognized the Aethelwing in her and clearly hated it, even with Victor whispering words of comfort, of encouragement.

"Easy," she heard Stephen say behind her. "They're almost through."

"Right." Deor said through clenched teeth. Her muscles ached.

Then the last of the vampires was through, and she and Victor breathed a sigh of relief.

"We'll keep it open," Victor said. "Just in case we need to get through in a hurry."

"Right." Deor nodded.

As Victor and Deor held the portal open between them, Rafe beckoned to the vampires already through. Victor didn't need him to help with the portal. The land heard Rafe as heir, but there was a level of power flowing through and between Victor and Deor like Rafe had never experienced before. He could do more good defending Victor's back with his sword. In the distance, a shout and the clash of swords broke out. Only about half of the vampires were through and already the parlor was crowded to capacity. The time for secrecy was over.

"This way!" he shouted at the vampires and charged out of the room with Donovan hot on his heels.

A melee had broken out in the corridor between armed servants and the Summer Court. The hall was already so crowded that the fighting was elbow to elbow, but Donovan's vampires swept through the crowd, mowing down Summer Court soldiers. The fight ended as quickly as it had begun.

"Quick," Rafe said. "We've got to sweep the castle before they can create defensive positions. Split up." He gestured in one direction. "A third of you head through the east wing," Rafe said. "You," he pointed at the second group, "Go with the butler to the watchtower to help Monjoie. The rest, follow me and Donovan. Vampires—do your worst."

Each group took off.

Rafe paused just long enough to slap a locking spell on his mother's workroom door. It wouldn't hold her, but it might buy Victor another minute or two. Sword raised, Rafe charged down the corridor in the direction of the guest quarters. He would take whoever he could find, but he wanted D'Nath.

Chaos reigned in Wellhall. Screams erupted and were suddenly cut off from all directions. Rafe slashed his way through Summer Court soldiers, hunting room to room for the Summer Court Sword. He rounded a corner alone to find a cluster of five soldiers holding a defensive position.

Five to one was more than he wanted to handle, but even as he closed on the first of them, a maid stepped out of a service closet and stabbed one in the neck with a toasting fork. A blur zipped by Rafe, and another soldier fell, his throat slit. Rafe made quick work of the next two, and the fifth tried to flee, but not fast enough to escape Donovan.

Rafe, Donovan, and the maid regarded each other in silence for a second over the bodies of their foes. Donovan saluted the maid with his knife, and she acknowledged it with a casual nod.

"The fellow you're looking for is staying in the garden suite, milord," she said to Rafe before taking up her position again in the closet like a sniper retreating under cover.

"Shall we?" Rafe said to Donovan, and they both took off again after their prey.

Just as the maid said, they found D'Nath and his command staff in the garden suite, all shouting. Donovan kicked down the door and elaborately bowed Rafe in. The room froze, every person in it clutching a mirror. D'Nath was dressed in his everyday military uniform, his white-blond hair unbound around his shoulders.

"You!" D'nath said, as if it were an accusation. "I knew you weren't dead." He flung his mirror aside and seized a sword. He eyed Rafe's robes. "And you're the fucking Ghost."

Rafe acknowledged D'nath's greeting with a small bow. "I've wanted to cross swords with you for a long time," he said. "Though I never thought it would be in my own house."

D'nath narrowed his eyes. "I'm afraid I don't have the leisure to indulge you today, boy." He charged at Rafe, sword raised and Rafe nimbly stepped aside, parrying the blow.

But instead of turning to redouble the attack, D'nath let his momentum carry him out into the hall where he took off at a dead run. At the same time, D'nath's aides lunged at Rafe and Donovan. In the flurry of blows and magic, Rafe lost sight of D'nath as he disappeared back down the way Rafe had come.

Rafe roared in frustration, hammering the people between him and the doorway.

"I'll handle these idiots!" Donovan shouted. "Go get him!"

Rafe charged into the hall after D'nath.

50

Across the room from Victor, the parlor door slammed open. Madeline, magic in her hands, stood there. "Victor!" Madeline's screech made Deor wince, and for a moment she thought she might lose her concentration and let the portal fall closed. Victor turned to see.

Madeline charged through the door, a freezing gust of wind preceding her, blowing back Deor's hair and making her shiver. "Traitor! You are no child of mine!"

Victor opened his mouth to talk, but before he could utter a word, a spear of ice shot from Madeline, catching Victor in the chest.

"No!" Deor cried as Madeline crowed in triumph.

Victor stumbled back and sank to the floor, one hand clutching the spear, the other still clinging to the portal, willing it open.

"No!" Deor repeated, but the portal was closing as Victor's strength ebbed. Deor drew all the magic she could and shoved it into the portal, holding it just long enough for her to leap across the threshold. Her stomach flipped and her vision blurred as she traveled hundreds of miles in a split second.

"Deor! No!" Stephen called behind her, but the portal snapped closed, leaving him in the palace.

Deor dropped down next to Victor and leaned over him. She put her hand on his face. "Victor," she said. "Victor, look at me!"

Victor focused on her. He reached up and rested his hand on her cheek. "It's fine."

"Yes." Deor nodded. "You're going to be fine." She could hear the hysteria creeping into her words. Her whole body trembled. She put her hand over his and tilted her face into his touch. "You can't leave me." She smiled, though she knew tears were streaming down her cheeks. "You promised you'd watch over me!"

He nodded. "The Winter Court is safe now. Wellhall is safe now. You're safe now."

"NO!" She leaned over him, pressing her face against his neck. "No," she repeated softly. "You're my Consort. I can't do this without you." Magic swelled inside her, filling her.

"Shhh," he said, and she felt his hand on her head, stroking her hair. "It's alright. It's your own magic, going back to you."

"Victor, you can't." She pushed back against the magic coming at her, willing it into him, willing it to give him strength. "Hold on, we'll get you help." But the magic was pouring into her now, and holding it back was like trying to stop a hole in a dam with her bare hands. "We can fix this," she said desperately.

"Deor."

"No!" She barked.

"Deor," he repeated. "Look at me."

She hauled herself up again and looked at him. He held his hand out to her, slick with blood and water from the wound and the melting weapon. She took it. "Don't—"

"Shh." He said firmly but gently. "This is the way it is supposed to be." He swallowed and paused, drawing in a few shallow breaths. "I chose this."

Deor clung to his hand. The surety in his voice was absolute and absolutely true. "I won't leave you."

"I know." He squeezed her hand. "Thank you." His eyes closed.

"Oh, how tragic." Madeline loomed over them, laughing. Magic filled her hands and poured off her, telling Deor to cower, to surrender, or be crushed like the bug she was.

Deor gently laid Victor's hand at his side. She looked up at the gleeful woman. Her whole body shook, and rage broke through the grief and flooded her. Sparks flared off her. She stood.

"You've killed your husband, all your children, and for what?" Deor spat at her, tears still rolling down her cheeks. "So you can be some puppet of the Summer Court?" She barked out a laugh. "You'll never be Queen of anything."

Madeline drew her hands to her sides and then thrust them out, sending a blizzard of razor-sharp icicles at her.

"No," Deor said softly. She didn't lift a finger, but sparks filled the air, and the icicles vanished to steam before reaching her. Deor flicked her hand out, and the sparkles coalesced into a sword of pure silver, pommel to tip. "I should have killed you in the alley."

Madeline's smile faltered, and she launched another barrage of icicles.

Deor raised her free hand, and her sparkles formed a shield, sending the ice bouncing harmlessly to the floor. The sword vibrated in her hand, not from fear, not even from rage, but from power. The power of the Winter Court poured into her at the Consort's death. She stepped toward the traitor.

Madeline backed up, first one step, then another, and Deor raised her sword, driving Madeline back.

"You can't!" Madeline said when her back hit the wall. "You won't kill me. You can't kill me! That's not justice. You'll be just like your father."

"No one can be perfect all the time." Deor thrust the blade into Madeline, feeling the resistance as the tip struck the breast bone. She shoved all the magic she could into the sword, into the force of it, and it broke through with a *crack*. Then there was nothing but the sliding of the blade deep into the flesh, into the heart, until the hilt of the sword hit Madeline's body, bringing the women face to face.

Madeline gaped, blood gurgling from her throat and dribbling out her mouth. Deor leaned her whole weight against the sword and twisted it. Madeline's last breath rattled in her throat and a fine mist of blood splattered across Deor's face as the light died from Madeline's eyes. Warm blood covered her hands as she pulled the sword out. Madeline's corpse slid to the floor.

Deor turned and looked back at Victor. The spear was still there, still a frozen hunk of ice, Maybe that meant he wouldn't bleed out, that whatever was torn could be held in place. Her grip loosened, and the sword slipped from her hand, vanishing in a cloud of sparks. The room spun, and spots flashed before her eyes. The magic in the sparks, the shield, and the sword was gone, leaving her swaying. She dropped to her knees next to Victor and took his hand. The kingdom's magic poured into her, a chaotic rush from all sides she couldn't control.

The door burst open, and D'nath rushed through. He gaped a moment, looking around the room and down at Madeline. His eyes met Deor's. "Well, now. That's some nice swordwork." He took a few steps toward her.

"Stay back!" Deor said, giving it more energy than she felt. Magic sparked and failed to coalesce in her hands.

He paused. "You cheated."

Deor blinked at him. "What?"

"Vampires. Assassins. That's not the rules of war."

"War isn't a game. And I'd never win playing your way."

He half lowered the point of his sword. "Losing Wellhall is unfortunate," he said. "But I have a better prize in you." He held out his hand to her, dispelling magic flaring over her to quell her own. "Come along now."

"Fuck you." Deor said. Sparks flew off her and she curled her fingers, fighting her own magic for control.

Rafe, in a monk's robes, cowl thrown back, strode into the room, bloody sword raised.

51

Rafe scanned the room quickly. His mother lay dead on the floor and D'nath stood a few feet from Deor—what was she doing here?—kneeling over Victor's body.

"Rafe. You're alive?" Deor gaped at him. D'Nath turned, following her gaze, and swore.

"I am indeed." He moved further into the room, edging between D'nath and Deor. "Stand and fight me, D'Nath. Or have you become a coward?"

D'Nath laughed at that and swung his sword. "Don't trifle with your elders, boy."

Rafe brought his own sword up, his movements slowing as if he were at practice with Joan. He parried D'Nath's sword and struck back. D'Nath dodged the strike and attacked again, sword point quicker than the eye could follow. Rafe blocked every attempt. Muscle memory flowed through him. Slower. Slower. Every move deliberate. Every muscle used exactly as much as it was needed.

D'Nath renewed his attack, furious. He rained blows on Rafe, but Rafe slid past them, no energy wasted in flashy parries or counterattacks. He retreated before D'Nath, and his retreat drew D'Nath further from Deor.

"Stop. Running."

"Catch me." Rafe flicked his wrist and stabbed. D'Nath slid past the blade like a dancer. He was too good a swordsman to be caught in the hip the way Rafe had intended, but still, D'Nath seethed, his laughter gone.

Rafe couldn't dodge every strike. He parried again and again, seeking an opening to strike back. D'Nath was no fool. His attacks were fast, not reckless. Rafe's wounded hand faltered on the hilt, nerves cramping. *Did this hand do everything it could? Then it is enough.* Rafe shifted to a two-handed stance, wielding the blade like a quarterstaff. A peasant's weapon. A good style to parry with. Not a good way to get inside a master swordsman's defenses.

D'Nath sneered at Rafe's hold and attacked again. His sneer could not hide that he was panting. Rafe dropped into Swan Blade discipline and the tip of his sword sheared across D'Nath's collarbone like a swan's wing skimming the air. Red blood flowed across D'Nath's unprotected chest.

D'Nath swore in pain. He clamped his free hand over the wound, but his sword never faltered. "You've learned since you were my sister's toy."

Not long ago the jibe would have filled him with shame and rage, but now Rafe let it slide easily away. Rafe advanced, but this time D'Nath retreated. He stepped into the doorway and a portal opened for him. Rich, flowery scents like a garden in high summer flowed through it.

D'Nath looked past Rafe. Through gritted teeth, he said, "Pretender. Fraud. You will never be a true faerie queen." He stepped back through the portal and was gone.

Confused at D'Nath's sudden retreat, Rafe turned to look behind him. Deor stood there, clutching a sword of pure silver, her dress soaked with Victor's blood.

Deor stared at Rafe. His scar. His wild black hair swept around his blue skin. His strangely familiar brown robe. He stared back at her, his eyes unreadable.

"You're the Ghost," she said. A sob that was half a laugh broke out of her. "I should have known." She turned the sword blade toward herself and plunged it into her chest reabsorbing the magic. It didn't matter what Rafe was or why. She had to help Victor.

Her entire body thrummed with overflowing magic. Her muscles trembled and twitched with exhaustion as if she'd been running a marathon and drinking espresso at the same time. A mirror. She needed a mirror to call a healer.

But Rafe pushed past her, calling Victor's name. He swept her Consort's body up in his arms, calling out to someone she didn't know. Seagulls screamed and she smelled seaweed on sun-warmed rocks. Rafe took a step and vanished.

Deor reached for him, for Victor, but it was too late. They were gone. "Mirror!" she screamed. Somewhere in this room had to be a mirror that worked. "Mirror. Find Stephen. Stephen! Help me!"

In her dress pocket, her mirror vibrated frantically. She drew it out and a frantic Stephen appeared.

"Are you okay?"

"No," Deor said. "I need you." The tears flowed over her cheeks. She didn't know when they had started and she couldn't stop them now.

"I'm trying to open a portal to you," Stephen said. "I need you to reach back to me."

Deor forced her feet to carry her to the doorway where D'Nath had made his portal and laid her hand on the frame. Stephen couldn't break into Wellhall, but she couldn't be kept out of her own Palace. She reached out with all her magic and the Palace practically ripped itself open making a portal for her.

Stephen reached through and pulled her back home. Immediately she was surrounded by the palace healers, searching her for wounds. Boomie flitted back and forth overhead, yowling.

"It's not my blood. It's not my blood. It's not my blood!" She had to repeat herself over and over before they stepped back.

She wrapped her arms around Stephen and sobbed, unable to say more than "Victor" and "Madeline."

"It's okay," Stephen said, wrapping his arms around her. "I've got you." He held her until she could breathe again.

"There's so much magic," Deor whimpered as she clung to him. "I can't hold it all. All of it came back when Victor…"

Stephen cradled Deor against him, and she clung to him.

52

Hours later, after the palace healers had bullied her into taking a shower and changing her clothes, Deor lay on a couch, surrounded by a cloud of magic sparks. Stephen paced nearby, giving her updates from Barty in the war room as they came in. She'd only agreed to this compromise after Mac laid out in dire terms how the kingdom would suffer if the monarch collapsed from magical exhaustion. Her muscles twitched and jumped. The blood rushed through her head, pounding at her eardrums. The untethered magic of the kingdom pulsed through her and her heart raced as if she were running full speed. Brand lay full length on the couch with her, his massive head resting on her stomach. Boomie purred aggressively in her ear, as if he could cure her heartache by sheer will. Stroking his head helped.

She closed her eyes and concentrated on the feel of Boomie's stone head under her fingers, the anchor he provided to the Palace and the kingdom. She imagined the floods of magic flowing down into the earth, spreading out into the Winter Kingdom. Her heart slowed its pace a bit. Still, Victor's absence was a gaping hole in her and in the kingdom.

Stephen came over and pulled up a chair. "It's over," he said. "Wellhall is secured. The siege at Northfalls has broken and the Summer Court is retreating. They did it. You did it. Your plan worked. We won."

Tears flowed out of Deor's eyes again. "We won."

Boomie purred louder and she hugged him to her chest. Wiping away the tears, Deor pulled herself out from under Brand and hugged him too. "We won, Brand."

As the two animals ran and flew in crazy circles around the room, Deor and Stephen hugged each other for a long time. Finally, Deor pulled back.

"I have to go downstairs. I've got work to do."

Stephen nodded and she was grateful that he had the sense not to argue with her or demand she ask a healer's permission. "Tell everyone to meet in the Amber Room. I'm going to wash my face."

Roger and Arthur stood at one end of the Amber Room with Ivan. Unlike Deor, they had not had time to wash and change. Bartholomew was there, too, unbloodied, but with deep lines of exhaustion around his eyes. Genevieve, Astarte, and Chloe stood as well. Astarte and Robbie had portaled back as soon as victory was declared.

Everyone bowed or curtsied deeply as Deor walked into the room. The only person sitting was Bill. Of course. Deor shook her head. Academics and bards.

Deor gave everyone a tight smile and gestured at the table. "Everyone have a seat." She pulled out the chair at the head of the table and sat next to Bill. He reached out to her, palm up, and she squeezed his hand tight for a moment. Stephen sat down on her other side.

Everyone sat and looked to her. "Well done, everyone," she said. "Well done. And thank you. The Winter Court has survived because of you." Her voice caught in her throat as she thought of all the people who had not survived. She tightened her grip on Bill's hand.

Barty stood. "Three cheers for our Regent, Princess Deor!" he shouted and the room shook with the resounding cheers around the table.

Deor shook her head, waving them to silence with her free hand. "Thank you, but no," she said. "I can't... We have so much to do. Victor is dead. Madeline is dead. And Rafe is alive. At least he was for the half minute I saw him. He took Victor and vanished. I don't know where."

She ruthlessly stamped down all the thoughts of Victor's funeral, of what she would do if Rafe wouldn't let her see his body.

"Rafe is alive?" Astarte said, hand over her mouth. "How?"

"I don't know." Deor shook her head. "I didn't have a chance to ask him."

Barty raised a hand. "Rafe has not contacted us, but Donovan has. He says that Wellhall is secure and he is holding it with the help of someone called Luc Monjoie because there aren't any living Farringdons on hand? Does anyone know who Luc Monjoie might be?"

Stephen swore in three languages and Deor put her hands over her face and laughed. Clenching her hands she pulled herself back together and said, "Is he on our side?"

"Donovan seems to think so. Says he helped them take Wellhall. Apparently, D'nath managed to escape in all the chaos and someone killed Madeline."

"That was me," Deor said. She held up her hand for silence. "We cannot spend all night shouting questions at each other. So I want everyone to report on what they know. Then we can ask questions. Roger, would you start us off, please? What is the situation at Northfalls and how much emergency food do you need us to send?"

Roger rose from his seat and bowed to Deor. "Your Majesty, it seems we don't need resupply after all."

"Damnedest thing I've ever seen," Arthur chimed in. "Once the battle was over, the magic was gone—all of it. The water, the food, it's all fine. Like it was some kind of glamour, except we tested the food to see if it was a glamour, and it was definitely, provably spoiled. Now, it's fine. I've never seen anything like it."

"I've never even heard of anything like it," Bartholomew said. "And that's troubling."

"Yes." Roger said. "But let's not trouble about it now. My people are scouring the castle for any signs of magic that doesn't belong. The physical walls of the fortress will need repair, but the magic shields will be fully restored by tomorrow morning."

"Winter Court deaths?" Deor said, trying to keep her voice from trembling.

"Very few," Roger said. "Brave fighters." He passed a single-page written list to Genevieve, who took it gently, reverently.

"We'll see that their families are notified in the gentlest way possible."

One by one, each person around the table gave their reports, ending with Deor herself. She kept her description of what happened to Victor and Madeline as spare as possible, fixing her eyes on the amber-covered wall opposite her. "I don't know where Rafe is," she concluded. "Or what he did with Victor."

"Are you sure Victor is dead?" Astarte asked, her voice soft.

"The kingdom's magic has returned to me," Deor said. Around the table, a hush fell and more than one person wiped their eyes.

Deor nodded once, sharply and scanned the room. "What do we do next?"

"Now we start preparing press releases," Astarte said. "Genevieve? You'll help with those?"

"Yes, of course." Genevieve smiled at Deor. "We'll have an initial statement of victory out to the press tonight and a more detailed announcement from the Regent on the mirrors tomorrow. If that's alright with you, Your Majesty."

Deor nodded her agreement.

"We'll need to gather the names of the Wellhall dead," Astarte said. "We must notify the families before we release any names to the public."

"Right." Deor nodded. A wave of relief washed over her. Astarte knew what to do, and Deor could trust her to do it. Same with Genevieve. She pursed her lips. "We'll have memorials," she said suddenly. "Here, Northfalls, and Wellhall if it is possible. For those who died, faerie and vampire" She looked at Ivan. "We'll honor everyone who died fighting for or with the Winter Court."

Ivan bowed. "Thank you, my Lady Regent."

Deor turned to Barty. "What about the Summer Court? What do we say to them?"

Bartholomew cleared his throat. "We need to negotiate the return of prisoners, the few we have, to the Summer Court. I understand there are none at Northfalls, but Wellhall has a dungeon full. And a job sorting out what to do with the Winter Court faeries who sided with Madeline." He paused, seemingly waiting for an answer.

"I have no intention of beginning the peace with a string of executions," Deor said. A sigh of relief went around the table.

Barty said, "Good lass." He added, "I can handle the prisoner exchange if my Lady wishes?"

"Please," Deor said, nodding. "What else?"

"The vampires," Stephen said. "We need to open the portals to return them home. As soon as they are back here, we can get them home."

"Yes," Deor said. "Though if any want to stay for the memorials, they are welcome." She looked at Ivan and Chloe. "I hope you will stay."

"I think so," Chloe said.

"Okay," Deor straightened. "That sounds like we have a plan, then."

"Pardon me, Your Majesty," Arthur spoke. "I need to tell you something." He scanned the room. "Perhaps it is only suitable for those in the inner circle of the Court." He looked at Ivan and Chloe. "I'm sorry."

Ivan shook his head. "No need to be sorry." He stood. "We'll step out and start making preparations with our own people." He and Chloe left the room.

"So," Deor looked to Arthur. "What is it?"

Arthur ran a hand through his hair. "Treason," he said. "I have committed tre—"

"Don't be ridiculous!" Roger snapped at him.

"I struck—"

"No!" Roger insisted. He turned to Deor. "When your father escaped with me to Northfalls, of course, I welcomed him. The longer he was unable to return to the palace, the angrier he became. And the more violent."

Deor nodded but said nothing. She remembered the shiner Arthur had. "The last straw for me was when he raised a hand to Pookie." Roger flushed with anger, his lavender complexion darkening to the color of an angry bruise. "Arthur stepped in and took the blow." He looked at Arthur. "I owe you a great debt for that."

"It was my duty."

"The King was kept in his quarters after that. He remained moody and violent. Then, he stopped. He suddenly was less angry. I thought perhaps he had spoken to you, and you had comforted him."

"No," Deor snorted.

"I know that now," Roger said. "He grew happier as the Summer Court's attacks on our defenses increased. Shortly before the poisoning of our food and water, Arthur found him..." Roger shook his head.

"I found him communicating with the Summer Court commander," Arthur continued for Roger. "He was planning to help them into Northfalls. I believe—though I don't have proof—that he somehow helped with the poison attack."

Deor's jaw dropped. She had never considered the possibility of Finn turning on the Winter Court. Turning on her? She was sure he would. But betray his own nation? Beneath her, the whole of the palace seemed to shudder.

"The King is a traitor," Deor said softly, as though doing so might soften the blow. The room echoed with her decree, and the people around the table winced.

"I am as well," Arthur said. "When the King's treason was discovered, he attempted to break our defenses himself. I had to stop him."

"Arthur punched him in the face. Knocked him clean out. Beautiful shot." Roger stared at Deor, daring her, it seemed, to challenge his interpretation.

Arthur stood. "I won't resist arrest, Your Majesty. I laid violent hands on the King."

"Sit down," Deor commanded. Arthur sat. "The only thing even remotely treasonous in what you did might be that I didn't get to see it for myself. The man betrayed us all—he'd have gotten all of you killed and our people enslaved." She shook her head. "Jesus. He's worse than Madeline."

No one around the table objected.

"If you need a pardon, Arthur, you're pardoned. For everything."

He gaped. "Thank you. I'll gather my things and be out of the palace by this evening."

"Oh no." Deor shook her head. "You don't get off that easy. You have knowledge and skills that I need. You'll stay here and help us put this kingdom back together." She looked at Bartholomew. "What do we do with Finn?"

"He is not staying at Northfalls," Roger declared.

"Arrest him and put him in the Tower?" Bartholomew asked, sounding uncertain.

"That will only cause more problems," Deor said. "It will bring the Winter Court closer to civil war than ever."

"The lake house," Astarte said. "It's literally a house on an island in a lake. Some king eons ago had an island built there. It's meant to be a peaceful place, and Finn enjoys it. It has all the comforts of home and—"

"Can be guarded easily by a handful of trained soldiers," Arthur finished. "Nothing will get in or out without your knowing about it."

"Done!" Deor said. "Arthur, take whatever people you need to Northfalls and help get the King moved to the lakehouse and settled as fast as you can. Whether he wishes to go or not."

"Yes, Your Majesty." Arthur rose and headed for the door. He paused and looked back. "I should have listened to you," he said. "You saw him for what he was. I'm sorry. Whatever you need me to do to make up for my error, I will. I put the whole kingdom in danger."

'You're forgiven, Arthur," Deor said. "You made a mistake, and you did it for logical reasons. You're no traitor. We all do the best we can do with what we've got. I've got a catalog of wrongs and mistakes too. We've got to do the best we can, moving forward. So let's just say this right now, for all of us. Whatever we did, whoever we were, before the war, that's done. We carry our best forward, and leave our worst behind." Everyone murmured their agreement, nodding.

Deor stood. Her stomach growled and she realized she hadn't eaten anything since the night before. "Right." She looked around at everyone. "Food first. Astarte, please talk to the kitchen and get food sent to my office. Genevieve when you've dealt with the press release, please come help me write my speech. Assuming he comes back, Rafe is now Duke of Wellhall so I would like to know if and when he returns. Anything that can wait until tomorrow waits. We all need rest. We'll meet tomorrow morning, here, at eight a.m. for breakfast. We'll work out all the details of moving forward then. Thank you all."

53

Rafe settled into one of two wingback chairs in front of the fire in what was, now, his own parlor. It had been his mother's. Not the one with the portal where she had died, but one she and her family had used most days—so Monjoie had explained. When Rafe had been trekking in the woods, playing pirate, and planning the invasion of Wellhall, the idea of being *the Duke of Wellhall* was far away, a dream. Now, the reality of it was dawning. He had a household to run, and he had no idea how to do it. He shook his head. More of a reason to enlist Monjoie's help.

Rafe closed his eyes and rubbed his face. Victor was gone. He would mourn, but later. There was still more to do tonight.

He went to the side table and picked up two snifters and a bottle of some of the finest goblin brandy. He returned to his chair. Luc would be here soon. He set the glasses on the table between the two chairs and poured a dram into each. He took up one and sipped.

A few moments later, on time, there was a knock at the door.

"Come in, Luc," Rafe said.

The door swung open, and Luc came in. "Good evening, Your Grace."

"Have a seat. And a drink." Rafe gestured at the chair.

Luc sat.

"Victor is not coming back," Rafe said at last. "They think he might survive, but if he does, he will be like Evelyn and Joan."

"Madeline was good at killing," Monjoie said softly. He picked up the glass and took a sip.

Rafe swirled the brandy around the glass, more for something to do than because he gave a damn about its quality. "Caedmon told me that we'll forget. Not all of it, but our memories will fade—to protect them and us from the Enemy."

"What about everything we went through?" Monjoie met Rafe's gaze.

"We won't forget, Luc. I promise." He sighed and put his feet up on the ottoman in front of him. "For now, let's just sit and have a drink. To Victor."

Monjoie echoed him and took a sip of the brandy. He sat uncomfortably straight, perched on the edge of his chair.

"So," Rafe said. "My mother has been put underground. The blood stains are being scrubbed out of the carpets. And the Regent is safely back in the palace. No doubt she'll want to speak to Wellhall soon. This is our last quiet moment before everything erupts again."

"Yes it is, Your Grace," Luc said.

With an ugly jolt, Rafe realized that for Luc this wasn't a comfortable moment to unwind with a companion in arms, but a command performance with a new lord.

"You don't need to address me by my title, Luc. I thought we decided on a first-name basis. Or do you prefer the distance?" Rafe hadn't thought about what would happen after retaking Wellhall, not really. Perhaps Luc wasn't interested in a friendship.

"No—first names are fine... Rafe." He managed to choke the word out, but it troubled him. Clearing his throat, Luc set down his glass and stood facing Rafe. "I know I'm not a Farringdon, and if I were it would only make what I did to Victor even more inexcusable. I know that the Regent hates me—understandably so—and she'll want justice for all of my treason. I'm planning on turning myself over to her. There's no need for her to have to pry me out of Wellhall. I just ask, if you can, please protect my family. Don't let them be punished for my crimes."

Rafe stood to face Luc, putting his hand on the man's shoulder. "I wouldn't harm your family even if you were ten times the traitor. I can't forgive on Victor's behalf. Only he can decide that." Luc closed his eyes for a second and nodded as if accepting a death sentence.

"But," Rafe said, his hand still on Luc's shoulder, "I, too, have done all the wrong things for what I believed were the right reasons. I understand.

And I've seen your loyalty in the field. I see how much the people here trust you. Whatever crimes you've committed, I pardon you."

"Thank you, Your Grace." Luc's voice was harsh as he said it.

Rafe pulled him into a rough hug, pounding him on the back perhaps harder than he needed to before letting Luc go. "I had too little time with Victor. I'm not about to hand over for execution the only brother I have left."

Eventually, they sat down again, still wiping their eyes. Rafe poured both of them more brandy. Luc saluted him with his glass. They drank their brandy in silence, enjoying the crackling of the flames. It reminded Rafe of the tiny, furtive campfires they had lit while in the woods, fighting the Summer Court. All in all, he preferred the bright, open fire in front of him and the comfortable chair over a damp log to sit on.

"Of course, the Regent may not agree with you," Luc said. "She may demand my head be placed on Tower Bridge."

"She can try," Rafe growled. "But she'll need a better army than the one she's got to get you out."

Luc glanced at him. "I'm not worth risking Wellhall for. You have to think about all your people. They don't need another war."

"I am thinking about my people," Rafe said. "How well would they trust me if I bought myself safety at the expense of one of their own, especially one who sacrificed so much for them? They barely trust me now as it is." Rafe grinned as an idea struck him. "No, I have a better idea. I will make you Seneschal."

Luc laughed. "You're drunk."

"Not at all. This is only my second glass. You know this area. You know the people, and they know you. They trust you. If they see you willingly supporting me, that will go a long way toward earning me their trust. Besides, the things I don't know about my own land and people could fill volumes. I'm going to need your help to be a competent duke." Rafe leaned forward from his chair, smiling at Luc. "What do you say?"

Luc regarded Rafe for a few minutes, a half-smile on his face. "I would be honored."

54

Deor stood on the balcony of her suite and stared at the palace gardens below her. Summer was in full swing, with warm sun and blossoms in full bloom. In a moment, she would be leaving for the Wellhall memorial service. Following that would be the private funeral for Victor at the Farringdon family mausoleum. She wanted to go to Victor's funeral, but not as the Regent. She wanted to go as an ordinary person who had lost someone she loved.

The magic that he held for her had poured back into her, and she still held it. She had to choose a new consort, and soon, but she and Victor had an intimacy that felt irreplaceable and made the thought of choosing a new consort unbearable. Maybe if she'd been pure faerie, or even if she'd been raised in the Winter Court, the exchange of magic between them wouldn't have had so much power. A small part of her was missing, like he still held a bit of her magic, and that left a hole, not unlike a tiny speck of dust under a contact lens—something that made itself known all the time.

If that wasn't enough, then there was Rafe and the Farringdon duchy. Though Rafe was the only living Farringdon, acknowledgment of the new Duke by the monarch was necessary. For literally every single transfer of Wellhall power mentioned in the records the new Duke had presented himself at court. The thought of Rafe kneeling in front of her made her ill.

Thinking about Rafe at all made Deor twitch. Relief at his being alive.

Rage at his leaving. Betrayal at his choice not to trust her enough to tell her he had returned. Grief that whatever they had was over and done. All of those tumbled over each other like a ball of fighting cats,

"You don't have to go," Stephen said.

Deor started and turned. "I didn't hear you come in." She smiled when she saw him. They had a friendship that reminded her of her relationship with Bill. Stephen had stayed with her through her time in the Tower. He'd been Shield during the war. He never made her feel like she had to perform. In many ways, she had more in common with him than any other person in the palace. Neither were raised as nobility. Stephen's parents were gentry, landowners and farmers. Not wealthy, by any means, but certainly not poor. Together she and Stephen could laugh at the weird things the nobility did, their exquisite etiquette and mannerisms.

It helped, too, that she was not attracted to him the way she had been to Victor. And even if Stephen had been attracted to women, he only had eyes for Charles. That relationship was another thing Deor liked about him. Though Stephen and Charles hadn't been together long, they had such an easy fit with one another, they felt like a couple that had been married for decades. More stability, she realized, was what she craved.

"I know this is going to be hard for you," he said.

"It is." Deor smiled softly. "But it will be good for me too. I missed my grandmother's funeral. I'm not going to miss Victor's." She stared at him for a long moment. There was no reason to put it off any longer. She looked him in the eye. "I want to ask you something. About you being Shield."

"I know what it is."

"You do?"

"Arthur is better suited for the job. You want me to step down so he can take over the position again, right?"

Deor blinked a couple of times. "Not exactly. I am thinking of Arthur for Shield. He is good at it. But I wouldn't take the job from you, either. I wanted to know if you would be my Consort. Most of the time it's a position filled by a family member, and I'm short of those. I trust you more than I trust anyone else—even more than I trust my own judgment sometimes. But if you don't want it, that's fine. I'm happy to keep you as Shield."

"What?" Stephen looked genuinely shocked. "I... I don't know what to say."

"Take some time to think about it," Deor said hurriedly. "No rush."

Stephen nodded, brow furrowed. After a moment his expression cleared. "You know what? Yes. Yes, I'll do it." He reached out and touched her hand. A shock of magic passed through them both. "Wow," he said. "It really is that easy." A small breeze whirled around them.

Deor laughed, and a flutter of sparkles drifted from her toward him, absorbing into his skin as they touched him. She drew a deep breath and let it out. "I can feel the magic receding," she said softly. "It's like I can breathe again."

"Yeah," Stephen said, his golden eyes sparkling. He waved his hand, and the breeze around them intensified, then tightened, spiraling down into a mini-tornado that he balanced in the palm of his hand. It shrank until he closed his hand around it, and it was gone, magic reabsorbed into him. He held out his hand to Deor, and she took it.

55

Rafe waited on the stairs of his palace. He wore the dark blue of the Farringdon house. A perfectly-fitted suit, not a uniform, with an open-collared shirt in a pale blue. His hair was pulled back, and the scar on his face was left unglamoured. Assane, now the head of Wellhall's guard, waited at the portal at the entrance to the palace courtyard. He nodded at her.

Assane turned to the portal. A moment later, it opened, revealing Deor and Stephen waiting to come through with a small group of servants. She wore a plain, black, floor-length dress, with a modest neckline and sleeves to the elbow. Her hair was down with the sides held back with pins, still short from Arthur's shearing. Her gray eyes were stern. Next to her, Stephen stood in uniform. Rafe's gaze almost glided over the badge he wore without noticing it. The Consort badge. A chill rolled off him, and he struggled to contain it.

Then he heard the barking, and his face lit up. Jake and Sam bolted from the portal, charging at full speed. He ran down the last of the steps and crouched down, catching both dogs as they barreled into his chest, knocking him back onto his ass. They sniffed him all over and barked. Sam danced back and forth, giddy. Jake leaned into Rafe, his paws on the man's shoulders, and licked his face. Finally, Rafe pulled himself from under the massive beasts and cheerfully commanded them to sit. He turned his attention to Deor.

"Lady Regent," he said bowing. "Thank you for caring for my boys. You are most welcome to my home."

"Thank you, Your Grace," Deor said. The title wasn't formal yet, but she used it anyway. Next to her, Brand whined. "Go say hello."

Brand ran up to Rafe and sat in front of him, tail wagging. He barked once.

"Hello Brand," Rafe said, bending down to pet him. "You've grown, haven't you?" Brand yipped and jumped up, resting his paws on Rafe's chest. Rafe laughed and rubbed Brand's ears. "You're a good boy, aren't you? Yes, you are."

"Sir, shall I see everyone inside and settled?" Luc had come from the palace and was standing on the steps behind Rafe. He wore Farringdon blue, and, like Rafe, it wasn't a uniform, though it echoed the Duke's suit. Over his heart was a badge, the Wellhall fountain, with the marking of his Seneschal.

Anger flashed across Deor's face for a split second and then was gone, smoothed away in a carefully schooled neutrality. She managed a small, tight smile as she approached him. If Rafe hadn't known what to look for, he'd have missed the flash of silver in her eyes.

Rafe turned to Luc as he made his way down the stairs. "Yes, Luc, if Her Majesty is ready?" He glanced at her.

"Of course. I'll follow you." She smiled.

"Your Majesty," Luc said to Deor with a small bow. "You are most welcome here," he added again. "I'll let you get settled, then we'll discuss tomorrow's events."

As she and her Consort approached, Rafe turned, as did Luc, and led them up the stairs.

"I do want a moment to speak with you and your Seneschal." She paused. "Alone."

Luc stiffened slightly.

"I thought you might," Rafe said. He continued up the steps without another word.

After they settled in, a servant led Deor, Stephen, and Brand to Rafe's office. Rafe rose from his seat behind a large desk. "Shall we sit at the conference table?" He gestured to his right. Monjoie stood waiting by a large round table carved from dark wood. Somewhat comfortable-looking chairs surrounded it.

Deor nodded and moved to take a seat.

From behind Rafe's desk, Sam came bounding up to her, wagging his tail. She couldn't help but smile and patted him on the head. Brand barked cheerfully at Sam. "Hush," Deor said gently. Brand wagged his tail.

"Will your Consort be staying as well?" Rafe asked.

"Yes," Deor said, looking up to meet his gaze. Next to him stood Jake, staring at her. "I hope you don't mind that I brought Brand." She rested her hand on the dog's head.

"Of course not." Rafe moved to the conference table and waited.

Deor took a seat opposite the side where Rafe stood, and Stephen sat with her. Monjoie and Rafe sat as well. They all stared at each other for a moment. Finally, she spoke. "Thank you again for having the memorial and for inviting me to Victor's funeral. How will that work?"

"We're holding a funeral service at the door to the family mausoleum."

"I see," she said, not knowing what else to say. She rubbed a hand across the bridge of her nose. "And the memorial service for Wellhall is tomorrow morning?"

"Yes." Rafe nodded. He let out a sigh and seemed relieved that she'd changed the subject. "We're having it in the center of the city. It's a beautiful park, especially this time of year. There's a memorial there to soldiers of past wars."

"I'll give a short—very short—speech, honoring those who helped retake Wellhall—I'm using the list you've given me. So if there are any changes, you need to let me know."

"No changes." He frowned. "Every name on that list deserves the highest honor. Both those who died and those who survived."

"I know," Deor snapped, surprised at her own anger.

Rafe recoiled slightly. "Was there anything else?"

"Yes." Deor shifted her gaze to Monjoie, who, to his credit, held her gaze, though he cringed back a bit. Her eyes were probably a bit silver. She'd sworn that if she ever got this close to him... *Stop it. You won't help anything by dwelling on vengeance fantasies.* "You were a vital part of Madeline Farringdon's attempted coup. For that you should pay with your life—"

"He was a vital part of winning the war!" Rafe interrupted. "Without him, we could not have won." He sat back and crossed his arms.

Deor blinked at him and returned her attention to Monjoie. "All evidence suggests that you have for decades been Madeline's spy. I've no doubt that you were involved in the multiple attempts on my life," she flicked her gaze to Rafe, "and the near-death of Lady Astarte's daughter Robbie." She returned her gaze to Monjoie.

Monjoie shifted uncomfortably. "Your Majesty, I do not deny—"

"Don't say another word, Luc!" Rafe snapped. He glared at Deor. "Monjoie's service has more than made up for his crimes."

Deor raised her eyebrows. "And who are you to make that judgment?"

"I am—"

"I'd think carefully before you said another word." After a moment she continued. "Monjoie, you are accused of treason—"

Rafe burst out again, "I will not stand by and let you—"

"Stop!" Deor slammed her fist on the table. Stephen gently squeezed her other hand. "You will not interrupt me again."

"You cannot—"

"I can, Your Grace. In fact, it might be argued that it is my duty to protect this kingdom."

"You think—"

Deor stood. "You know nothing of what I think. Nothing."

Rafe stood. "I know enough!" He paused, getting himself under control. "Now listen—"

"No." Deor's voice was soft but edged with power. "I do not know what has caused this uncontrolled outburst, Your Grace, but I seem to remember you have, for decades, been excellent at keeping your mouth shut when a monarch talks. I fail to see why you are struggling so much with it now."

Rafe gaped.

"If you continue to find it difficult to contain yourself, my Consort can escort you outside so that Monjoie and I may continue our conversation in peace."

Rafe glanced at Stephen, and Deor did too. He sat perfectly still, his hand still holding hers, a placid expression on his face, watching.

Deor sat. "Now, either sit down and shut up, or leave."

"Please, Rafe," Monjoie said quietly. "We talked about this."

"I'm not letting her take you out of here," Rafe said gently, but loud enough for Deor to hear it clearly. He sat.

"As I was saying, Monjoie, you are accused of treason." Deor glanced at Rafe, and a gust of frozen air buffeted her. She rolled her eyes. "That said, the list of my father's wrongs is long. And were I to go down the list of those who have, in one way or another, large or small, betrayed him, there would scarcely be any nobility or gentry left."

"What?" Monjoie said, eyes widening.

"You are not the only person to find yourself in this position. And so you, with the scores of others, including Arthur Maerwhere, are pardoned. The only way to move forward is to take only what we need and leave everything else behind. What the Winter Court needs now is a strong, loyal Wellhall." Deor stood and looked down at Rafe. "I don't know, Your Grace, what offends me more. That you think I am so cruel as to arrest a hero of Wellhall the day before he is to be honored for his valor, or that you think I am so stupid."

Rafe winced and rose. "Your Majesty—"

"Save it." Deor looked to Stephen. "Shall we?"

Stephen rose. "Yes." He looked to Rafe. "Her Majesty and her retinue will take supper in her quarters. We will see you tomorrow morning at the memorial, Her Majesty will recognize you officially as the Duke of Wellhall." He tucked Deor's hand into his elbow. "Have a good evening, Your Grace."

A servant hurried to open the door, and Deor and Stephen passed through, Brand at her heels. The servant escorted them back to their quarters on an upper floor.

When the door closed behind them, Deor's shoulders sagged. She made her way across the room to the wall of windows looking out at the sea far below the cliff-topping castle. Silent tears ran down her cheeks until she let out a small sob. Brand pressed his body against her side.

Stephen gently put his arm around her.

She turned toward him and let him wrap her in a hug. She pressed her cheek to his chest and wept. She let the grief run its course, which given how weary she already was, didn't take long.

"I think Rafe was just afraid for his friend," Stephen said.

"Yes." Deor sniffed. "But he actually thought I'd come here and, what, have Monjoie hanged in the town square?" She stepped away and wiped her eyes. Next to her, Brand whined and knocked her hand with his head. She knelt down and hugged him, burying her face in his fur. "I know you'll miss Jake and Sam," she said. "I will too." She stood. "Thank you, Stephen, for keeping me steady."

"No problem. After tomorrow all this will be done."

"Thank God."

56

Rafe led the informal procession through a small copse of fir trees. The Farringdon family mausoleum was not far from the castle itself, though it couldn't be seen from it. Inland from the ocean, the soothing crash of it on the cliffs beneath Wellhall could still be heard.

A small group followed Rafe, including Luc and a number of the servants from the house, most of whom had known Victor since he was a child. Some of the Wellhall guards came too.

The Regent and her Consort remained at the end of the group. As he made his way through the trees, he had to admit, the memorial service had been perfect. Deor had not been lying when said her speech would be short. She'd focused solely on those who had fought and praised many by name, including himself and Luc. Deor had asked for those involved in the fight for Wellhall to read the names of those who had died fighting: Assane and Zaya did the honors. Donovan stood for his people, too, clearly moved by those losses, though stoic. Once her speech was done, Deor had stood by, occasionally wiping a tear away.

Now, she was a few yards behind him, but he could feel her. Finn's dangerous, selfish attempt to make Rafe heir had bound him and Deor together in a way neither understood. It was that connection that gave them such a rapid and easy intimacy. What they had shared hadn't been real—at least that's what he kept telling himself.

When they emerged from the woods into the clearing, Rafe blinked back tears. His only visit to this place happened during his brief return to Wellhall before Finn had come for him and taken him "home." He had found this place beautiful, made of white marble, though he had pretended it hadn't moved him. He'd wondered then, some sixty years before Finn would try to make him heir, if he'd be buried there, or if his connection to the King severed him from Wellhall forever.

The building was a single story with one set of massive doors. They passed through the summer sun and into the cool quiet of the house of the dead. It reminded him a bit of the sanctuary at Mont Saint-Michel, peaceful. Victor's space was next to Edgar's. Rafe had Madeline laid to rest here, too, though part of him wanted to toss her body out for wild beasts. She was a Farringdon, good or bad, and had to be remembered.

Rafe drew a deep breath and turned to face the small group. His mouth went dry. He looked—really looked—at Deor for the first time. She was dressed in traditional, perfect, funeral garb—almost. She had eschewed the veil, though, the mark of a widow. Her dress was a combination of what someone might wear to mourn a friend and a spouse. In an unusual choice, she had worn her house colors, not Victor's. Perhaps a political statement of some kind? She was crying, and from the look of her, she had been crying the whole walk here.

Luc cleared his throat. "Would you like me to begin?"

Rafe looked at him and smiled. "Please."

"I knew Victor since I was a child," Luc began. Rafe let his mind wander, pulling up memories, far too few of them, of he and Victor together. He let the tears fall.

Deor drew in a deep breath and let it out with a shudder. She had been crying for days, and today had been no different. Tears at the memorial. Tears on the walk here. Tears now. On the walk here she had watched Rafe carefully, through tears, as he led them. He was in blue, not black. In fact, she was the only one in black. Everyone else wore Farringdon colors, except Stephen, who wore his dress uniform.

Monjoie's words were kind and filled with love and regret. She had tuned out the specifics, but the tone carried into her thoughts. As Monjoie finished, another person, Victor's valet who had been with Victor since he was a boy, spoke. Round it would go, until everyone had their chance to say something. Rafe, being the head of the house, would speak last. At least if the funeral followed the traditional scheme according to Genevieve.

She was reminded of her mother's funeral. Many different people had spoken, including Deor's grandmother, some of her mother's dearest friends, and even Bill. When the time had come to look at her, she hadn't been able to speak. The pastor asked her if she wanted to come up, and she could only shake her head and keep crying.

"Your Majesty?" Rafe's voice cut through the memory, and she jolted slightly.

She blinked until tears fell and her vision cleared. Everyone stared at her expectantly. "I'm sorry."

"Do you want to say a few words?" Stephen asked her softly. "His Grace is giving the floor to you if you want it."

"No." Deor's answer came too quickly, she knew, but she couldn't help it. As the word left her mouth she met Rafe's gaze for the first time that day. A good trick that both of them had pulled off together, avoiding each other's eyes. "I…" His eyes were a perfect blue. Beautiful. And hostile. "I'm sorry," she repeated, this time directly to him. "I…" She needed to stop saying *I*. This wasn't about her. It was about Victor.

"Yes?" Rafe said, eyes narrowing.

"Victor meant the world to me," she said, the words coming out rushed and, at least to her own ears, shallow.

Rafe snorted quietly.

"He was the reason I survived. He saved the Winter Court, but he also saved me." She couldn't take her eyes off Rafe. "He took on his shoulders a great burden, and he…" She shook her head; her voice was trembling and tears were starting to cloud her vision. "Now he's gone." She looked Rafe right in the eye. "He was my friend. He was my Consort. He was the Winter Court's hero."

"Thank you, Your Majesty," Rafe said drily.

Deor turned to Stephen and let him put his arm around her. She stopped holding back and let a sob come. Here, where she was supposed to be letting go, Victor felt closer than ever. There was some part of him that was still with her—or, rather, some part of her that was with him. Her mother's death had left her feeling empty, but that was more a metaphor for the pain. This was no metaphor. A piece of her was missing.

Rafe walked past her, close enough that she could feel the chill, as he led them out of the building and back to the palace.

57

eor stood before the door of Rafe's study and drew a deep
breath. After the memorial and the funeral, she'd sent him a
note asking if she might speak to him in the morning before
she was to leave. He'd offered to see her in his study. She wiped her hands
on her dress. She'd brought Stephen with her to the door, but not to come
in for the conversation. Brand was with the servants preparing to portal
home.

She knocked softly and waited. She was about to knock again when
she heard a voice. "Come in."

Deor turned the handle and pushed open the door. The study was
small. There were two wingback chairs and a sofa, a small coffee table,
and two side tables in front of a fireplace. Today was warm enough that
there was no fire, and the windows on the far wall were open, letting in a
breeze of salty sea air. Rafe stood by one of the chairs, a glass of something in his hand. For a split second, she couldn't help but think about the
first night they were together, him in lounging pants and holding a glass
of whisky. That was nothing like this moment. He was fully dressed, and
she was too, but even more, a cool civility hung in the air, the perfect
opposite of intimacy.

"Thank you for seeing me."

He nodded. "Please," he gestured at the chairs, "sit."

Deor sat in the one closest to the door, and he sat in the other.

Rafe set the glass on the side table. "What can I do for you, Your Majesty?"

Deor smoothed the already perfect line of her skirt and folded her hands in her lap. This was a bad, bad idea, but it was too late to turn back now. "I wanted a chance to talk to you, just the two of us. We haven't been able to do that since—"

"I remember." He stared at her. He wasn't sending off waves of cold, which surprised her, given his stiffness. She should be chilled to the bone. Perhaps he'd gotten it more under control.

"I wanted you to know that if you want to be Sword—"

"Ha!" Rafe barked out a laugh. "No. I do not want to be your Sword."

"Oh." Deor reeled a bit. "I understand if you need some time away to handle Wellhall—"

"I've handled Wellhall just fine, thanks."

"I know that!" Deor insisted. "That's not what I meant. It's just that I thought you liked being Sword?"

"I did once," Rafe nodded. "But that was a lifetime ago."

Deor nodded and looked down at her hands folded in her lap. She hadn't come here to ask if he wanted to be Sword, not really. She wanted to know if he still wanted *her*. "I thought... I mean..."

"For someone who has never seemed to be at a loss for words, you seem strangely out of your text." A chill blew from him—small and controlled.

"We were friends," she said. She blinked. Tears were threatening again. "I thought we were."

"We were," he acknowledged. He picked up his glass and sipped from it, not taking his eyes off her. He hadn't offered her any. "But then you fucked my brother, and he died."

Deor gasped, the crass framing of her and Victor stabbing her in the chest. "We... It's complicated," she finished. She wanted to explain that it had happened only once, a response to the intimacy of the magic they shared and to their grief. But she also wanted, needed, to protect their relationship and the intimacy they shared.

"Complicated." Rafe's eyebrows shot up. "It didn't seem complicated to me."

She frowned. "What did Victor say about it?" She hadn't even thought about what Victor had shared about her with Rafe.

"Victor didn't tell me anything. He didn't need to. Seeing him leaving your room, half-dressed, and you wrapped in a sheet was clear enough."

Deor's jaw dropped. She started to speak, stopped, and tried to start again. Thoughts whirled through her head. "Are you talking about the Proving at Mont Saint-Michel?"

"Yes." He crossed his arms and stared at her.

Deor tried to remember the specifics of that morning. She had assumed they were safe from prying eyes, and it hadn't even occurred to her to look up and down the hall, to whisper, to hide. Those thoughts were shoved aside when realization dawned. "You were there."

"Yes." He nodded.

Anger flooded Deor, and her eyes went silver. "Why the hell didn't you say something?" Deor flung herself from the chair and barely stopped herself from lunging at him, grabbing him by the lapels and shaking him.

"It's complicated," Rafe parroted, though he seemed unsure.

"You just decided that because I *might have* had sex with your brother, while you were presumed dead that you didn't need to say anything to me. What were you doing there?"

Rafe stood, forcing her to look up at him. "In the fight for Finn, both Luc and I were washed out to sea, fell through one of the thin places between Fae and everything else, and ended up at the monastery. They took us in and nursed us back to health."

"That doesn't explain anything!" Deor snapped. "It was very nice of them to help you, I'm sure, but why didn't you say anything?"

Rafe ran a hand through his hair. "It doesn't matter now. All that matters now is that I was needed more there than here. I could do more good there than here."

"And now you can do more good here?" Deor crossed her arms and glowered at him.

"Yes," Rafe snapped. "I felt Madeline's betrayal through the whole of my body." He shuddered. "And when Luc and I arrived, we discovered what Madeline had done. We figured we were of more use here."

"Hm. Nice. So you didn't give me any chance to have an opinion on that?"

"No." He shook his head. "Victor and I agreed that we wouldn't tell you I was alive until our attack on Wellhall happened, for better or worse. We agreed that it would cause too much confusion."

"So, let me make sure I understand." Deor drew a deep breath but didn't bother to try to ease the silver of her eyes or nails. "You knew that war was coming, and on multiple occasions had the opportunity to resume your post, or at least tell people you weren't dead. Instead, you played at being a monk until it had to do with *your* land and *your* title, and then you came back and played Robin Hood in the forest. How delightful! And exactly what were you doing when your brother was stabbed through the chest by his mother? Off having tea with Monjoie? Deciding where you'd hang your ducal portrait?"

"I was fighting D'nath!" Rafe snapped.

"I see." She wanted to drop back into the chair and cry again. "So you're a hero and I'm, what? The slut that ruined your brother?" Deor chuckled grimly. "What a very Finn-like attitude."

"Victor is dead," Rafe said.

"I know. I felt him die." Deor wanted to scream that his death had taken a piece of her, that she knew she would never, ever feel whole again, but she held her tongue. She didn't owe this man an explanation for anything. Finally, she spoke again. "I thought we were friends. I thought we might mourn Victor's death together."

Rafe snorted his derision. "Victor deserved much better than he got."

"That does seem to be the one thing we can agree upon. The wrong brother died." She gave a small curtsey. "I shall not trouble you any further, Your Grace." She turned on her heel and left, closing the door gently behind her.

Stephen stepped forward from where he leaned against the wall and reached for her. "That did not go well," he said, taking her hand.

"No." Anger radiated off her, she knew. "He was," she shook her head. "He was mean to me." She turned to look at him. "I sound like a child. But he was so...mean."

"I'm sorry," Stephen said. He took her hand. "You don't have to have anything to do with him. He's in Wellhall. You're at the palace. You've got more than enough to keep you busy. I imagine he won't have any reason to come to the capital for a while, and even when he's here for Parliament, it won't be your problem."

"Right." She drew in a deep breath and tried to clear her head. "Great, let's go."

58

The next morning, Deor held her first official cabinet meeting. Everyone was seated around the table. Bartholomew and Arthur —her Sword and Shield; Astarte, her Chamberlin; Genevieve, her Majordomo; and Bill, her friend. "Good morning." She smiled and took her seat, Stephen next to her. In front of her was her tablet, with an agenda. God bless Genevieve. "What's on the docket?"

Genevieve cleared her throat. "A lot, actually."

"Alright," Bartholomew said. "My turn…"

One by one they went around the table, laying out the next steps, talking about potential avenues of action, taking care of household and national business. Finally, it was Genevieve's turn.

"So," Genevieve said. "You have a lot of positive feeling behind you right now. Parliament will reaffirm you after one hundred days, possibly sooner. But the people still don't know you. They want to, but they don't."

"I know." Deor frowned. "I feel the whole nation, but I also feel like I hardly know anyone. I haven't seen ninety-nine percent of the land!"

"Exactly," Genevieve smiled, relief clear. "So I have an idea to help with that." She paused for dramatic effect. "A Royal Tour."

"You mean like when a king travels the countryside staying with people?" Deor asked.

"Yes! The people will get a chance to see you, talk to you!"

"Kings did that in the human world to bankrupt people. I'm not doing that." Deor frowned.

"Of course not!" Genevieve insisted. "You aren't your father. You're going to do this your way, which, I think, will be with a small number of people. Me, Stephen, Melanie, and a few guards and servants. We can stay with noble families—the Count or Duke—but we can also stay other places, like the McIntyre's inn."

"Okay," Deor nodded. "A few days in each place?"

"Depending on the size, maybe a couple of weeks. But yes."

"There are a lot of places. I'd be gone for months."

"If you did it all in a row, yes, it would take about a year. But you don't need to do it all at once," Genevieve confirmed. "We can put together a schedule where you are traveling a few weeks at a time and then home again."

"That sounds manageable." Deor let out a breath. She loved and hated the idea. She wanted to see the country, *her* country. But she also wanted to curl up in her room and not leave it for a year. This sounded like it could be a balance of both.

Genevieve stared at her expectantly.

"You already have some of it planned, don't you?" Deor smiled.

"Yes." She laughed. "I've got a seven-year tour schedule entirely mocked up."

"I'm convinced," Deor said. "Where do we go first?"

"My home," she said with a smile. "My parents are noble and have a small county. They'd love to meet you. It will be a friendly, easy trip, to get you used to it."

"You're from Wellhall," Deor said darkly.

"I am from a county inside the duchy, but nowhere near Rafe," she said gently. "I've got it all set. Seven years. Wellhall is last."

Deor laughed. "Perfect. Thank you so much."

"You're welcome." Genevieve beamed.

"So," Deor scanned the faces around the table. "It looks like we've got some plans, so let's get on them." She stood. "Once again, thank you all. I never would have made it through any of this without every single one of you."

As everyone smiled, stood, and spoke their optimism, a small chill ran over Deor. The palace's power had settled on her, confident in her, but there was something missing, something nagging just a little bit. Everything seemed fine now, *seemed* being the operative word. Her thoughts drifted back to her mysterious visitor, Puck, his power, and the looming threat she felt. She hadn't seen the last of him. She was sure of it.

Months had passed since Rafe had become the Duke of Wellhall. Every day brought something good and bad as he sorted out the mess left by the Summer Court and his mother's treason. Even most suppers involved work, as he hosted the newly freed mayors of nearby towns, hearing their concerns, and their need to simply vent in his direction about all the harm that had been done by his absence all these years. He might be Duke of Wellhall, but it was clear his people expected him to earn their respect.

That particular morning, as Rafe sat at his desk trying to make his eyes focus on a report about the state of the fishing fleet, Donovan sauntered in. Despite the fact that they were indoors, he wore dark sunglasses.

Rafe laughed. "Are you really feeling the sunlight that badly, or are you just trying to look mysterious?"

"Little of both." Donovan sighed and threw himself down in a chair without waiting for an invitation. "So I have a proposition for you. I think you'll enjoy it."

"I'm listening."

"Some allies of my mother-in-law are having a small problem with mischief makers in their town. I was wondering if you could help them sort it out."

Rafe gave Donovan a quizzical frown. "Your mother-in-law? Who not only lives in the human world, but lives on the other side of the globe in America? And she wants my help?"

"More or less. She wants faerie help, and she deputized me to find it. She's hesitant to ask for favors from either Court for obvious reasons. But since the two of us are friends…"

The word *mischief* clicked in Rafe's brain. "Goblins?"

"Maybe. I was thinking we could go together, look around a bit, and then you could have a much-deserved vacation."

Rafe drummed his fingers on the table. Truth be told, he'd love the chance to get out from behind this desk and stretch his muscles a bit. Holding office always seemed to involve so much damn paperwork. But his people needed him here. He couldn't just run off on an adventure to the human world. Or could he?

Donovan peered over his sunglasses and said, "When was the last time you had a vacation?"

"A real one?" Rafe considered it. "Years."

"Then you're overdue. Come out to California as my guest. If you get to break a few Goblin heads in the process, it'll just be an unfortunate coincidence."

"That does sound like fun," Rafe admitted. He guiltily shuffled a few of the papers on his desk.

Donovan's voice was wheedling. "You can swim in the Pacific. I bet you'd love surfing. I'll teach you to ride a motorcycle."

Rafe had seen moving pictures of Donovan's motorcycle, a giant two-wheeled iron machine faster than any horse. "Luc is doing a fantastic job as Seneschal," Rafe said. "And I'd have my mirror if an emergency came up." And, he added to himself, California was the other side of the world. As far away from the Regent and her court as he could possibly get. He heaved a deep, happy sigh and grinned at Donovan. "When do we leave?"

THE END

ACKNOWLEDGMENTS

First, to the amazing project manager Erin Penn, who kept track and kept us on track. Next to our amazing editors. Lucy Blue for great advice on how to make our book so much better. For Tuppence Van der Vaarst for her great catches in copy edits. Finally, for Kristen Gould, whose work with commas is unmatched. Thanks to all of you. To Natania Baron for her amazing covers. To John Hartness for believing in the project.

Now to the folks outside of the project. In particular to our D and D group: Kalvith, Moon, Roque, and Ash (or maybe it's Chris, Dan, Justin, and Erica), who have given us many great laughs in dozens of sessions. And to Jack, the GM, whose amazing stories and ability to put up with our shenanigans is second to none. We've learned so much more about storytelling from all of you! And Justin, thanks for harassing us about when this book was coming out. Now you have it. We hope you love it as much, nay, more than we do! Thanks again to all of you.

ABOUT THE AUTHORS

Sarah Joy Adams has written five novels, a few short stories, and too many drafts to count. Her novel *Steel Mill Vikings* was shortlisted for the Manly Wade Wellman Award. Having survived earthquakes, forest fires, and teaching Middle School she no longer fears death. She is now happily the director of the Writing Center at a rural university. She can be found on Facebook and Bluesky under her name, and on Tiktok at changeling_writer. Her website is www.sarahjoyadams.com.

Emily Lavin Leverett is a writer, editor, and medievalist. She writes two fantasy series, *The Eisteddfod Chronicles* and *The Wolf and the Nun*, a paranormal historical romance based on the writings and life of twelfth century abbess Marie de France. When she's not writing about faeries and werewolves, she teaches and writes about medieval pop culture. She lives in North Carolina where she, her spouse, and their cats, are avid Carolina Hurricanes Fans. She can be found on X, Facebook, and Bluesky under her name and at www.emilyleverett.com.

MORE BY THESE AUTHORS

Sarah Joy Adams & Emily Lavin Leverett

The Eisteddfod Chronicles

Changeling's Fall

Winter's Heir

Traitor's Spring

Sarah Joy Adams

The Kinslayer Saga

Steel Mill Vikings

Emily Lavin Leverett

The Wolf & The Nun

The Wolf in the Cloister

The Enchanted Rose

The Song of the Black Wolf

Emily Lavin Leverett (editor)

The Big Bad

The Big Bad II

The Weird Wild West

Lawless Lands

Predators in Petticoats

FRIENDS OF FALSTAFF

Thank You to All our Falstaff Books Patrons, who get extra digital content each month! To be featured here and see what other great rewards we offer, go to www.patreon.com/falstaffbooks.

PATRONS

Dino Hicks
John Hooks
John Kilgallon
Larissa Lichty
Travis & Casey Schilling
Staci-Leigh Santore
Sheryl R. Hayes
Scott Norris
Samuel Montgomery-Blinn
Junkle
Vickie DeSantos
Quincy J. Allen
Allison Charlesworth

Thank You for Supporting Independent Publishing!

We believe that you should be able
to read your books, your way.
That's why this Falstaff Books
print edition includes a digital copy
at no additional cost!

Just scan the QR code with your device,
follow the directions on Prolific Works,
and enjoy!
You can also join our newsletter when prompted,
and never miss an awesome Falstaff Release!

FALSTAFF
BOOKS
WWW.FALSTAFFBOOKS.COM